A WOMAN'S PLACE

They were known as the two Graces, though only one of them was called Grace.

Grace Calthorpe lived in a large detached house in the wealthy part of Beckersleigh, where the wide macadamed roads sloped gradually towards the rich green moor that dominated the town. On either side of the roads were high walls or privet hedges, double gates of matured wood or wrought iron, leading to double-fronted houses made of warm red brick or grey Yorkshire stone. Garages built for two or three cars and a gracious acre or two of cultivated garden completely isolated each house from those on either side.

At the poor end of town, where Agnes Rivington came from, the narrow cobbled streets sloped steeply, the rows of houses built in a single ascending line, each roof slightly higher than the one below. The moorland here was bare and craggy, scarred with the effluence of the nearby pits. But for children who had nowhere else to play, it was a paradise.

The two Graces, secure in their natural superiority, cared little about wealth or the lack of it. From their first days at school together, they remained inseparable, admired and aloof. Not only were they better looking than their peers; they were taller, cleverer, more articulate, amusing and better at games, and by the time they were sixteen they had acquired a glamour that, as far as anyone else could see, they would have for ever. Like their mythological counterparts, the daughters of Zeus, the two Graces were destined always to be beautiful, lucky and clever.

ROSEMARY ELLERBECK
writing as Katherine Yorke

A Woman's Place

A Mandarin Paperback

A WOMAN'S PLACE

First published in Great Britain 1983
by Macdonald & Co (Publishers) Ltd
This edition published 1990
by Mandarin Paperbacks
an imprint of Reed Consumer Books Ltd
Michelin House, 81 Fulham Road, London SW3 6RB
and Auckland, Melbourne, Singapore and Toronto

Reprinted 1994

Copyright © Katherine Yorke 1983

A CIP catalogue record for this book
is available from the British Library
ISBN 0 7493 0480 4

Printed and bound in Great Britain
by Cox & Wyman Ltd, Reading, Berks

AUTHOR'S NOTE

The town of Beckersleigh is not to be found on any map of Yorkshire, or anywhere else that I know. It exists only in my imagination as a typical small town built on the side of the Pennines. Such towns with their sloping terraced houses, their narrow cobbled streets and the more prosperous areas will be familiar to anyone who knows the North of England.

It is a town of mixed industry, and has a definable but changeable class structure. Like Beckersleigh itself, all the people who feature in this book are the product of my imagination.

Although this is a work of fiction, I would like to record the debt I owe to Sheila Hudson and Sheila Duncan, who spent hours discussing with me the early days of the Women's Liberation Movement and how it has developed since. Their first-hand experience and memories of the mood of the time when it started in this country about ten years ago were invaluable.

K.Y.
LONDON 1983

Part One

CHAPTER ONE

THEY WERE KNOWN AS THE two Graces, though only one of them was called Grace.

Grace Calthorpe lived in a large detached house in the wealthy part of Beckersleigh, where the wide macadamed roads sloped gradually towards the rich green moor that dominated the town. On either side of the roads were high walls or privet hedges, double gates of matured wood or wrought iron, leading to double-fronted houses made of warm red brick or grey Yorkshire stone. Garages built for two or three cars and a gracious acre or two of cultivated garden completely isolated each house from those on either side.

At the poor end of town, where Agnes Rivington came from, the narrow cobbled streets sloped steeply, the rows of houses built in a single ascending line, each roof slightly higher than the one below. The moorland here was bare and craggy, scarred with the effluence of the nearby pits. But for children who had nowhere else to play, it was a paradise.

The two Graces, secure in their natural superiority, cared little about wealth or the lack of it. From their first days at school together, they remained inseparable, admired and aloof. Not only were they better looking than their peers; they were taller, cleverer, more articulate, amusing and better at games, and by the time they were sixteen they had acquired a glamour that, as far as anyone else could see, they would have for ever. Like their mythological counterparts, the daughters of Zeus, the two Graces were destined always to be beautiful, lucky and clever.

In the middle, commercial part, of the town were the boys' and girls' Grammar schools, and here Grace and Agnes used to rendezvous each day.

'Dad wants me to leave,' Agnes said breathlessly one morning, having run all the way down the hill to tell Grace the news.

'Leave?' Grace exclaimed incredulously. 'Leave school?'

'Yes. Dad says it's time I was contributing to the family.'

'What a silly idea! How can you contribute to the family?'

'Through my wages. Dad doesn't earn as much on surface work as he used to on the coal face, and he wants to make sure that Paul has everything he needs.'

'Why should Paul have everything *he* needs?' Grace said with a note of contempt for the gangling, spotty boy whose head was forever in a book.

'Because he's the boy. Men come first in this world.'

'I don't see why they should.'

'Neither do I! Let's go in. There's the bell.'

It wasn't taken seriously at first that Agnes would leave at the end of her fifth year with only O Levels. It had always been supposed, indeed taken for granted, that the two Graces would both aim for Oxbridge. But that was before Albert Rivington had come out of the pit with pneumonicosis. Now, a safe but poorly-paid job had been found for him on the surface, winding down the cage that took the men to the bottom. After that, in his mind, there was no longer any question of Agnes going to university.

'No question,' he said to Mrs Armtree, the headmistress. 'There's not the brass.'

'But Agnes might get a scholarship, Mr Rivington. There would be very little to pay.'

'We couldn't afford to pay anything,' Albert Rivington said firmly, twisting his cloth cap in his hand. His thin neck made his Adam's apple seem very prominent. His collarless shirt was spotless and neatly fastened at the neck with a brass stud, but his grey suit was a little threadbare, baggy because he had lost so much weight since the illness was first diagnosed.

Although his daughter had been one of her star pupils Mrs Armtree had never seen much of Mr Rivington; but she knew the sort of man he was. Agnes had many of his qualities. He was a principled, decisive man, not easily deflected once his mind was made up. But she felt she owed it to her pupil to try.

'It would be an awful pity, Mr Rivington, not to give Agnes the chance to go to university,' she said warmly.

'Her brother is going.' Albert's face showed the intense pride that he felt at his son's achievement. 'He got a major scholarship.'

'I know, and that's wonderful. But Agnes is just as clever.'

'Agnes is a girl.' Albert's voice was flat, final. 'Women don't have the same need for education.'

Cynthia Armtree, B.A., straightened her already smooth skirt over her knees. 'I don't altogether agree with you there. Education for women is just as important as for men. Women have a very important role to play in life, and a good education equips them better for it.'

'Mebbe – for them as can afford it.' Albert's gaze was steady as he raised his eyes to meet hers. 'We can't. We need the money that Agnes can bring in. She knows it and she's willing to do it.'

'I'm sure she is – for *your* sake.' Mrs Armtree began to feel angry with this bleak, dogmatic man with his pointed nose, his thin lips, his steely eyes and the greyish hue that years at the coal face had given to his skin. 'She is willing to do it because she feels it is her duty.'

'Aye, and so it is.'

'But it is also a sacrifice!' Mrs Armtree's voice was tinged with frustration. 'Agnes will never have the opportunities she could have had.'

'She'll marry sooner or later.'

'Is that all you think a woman should do, Mr Rivington?'

He looked at her appraisingly, as only a man can look at a woman, a crooked smile on his lips.

'It's all most of them do, and right enough that they should do it. I only allowed my wife to go to work when Agnes was old enough to look after herself. I wouldn't let her go out before and I'm sorry I had to then. But . . .' Albert broke off in a fit of coughing. Mrs Armtree was suddenly aware how thin his chest was, so concave that she could even see the outline of his rib cage as he breathed in painfully.

'I had no choice,' he finished in a whisper. When he breathed, she could hear the erratic, squeaky rhythm of his dust-filled lungs.

Pleadingly, gently, she tried again. 'If Agnes were to go on to higher education, Mr Rivington, even complete the sixth form, she'd get a good job with good pay. What could she do now?'

'There are vacancies in the mill along where my wife works. I'm not saying it's ideal, but it's regular money.'

Yes, Mrs Armtree thought bitterly, he really *would* let his lovely, talented daughter work in a mill; but how would he feel if his clever son had to go down the pits?

'I see I can't convince you, Mr Rivington. Does her mother agree, too?'

'Of course,' Albert said, surprised. 'The whole family agrees with me.'

No one questioned what Dad said. He was a good and just man, and Agnes loved him. His was a home where the highest principles were upheld and national issues were constantly debated and discussed. Books were read and records were played, and although some people in the town had television sets, the Rivingtons hadn't – nor did they desire one. Most evenings after tea, Albert attended a meeting; sometimes to do with the Labour Party, sometimes the mining industry, or civic affairs. When he came home the family all had tea and bread and butter together, before going to bed.

Dad was usually gone by the time they came down in the morning. He had had his breakfast, lit the fire and gone off to the pit to let down the early morning shift in the big wire cages. Mother followed him shortly after to lay the breakfast table for Agnes and Paul. When Agnes came home at four, she would wash up the breakfast things, tidy the house, and get things ready for high tea at six o'clock.

Paul did nothing in the house. He wasn't expected to, because he was a male and he was clever. The only things that Dad did were to light the fire and make his own breakfast of tea, bread and margarine and jam. His wife cut his sandwiches, wrapping them in greaseproof paper and packing them in his tin box the night before. He made some tea in a Thermos and packed it with the lunch box in his canvas bag. He was always gone before daylight.

'Your father had words with Mrs Armtree,' Kathleen Rivington said to her daughter as they sat by the fire that night, while Paul worked upstairs and Albert attended a meeting of the GMC of the Labour Party.

'What did she say?' Agnes brushed her hair back from her face. Her hair was dark brown and thick with a natural curl, and her eyes were an unusual clear tawny, flecked with spots of yellow and grey.

'She was sorry. She said you were a bright lass.' Mrs Rivington picked up the pullover she was knitting for Paul. 'Well, we all know that. But your Dad said there was no question of anything more. He told her we need the money and why. You understand that, don't you, Agnes?'

'Oh, yes,' Agnes said, looking into the fire, her eyes widening. She and Grace had often fantasised about the days they would spend at university together. London always seemed to be the goal. Not Oxford or Cambridge, but London. 'I'm sorry, but I do understand. Happen I'll get the chance to study when Paul is through.'

'It'll be years before that. His medical studies go on for seven years and then maybe he'll want other qualifications. By that time I dare say you'll be wed and looking after your own children – and see what time that gives you for study!'

'I suppose so.' Agnes looked at the coal settling deeper in the grate. She was aware of her mother staring at her.

'*Are* you disappointed, Agnes?'

Agnes sighed. 'I suppose I never *really* thought seriously of going further. I knew there would be difficulties with Dad.'

'Why with your father?' Kathleen said sharply, defensively.

'I know Dad doesn't really approve of women being educated.'

'It isn't that he doesn't *approve*, love. He doesn't think it's necessary. And I'm not sure that I do. Where has education got women?'

'It's got some of them into Parliament. And there are women doctors and lawyers.'

'And do they do that as well as men?' Kathleen's tone became derisive. 'I'd prefer a man doctor or lawyer any day to a woman. As for women politicians, I can't name one!'

'Barbara Castle, Edith Summerskill . . .'

'All right, all right – there are one or two. But are they *necessary*?'

'They have a right.'

'Oh, rights . . . get on with you! We're equal to men, is what I say, but we do things different. I believe in the old way of life, and so does your father. You're a pretty girl, Agnes. You'll work a year or two and then you'll get wed.'

'*Then* what about the money coming into the home?'

Kathleen pursed her lips. 'You'll have made your contribution. That's all we ask. We don't want to stand in the way of your happiness. Eh, sometimes I think it's a pity you got a scholarship to the Grammar. But there, you've always done as you were told and your ideas have never been too grand – even if your best friend is Grace Calthorpe.'

'What's Grace got to do with it?'

'Well . . . her family, to begin with. Much richer than ours – even if her grandfather did work in a mill like me. Or was it her great-grandfather?'

'The great-grandfather; he started the firm.'

'Grace's a good girl, a nice girl. And she's been a good friend to you. But Agnes ...'

'Yes?'

'Don't expect your friendship to go on.'

'Why not?'

'Well, if you're in the mill and she goes to the university ... your ways are bound to part.'

'Oh, our ways won't part. I don't want to work in the mill, anyway. No one says I have to, do they? I can do other work – in a shop or an office, maybe. That's what I'd rather do.'

Kathleen was disappointed. Sometimes mothers and daughters worked at the looms side by side, as fathers and sons did in the pits. She had always assumed that when Agnes left school she would work with her.

'It's not a bad life in the mill. You get used to the noise.'

'I don't want to, mother. I could work in an office and get some sort of qualification. That way I might get a better job eventually.'

'Qualifications!' Kathleen said in disgust. By twenty Agnes would be wed, if not before. Everyone said so.

Mr Calthorpe was a wealthy carpet manufacturer and Albert had never been to his home before. He knew where it was and how to get there, but he had never been inside, never having been invited. The friendship of the children did not extend to the parents. But tonight Albert had found a note under the door from Mr Calthorpe, asking to have a word with him. He didn't tell his family, because he knew what it would be about. It wouldn't make any difference. His mind was made up.

Albert stood on the golden Calthorpe carpet which covered the hall and led up the broad staircase to his right. The carpet was springy underfoot, like the moorland turf near the golf club, which he and his friends skirted on their way to shoot rabbits on the moors. On the carefully tended turf of the club he had often seen the golfers teeing up; men like Mr Calthorpe, portly and privileged. But Albert did not envy them. He knew he would never be a member of the golf club, not did he wish to be. Looking around him now, Albert could never recall ever having been inside a house such as this, but although he felt nervous, he wasn't envious or intimidated; it was just a matter of adjustment – like going underground for the first time.

14

The walls of the hall were covered with a heavy flock wallpaper. Everywhere was white and gold. A white marble table and two white chairs stood to one side of the hall, their seats upholstered in gold satin. A large decorative urn of twigs and berries stood on the table, together with a silver tray, on which were one or two letters ready for posting. The lights of the chandelier hanging from the ceiling cast a white glow on the golden carpet and made a kind of halo round Henry Calthorpe's partly bald head as he drew his guest into the warmth of the house.

'Come in, come in,' he said, jovially rubbing his podgy hands together. 'Nasty cold spell we're having.'

'Nasty,' Albert agreed. It never occurred to him to remove his cap. He followed Mr Calthorpe through the double doors into a room that could have contained two houses of the Rivingtons' size.

The gold carpet covered the floor; between two long facing sofas was a large patterned rug, and in front of the chairs scattered about the room were smaller ones. The chairs and sofas were covered with a shiny material which Albert couldn't name, but it had a thick weave and was rich and almost opalescent, like the wallpaper – a heavy-blocked silver fern motif on a dull gold background. At the long windows, velvet curtains hung to the floor, a soft brown, the colour of the bark of a stripped tree. A fire roared up the chimney in the huge grate.

'Good colliery coal this,' Henry said, ushering Albert to a well-upholstered chair by the fire and putting a glass in his hand.

Albert gingerly sat down and scratched his forehead under the peak of his cap. His large calloused hand comfortably encircled the thick cut-glass whisky tumbler. 'Aye,' he said, sipping his whisky.

'I'll come straight to the point.' Mr Calthorpe sat opposite Albert and stretched his neatly trousered legs in front of him. 'It's about your Agnes.'

'I thought it might be.'

Henry Calthorpe chuckled. 'Oh, you did?'

'Well, what else?' Albert looked at him without smiling. They knew each other's measure, man to man, whatever the gulf that money created between them. 'The answer is as it was, Mr Calthorpe. Agnes is leaving the Grammar at the end of this term. She doesn't want to work at Martin's Mill alongside her mother; but she'll take some job in the town.'

'She's a very bright girl. She'd be a credit to the town as well as to you and the school if she went to university.'

'Well, she's not going. We've never lived beyond our means, Mr Calthorpe, and we're not starting now. My son Paul is going to Oxford University. That's honour enough for this family.'

'It is an honour. You should be proud of him.'

'I am that.'

'Have another whisky?'

Albert held out his glass. 'I'm not against education for women, and our Agnes has done well. What she's learned at the Grammar is more than I or her mother ever learned. It'll give her a good start in life, I dare say. She's taking eight subjects in O Levels. If she wants to work in an office and not the mill, I'll not stand in her way. I see the point of that. She's bright and she can learn shorthand and typing. I warrant that'll be far more use to her than a degree from the university. She says she's no wish to teach, so why should she go to a university?'

Henry joined his fingers into a church steeple and peered over the top of them. He liked good food and drink and the comforts of life, and it showed in his rounded face, the slight paunch under his waistcoat. When he opened his mouth, two gold crowns shone on the left side of his lower jaw and one just off-centre on the upper. His cheeks were smooth and he smelt of expensive after-shave. His eyes were very blue, like Grace's.

'I'm inclined to agree with you. Both our daughters have the advantage of good looks, and they'll not want for admirers. But if you wanted, I could help and you could pay me back ...'

'Well I don't, and I can't. I don't want your help and I can't pay you back. I don't want debts of that kind.'

Henry was unperturbed. He spread his hands and glanced at the slim gold watch on his plump wrist. 'Agnes could pay back ...'

Albert stood up and put his half-full glass on the table.

'Mr Calthorpe, I'm surprised you should suggest ...'

'Grace asked me. I'm sorry if I have embarrassed you. No hard feelings?'

'None at all.'

The two men shook hands.

'He's such a proud bastard,' Henry Calthorpe said, puffing smoke into the air as he lay propped up on the pillows after making love to his mistress. He made a habit of discussing everything with her now

– but first things first. They made love and then they had a chat, never the other way round. All the same, he was beginning to attach considerable weight to Rose's opinions.

'You can't blame him,' Rose said, stretching languorously, pulling the sheet up to her chin and peering at Henry over it. After he made love his face was very red and the blue of his eyes was very pronounced.

'You think I shouldn't have offered?' Henry glanced at her through the smoke.

'I suppose you had to seeing as how Grace asked you; but people like Albert Rivington have their pride.'

'Don't I know it! I have any number of Albert Rivingtons working for me. Yes, I'm sorry I asked now. I didn't want to hurt his feelings.'

'But you didn't want to hurt Grace either.'

'No. She begged me to ask. She's so attached to Agnes.'

'I know. Maybe it's a good thing for them to part.'

'What do you mean?'

'Well, they're getting on, aren't they? Girls of that age should be thinking about boys.'

'I hope you don't mean anything funny.' Henry stubbed out his cigarette and sat on the side of the bed.

'Oh, I don't think there's anything funny about Grace!'

'But you've never seen her.'

'I have, from a distance. I saw her in Marks and Spencer in the High Street, with your wife.'

'I don't know what they shop there for.'

'Don't be so stuffy! They're very good, especially for undies.'

'Well *you've* no need to buy your undies there.' He looked at her flimsy lingerie, neatly arranged with her nylon stockings on the chair by her dressing table.

'I don't.' She put out a hand and touched his thigh. He was quite repulsive naked, she thought, with his folds of flesh and his reddish fair hair sprouting all over the place. He had no waist at all and his torso was a thick, straight line from his shoulders to his thighs. ' People wonder where I get my money from.'

'Tell them it's your war widow's pension.'

Rose giggled. 'They'd never dare ask me. Anyway, you've no need to worry about Grace. She looks very normal to me. I wouldn't dream of sending her to university unless she's really keen herself. It's a waste of money. Some man will snap her up!'

17

'I hope someone snaps up Agnes, too,' Henry said, struggling into his combinations, a garment he had worn all his life and would continue to wear until he died. To Rose's eyes he looked even more comical in them than he did naked, but hers was not to criticize. After all, he paid the bills. He owned the house she lived in and the furniture inside it; he paid the gas and electricity and bought all her clothes. Henry, meanwhile, imagined that Rose had no life of her own outside of him, and took immense satisfaction in having such a youthful, good-looking woman as his possession.

When he was dressed, he kissed her perfunctorily.

'Until tomorrow,' he said, and she smiled at him as she opened the door. Adjusting his hat, he walked down the path, as usual looking to right and left as he came to the garden gate. His car was a short walk around the block. She often wondered what he would do if he saw anyone he knew in the street. Would he scuttle back? Or would he simply nod and pass the time of day?

It was one of the few things about Henry Calthorpe that she didn't know ...

CHAPTER TWO

QUEEN ELIZABETH II HAD BEEN two years on the throne when Albert Rivington let it be known that his daughter Agnes was to leave school at the end of her fifth year. It never for one minute occurred to him that he was blighting her life or depriving her of a career. The Queen had not been to university, nor was she known for her scholarship. She was a nice ordinary young woman who had been photographed in overalls, with a spanner in her hand, during her war service in the ATS; she had married a nice young man of her own sort, but without wealth. Albert failed to see why his pretty daughter Agnes shouldn't be like the Queen and settle down and marry after a year or two in some ordinary job.

So Agnes left school in July with eight O Levels and went to Blackpool for two weeks' holiday with her family. When they returned, she set about looking for a job.

Meanwhile, Grace's family went to the South of France, where the climate suited Mrs Calthorpe's delicate health. Mother and daughter stayed there for almost six weeks, but Henry came back after two and spent more hours than usual in the company of his warm, accommodating mistress.

In September the two Graces met after nearly two months apart, and for the first time Agnes became aware of a difference between them. At school the two Graces had complemented each other: Agnes was quiet, Grace ebullient; Agnes was thoughtful, Grace spontaneous; Agnes considered everything carefully, Grace took risks; Agnes smiled but was inclined to be serious; Grace seemed illumined by inner happiness and laughed a great deal, as though her exuberance could not be contained.

Now Grace was very tanned and her ash-blonde hair was drawn back from her forehead, giving her a very sophisticated, grown-up look. Her breasts seemed larger too, and her hips more rounded and womanly. She wore pale pink slacks and a white blouse that showed her deep cleavage. Agnes felt pale and dreary beside her, in her twin set and skirt.

They sat in Grace's 'den' at the top of the house, Grace lounging on the daybed, Agnes sitting upright in the armchair in front of the gas fire.

Grace's room was pretty, chintzy, still showing the tastes of a girl rather than a young woman. There was a cluster of favourite dolls on an armchair, and the few books on the shelves were the treasured books of childhood: the adventures of Mumfie the elephant, the stories of Mary Plain the bear who lived with her family in the bear pit in Berne. The curtains and matching bedcover were of pretty glazed cotton with tiny rosebud hearts in pink and blue, and the furniture was white and fragile, as though it was really meant for a dolls' house but was several sizes too big. The wall-to-wall Calthorpe carpet was a deep pink. The only signs of Grace's dawning maturity were a new washbasin and a larger wardrobe to house her growing collection of clothes.

But if her room had not changed much, Agnes thought, Grace had. She was poised on the brink of womanhood. Agnes hardly knew whether to be glad about it or sad as she looked at her and saw how much taller she seemed since her summer sojourn.

Grace addressed the ceiling. 'I can't believe school starts tomorrow and you won't be there.'

'I know.'

'Don't you hate the idea?'

'I do now!'

'I was always amazed how you never seemed to *care* – not really. You went through your last term as though it was the most natural thing in the world.'

Agnes shrugged and scraped her hair back from her head, trying to get it to look like Grace's.

'Of course I cared, but what could I do? I knew Dad's mind was made up. I've never known him change his mind about anything serious.'

'I don't think I can bear it without you there! I've told Daddy I want to leave too.'

'What did he say?'

Grace laughed. 'What do you think he said? He said he had paid to give me a good education and he wasn't going to let me throw it all

20

away now. He says I'm his only child and he expects a lot from me. He wants to see you, by the way.'

Agnes frowned. 'I hope he's not going to offer to pay again. That caused no end of trouble last time.'

'Oh, no! He knows exactly where he stands with your dad! No, he's got a suggestion that you might like and your father might accept. Don't you think the world is dominated by men, Agnes?'

Agnes gave a fleeting smile. 'Why do you say that?'

'I never thought about it much before, but it really struck me with your father and his attitude towards school. He never stopped to ask what your mother or anyone else thought.'

'No, but Mum would have agreed with him. She may not always agree on little things, but she does on basics.'

'And this was basic?'

'Very. Father believes that Paul should be educated no matter what – that he should be a doctor and be successful. This'll give him enough pride to last him for the rest of his life. It'll make up for all the years spent in the pit; the illness, the lack of money. He knows that after Paul no one in our family will ever go down the pit again. We'll be middle class, like you. *We* won't be; but our children will be, Paul's and maybe mine.'

'Depending on whether you marry a miner or a teacher.'

'Yes.'

'I still think it's unfair. Daddy doesn't carry on like that in our house. Even though Mummy's an invalid she rules him, and I can do what I like because he adores me. Women rule here, not men.'

'Well, they don't in our house.' Agnes laughed and got up, pulling down her skirt. 'I'd better get back. I said I'd help mother wind some wool.'

'Come and see Daddy first.'

Mr Calthorpe was sitting on one side of the fire in the gold and white drawing room and Mrs Calthorpe on the other. He put down the paper, stood up and kissed Agnes, then he held her away from him and looked at her.

'My, how you've grown! You're quite a young woman.'

'I was thinking that about Grace,' Agnes said, blushing slightly. 'Maybe it's because I haven't seen her for a bit.'

'Well, come and sit down and tell us what you've been doing, Agnes. Grace won't know what to do at school without you. Have you got a job?'

'I'm working at Millers, the stationery shop in the High Street. I do the books and odd little chores like making tea.'

'It doesn't sound very worthy of a girl with eight O Levels.'

'They say there are prospects.'

Henry Calthorpe sat down and shook his head. 'I'm very sorry your father ...'

Mrs Calthorpe looked sharply at her husband. 'Oh, Henry, don't go over all that again. We quite understand why Agnes's dad didn't want help. He could never pay it back.'

'I wouldn't have needed paying back!'

'Dad doesn't see it like that ...'

'I know, love, I know,' Mr Calthorpe said quickly. 'But what I want to propose this time should be quite acceptable to your father. If you like Millers and think you have prospects, all well and good; we'll leave it at that. But Millers is a very small concern. It would take years to get anywhere there, don't you think?'

Agnes lifted her eyes from the richly patterned rug and looked straight at Mr Calthorpe.

'I don't know. It was all the Labour Exchange had that was at all suitable. I didn't want to serve behind a counter or work in a mill. And I hadn't any secretarial qualifications or skills.'

'And what are they paying you?'

'Four pounds a week.'

Mr Calthorpe sat back and grunted. 'Well, that won't do very much for the family fortunes. That's only just over two hundred pounds a year!'

'I keep ten shillings for myself and give the rest to Mum.'

'I hope Paul appreciates all this.'

'Paul didn't ask me to do it!'

'Oh, I know that, love, I know that.'

'Come to the point, Henry,' Mrs Calthorpe interjected, snipping off a piece of thread from the table runner she was embroidering. 'You'll take all week to get to it if you go on like this.'

'I was just establishing the facts, dear. The point is, Agnes,' Mr Calthorpe said, getting up and taking a cigarette from a green onyx box, 'that I could offer you a job at our factory – in the office, of course. We need a bright, quick girl, a good learner. And there really *are* prospects. I'm willing to pay six pounds a week and give you shorthand and typing lessons as part of the job. Now, what do you think your father will say to that?'

'What do *you* say to it first, dear?' Mrs Calthorpe smiled at Agnes. 'Does the idea appeal?'

Agnes wasn't sure whether the idea of being an employee of Grace's father appealed or not.

'I'm not doing it as a favour, mind,' Mr Calthorpe said. 'We really do need a bright girl, a school leaver. If you don't take it we'll get someone else just like you; but we'd prefer to have you.'

'We're very fond of you, Agnes,' Mrs Calthorpe said warmly. 'We think of you as a sister to Grace – you've always been that close. We don't want you to lose touch with her or with us, so say you'll think about it.'

'I'll talk to my father,' Agnes said. But already she knew she wanted to do it.

'Oh, make him say yes!' Grace ran over to her and clasped her arm. 'Shall I come over and talk to him too?'

'Oh, no!' Agnes exclaimed, gently freeing herself from Grace's grip. 'This'll need all of mother's skills, and mine. But if I can, I'd like to! Thank you, Mr Calthorpe.'

He went over to her and kissed her cheek. He smelt of tobacco and a spicy after-shave. Her own father never smelt of anything except sweat when he came back from the pit and carbolic after he had had his weekly bath in front of the fire. At the Rivingtons', the lavatory was outside, and they still didn't have a bathroom, though the Council was supposed to be putting one in soon. Goodness knows where they were going to put it.

When Agnes returned home that night and told him about Mr Cathorpe's proposal, her father's reaction was predictable. His thin nostrils quivered.

'That man has a bloody nerve!'

'It's not charity, Dad!'

'I don't care what it is! I'll say no, and he knows it.'

'Albert ...' Mrs Rivington said placatingly, still at the table where they had just finished tea. Her husband stood by the mantelpiece lighting his pipe with a spill from the fire.

'No, I mean it, Kathleen. They're the Calthorpes and we're the Rivingtons. We live at opposite sides of the town.'

'Dad, this is 1955! You'd think you were in the nineteenth century.'

'Aye, I know. You'll be telling me that we're all equal, we fought side by side in the war. Well, we aren't. Mr Calthorpe is a factory-owner and I'm a pit-winder. Neither of us fought in the war, me because of my health and him because he had a reserved occupation. But if we had, I'd have been a private and he'd have been an officer.' He held up a hand to cut off Agnes's protests. 'Oh, yes, he sent his daughter to the same school as you. But he paid full fees while you had a scholarship.

'I can understand you and Grace being friends. You're both clever, bright lasses, drawn together; but mark my words, you'll grow apart. You're working class and they're not, and this society is based on class, whether you like it or whether you don't. Now then.'

He puffed at his pipe and looked at the ceiling.

'I don't see what that has to do with me working at Calthorpe's!' Agnes raised her chin and looked at her father. It was unusual for her to contradict him, but she was going to now.

'It has everything to do with working there. Why does he want you in the first place?'

'He said he needs a bright girl.'

'Let him get one, then. There are plenty about.'

'He wants *me* there, Dad.'

'But *why*?' Her father pressed the tobacco firmly into the bowl of his pipe and applied another spill to it.

'Because he likes me. He knows me.'

'Aye. It's his form of charity.'

'It isn't that at all, Dad!'

'Well I say no. You carry on at Millers and see how you get on. You haven't given it a chance.'

'I know how I'll get on at Millers: I'd never get anywhere if I worked there for the rest of my life.'

'Well, you'll be wed, like everyone else. But I suppose you want to try and be different. I suppose that's not good enough for the likes of you.'

'Oh Dad ...' Tears came into her eyes. Her mother coughed and pushed her tea cup away.

'I think you're being unreasonable, Albert.'

Albert Rivington looked at the wife who never contradicted him – at least never in front of the children.

'You stay out of this!'

'Albert, Mr Calthorpe is only offering our Agnes a better job. I think it's nice of him.'

'It's charity!'

'It is *not* charity, Dad! I'll be paid a wage for the work I do.'

'*I* know what's in his mind. I know his sort. They want to own you by giving handouts that make you beholden to them, just like all bosses. That's why I want to see a country run *by* the people *for* the people, and by God, one day we'll get it.'

Albert knocked out his pipe and went over to get his cap. 'I'm going to play darts. I'll be back ...'

'Just a minute, Dad. We haven't finished!'

Albert frowned. 'The last word has been said, Agnes. No!'

'I want to work there, Dad.'

'No!'

'If I can't work there, if you won't let me, I'll leave here, Dad. I'll go to London. I'll ...'

'You'll do no such thing!' Albert stalked over to her, cap in hand, his pipe pointing accusingly.

'I will, Dad! I didn't argue with you about leaving school. I knew you needed the money, and Paul's future is important to all of us. I agreed to that and I didn't argue. But I'm arguing about this! I think you're being cruel and unreasonable and I won't be bullied by you and told what to do for the rest of my life. I'm no longer a schoolgirl. I'm a working girl. I pay tax ...'

'You're sixteen years old ...'

'I'm old enough to do a day's work. I can make my own decisions now. And I won't be told what sort of work I'm to do!'

'I think she's right, Albert.'

Kathleen spoke tremulously. Years of agreeing with Albert had taken their toll. But she didn't want Agnes to be what she had always been: a timid dutiful wife, terrified of her husband's anger. Albert was a good man and often he was right. He didn't get drunk and he didn't knock her about as some men did; he was considerate and a good husband and father. But he was a domestic tyrant too. In this small house, Albert Rivington controlled the lives of those around him like some medieval baron.

'I don't know what's got into the pair of you.' Albert put his cap on his head.

'I'll not change my mind, Dad, so you'd best decide before you go out.'

Albert looked at his daughter and saw the rebellion in her eyes. She was serving him notice! There and then he realised that she would go through with her threat. She was stubborn like him, and cleverer too. She would go to London and make her own way there. He would never be able to bring her back, even though she was under age. Not once she was gone.

'You can do what you like!' Albert said. 'If you want the Calthorpes' charity you can take it; but don't say I didn't warn you. And don't come running to me when you find you've done the wrong thing.'

He tightened his muffler about his neck and slammed the door behind him.

Agnes gazed at her mother and smiled through the tears that were suddenly falling. Mother and daughter hugged each other, clinging together, just as together they had defied the head of the family.

'You did right!' Kathleen said at last; then suddenly she drew away, ashamed of her emotion. She was not a woman given to kissing and holding; she was not a toucher. Shyly she started to clear away the tea things.

'Your father's very stubborn, very proud. He felt the pit gave him a surface job out of charity, so now he works harder than anybody else. He can't see that sometimes people do things with their own interests at heart. No doubt Mr Calthorpe is right glad to have a girl like you who's clever and keen to work for him – someone he knows. He's the lucky one, not you; but your father can't see that.'

'I'm lucky, too,' Agnes said, getting a tray to help her mother and piling up the crocks one on top of another, sturdy white cups and plates with a plain blue line round the rim. 'It's like death working at Millers. I hate it!'

Now Kathleen heard the truth for the first time. Agnes had never uttered a word of complaint. Kathleen put her head on one side and went into the kitchen. Her daughter was like her; she kept herself to herself. It was a good North Country characteristic, but it also brought its own suffering. You seemed to carry an awful burden inside you which you could speak to no one about. How many nights had she lain alongside Albert, bitterly resentful of something he had said or done or forbidden her to do, yet accepting it because it was how her mother had been before her, and her mother's mother before that. Her Agnes, too and Agnes's daughters. But no! Kathleen turned on the tap and sluiced the plates before washing them. *They* would be different, and Agnes was turning out different too.

* * *

Agnes made progress at Calthorpes. Two evenings a week she went to shorthand and typing classes at the Polytechnic; but although she still insisted that she didn't mind about leaving school, she skirted it whenever she could, so that she would neither see people she knew nor be seen by them. It was envy rather than shame that motivated her. To be a sixth former! How they had looked up to the girls in the sixth form – and to think that Grace was a prefect now!

'Everyone misses you,' Grace told her. One night a week she went over to the Calthorpes' as she used to do. Only now she went from the factory for supper rather than from school for high tea. 'Do you miss school?'

'Not a bit!'

'You make yourself say that. I think you do.'

'Why should I miss it?'

'I *hate* school without you. I want Daddy to let me leave and work at Calthorpes, too.'

Agnes exploded with laughter, releasing a tight, pent-up feeling she felt almost continually in the pit of her stomach whenever she saw Grace. She knew it was envy and longing. In spite of what she said, she missed Grace terribly, and the school. She didn't like being a woman, wearing lipstick and women's clothes and shoes. She still wanted to be a schoolgirl.

'Whatever did your dad say?'

'He said no, of course, but I've told him I'm not staying on at school. I'm leaving in the summer. Agnes, did you ever know a boy called Johnny Henley?'

Agnes screwed up her nose. 'Why should I?'

'I like him. I think he's in the year below Paul at the Grammar.'

'I don't remember him.'

'He's got rather a spotty face, but nice eyes. Don't tell my dad, but we're dating.'

Agnes felt herself go red. Did that mean Grace was in love with Johnny Henley?

'When do you see him?'

'After school. We meet in the park. We can't do much else and it's ever so cold! I think as I'm sixteen I'm allowed to have a boyfriend, don't you?'

A boyfriend! Did they kiss? Agnes hated the idea of someone kissing Grace. She still felt that boys were silly, and as she and Grace had always had so much in common, she had expected Grace to feel the same way.

'What ... what do you do?' she asked, looking at Grace, still with her colour high.

Grace giggled. 'What do you mean "do"?'

'Well, when you're together.'

'We talk and that.' Grace still had on her school uniform, her gymslip and white shirt, red tie and heart-shaped prefect's badge.

'Do you kiss?' Agnes wanted to know. Her eyes were burning as she looked at Grace.

'Oh, what a thing to ask! Don't be daft!'

Agnes was at a loss to know whether this meant yes or no. She felt very uncomfortable; suddenly they seemed to be on strange, hostile ground. She hoped Grace didn't do anything else; didn't let a boy touch her in ... in that way – pull down her pants and look at her. Agnes knew what went on behind the great slag heap at the top of the road.

'Johnny has a friend called Max,' Grace said. 'He said we should get together, the four of us.'

Agnes was angry.

'I can't meet in the park after school.'

'At weekends, then.'

'I'm not interested in boys!'

'You will be one day.'

'Don't talk like that. Boys are so soppy.'

'You're right,' Grace said with a sigh, the silly, unfamiliar smile leaving her face. She started to unroll her stockings and remove her gymslip and shirt. 'I really think they're soppy too. I'd rather talk to you than Johnny. We never have anything to say to each other. All we do is hold hands.'

'Is that all?' Agnes felt tremendous relief.

'Of course.' Grace turned to her and gave her a sly look. She groped in her wardrobe and drew out a bright blue pleated dress with a yoked bodice. As she put it over her head, Agnes noticed how big her breasts were in her brassiere – much bigger than hers. Grace's breasts completely filled the cups, whereas hers always had a little empty peak at the front.

She felt envious of Grace having womanly breasts like that, a boy who held hands with her in the park, a nice home, a doting father and mother, and a chance to go to university ...

Grace had finished doing up her dress and as she fastened the belt, Agnes saw that she was looking at her rather strangely. Perhaps she recognised the envy on her face, something that Grace had never seen before and never expected to see.

'Let's go down to tea,' she said, slipping her arm through her friend's and giving it an extra squeeze for comfort. 'Mummy'll be waiting for us.'

CHAPTER THREE

MR CHESTER LOOKED AFTER THE Accounts Department at Calthorpe Carpets. He had been wounded in the war and walked with a limp, but people said he put it on, because on some days it was more pronounced than others.

Fred Chester lived in a village on the far side of Beckersleigh with his wife and four young children and as he passed the bottom of Enderby Street, where Agnes lived, he got into the habit of offering Agnes a lift home at night. Agnes was grateful for the ride in the winter, when it was cold and raw; but in the spring and summer she preferred to walk, especially after sitting all day in a stuffy office.

Agnes worked in the office next door to the Accounts Department at Calthorpes, helping to process orders for the carpets. She soon learned that there were many different qualities of carpet and all kinds of different uses. Calthorpes supplied a lot of carpets for Government departments, and apparently this was why Mr Calthorpe had not been called up during the war.

Mr Chester opened the door of his black Vauxhall Wyvern and leaned out. 'Can I give you a lift home, Miss Rivington?' He said this every time.

Agnes looked up at the sky. It had been a warm and sultry day and she was looking forward to a walk along the edge of the moors, where she would feel the benefit of the cool breeze. She smiled. 'No thanks, Mr Chester. Not today. I fancy a little walk on the moors – it's been so hot.'

'I'll drive you to the top of the hill, then.'

'Oh, please ...'

'Go on. It's no trouble.' He patted the passenger seat, and Agnes got in beside him, feeling faintly annoyed.

'I really don't need a lift in the summer, Mr Chester. Walking to and from work is the only exercise I get.'

Mr Chester didn't reply and the car climbed laboriously up the hill to the road which ran along the edge of the moor.

'That'll do nicely, thanks very much.'

He reached into the back seat for his jacket. 'Mind if I come with you? I wouldn't mind a walk, too.'

'But won't you be late?'

'Oh, I often drop in for a pint on the way home. My wife will think I've done that.'

The remark made Agnes feel uneasy. Why should he lie to his wife? She glanced out of the window, but there were no houses or people in sight. On every other side was the moor, empty and desolate, with the great pyramids of the slag heaps just visible in the distance. Agnes made to unfasten the door but the moment she turned, she felt Fred Chester's arm slide round her waist. She looked back with startled horror. His mouth was slightly open and moist and his eyes were bright. Even on his best days Mr Chester was not a particularly attractive man, but now he looked repulsive.

'Please don't do that, Mr Chester!' She put her hand on his arm, but he sidled the other one round and clenched his hands over her stomach, gripping her whole body in a vice. 'Mr Chester! Please!'

'Oh, come on, Agnes.' He pressed his cheek against hers; it was sweaty and bristly, utterly loathsome. She struggled, but his grip tightened and his long, moist tongue tried to lick hers. His breath smelt slightly and she felt nauseated. She tore at his hands, turning her head away.

'Mr Chester! Stop it!'

Ignoring her, he moved one hand up to her bosom while with the other he tried to reach under her skirt. Her arms flailing she felt close to tears, her heart pounding as hard, if not harder, than his. Suddenly desperate, she leaned down and bit the wrist of the hand that was trying to caress her bosom.

'Little bitch!' With a yell of pain he withdrew the other hand and clasped his wrist to his mouth, eyeing her savagely. 'What did you want to do that for?'

'What did *you* want to do *that* for?' She tried to draw her skirt over her knees.

'Give over, Agnes. You've been giving me the come-on ever since I first set eyes on you. You must have known I fancied you.'

Agnes looked incredulously at him. 'What would your wife say?'

Fred Chester gave an ugly little laugh. 'She wouldn't know, would she?'

'I might tell her.'

'Oh, no you wouldn't! She wouldn't blame me anyway. She'd blame you! And she'd be right. You shouldn't have given me the come-on. You girls are all the same. You lead men on. They call you cock-teasers. Your friend Grace Calthorpe's one. Oh, she's one all right, from what I've heard.'

'Grace Calthorpe is no such thing, and nor am I!'

'You might not be, Miss High and Mighty Rivington, but she is. You don't know what goes on in the park after school, especially in the winter when it's dark. Miss Calthorpe is *very* active then, from all I've heard.'

'You're disgusting!' Agnes said. She held the door handle and pushed it downwards. 'I'm getting out. Please don't offer me a lift again.'

'Oh, you can be sure I won't, Miss High and Mighty!'

'And don't call me that!'

'Everyone else does, didn't you know? They think you're too big for your boots at Calthorpes. Miss High and Mighty, a personal friend of the boss. Don't you notice all the special little privileges you get?'

'I don't get any privileges!'

'Well, I've never known a junior office girl get moved around as much as you do. Anyone would think you were going to take over the firm! Six weeks in this department, five weeks in that. They say he pays for your shorthand and typing classes. He doesn't do that for anyone else, or move them about. An accounts clerk stays an accounts clerk, an invoice clerk an invoice clerk. Learning the business are you, Miss Rivington? Does he have a high position in mind for you? Secretary, maybe? No one likes you at Calthorpes, Miss High and Mighty. You're too much in favour with the boss. No one dares offend you in case you tell him. I've always stuck up for you because I liked you; but I won't any longer. I'll tell them you're a cock-teaser, just like Grace ...'

Agnes flung open the door, tripped, recovered her footing and then ran towards the moor. She ran until she was breathless and then she stopped and looked over her shoulder. He was still standing by the car watching her and she thought he was going to wait until she was exhausted and then follow her; but as she began to run again she heard the engine start up and, glancing back, she saw him reverse in the road and drive back the way he had come. She slowed down, feeling sick and disgusted. She wished she could tear off the dress he had pawed and throw it in a ditch. She felt unclean, contaminated.

When she arrived at the 'slag' she was greeted by several children she knew playing there; but she ignored them and ran all the way down the street until she arrived at her own home. Before she got to the door she slowed to a walk and took a deep breath. Her father would kill her if he ever found out what had happened – even if it wasn't her fault! She had never told him about taking lifts from Mr Chester. Perhaps in her heart she had known it wasn't wise.

Agnes opened the front door and prepared to climb quietly upstairs to her own room, but she had only gone a few steps when the sitting room door opened. Paul stood there. Her face lit up with joy and she ran into his arms, raising herself to kiss his cheek. He seemed to have grown even taller during his year away at Oxford.

'Paul! When did you get back?'

'At lunch time.'

'Where are Mum and Dad?'

'They've gone to Auntie Edna's to see Doris's new baby. They told me to stop here and wait for you.'

He stood back, smiling, and she went into the sitting room. A teapot and teacups were set out on the table.

'Mum said we're to have a cup of tea and then join them at Auntie Edna's. Here, it's still hot.' He poured her a cup and held it out to her.

'Ta.' She took the cup, but as she lifted it to her lips, her hand trembled. It shook so violently that she quickly put the cup back on the saucer and sat down. Paul looked at her with concern.

'What's the matter? You look upset.'

'I've – I've been running.'

'But why? You look as if you've had a shock.'

Seeing his concern, Agnes suddenly felt unable to restrain her tears.

'Here,' Paul said. 'Here, what's up?'

Agnes cried and cried and said nothing. She couldn't ever remember losing control like this.

Paul put an arm round her shoulders and let her cry. 'You must tell me what happened. Did someone follow you?'

Agnes shook her head 'It's – it's nothing.'

'Agnes. Tell me. I'm not going over to Auntie Edna's until you do.'

'Well, it's such a silly thing. There's this man at work ...'

By the time she finished pouring out her story, Paul's face was a study in rage.

'I'm going to see that swine and beat him up!'

'Oh, Paul, no! Besides, it's not so much what he did as what he said. I thought they liked me there. Why should they call me Miss High and Mighty?'

'I'm sure they don't,' Paul protested.

'But what if they do! He wanted to hurt me, but I'm sure it's true. I'd better leave Calthorpes if that's what they think.'

'Oh, that's ridiculous! Why should you leave when you're doing so well?'

'I knew I was silly to take a lift from him,' Agnes said bitterly.

'You mean you *knew* he fancied you?'

'Oh no! Nothing like that. I never thought he fancied me for a minute. But I still knew I was silly – that it was wrong. That Dad wouldn't approve if he knew.'

'Why did you do it, then?'

Agnes shrugged. 'I thought it was kind of him to ask. When it's cold it is nice to have a lift home. And he never touched me before, or so much as hinted ...'

She looked at him pathetically. She hadn't told Paul what Mr Chester had said about Grace, or about cock-teasing. She couldn't bring herself to mention things like that. She felt sodden with shame and guilt and humiliation. That someone should think she was *that* sort of girl! As for Grace, she didn't dare ask herself if what he said could be true.

'Well,' Paul said, 'you must never take a lift from him again. That sort of thing passes over. It may be unpleasant for a day or two ...'

Agnes buried her face in her hands. 'I don't feel I can ever look him in the face again.'

'If you're going to stay at Calthorpes you'll have to; but be polite to him, that's all. Do you like it there, really?'

He sat down and got out a cigarette. She had never seen him smoke before. He suddenly seemed so distant and grown up, with his long thin face and his mop of curly hair. He looked like a man now, no longer a boy.

'Yes, I do. The work's varied and interesting.' Her voice grew bitter. 'Even if it is laid on especially for me.'

Paul stood up and blew smoke at his reflection in the mirror over the mantelpiece. He gazed down at Agnes's bent head. He loved her and he felt guilty about her, because he had been given opportunities and she hadn't. He bent down and touched her hair, running his fingers through her thick curls. It was an unfamiliar gesture and when she gazed up at him she saw tenderness and love in his eyes.

'You'd best go and change,' he said rather brusquely. 'It'll never do for Auntie Edna to see you like that.'

When, a week or two later, Mr Calthorpe sent for Agnes, she felt sure it was something to do with Mr Chester.

He didn't get to his feet when Agnes came in, but leaned back in his padded swivel chair, pointing to a seat with a hand that held a large, glowing cigar.

'Ah, come in, Agnes, love. Take a seat now and make yourself comfy.'

Agnes did as she was told and gazed at Mr Calthorpe apprehensively.

He leaned forward, beaming. 'Now, I'll not eat you. Don't look so frightened!'

Agnes swallowed.

'Are you happy here, Agnes?'

'Very happy, Mr Calthorpe.'

'Good, good.' He sat back, edging his chair away from his desk. 'I hear nothing but good reports. I ask about you regularly, you know. I take an interest in you. Don't think I sit here in my grand office, indifferent to the welfare of my staff. I don't.'

'I know that, Mr Calthorpe.'

'Well, I'm glad you're happy. I'm happy too – and I think that you have a future here, as far as a girl with your looks wants a future in an office. I bet you've got a boyfriend or two, eh?'

Agnes met his gaze. 'Oh no, Mr Calthorpe. My father thinks I'm too young.'

'Ah, keeps an eye on you, does he? Well, maybe he's right.'

Mr Calthorpe got up and started to pace up and down the office, which, like his home, was fitted with the finest all-wool Calthorpe carpet. 'A lot of young people are too easy going these days; their parents don't take enough care of them. I don't mind them going out in groups – no harm in that; but I don't like all this dating. Now, you'll go out in a group, I imagine, of a Saturday night?'

'I do sometimes, Mr Calthorpe; but I don't like dancing very much. Some of my friends go dancing at the Hippodrome on a Saturday; but I'm not very interested in that.'

'You don't see as much of Grace as you used to, do you?'

'No, Mr Calthorpe.'

'That's a pity. You were always a good influence on her. She goes to the Hippodrome *every* Saturday. I thought you went with her.'

'I do, sometimes.'

'I had the impression you were always there, from what she told me.'

'I'm there quite a lot,' Agnes improvised hastily, 'but not *every* Saturday.'

Mr Calthorpe sat down rather heavily.

'Are you sorry you left school, Agnes?'

'No, Mr Calthorpe.'

'Are you sure?'

'Yes.'

'Because you're a bright girl. More serious than Grace. I wish now you'd stayed on and helped her. I wish I'd done more to try and persuade your father. You see, Grace has fallen off this year. She doesn't work and she makes no bones about leaving at the end of the year. Mrs Armtree says she's completely lost her concentration since you left. There's no competition, so she doesn't enjoy her work any more. She just likes dancing and having a good time. I worry about her. Now look, Agnes, I want you to do something for me. I want you to try and spend more time with Grace. I'd like you to go dancing on a Saturday, go round to the house more, keep an eye on her for me ...'

'But Mr Calthorpe, I can't do that. She'd resent it like mad.'

'She needn't ever know I asked you. I'm very worried, I don't mind telling you. I keep on hearing rumours about Grace ...'

'What – what sort of rumours?' But as she carefully studied the carpet on the floor, Agnes already knew the answer.

'Oh, silly things – that she sees boys in the park. Her mother's worried about her too. I'd like you to try and persuade Grace to stay on at school, get her A Levels, go on to university or teachers' training, *do* something with her life. Would you try? For me. Agnes?'

Agnes looked up at Mr Calthorpe and nodded without saying anything. She knew it was hopeless to make any promises. She knew Grace!

* * *

Agnes knew it was impossible to talk directly to Grace. But she did arrange to go dancing with her and a group of her friends, and Paul. Paul disliked dancing as much as Agnes, but he agreed as soon as he knew Grace would be there.

It was the Saturday after Easter, and the Hippodrome was packed. As soon as Agnes arrived she regretted her decision. Brightly-coloured lights revolved, casting a lurid glow over the dancers, and 'Rock Around the Clock' thumped away at ear-splitting volume while the couples gyrated madly on the dance floor. She and Paul stood, scanning the faces.

'I don't think Grace has come,' Paul said. 'I can't see her anywhere.'

'Oh, there's Connie,' Agnes pointed into the dark. 'She used to be at our school. I work with her at Calthorpes.'

Agnes waved a hand as Connie bobbed past her, partnered by a tall, thick-set young man. As he threw her to one side in time to the deafening music, Connie saw Agnes and stopped.

Connie Shilton was a heavily built girl but, incongruously, with the cumbersome body went a pretty face, slanted eyes and full, sculptured lips. Her plucked eyebrows curved down at the sides and a thick curtain of dark hair neatly framed her oval face.

Connie was sexy; the big body and large breasts did not merely hint at voluptuousness, they proclaimed it. She had good legs and danced like an athlete, her heavy hips gyrating, the sweat pouring down her face from beneath her fringe. Now she was panting for breath and her face was flushed.

'Fancy seeing you here, Agnes! This is Mike.'

The young man with her smiled, his feet still shuffling to the rhythm of the music.

'This is my brother, Paul. Have you seen Grace anywhere?'

Connie nodded. 'She's over with a crowd by the band – surrounded by men, of course. This is Mike's brother Jeff.'

As if by magic Connie drew a thin young man out of the crowd and pushed him towards Agnes. 'He wants to meet you.'

Both Agnes and Jeff looked embarrassed, while Connie laughed and led Mike back on to the dance floor.

'Do you want to dance?' Jeff murmured awkwardly.

'If you like.'

Paul gave Agnes a wave and sauntered off.

'Do you come here often, as they say?' Jeff asked with a nervous smile. He had a thin face dominated by a pair of large, horn-rimmed spectacles, and his hair was thinning on top.

'No, not much. We were meant to meet up with Grace Calthorpe tonight, but we couldn't seem to find her.'

'You can always find Grace where the boys are,' Jeff said. 'She's got quite a reputation in this town!'

Paul, meanwhile, had been circling the dance floor, viewing Grace Calthorpe from all angles. He wanted to dance with her, but somehow he lacked the courage to ask her. She had never taken the slightest notice of him in all the years she had been his sister's best friend; what if she rebuffed him now?

He was helped at last by the music, which changed from rock and roll into the smoochy 'Stranger in Paradise'. Seeing Grace temporarily without a partner, he went quickly up to her, arms extended and, to his amazement, she slid into them, smiling into his face, her hips moving sensuously in time to the music.

Grace had indeed a reputation in the town. In his last year at school, Paul had heard much sniggering in the locker rooms about Grace, and what she would do in the garden shed in the park for favoured sixth-formers. Most of it he had found hard to believe, and certainly he would never have dreamed of talking about it to his sister. But the stories had inflamed his dormant passions, just as they had inflamed those of every other youth in the town. Those who boasted of seeing Grace in the nude were regarded with envy by the less fortunate.

Now that he felt those much-talked-of breasts pressed against his chest, his heart began to pound with excitement. He put his face down and leaned it against Grace's cheek. As his hands circled her back, he could feel the straps of her brassiere, and the erotic image this induced was overwhelming.

'How are you liking Oxford, Paul?' Grace asked, as though unaware of the tumult she was causing.

'I like it very much.'

'I must say you've changed.'

'How?' He held her away and looked into her eyes; they glistened, suggestively, invitingly. He swallowed.

'Just older, that's all. I haven't seen you since you left the Grammar ...'

Grace continued to dance with Paul all evening. The bevy of boys who waited for the privilege swarmed on her every time a number finished, only to be rebuffed. She and Paul hardly spoke at all until he began to walk her home, surprised and gratified that she had rejected so many offers of lifts.

'I enjoyed that, but I needed some air,' Grace said, linking her arm through his. 'Do you mind?'

'Mind what?'

'This.' She nudged him. 'Linking arms.'

'Of course not.'

'Do you think Agnes minded having to go home with Connie?'

'I don't expect so. They've known each other for ages.'

As they walked up the tree-lined road that led to the better end of town, Paul longed to draw her into the shadows and kiss her, but he didn't dare. He had never in his life kissed a girl the way he felt he now wanted to kiss Grace.

'I wish you hadn't left town,' Grace said. 'You're different from the other boys.'

'I come home at the vacations. I won't be here in the summer because I'm doing a holiday job in France, but there will be other times.'

Grace stopped and looked at him.

'Time doesn't mean much to you, does it, Paul?'

'How do you mean?'

'It doesn't seem immediate. Is it because it's going to take you so long to be a doctor?'

'I never thought of it like that.'

'I feel I'd like to see you here and now, but you don't seem to feel like that at all. Aren't you interested in girls?'

'It's not that!'

'I know: you're too busy with your studies. I couldn't care less about mine. Daddy's going to let me leave school this summer; or rather, I'm going to *make* him let me leave.'

'How?'

'Just by nagging. I've no ambition at all, you see. Does that shock you?' She let her hand slip and her fingers slid into his palm.

'No,' he replied carefully, conscious of the intimacy of the gesture. 'A girl doesn't *have* to have ambition, though there are a lot of girls at Oxford, you know.'

Grace laughed derisively. 'Blue stockings!'

'They're attractive, intelligent girls like you; like you and Agnes.'

'Agnes has no ambition either.'

'Are you sure?' Paul let Grace's hand fall and lit a cigarette. 'I'm guilty about Agnes. I feel that Dad put me before her quite deliberately. Agnes has a fine brain – she could have gone to university if she'd chosen to.'

'Oh, she didn't want to go,' Grace said. 'I'm sure of that. Women just wait around to get married and that's the truth!'

'Agnes doesn't just want to get married!' Paul exclaimed angrily. 'She's keen on her job, and she's going to study at the Poly.'

'She'll give it all up when the right man comes along, though,' Grace said cynically. 'All women do. Even your blue stockings. Just you wait and see.'

'You sound bitter,' Paul said with surprise and tried to take her hand again.

'I'm not at all bitter.' Grace threw back her head and gave a provocative, sexy laugh. 'I'm realistic. I look around me and that's what I see.'

They had reached her house now, and Paul stood uncertainly by the gate, wondering if he dared kiss her. Then he saw a light come on over the porch, the front door open and Mr Calthorpe appear on the steps, lighting his pipe.

'Too late!' Grace whispered. 'Shall we meet again before you go back?'

'Of course,' he said eagerly, thinking about the shed in the park. 'I'll give you a ring.'

'No, I'll call you. I don't want Mum and Dad to know that we're dating. They don't really like me going out on my own. They say I'm too young. Safety in numbers.'

'You can't call me. I'm not on the phone.' Paul decided this was the rebuff he had been dreading. She was a tease; people said she wasn't genuine, and they were right.

'I'll find a way. I'll get a message to you through Agnes.'

'Why, it's Paul!' Mr Calthorpe said, reaching the garden gate and holding out his hand. 'Did you have a good time?'

'Yes thanks, Mr Calthorpe.'

'I hear you're doing very well at Oxford, Paul. A credit to your family.'

'Thank you, sir.' Paul threw away his cigarette and stared into the eyes of the man whose daughter he wanted to kiss. Mr Calthorpe put an arm proprietorially round Grace and ushered her through the gate.

'See you again, Paul. Thanks for seeing Grace home.'

'Thanks, Paul,' Grace said without looking at him. 'Night.'

'Night.'

Paul watched them go into the house and the door shut behind them. Then the light went off in the porch and he turned to make his way slowly, thoughtfully, down the hill.

CHAPTER FOUR

GRACE HAD A FUNNY LITTLE SMILE on her face; a smile that few people who knew her would have recognized. But Johnny Henley knew the smile well; in fact, he found it almost as intriguing as the rest of her body. His eyes travelled upwards from the toes of her feet, remaining for a long time on the pointed tips of her nipples and finally coming to rest on her face. That arch little smile was furtive and naughty. It said 'so far and no further'. It was tantalising, and yet he knew she meant it for now. Johnny Henley was a year older than Grace and had left school to become an apprentice draughtsman. He sighed and licked his lips. He would have her one day – *all* of her.

'You've got a very red face,' Grace said prosaically, slightly altering her statuesque pose. One leg was slightly crossed over the other, the knees touching, so that that very special place between her legs remained hidden by the wiry triangle of hair at her groin. 'You look ugly when you go so red.'

Grace liked to taunt the boys who gazed at her, insulting them, belittling them, all the time knowing they were too mesmerised by her nudity to reply.

'You shouldn't lick your lips, either. It makes you look coarse and gross.'

She put her hands under her breasts, cupping them, pointing the nipples at him like two pistols. She smoothed her hands down across her ribs, over her waist, letting them rest by her hips. Then she joined her hands in front of her groin, and turned her head in profile for the final pose.

'I think I might be a model,' she said. 'With clothes, of course!' She turned her head sharply and looked at Johnny. 'That's enough for today. Now you can go and look out of the window while I get dressed.'

This was the form. They were never allowed to watch her dress or undress. Even in the gardener's hut in the park, which had been risky because there was no lock on the door, they had to wait outside until she was ready; then they trooped in, one by one, and one by one trooped out. Here there was no safety in numbers. Grace knew she could only control one at a time. Singly they were afraid of her, because she was Grace Calthorpe.

She had never brought a boy up to her room until today. But now that Johnny had a job, he couldn't get to see her in the park, and she had promised him a last peep before she stopped altogether. One last peep for Johnny, her favourite, Johnny the most handsome, the most persistent, the one who had started the whole thing off. But he had been told he must behave, just the same as when they were in the gardener's hut.

'Just two minutes more,' Johnny begged, his eyes fixed on her breasts; but Grace was unmoved. She put her hands on her hips and imperiously ordered him over to the window.

Just then, the door opened and Mr Calthorpe appeared, staring in amazement at his daughter, unable to believe the evidence of his eyes.

Grace grabbed at the clothes which lay neatly folded on her bed.

'What are you doing, Grace?' Mr Calthorpe spoke in a very ordinary voice, as if he had simply come in and found her reading the paper. 'What's this boy doing here?'

'It's Johnny Henley, Daddy,' she heard herself mumbling.

'But what's he doing here?'

Grace stepped hurriedly into her panties and caught up her provocative breasts in her brassiere. When she faced her father, she was still pulling her light summer dress down over her head. Her face had never burned so much before, even on that day when she had first taken off all her clothes in the garden hut in the park because of the entreaties of Johnny who was really her first date, 'just to see a bit more, Grace, please.' A bit more, a bit more, then all. After that first time it was comparatively simple. She enjoyed it and she enjoyed the power it gave her; the lust in their eyes, the denial of satisfaction that was hers to deny ...

'You might have knocked, Dad.'

'I didn't think you were here, or I would have done.' Puzzled, he turned to Johnny. 'I don't know what you think you're up to, young man, but I've a fair idea ...' He turned back to Grace as though pleading for some perfectly innocent explanation.

'I'm sorry, Dad.'

'You mean you actually were …?'

Grace nodded her head. Mr Calthorpe's face seemed to swell and went even redder than Johnny's.

'Get out of here, Henley!'

Johnny didn't even stop to look at Grace's father, but snatched his jacket from the chair by the bed and slunk out of the room. Then Henry Calthorpe sat on the bed and started to weep …

Barry Holloway ran his eyes over the new term's influx of students and wondered how many would be left by the end of the year, never mind the following summer. One of the disheartening things about adult education classes was the speed with which enthusiasm gave way to indifference.

Barry's course on the Origins of Socialism began with the 1848 Revolution in Europe. It was the third year that he had given the course and each time he tried to add a bit of new material, if only to keep his own interest from flagging. He cleared his throat and began:

'The causes of the revolution that swept through Europe …'

Agnes had seen him about the corridors and in the canteen the previous year, when she'd been learning shorthand and typing. It had decided her that she would do the course in politics as well as literature when she got her diploma. Barry Holloway was a big man with black hair and a beard. He wore clothes casually and was slightly scruffy, his tie never quite centred, his shoes never polished. He looked intellectual and passionate, and both aspects appealed to her. As he talked, she found she was looking at him, appraising him, rather than listening to what he said. She saw his eyes on her and hastily started to make notes.

She thought about him a lot the following week and soon realised that Thursdays, the day of his class, was all that she really looked forward to. But the following week he was ill and someone else took his place. He was away for three weeks and when he came back he looked thin and pale. He apologized, saying he had had a very bad bout of 'flu, and left immediately the class was over.

It was nearly Christmas when Agnes first spoke to Barry Holloway. He had been detained by one of the class bores and she was standing nervously by the door, hoping to catch him before he slipped away.

'Yes?'

'I wondered if you could suggest some extra reading?'

'You've got through that list?'

'Yes.'

'Well, I'm amazed! Most people don't even read a third of it.' His eyes showed interest. 'It's Miss Rivington, isn't it?'

'Yes.'

'Are you any relation to Albert Rivington of the Labour Party GMC?'

'He's my father.'

'Oh, so that's why you're interested in politics?'

'Maybe.'

'Look, I'll have to make another list for next week. Is that all right? I've got to fly now.'

'That's fine. Thank you.'

On Thursdays after his lecture Barry Holloway spent the night with his mistress. It was their one night together, the one time of the week it was safe. He saw her at other times, but Thursdays they slept together all night. Because, punctilious man of habit that he was, Henry Calthorpe always went to Leeds and spent the night with his brother.

Rose Munday was ten years older than Barry Holloway and they had only met by the merest chance, because she didn't move in the same circles as a young aspiring politician, especially a Labour one. Although he was a Yorkshireman, Barry did not come from Beckersleigh and when he had first started teaching at the Polytechnic he had lodged with some people called Singer who lived in the town. Mary Singer was a friend of Rose Munday who chanced to be there for dinner one night when Barry was at home.

Afterwards Barry drove her home and she asked him in. They went straight to bed. It was only some time later that he found out about Henry Calthorpe, but by then he was in no mood to abandon their relationship ...

Rose Munday gave Barry Holloway sex and good food. She always had a meal ready for him when he came, and he would always stop off at the off-licence on his way there to buy a bottle of wine. He looked forward to Thursdays, and felt better on Friday for having spent the night with Rose.

Rose had a tasty hotpot and some cheese ready the Thursday after Agnes first spoke to him. She took the bottle from him at the door and then helped him off with his coat.

'It's cold!' he exclaimed, kissing her lightly and then going eagerly to the sitting room, where a huge fire burned in the grate. He stood there rubbing his hands while she brought him a glass of beer, as usual.

'You are good,' he said gratefully and turned and kissed her more passionately. She had a good figure with large breasts and she always wore very high heels and nylon stockings with straight seams. She had her hair done twice a week and the style never varied; curly round the bottom, waved over the ears and smooth on top. Barry guessed she took a long time getting ready for him because she was conscious of the difference in their ages.

They usually ate by the sitting room fire because it was warmer than the dining room, and she would set a table cosily with fresh linen and shining cutlery and two large cut-crystal glasses for the wine.

They talked like an old married couple reviewing the week, but with a little anticipatory edge of excitement: they were lovers, and knew that in the course of the night they would explore each other's bodies intimately. They hadn't met since the previous Thursday because Barry had been busy; when he had been free, Rose had warned that it wasn't safe to visit.

'You've been seeing a lot of him, then?' He kept his voice casual, but he could not conceal his jealousy of Henry.

'Well, he's been over for this and that. His wife's ill and he doesn't know whether or not to send for his daughter. He's like a child. He wants advice and support all the time.'

'Is she seriously ill?'

'She has a bout of bronchitis every winter, and she's got a bad heart too. I think he's a bit more worried than usual, yes.'

'Where's the daughter, then?'

'At finishing school in Switzerland. Don't you remember all that fuss last summer when he found a boy in her room?'

'Oh, yes. He caught him with no clothes on.'

'No, *she* had no clothes on. The boy swore he was just looking.'

Barry laughed and gulped his wine, his eyes sparkling across at Rose, already imagining her naked.

'I bet he was, too,' Rose continued. 'Some girls just love taking their clothes off and tantalising men. That would be Miss Calthorpe, if you ask me. She's just the type.'

'Oh, what type?' Barry put down his knife and fork.

'A cock-teaser. She's very pert and pretty.'

'You know her, then?'

'Well, I've never met her, but I've seen her. She has very blonde hair and she's tall ... Listen, I don't know why I'm telling you all this.' She reached across and touched his nose. 'Saucy. You're interested, aren't you?'

'Of course I'm not. I suppose she'll only be about eighteen. I prefer the more mature woman.'

'Get away with you!' Rose sighed with pleasure and went to fetch the cheese.

'Don't bother with the cheese,' he said. 'We can have it afterwards.'

She knew that thinking about the young girl taking her clothes off had made him feel sexy. She didn't mind, so long as it made him want her.

The following spring Mrs Calthorpe, who had never enjoyed good health, had a heart attack and Grace was sent for; but by the time she came home her mother was better and in no danger. She was even sitting up in a chair in her room. But she looked a lot older.

'I think I should be home looking after you, Mummy.'

'Don't be silly, darling. What can you do? You're enjoying Switzerland, aren't you?'

Grace made a face. 'It's like a prim girls' school!'

Suddenly she heard the front door close and voices in the hall. There was a new addition to the house in the shape of a housekeeper, but the female voice she could hear was young.

'Agnes!' Grace said and leapt to the door, flinging it open. She held out her arms and her friend ran into them. They embraced and then stood looking at each other.

'I think you've put on weight!'

'And *you're* skinnier!'

'I'm not!'

'Well, I haven't!'

Instinctively they held hands and Grace drew her into the room. 'Mummy, hasn't Agnes put on weight?'

Mrs Calthorpe put her head on one side. 'She was very thin before. She looks bonnier. Yes, you look very bonny, Agnes. And thank you for your flowers.'

'I would have come to see you, Mrs Calthorpe; but they said no visitors.'

'I know. I hope you'll stay for supper, Agnes, I've missed you. Why, you're both eighteen! Imagine! I can't believe it, can you, Henry? I remember them as little scraps holding hands just as they are now and standing in their long gymslips in front of the fire.'

'Aye, I do remember, dear,' Henry said looking at them and wishing they had always stayed as simple and as innocent as they were then. Grace certainly wasn't innocent any more; he didn't know about Agnes, though he had heard one or two stories about her and Fred Chester.

'I dare say you and Agnes would like to go upstairs and natter,' Mrs Calthorpe said. 'With us going over to Switzerland for Christmas, you haven't seen each other since last summer – you'll have a lot to catch up on. Go off with you, now! Supper's at seven.'

The den looked terribly tidy, almost alien. The bed had been turned round so that it stood on its own in the middle of the floor. Grace immediately pushed it against the wall as it used to be and flopped down on it, legs crossed, one tapping the air. Agnes could see the top of her stockings and her suspenders.

'I don't care for this housekeeper woman one little bit. She looks like a governess from a Bronte novel,' Grace announced.

'She does look rather severe. But your mother needs someone; she looks very ill, Grace.'

'I think I should come home.' Grace frowned. 'I hate that school anyway; it's like a convent. You never see a male face except the husband of the *directrice*, and he's about sixty.' Grace glanced at Agnes. 'Have you got a boy-friend yet?'

'No.'

'No one at all?'

'No. There's a man I rather like, but he takes no notice of me.'

'Make him take notice! Who is he?' Grace was really interested.

'He's a lecturer at the Poly.'

'How old?'

'Oh, mid-twenties.'

'What's he like?'

'Very tall, with a black beard and curly black hair that falls over his eyes. He looks a bit as I imagine Heathcliff looked.'

'And you're very like Emily!' Grace swung her legs off the bed. 'You're very naive about men, Agnes. Trust you to fancy someone you can't get.'

'Who says I can't get him?' Agnes was annoyed. 'I've never tried!'

'But you've never liked any boys, have you? You know – in the normal way. Gone out with them, had dates, held hands.' There was a goading note in Grace's voice.

'I never took my clothes off in front of them, if that's what you mean!' Agnes spoke furiously.

Grace blushed, but her eyes shone with anger. 'Don't be cheap!'

'It's *you* who were cheap.'

'I don't know how that story got about. Dad wouldn't have told anyone.'

'Well, everyone knew. Even Paul knew. He told me that he'd heard you did it for a lot of boys, said he wished he'd been one of them!'

'Oh, did he?' Grace leaned back on her hands and moistened her lips. 'I must say I rather fancied Paul when I saw him again last Easter. He used to be all spotty, but I thought he'd developed sex appeal. He asked me to call him after that dance, but I never did.'

Grace thoughtfully gnawed a fingernail. The reason she hadn't called him was because her father didn't want her to. And she hadn't cared enough about Paul to defy him.

'I don't want you getting too involved with the Rivingtons,' he had said. 'Remember, they're not our sort.'

'But you like Agnes.'

'I do, love, I do; but that's different.'

Grace knew what her father meant. Her friendship with Agnes was one thing; with Paul Rivington it was another. After all, the Rivingtons had no money and Paul had years to go before he qualified as a doctor.

Agnes's voice brought her back to the present.

'I don't know how you could have taken your clothes off like that, Grace.' She was determined to press the point. 'How could you bring yourself to *do* it?'

'Well, I can, or rather I could. I don't know if I would now. Maybe it *was* a bit silly.'

'How many boys were there?'

'Oh, only three or four. Johnny Henley and Frank Barrow and John Cappell and ...' She laughed. 'I can't even remember who the other one was! They were all pretty silly. No, I won't do it again.'

Agnes was not convinced. There was an animal quality about Grace that she hadn't remarked on before. She looked more sophisticated than ever now, with her hair braided into a chignon, a single row of pearls round her neck, a ring on her middle finger.

'Who gave you the ring?'

Grace looked at her hands. 'That? My mother. It's a real sapphire!' Her voice softened. 'Whenever I go away, she's always afraid she'll never see me again.'

Grace was silent, and Agnes was conscious that a new rapport had built up between them in the short time since they had been in the room. When Mr Calthorpe had sent for her at the factory that afternoon and suggested they left work early, she had wanted to say 'no', to delay the moment of meeting Grace again. But as soon as she saw her, smiling at her from the door, arms extended, she knew it was all right. Better: she had even found the courage to speak her mind, to tell Grace what she thought of her.

'Don't you wonder what you're going to do with your life, Agnes?' Grace sighed deeply and turned her head.

'*Do?*'

'Well, are you happy as you are?'

'What else is there to do?' Agnes shrugged.

'I can't understand you. You're a thoughtful person, yet sometimes you behave like a half-wit. You should have stood up to your father much more. Just think – we'd be in the upper sixth now, going on to university. Our lives would be opening up in such an exciting way. Now I feel they're closing in, suffocatingly!'

'Oh, come on! You've been to Switzerland, Grace. I've never even been to London. And you could have stayed on at school if you'd wanted to.'

'No, I couldn't. Not without you. You don't know how much I depend on you, how much you really matter to me. And you hardly ever wrote, Agnes.'

'Nor did you!' she retaliated.

'Believe me, I was stifled in that place. I had simply nothing to write about.'

'And I thought you were having a wonderful time. I did feel a bit jealous.'

'Don't you like it at Calthorpes?'

'Yes, I do. And I have my night classes.'

'But it's not really you, is it? We *should* have gone to university. We *should* have gone to London.' Suddenly Grace jumped up and gripped Agnes's hands. 'Agnes, we still can! What's to stop us going to London?'

'Money!'

'We can get jobs,' Grace said airily.

'What jobs?'

'Well, you can get a secretarial job and I can work in a shop. Oh, Agnes, it would be heaven! Imagine sharing a room, going to the theatre, dancing ...'

'My Dad would never let me go.'

'Oh, your dad!'

'Yours wouldn't either. He'd say it would give your mother a heart attack.'

'Well, I'm not staying in this rotten hole all my life. I'll go mad in Beckersleigh, Agnes.' Grace was petulant.

'We'd better go down for supper,' Agnes said quietly, getting up and tugging Grace by the hand. 'We can talk about it some other time.'

'Agnes Rivington.' Barry Holloway smiled as he put her essay on her desk. 'Very good,' he whispered. 'Could you see me about it afterwards? John Turner ...'

Agnes put her hands on her hot cheeks. A-minus. It was the highest mark she'd ever had! But why did he want to see her?

'I think you put too much emphasis on the influence of Marx on the early Socialists,' Barry Holloway said gravely after the class, sitting at his high teacher's desk. He studied her paper, flicking over the pages. 'But really that's all. Otherwise it's very good. Hey, would you like a coffee?'

Agnes looked at her watch. She was always expected home straight after the class ...

'It's all right if you haven't got time,' Barry said, noticing her gesture. 'Have you got a date or something?'

'No – no. It's my Dad,' Agnes said. 'He gets anxious if I'm out late.'

'I'll see you home if you like.'

'It's perfectly all right. I'd like a coffee, though, thanks ...'

As they walked to the canteen, she was very conscious of his height, of a powerful quality in him that made people look at him as they walked down the corridor, lined with its faded yellow tiles. He told her to get a table while he got coffee. He brought two cups back and a packet of Marie biscuits.

'So your father's anxious about you getting home?'

His direct look made her feel nervous and she lowered her gaze like a shy schoolgirl. 'Well, he *is* a bit fussy.'

'How old are you, Miss Rivington?'

'Nineteen in October.'

'I'm twenty-six', Barry said. 'I hope you didn't mind me asking.'

'Not in the least.'

'I thought you'd be about that but I wasn't sure. You look a lot older.' He held up a hand apologetically when he saw her start. 'I mean that as a compliment – you know, twenty or twenty-one. It's just that you have a self-assurance most girls your age don't have. Where do you work?'

'At Calthorpes, in the offices.'

Barry gave a slight start and hid his face in his coffee cup. She misinterpreted his silence. 'You know, Calthorpes the carpet people.'

'Oh, I know Calthorpes. What's the old man like?'

'Mr Calthorpe? He's not really old – he's nice. He's good to his workers, even though he's a Conservative.'

Barry laughed. 'His daughter's pretty free with her favours, I hear.'

Agnes went scarlet. 'Grace Calthorpe is my best friend.'

'Oh, I'm sorry. I shouldn't have said that. It was probably just a rumour ...' He drained his cup to the dregs. 'But it's true her father sent her away, isn't it? Because of ...' He enjoyed seeing Agnes's confusion. She was an attractive girl, the antithesis of what he imagined sexy Grace Calthorpe to be, with her penchant for displaying herself nude. She had very curiously coloured eyes and the sun had brought out the freckles on her face. Tonight she had on a simple cotton frock with a round neck and a belt that tied at the back. She wore no stockings and sandals on her feet. In fact, she didn't look older than her years; if anything she looked younger. He'd said what he had said to flatter her. He saw her as the sort of bookish girl who was shy with men and was kept on a short rein by her possessive father. All the same she intrigued him ...

'Grace was going away anyway,' Agnes said defensively. 'Her father thought a year away would do her good. As it is, she's having two. She's not coming back even for the summer holiday. All the family are going to France.'

'I expect you miss her.'

'I do. We were very close at school, but now our lives are very different. My father's a pit winder and hers is one of the richest men in Beckersleigh.'

'But you've made other friends, haven't you?'

'Not many. There are girls I knew at school who I see occasionally. But I like it best when my brother comes home and I go out with him and his friends.'

'What does he do?'

'He's at Oxford, studying medicine.'

'Oh, yes, I've heard about him. But didn't you want to go to university? It's obvious you were really bright at school – your essays are excellent.'

'I wasn't that keen on university,' Agnes glanced at her watch. 'It's time I was getting home.' She looked at him questioningly. 'You hardly ever stay behind on a Thursday, do you? You always seem to dash off.'

'I go and see an elderly relative,' Barry said, stacking the cups. 'But she's not very well this week. She depends on me a good deal.'

'Oh, I am sorry! I hope she'll soon be well.'

Rose felt very hot but kept the sheet over her. She was aware that she was getting a bit overweight and if she just lay flat on the bed the flab spread. It was Monday afternoon, a day he often came because he had no classes.

'What's wrong with Thursdays?' she said.

'Well, it's a bit complicated with students and things.'

'It never used to be.'

'Well, they like to chat afterwards. They're a very interesting lot, the ones who take politics.'

In fact, late in the summer term there were only six of them left, and only one of them wanted to stay behind: Agnes Rivington. But she interested him. He didn't want to start asking her out, but he liked talking to her after the lecture, casually over coffee. Besides, her father was on the General Management Committee of the Labour Party and Barry was anxious to be a candidate in the local elections. He wanted Agnes to speak well of him to her father, but he was cautious of getting involved with the old boy's daughter.

'I think you've got another girl,' Rose said, lighting a cigarette.

'That's a silly thing to say.' Barry looked away.

'I'm sorry, love,' she said placatingly, feeling slightly panicky. She was terrified of losing him – she would never get such a young vigorous lover again. Imagine putting up with the likes of Henry Calthorpe for the rest of her days! He had no finesse; no refinement in the art of sex. She put out a hand and timidly caressed Barry's chest. She wondered if he realised that he intimidated her. She tried not to let him see it, but there was a hardness about him that scared her to death at times. To her relief he smiled and took one of her nipples quite roughly between the finger and thumb of his left hand.

'It *was* a bloody silly thing to say,' he said, squeezing it tightly; but she could see he was laughing.

Rose smiled and turned on her side so that the hair at their groins touched and her large breasts brushed against his chest. He put his mouth on hers and kissed her, thoughts of Agnes Rivington vanishing altogether ...

CHAPTER FIVE

GRACE CALTHORPE WAS TWENTY when she came back to Beckersleigh to settle. She had been away two and a half years: two years at her finishing school in Switzerland and six months in Paris, where she went to perfect her French. Paris was wonderful, so different from the provincial Swiss town where she'd been educated, and Beckersleigh, where she'd been born and brought up. She felt she could have stayed there forever.

But in January 1959, Mrs Calthorpe had a severe heart attack and was confined to bed.

Grace found it hard to settle down. She had drifted away from the casual friends she had had at school and the people she used to go dancing with at the Hippodrome. She came to depend heavily on Agnes, but at first even the two Graces had difficulty establishing a rapport; each had changed.

Grace saw a pretty but rather provincial girl with short brown hair, little make-up, a brown tweed skirt and a green twin set. She felt she had left Agnes behind; yet for the moment she was all she had, here in Beckersleigh.

Agnes saw a stranger. Grace seemed taller, thinner, more stylish. She dressed with an elegance that she could never have acquired at Beckersleigh. And her hair seemed more golden, streaked at the front as though she spent a lot of time in the sun, even in the depths of winter.

Grace complained a lot. Agnes found her trying, but her father found her impossible.

'I wish she'd get married!' Henry Calthorpe said one day to Rose. 'It would please her mother too. She'd like to see her settled before she ...'

Rose Munday looked at him sympathetically. 'It's that bad, is it, Henry?'

'Yes, she'll not last the year; but she's anxious about Grace. She knows she's restless.'

Henry took a cigarette from the bedside table. They hadn't made love yet, although they were in bed. He hadn't felt up to it and, in many ways, he wanted sympathy more than sex. Rose didn't seem to mind.

'Did your wife ever find out about the ... er ... incident?' She glanced at Henry and saw him frown.

'Good God, no! It would have killed her. It nearly killed me, I can tell you, seeing my daughter in the nude with that boy staring at her.' He shook his head. 'I've never wept like that before or since. Still, it helped me and it helped Grace. It was better than shouting. She promised me she'd never do it again. But she's restless – I know she doesn't sleep well, because I hear her going down to the kitchen to make cups of tea at all hours.'

'You're sure she's not seeing a man off the premises?' Rose started to smile, but regretted it when she saw his face. 'Sorry, love. It was just a bit of fun.'

'Well, it's not funny. And it's time I went.' Henry stubbed out his half-smoked cigarette with a swift, angry movement. Instead of leaning over her and kissing her as he usually did, he got out of bed and climbed into his trousers. Rose got out and put on her satin housecoat. She went round to the other side of the bed and helped fasten the top button of his shirt, which he always found difficult. He stared down at her without smiling.

'I didn't mean it, love, you know that. It was just a tease. I wouldn't say it if I thought it was true. Forgive me?' She passed him his collar and he fastened it at the back and then drew it round to the front. She held out his tie and he took it.

'I don't like jokes about my daughter. She's my only child. All I've got. When I heard there was talk about her, I was upset and when I saw her naked, I was shattered. But I like to think it was an adolescent phase. I trust her. But I wish she'd get married, all the same.'

Rose turned and brushed his jacket before handing it to him, the expression in her eyes sympathetic, understanding. She knew he wasn't telling the truth ...

The sets were even and the games were even in the third set. Grace's tennis was good and Agnes's even better. She was partnered by Jeff Orchard and Grace by Stephen Hetherington, whose father owned one of the steel mills. She and Grace were better than the men, but Stephen was better than Jeff. Stephen had been away to school and was now at King's College, London. Jeff Orchard had just finished training as a teacher. The third set went to seven games and there were several deuces before Agnes and Jeff finally clinched the match. The couples shook hands at the nets to sporadic applause and then they went and collapsed on the grass at the side. Stephen was very fair and his face and neck were red and running with sweat. Jeff's glasses had misted over and he was wiping them on his handkerchief.

'Mummy said we're to go to the house for tea,' Grace said.

'I thought we'd have tea here,' Stephen looked at the club house. 'On me.'

'Mummy will be disappointed if we don't go.' Grace sat up, linking her hands around her knees.

'Okay, but let's have a lemonade now.' Jeff sat up and put on his demisted spectacles. 'I'm terribly thirsty.'

'Good idea.' Agnes rose to her feet, feeling tired but exhilarated. It had been a good game and anything that matched her with Grace made her feel better.

'I do think we should get home to tea,' Grace said, pursing her mouth as she always did when she meant to have her way.

'Oh, just a cool drink, Grace!'

'If *your* mother had said you'd better get back,' Grace said spitefully, 'you'd get back double quick, and you know it.'

Agnes glanced at her and frowned. 'I'm sorry. If you feel that strongly let's go straight to your house.'

'No. *I'm* having a drink!' Stephen said. 'It won't take ten minutes and I'm parched.'

'Tell me where you've put your car, Stephen, and I'll wait for you,' Grace said.

'Oh Grace ...' Stephen started to redden again.

'No. I'm serious. I don't want a drink anyway. In fact, I think I'll walk up the hill. Are you coming, Agnes?'

Agnes looked from Grace to Jeff to Stephen. She knew that Grace was really giving a command. 'I *am* actually very thirsty,' she said. 'We won't be a moment ...'

Grace took her cardigan and her bag with her racquet and walked swiftly towards the exit.

'I'd better go after her,' Agnes said resignedly.

'Oh, we'll all go!' Stephen got his car keys from his tennis bag. 'Miss Calthorpe *must* have her way, mustn't she?'

'But her mother *is* very ill.'

'I don't see what difference five minutes makes. Hey, Grace,' Stephen called, and started to run.

Grace stopped and looked behind, a little smile forming on her mouth. 'Hurry up then,' she said impatiently.

'She's bloody well determined to have her own way, isn't she?' Jeff muttered. '*My* throat's cracked.'

'Oh, we'll soon be there once we're up the hill.'

As they walked past the club house to Stephen's car, a rather old sports car drew alongside. A bearded face looked over the windscreen and smiled at Agnes.

'Hello, Miss Rivington. Remember me?'

'Of course I do!' Agnes said, smiling nervously, somewhat taken by surprise. 'Grace, this is Barry Holloway who used to teach me politics. He's a city councillor now and Parliamentary Labour Candidate.'

Barry had given up taking evening classes since the increase in his civic duties. A prominent city councillor, a man who concerned himself with causes, had more opportunities of displaying himself in the public eye than one who took evening classes, though he still kept on his lectureship at the Poly during the day.

Barry got out of the car, shook hands and flung his jacket into the back of the car. 'It's too hot for this. Have you been playing?'

'Three strenuous sets,' Grace said, laughing, her eyes flashing as she looked at him. 'And we were beaten!'

'I don't believe it!' Barry Holloway returned her bantering tone. '*The* Miss Calthorpe. I've heard so much about you.'

'Oh?'

'Only good things, I assure you. Why don't you all come and have a drink with me? Agnes can tell me what she's been doing since I stopped teaching her politics.'

'Oh, I'm sorry ...' Agnes began.

'We'd *love* a drink,' Grace said smoothly. 'We were just going to have one.'

She smiled sweetly at Stephen, who started to say something and then thought better of it. He opened the boot of his car and put in his bags. 'I don't believe it,' he muttered under his breath as Agnes threw in her bag and cardigan. 'Talk about nerve!' But Grace and

Barry were already walking towards the club house, deep in conversation.

Barry was looking towards her as Agnes entered.

'What will you have to drink?'

'Something long and cool.'

'Miss Calthorpe is having lager.'

'Grace, *please*,' Grace said, laughing. 'Miss Calthorpe sounds terribly formal.'

'I'll have lemonade,' Agnes said, hoping he wouldn't think her childish.

'I understand you're back in England permanently now, Grace.' Barry, smiling, passed her her glass. 'How's your mother?'

'A bit better, thanks. But how do you know so much about *me*?'

'I hear a lot of things on the Council.'

'But my father's not a councillor.'

'No, but he's an important man. I know a lot about him.'

It amused Barry to think that he shared a mistress with this girl's father, and there was an air of titillation in his tone which Grace mistakenly took for flirtatiousness.

'I suppose you know a lot about everything,' Grace said. 'Do you think there will be an election?'

'No doubt about it,' Barry said confidently. 'All these things Macmillan promises that he can't fulfil. Never had it so good – my eye! What about the cotton industry? No, you can't trust a Tory. No offence meant. Are you a Tory, Grace?'

He looked at her, his eyes crinkling as though expecting her to say she was.

'No, I'm a Socialist, of course, like Agnes. We've always been very close in everything. We were called the two Graces at school.'

'Why not the two Agnesses?' Jeff said, putting his foaming glass of beer to his lips.

'I'd have thought it was obvious if you knew your mythology,' Grace said scornfully. 'The three Graces.'

'I didn't know you were Labour!' Agnes laughed. 'It's news to me.'

'I'm not a member of the party; but when I vote I'll vote for you, Mr Holloway.'

'That's just what I came here for,' Barry said, looking around. 'Really?'

'No, actually I came to meet a man who has some ideas about

municipal building. He's not here, though.'

'Who is he?'

'Keith Winchester. From London. Do you know him?'

'No.' Grace looked at her watch. 'We have to get back to our house for tea. Would you like to come?'

Barry shook his head. 'I'd like to, but I can't. I've got to meet this man, and after that I've got a committee meeting at seven-thirty.' He shrugged his shoulders. 'It's all go, I'm afraid.' He turned to Agnes. 'Now, young lady, are you keeping up with your studies?'

'Not politics. Literature and creative writing.'

'Creative writing! Have we a budding novelist here?'

'Just short stories so far.'

'Agnes always wrote stories,' Grace volunteered. 'She was very good. She's wasting her talents working for my father.'

'You're still at Calthorpes?'

'Yes. I'm secretary to the Production Director now.'

'She should have gone to university,' Grace persisted. 'We both should.'

'Then why didn't you?'

'There was an economic reason for Agnes. I just didn't care enough. I'm not ambitious, not in the least.'

'Oh, you look very ambitious to me,' Barry said, laughing. 'I think you're a very smart young lady indeed.'

'I'm smart,' Grace acknowledged with her sexy little half-smile, 'but not ambitious.'

'Then what do you want to do in life?'

'Have a good time!' Grace glanced at her watch. 'Come on, you lot! We'll be late for tea. 'Bye Mr Holloway. Good luck in the election.'

Barry held up a hand. 'Thank you. Ah, here's Keith.' He waved to a man who stood at the door of the bar. 'Over here.'

The stranger raised his racquet. He was dressed in immaculate whites and a striped blazer. He was a tall man with a strong face and very fair sparse hair, but he walked with the confident gait of an athlete. He took Barry's hand.

'Hi. I wondered if you'd want a game.'

'I haven't time,' Barry said, 'I'm sorry.'

'That's all right. I booked a court, but there are sure to be others wanting a game.' He looked at the group around Barry. 'Anyone here?'

'We've just played.' Stephen held out his hand. 'I'm Stephen Hetherington.'

'Very rude of me,' Barry said, quickly making the introductions. Keith Winchester smiled and shook hands.

'Hetherington?' he said. 'Any relation to Alloyed Steel?'

'The son.' Stephen gave a rueful smile. 'Due to join them in October, alas.'

'Why "alas"?'

'Well, I've had three years at King's in London, studying engineering. I don't really fancy being cooped up in Beckersleigh again; but Dad wants me here.'

'I'm sure he does, and as long as Labour keeps its hands off steel you'll have a good future.'

'How do you mean, "keeps its hands off steel"?' Grace asked.

'It plans to nationalize steel,' Keith said. 'It's been planned since '45, but the Tory comeback in '51 put paid to that. They're determined to make something that runs well run badly, like coal.'

'Steady on!' Barry said, smiling amiably enough, but with a warning light in his eyes.

'I'm sorry, Holloway, but you know how I feel. I respect your opinions, but I don't share them.'

'I hope you don't want to nationalize the carpet industry, Barry.' Grace assumed a tone which Agnes hadn't heard before: that of the frail little woman. Barry smiled at her in just the patronising way he was expected to.

'Ideally, Labour would like to nationalise everything. That's what all the fuss is about in the Party at the moment. Gaitskell wants to repeal Clause 4, which aims at eventual total nationalisation.'

'And where do you stand?'

'I'm with Gaitskell.'

'I thought you'd be a Gaitskellite!' Jeff Orchard jeered derisively.

'Jeff's a communist!' Grace whispered.

'I'm *not*. I'm a real socialist, a member of the Socialist Party of Great Britain. But I support complete nationalisation of everything.'

'That's what my Dad says too,' Agnes said.

'Oh, I know your dad!' Barry laughed. 'He thinks I'm a pink Liberal.'

'I think he likes you, though.' Agnes smiled at him. She liked him too. She had never been so attracted to any man. She saw understanding dawn in his eyes and lowered hers, embarrassed.

'We must go,' Grace said. 'Nice to meet you, Mr Winchester. Don't pull down all our town, will you?'

'I'll make no promises,' Keith Winchester said. 'A lot of it could do with pulling down and nice tall blocks built in their place, leaving lots of open spaces ...'

'And lonely people ...' Jeff began, but Agnes took his arm.

'Don't let's fight. See you again, Mr Holloway.'

'I thought I was Barry by now?'

'Barry,' she said, repeating it again silently to herself: *Barry*.

'I like Barry Holloway,' Grace said thoughtfully as she took a large bite of cream cake. At the Calthorpes, afternoon tea was being served on the lawn at the same time the Rivingtons usually had their main evening meal. The Rivingtons called it high tea, and it was eaten between five-thirty and six, after everyone had got home from work. Supper was bread and butter and tea, or sometimes fish and chips at nine or so. But the Calthorpes had afternoon tea and then dinner at eight. Dinner-time to the Rivingtons was lunch-time to the Calthorpes.

The shadows were lengthening on the lawn, but the breeze that usually blew down from the hills was still.

'Is that the candidate, dear?' Mrs Calthorpe asked.

'Yes, mother, the Labour candidate.'

'He had a strong fight to be selected against the Trots,' Stephen said. 'I admire his guts, if nothing else.'

'If you mean by "the Trots" the Left Wing of the party, you can count me in on that.' Jeff's eyes, gleaming through his round spectacles, looked angry. 'We're the pure socialists.'

'Oh, I do hope we're not going to have a row!' Mrs Calthorpe said breathlessly. 'They do upset me. We're Tories and I think Mr Macmillan has done very well for the country.'

'Grace said she was La –,' Jeff began, but Grace interrupted.

'You heard what Mummy said about not wanting an argument. You know perfectly well I just said that for fun.'

Stephen stared at her. 'I thought you were serious!'

Mrs Calthorpe laughed. 'Grace is far too mercenary to be a socialist.'

'Oh Mummy, that's not fair! Anyway, I don't care who wins.'

Mrs Calthorpe looked at the boy she would very much like for a son-in-law. Stephen was twenty-two, good-looking and rich. An alliance between the Hetheringtons and the Calthorpes would unite two of the wealthiest families in town. It would be a safe, solid match. But the trouble was that Stephen lacked Grace's sophistication. Although he was two years older, he seemed far less mature than she, and in her heart Mrs Calthorpe knew that Grace needed a much stronger man.

'I wonder how old Barry Holloway is,' Grace mused.

'He's twenty-eight.' Agnes glanced at her. 'He told me he was twenty-six two years ago.'

Grace looked at her sharply. 'And why did he do that?'

'He just asked my age and told me his.'

'Why?'

'We were having coffee after one of his lectures.'

'Oh were you? I didn't know you were that intimate.'

'We weren't "intimate". We met once or twice after lectures. Then he became a councillor and that was that.'

'Oh, don't fall for the Labour Candidate please, dear,' Mrs Calthorpe said with mock anxiety in her voice. 'That would distress your father.'

'Of course I won't fall for him, Mother. I just wondered how old he was. It doesn't mean I want to marry him.'

'He won't get in anyway,' Stephen said, getting to his feet. ' People in this town know which side their bread's buttered.'

'I'm not sure.' Jeff got up and knocked his pipe out against the trunk of the tree. 'The cotton issue has made them very angry. There's too much unemployment in the north.'

'Labour makes them uneasy, though.' Stephen glanced at his watch. 'Would either of you girls like to see this new film "Room at the Top"? It's about a working-class boy who ...'

'I know – I read the book,' Grace said, stretching. 'I don't mind. Agnes?'

'I'd like to see it,' Agnes said, 'but not tonight. I've got a lot to do with my studies.' Agnes looked at Mrs Calthorpe and saw her approving smile. 'Can I wheel you in, Mrs Calthorpe?'

'If you would, dear,' Mrs Calthorpe smiled.

Agnes let go the brake of the wheelchair and slowly pushed it towards the house. Mrs Calthorpe seemed to be shrinking visibly before her eyes; she was like a tiny, wizened bird with large, luminous eyes.

'Did you know I have a room downstairs now, Agnes? In this hot summer weather I've been able to get out in the garden in the morning when it's cooler. But in the winter I'll go upstairs again.'

Agnes pushed her through the opened doors of her room and then turned the chair to face the garden. Jeff was saying goodbye and Stephen had sat down again.

'He's nice, isn't he, Agnes?'

'Very nice.'

'Do you think he's Grace's type?'

Agnes looked at him critically. 'Not yet. Maybe in a few years.'

Mrs Calthorpe nodded sadly. 'That's what I think. We do so like the Hetheringtons; but Grace seems to regard him more as a brother than anything else. Do you think he thinks of her in that way too?'

'I'm not sure. I think he likes Grace, but he's a bit afraid of her. Most men are.'

'Oh, Agnes, Grace has been such a worry to me since she left school. There's something so restless about her.' She looked up at Agnes. 'Why couldn't she take after you?'

'Dull,' Agnes said quietly. 'Steady and dull.'

'Agnes! You're not in the least bit dull. I just wish that you and Grace had somehow managed to stay together. It would have been so good for her. You needn't have gone away to university, but somewhere near like Leeds or Manchester. Grace just drifts from one day to the next. Spends all her time dancing or at the cinema. She never reads a book.'

'She said she'd read "Room at the Top".'

'Well, it was fashionable, wasn't it? No, Grace is drifting and I'm anxious about her. She should be married.' Mrs Calthorpe took Agnes's hand. 'And so should you!'

'Why does everyone think that the only thing a girl should ever want to do is get married?' Agnes was surprised by her own vehemence.

Mrs Calthorpe looked offended and dropped her hand. 'Well, it's natural! It's the thing most girls want, even if they do have a career. I think a girl who didn't want that would be *very* unnatural, I really do. And the younger the better, I think. I married Mr Calthorpe when I was twenty-eight and I think that's a bit old. Maybe if I'd been younger I mightn't have had such trouble with my pregnancies. I'm sure that's what caused my heart trouble.'

' Pregnancies? You had more than one?'

Mrs Calthorpe smiled sadly. 'Oh, Grace was just the successful one. I had five altogether, four ending in miscarriage. I was very ill every time, as well. No, take a tip from me; begin to think of settling down, and encourage Grace, too. She's just coming in.' Mrs Calthorpe waved as Stephen walked over the lawn to the front of the house and Grace came towards them. 'He's such a charming boy, dear!'

'Oh, Mother! Always matchmaking. He's too immature. I like a man of character.'

'Have you found one?'

'Not yet, but I'm looking.' Grace glanced at Agnes and went out of the room.

'I'll go and get my things,' Agnes said. 'Sure you're all right?'

Mrs Calthorpe leaned back in her chair and closed her eyes. 'Quite sure, dear. I'll just have a little doze.'

When Agnes appeared upstairs, Grace was in the bath.

'Is that you?' she called from the bathroom.

'Who did you think it was? Barry Holloway?'

'Oh, don't be like that!'

'Like what?'

'Jealous.'

'I'm not jealous! He doesn't interest me at all.'

'Well, he should. He's very handsome.'

Agnes went to the door and leaned against it, looking at Grace in the bath. 'He's never looked at me seriously. I think he'd want someone more sophisticated. Like ... you, perhaps.'

'Me?' Grace smiled and sensuously lathered a slim leg. Agnes thought that Grace was almost displaying herself in front of her, delighting in her slender body, her heavy, well-shaped breasts. Agnes looked good in the bath too, but not as good as Grace. 'I'm not a bit interested in Mr Holloway. I'd never want anything serious with him.'

'Why not?'

'Well ...' Grace lay back, scooping handfuls of water over her body. 'I'm not interested in what he does. Politics bore me, and he's too idealistic. He's obviously not very well off, and I like money. He wouldn't do for me at all; but he'd do for you. So make him choose you!'

'You sound like your mother,' Agnes said, exasperated.

'Oh, was she on about marriage again? She mentions it at least once a day to me. You'd think I was on the shelf! Good grief, I'm not twenty-one yet! I want to have a good time. But I can't imagine why *you* don't get married.'

Agnes stood up. 'Why me and not you?'

' Pass me the towel, would you?' Grace held out an imperious hand and looked at her. 'If I were you, I'd want to get away from your home, especially that tyrannical father of yours.'

'He's not a tyrant!'

'Well, I think he is.' Grace stood up and began drying herself. She made no effort to hide her body with the towel, but seemed to flaunt it. 'You're always running home to Daddy. If you're late he comes looking for you; you can't call your soul your own. Agnes, he's possessive and if you go on living there you'll *never* get married.'

Grace got out of the bath, the suds from her legs dripping on to the bath mat.

'I didn't know you were so hostile to my father.'

'I'm not. I'm thinking of you. I don't care a rap about your father; just his effect on you. It would drive me mad to be watched over like that!'

'I'll thank you to be more civil.' Agnes turned angrily and went into the bedroom to look for her bag with her tennis whites.

'I'm being perfectly civil.' Grace wound a towel round her head and came into the room, fastening a bath robe.

'I never say anything about *your* father.'

'You wouldn't dare!' Grace gave a nasty little laugh. 'After all, you work for him, don't you? You wouldn't dare say anything about him in case I told him and you got the sack!'

'I think that's a dreadful thing to say!' Agnes felt close to tears.

'Well, it's true. You're ruled by two fathers, mine and yours. You work for one and live with the other. Are you really content being a secretary at Calthorpes? Of course you're not! But you're too timid to do anything else! You're nearly twenty-one and you've never done anything. You've never even had a serious boyfriend! I think you're afraid of men.'

'And what about you!' Agnes was beginning to shout.

'What about me? *I'm* not timid with men!' Grace looked surprised.

'I mean why don't *you* leave home?'

'You think I don't want to?' Grace began shouting too. 'You think I like spending three-quarters of every day watching my mother slowly die? I read to her, push her out into the garden, push her back again, read more. We have dinner in front of the television and I tuck her up in bed at nine to go to sleep. You call that a life? You think I don't want to get out?'

Agnes was immediately contrite. 'I'm sorry. I forgot for a moment, you made me so mad.'

Grace seized her shoulders and shook her. 'I wanted to make you mad! Don't you see? I can't help my life – but you can help yours. Yes, I've been abroad. Yes, I've had boyfriends. But I'm stuck here. You're free! You don't seem to see it. You're quite content with things as they are and I can't understand it because there's so much I want and can't have.' Grace turned away in an agony of frustration and went to the window. 'And I tell you another thing. As long as you're my father's employee we can never be equal. Never!'

'You think I'm inferior to you?'

Grace turned, studied her as though she was appraising a painting. 'Not inferior. But I'm conscious of us as a family always being nice to you because we don't want you to think you're in any way different. But you are! You work for my father and he pays your wages. That *makes* you different.'

Agnes seized her bag and ran out of the room and down the stairs, the tears of rage and humiliation pouring down her cheeks.

CHAPTER SIX

AGNES DIDN'T GO BACK TO the Calthorpe house for the rest of the summer and she neither saw Grace nor heard from her. If Mr Calthorpe was mystified by the rift between her and Grace, he didn't say. Or maybe he felt as Grace did and she had told the truth. What had happened that day at the Calthorpe household Agnes never mentioned at home; never told her father, her mother or Paul, who appeared only briefly that summer in between working in a hospital in the South as a ward orderly. She kept her grief and her bitterness to her heart and then she threw herself into the campaign to elect a Labour Government at the 1959 General Election.

Beckersleigh had only once returned a Labour candidate, and that was in 1945 when disgruntled servicemen swept Labour to power. The tiny Labour majority had been wiped out in 1951 and the Tory majority increased in 1955.

Barry Holloway, the Labour candidate, had the disadvantage of being both an intellectual and a stranger, and he was running against a Tory candidate who was working-class and local. The Tory image was good in Beckersleigh; it was identified with thrift, hard work and enterprise. Even the workers didn't welcome the thought of nationalisation of the steel industry. But they were angry about the closure of so many collieries.

So Barry worked wicked hours and his supporters worked with him. Agnes didn't have a night free for weeks, or a Saturday or Sunday. Throwing herself into the fray helped her forget about Grace and her wounding, hurtful remarks. It also meant she saw more of Barry Holloway, who turned out to be dynamic, hard-working and had the gift of making his helpers feel that he cared about them and that he was grateful for what they did. The result was that they worked even harder.

One night Agnes was canvassing in a street near her own, working her way home. This side of the town, the Enderby Ward, was solidly Labour, but it wasn't neglected. Barry Holloway had the political sense not to make the bedrock supporters feel that they were taken for granted. Just as she was banging on the fiftieth knocker that night, there he was by her side.

'How's it going, Agnes?'

She looked round, her eyes wide with surprise, her heart racing. 'I didn't hear you arrive.'

'The others have gone down the hill to take some leaflets. How long have you been going?'

Agnes looked at her watch. 'Since six.'

'You must be all in.'

'I am.' She smiled at him and was rewarded by his brilliant grateful smile in return.

'Come and have some fish and chips.' It was a command, not an invitation. 'I haven't eaten all day.'

'Oh, I can't. My father doesn't like me being out so late as it is, with the nights drawing in.'

'Well, I'll tell your father I'm taking you for some fish and chips. What about it?'

'He might say no.'

'He's a real Victorian patriarch, isn't he? I tell you what, when the car comes back we'll ask them to take us to the fish shop and then tell your father. How's that? Ah, good evening!' Barry turned on the practised charm as the door opened and gave an old age pensioner five minutes' worth of uplift and good cheer, ending with: 'I know we can rely on you.'

'You can that, Mr Holloway.' He was very popular.

The old woman stayed with the door open, smiling, as he got into the car with Agnes and then closed the door, grateful that the country was, or should be, safe in the hands of fine men like Mr Holloway.

At the fish and chip shop Barry had double helpings; two large pieces of cod, crisp in its batter, and two portions of chips. Agnes had already had a good tea, but she felt quite hungry. The cafe wasn't crowded and they found a corner table, easing their way through smiling faces. Everyone knew who he was.

'I think the campaign's going well, don't you?' He salted his chips and lifted the mug of tea, looking at her over the brim.

'I think you'll beat Smethurst. Just.'

'Well, one vote's enough. One vote and I'll be in Parliament.'

'Is it what you've always wanted?'

'Always!' Barry looked at her. 'Since I was a very small boy. Even in the war I was against Churchill.'

'Are politics in your family?'

'No,' Barry laughed, 'not like yours! My father was a Regular Army Officer. He was killed at Tobruk.'

'I'm sorry.'

'It was a long time ago now.'

'Did your mother manage all right?'

'I had one sister younger than I and one older. We got by. My father left a bit of money and my mother got a job as a Welfare Officer in a munitions factory while the war was on. After the war she went into welfare work. Now you know everything about me. How's Calthorpes?'

'Fine.' Agnes wiped her mouth on a paper napkin. She knew that time was getting on, that her father would be waiting for her. Well, just this once he could wait; being here, with Barry, mattered more...

'And how's Miss Calthorpe?'

Agnes avoided his eyes. 'We don't see so much of each other these days.'

'Oh? Drifted apart? What happened?' It was the tone he used when he wanted to show the voters how interested he was in them.

'We had a kind of row. Well, my mother said the friendship would never last.'

'Why not?'

Agnes shrugged and sipped a mouthful of tea. 'Because of our different backgrounds. She said as we got older it would show.'

'And it has?'

'Yes.' Agnes's voice was bleak.

Barry thumped the table. '*That's* what we need – to get rid of class divisions.'

'I don't think you ever will in this country. It's so deeply ingrained in people.'

'No, it isn't,' Barry said firmly. 'It's an attitude of mind. If we had a government dedicated to the abolition of private schools and so on, it would disappear.'

'Grace and I were at the same school and it still shows. It's to do with money. It's not really class at all.'

Barry swallowed the last mouthful of fish and stared thoughtfully at her. 'You really are a very intelligent girl, you know.'

Agnes shook her head. 'It's nothing to do with intelligence! It's common sense. Grace is used to things that I'm not. She's indulged, and I ...' Agnes paused, groping for the right words.

'And you work?'

'Yes. I do what was expected of me and Grace is doing what was expected of her. When we were at school the differences weren't so apparent, but now our attitudes have changed too.'

Barry lit a cigarette and sat back, looking speculatively at the girl opposite him. He had developed a slight paunch due to the copious quantities of good Yorkshire bitter he consumed during the many social functions he dutifully attended. But he kept the flab at bay with plenty of exercise, and played rugger for the Beckersleigh Rovers and squash at the sports complex. In the steamy atmosphere of the cafe, sweat trickled from beneath his thick black curly hair, strands of which lay damp on his brow.

'How do you mean, your attitudes have changed?'

'I've become interested in study. Grace doesn't seem to be interested in anything except who the two of us are going to marry.'

'Well, that is quite important!' Barry sat forward to stub out his cigarette.

'But is it important to you?'

Barry looked amazed. 'Why should it be important to me?'

Agnes laughed with confusion. 'I don't mean who *we're* going to marry; but is who *you're* going to marry more important than anything else in your life?'

'Of course not! I don't even think of it. I'll marry in my own time, when I want. Otherwise it never enters my mind. But for women it's an important thing. It's different for men and women.'

'But *why*?' Agnes leaned over the table, gazing at him earnestly. He smiled, holding up his hands as though fending off an attack.

'Agnes, I see there are lots of things for us to talk about; but I must get you home to your dad.' Barry got up and reached in his back pocket for his wallet. 'Seeing you're a literary lady, you'll know your Byron. "Man's love is of man's life a thing apart.'Tis woman's whole existence".'

'I think that's rubbish!'

'Well, I think it's true, and the longer you live perhaps the more you'll come to agree.' He reached down and took her arm.

'I won't, because I think it's wrong!' Agnes shook herself free of his grip, resenting his male conceit. 'If it was right then, it's wrong now. It won't happen to me. I want to do something with my life besides thinking about marriage; but just yet I don't know what it is.'

The helpers had gone home, leaving the car outside for Barry. His bulk filled the whole of the seat of the small Ford Popular and Agnes was very aware of his presence, his particular smell, and the fact that their conversation had introduced a new intimacy into their relationship. In their brief meetings, they had never discussed anything personal at all. She was suddenly sorry that the distance between the fish shop and her home was so short ...

Barry drove silently up the hill and she could see he was tired. The door of her house was open and her father stood at the threshold with his arms folded, his pipe clenched firmly between his teeth.

'I hope we aren't too late, Mr Rivington,' Barry called out. 'I took good care of your daughter. Gave her something to eat.'

Albert Rivington opened Agnes's door without saying a word. She could tell he was angry.

'My wife's gone to bed,' he said shortly. 'I said I'd stop up for our Agnes.'

'I didn't realise it was so late.' Barry was apologetic.

'It's gone quarter to eleven, Mr Holloway. You'll be needing your sleep for the campaign.' Albert banged the door and turned towards the house, his hand on Agnes's back, not pushing her but steering her firmly to the front door.

'Just a minute, Dad!' she said angrily. 'I have to thank Barry for the meal and the lift.'

Barry leaned out of the window. 'There's no need to thank me. It's I who should thank *you* for all your help. When I've won we'll have a real celebration. See you soon. Night, Mr Rivington.'

He waved, put the car into gear and drove rapidly up the hill before turning at the top to drive down again.

Agnes hurried ahead into the living room, undoing her scarf. 'You made a fool of me in front of Mr Holloway, Dad!'

'I did no such thing,' her father said, removing his pipe from his mouth. 'He's no right to keep you out till nearly eleven. And "Barry" is it, indeed!'

'I'm twenty-one next month, Dad.'

'I don't care how old you are. You're still my daughter and while you live in this house you're under my care.'

'Then perhaps I should move out.' Agnes took off her coat with shaking fingers.

'Don't talk so daft!' Albert went to the sideboard and poured himself out a glass of bottled ale, as he sometimes did before going to bed.

'I'm not daft, Dad. But I'm old enough to do what I want and see who I like.'

'I let you go out every night campaigning, don't I? I never complain about that. But I like you to be home about nine, before it's properly dark. What will the folks next-door say if they see you arriving home at all hours with Barry Holloway?'

Resentment and anger made Agnes feel as though she had a tight knot in her chest. 'I don't care what the neighbours think, Dad! If they're that narrow-minded they can think what they like! Barry and I were having fish and chips at Meg's Cafe and talking. That's all!'

'Well, you can talk during the day. I'll not have you stopping out until all hours; you've a day's work to do tomorrow. Aye, and I have too.' Albert finished his ale and wiped his mouth with the back of his hand, belching as he did so. He was calm and in control, certain of his authority. 'Besides, I don't know why Barry Holloway's that interested in you; he's a lot older. You'd think he'd want to see women of his own sort.'

'Dad, there was *nothing* in it. I have never been anywhere with him before and probably never will again. He just happened to join the canvass at the end, and as I was finishing and he hadn't eaten, he said to come along with him.'

'Alone?'

'Yes.'

'Well, I don't like it.'

'Besides, what do you mean "women of his own sort"? What sort?' Agnes realised that in her anger she was in danger of losing control of herself. 'What sort, Dad? Educated? Refined? Middle class?'

'Don't be silly!' her father said, poking the grate, flattening the ashes as they fell into the pan beneath. 'You know what I mean. Barry Holloway's a man of the world. We've nothing in common with the likes of him.'

'What about politics?'

'That isn't basic. His father was an army officer.'

Agnes sat by the embers of the fire, linking her hands in front of her. 'Dad, I know what you mean, but I think you're wrong. We're not in the Twenties or the Thirties now. I don't believe in class warfare, Dad.'

'It'll be with us for a long time yet, whether you believe in it or not,' Albert said, winding up the clock on the mantelpiece. 'Come on, it's nearly half past eleven.'

'What about Paul?' Agnes's voice was taunting.

'What *about* Paul?' He looked at her.

'When Paul's a doctor he won't be in our class.'

'That's something else! Paul's my son. He's our blood.' Every time Albert mentioned Paul his voice changed and the expression on his face grew almost angelic. ' Paul will never desert his class; what happens with his children is something else, but I'll always be proud to have been their grandfather – a working man who drew the coal from the earth with his bare hands.' He held up his hands and gazed at them, gnarled now and arthritic.

'That's not the point, Dad! We were talking about what I do with my life!'

'I've not forgotten. Look, I trust you, Agnes. I know you're a good girl; but when the time comes for you to go with boys and consider marriage, I want you to choose someone like ourselves, a man who understands us and who we can understand. I don't want anyone like Barry Holloway for a son-in-law. Not in a thousand years! Him with his fancy ideas and posh accent!'

'He has a Yorkshire accent!'

'Well, you could hardly tell. It's not like mine, is it? Or your ma's. More like yours and Paul's. *That's* what education does for you – strips you of your birthright! I was always sorry you went to the Grammar, Agnes. I think going with Grace Calthorpe spoilt you. You know, I think if you'd left school at fifteen you'd be a lot happier now. You'd have found a working-class job, a working-class man and by now you'd be wed and settled like your ma at your age.'

Her father looked at her thoughtfully, sorrowfully, and she had no words to answer him with. She wanted to scream and rage at him, make him see what sort of future he was condemning her to. Couldn't he see how unfair he was being? Working-class drabness for her and her children; the endless struggle for money … But for Paul, for his son, there would be the chance to use his brain, to give his children a future of their choosing. She shook her head angrily, knowing he would never understand.

Agnes sat with her head bent as the recount came to an end. The Tory had narrowly won – but pray, pray that the recount went against him.

'I think he's in,' Connie Shilton said.

'Who?'

'Smethurst. Barry looks very grim.'

The recount had finished. The Mayor was talking to the candidates. Barry was frowning and Tom Smethurst had a sickly, relieved grin on his normally earnest face. That on his wife's was seraphic.

'Silly cow,' Jeff Orchard said, between clenched teeth. 'She's crowing. I wonder how she'd like to be the wife of the ex-MP?'

'Sometimes I think they only try for Parliament to win prestige for their wives.' Mike Orchard looked at Connie and put an arm round her shoulder. 'Should I try, love?'

'Who said anything about us getting wed?' Connie said and managed a smile.

Agnes now saw more of Connie and the Orchard brothers than anyone else. The Orchards were working-class boys and Connie a working-class girl like herself, and they lived in the narrow steeply-sloping part of the town. They all had a genuine concern for social conditions.

Connie and Mike were officially engaged, to satisfy her parents; but Agnes had no intimacies with Connie such as she had enjoyed with Grace.

Jeff had told her that Mike and Connie slept together, and he would have liked Agnes to sleep with him. He had now started to date Agnes regularly and, because he was a working-class boy teaching in a poor district of Leeds, Mr Rivington thoroughly approved of him. Agnes liked Jeff as an individual, but physically he repelled her. He was very thin with severe myopia and his thick-lensed glasses perched precariously on a thin pinched nose, so that he was forever pushing them up with his forefinger. There was always a slight body smell about him that she found unpleasant. It hardly qualified as BO, but it wasn't an attractive smell like Barry Holloway's.

Occasionally she let Jeff kiss her, but he was clumsy and his wet mouth felt unpleasant. Still, so long as their friendship remained platonic, she liked Jeff's company very much. He was sincere and dedicated and took an interest in her work and was sympathetic to her aspirations.

The candidates were now gathering behind the Mayor. The TV cameras had come to Beckersleigh because it was an indication of how the nation as a whole would vote. The Mayor cleared his throat and started to read out the results in alphabetical order. Barry was next to last.

'Holloway, Bernard Paul, 17,431.'

There was an enormous roar. Then he read out Smethurst's total. He had won.

Jeff was busily scribbling on a piece of paper. '94 votes!' he said. 'Smethurst's in by 94 votes.'

'I think there should be another recount!' Mike stood up, calling for a recount. The boos and the catcalls mounted in volume until the Mayor held up his hand and called for silence.

'The number of votes was the same both times, ladies and gentlemen. I see no need for a further recount.'

Tom Smethurst went with his wife before the TV cameras and made a good speech about it being a close-run thing. Barry Holloway chatted to his agent, until he too was called in front of the camera. He looked tense and unsmiling. Plainly he wasn't a good loser.

'It meant so much to him,' Agnes said, choked with disappointment for Barry.

Connie got to her feet, pulling Mike with her. 'It's a radical candidate we need here, not a Gaitskellite!'

'I think you're wrong. Beckersleigh has returned a Tory three times now – it would be frightened of the New Left.'

'It would be frightened of its own shadow!' Jeff sneered.

'Oh, let's go and speak to Barry,' Agnes said, impatiently. 'People are avoiding him, they don't know what to say.'

'I'm not going to speak to him,' Connie said firmly. 'Not after that row we had.' Connie had been one of the first to join the new CND Movement and had walked from Aldermaston to London the year before.

'He supports CND, Connie; it's just that he doesn't want unilateral disarmament,' Agnes said.

'If we don't, nobody will ...'

'Oh, come on, Jeff. Let's speak to Barry.' Impatiently, Agnes put a hand on his arm and then speedily withdrew it.

'Oh, all right, for your sake.'

He put an arm round Agnes's waist and they walked across the floor of the primary school where the count had been held.

Barry leaned down and kissed Agnes on the cheek. 'I see you don't desert the sinking ship.'

'You'll win next time!' She could feel his disappointment and longed to comfort him. 'It was very close. They're not deserting you, they just don't know what to say!' Her vehemence seemed to surprise her, and she faltered: 'You know Jeff Orchard, don't you?'

'Of course.' Barry shook hands.

'I canvassed in Leeds, I'm afraid,' Jeff said. 'It's where I teach.'

'Then I hope you have more success than I did. Are we going to have a coffee?'

'I don't know where we'd get it,' Agnes said. 'It's nearly midnight.'

'My God, so it is!' Barry, red-eyed, looked at his watch. 'We'll have to have it from the Thermos. I think there's some left.' He tilted the Thermos into a white mug. Nothing came out. He shook it and laughed. 'Nothing's coming right for me tonight. By the way, I got an invitation to Grace Calthorpe's twenty-first party, Agnes. Did you?'

'Yes, it came this morning.'

'I wonder why she asked me?'

'Maybe she thought you'd be the Member.' Agnes gave a malicious little smile and Barry pretended to be shocked.

'Surely she's not a social climber?'

'She's nowhere to climb to! She's at the top already.'

'We'd better be getting home,' Jeff said pushily, putting his arm once more around Agnes.

She saw Barry notice the gesture, saw the odd look that came into his eyes.

'Have you got a lift?' Barry said.

'Yes, thank you,' Jeff said abruptly, drawing Agnes away, his voice hostile. 'Better luck next time!'

Barry waved a hand and turned to greet someone else who had come up to him. 'See you at the Calthorpes',' he said to Agnes, ignoring Jeff completely.

'I think you were rude to Barry,' Agnes said in the car.

'Who was rude to Barry?' Mike and Connie were on the back seat.

'Jeff.'

'I wasn't.' Jeff turned into Agnes's street.

'It was your tone.'

'He didn't like seeing you with my arm round your back. He fancies you, if you ask me.'

'He's never looked at me!'

'I think Jeff's right,' Connie was serious. 'Every time I see you and him together he looks at you in a funny way.'

'I've never noticed it.' Agnes twisted in her seat, but even in the dark she knew she was blushing because she too had seen the look in Barry's eyes that night.

Jeff stopped five houses away from hers. He turned off the engine and turned to her, his mouth moving towards hers. Agnes backed away, glancing behind her. But the two in the back were entwined, panting.

'They'll not notice us,' Jeff said, clutching her. 'Come on.'

'I don't want to, Jeff. Besides, my dad might see. He'll be looking out for me.'

'I looked. The door's not open.' He took off his glasses and lunged towards her. But because of the awkward way she sat, his lips missed their object and pressed wetly against her cheek. 'Come on,' he said again, angrily. 'Kiss me!'

'No!' Agnes jerked away from him towards the door.

'They'll not notice!'

'It isn't *them*. I just don't want to.'

'Why not tonight? You do other nights.'

She couldn't tell him that he smelt, that she found him sexually repulsive, because she liked him. She couldn't tell him she didn't want him to kiss her because the only man whose kisses she wanted was Barry Holloway. She moved closer to him because she didn't want to hurt him and waited for the renewed approach of his eager, sticky tongue . . .

CHAPTER SEVEN

GRACE'S TWENTY-FIRST BIRTHDAY PARTY was held at the Conservative Club, a large converted country house on the right side of town, and all the best people were there: the Parsoes, the Hetheringtons, the Manleys, the Longleys. There were business acquaintances of Henry Calthorpe, a sprinkling of specially selected employees, numerous friends of Grace's, some civic dignitaries and various relations both from the Calthorpe side and her mother's side, the Armitages of Shipley.

Also there was Keith Winchester, who arrived early, shaking hands with Grace and bending to kiss the cheek of Mrs Calthorpe, who sat looking rather woebegone in a wheelchair at the end of the line. The intimate gesture was not lost on several onlookers who were interested to see Mr Winchester's easy familiarity with the Calthorpe family. In fact, he had already been invited to dinner several times, because Henry liked to encourage young talent; Mrs Calthorpe was beginning to wonder if at last they had found someone suitable for Grace.

In theory, Keith Winchester was eligible. He was good-looking personable and well-mannered. He dressed a little flashily in heavy silk shirts, but that could be attributed to his southern origins. He could converse on subjects of all kinds and, above all, he appeared to have ample means. It was probable that his family were lower middle, or even working class; but in the Calthorpe almanack, wealth and success came before class, perhaps even superseded it. Besides, Keith Winchester never talked about his origins and no one ever asked him.

After greeting Mrs Calthorpe, Keith moved easily through the crowd, smiling at a considerable number of people he seemed to know already.

Shortly after, Agnes arrived, feeling very lonely and rather uncertain as she walked through the imposing door of the club and

79

saw all the people gathered in the foyer. Grace spotted her as soon as she came in and broke away from her parents, running towards Agnes, both hands extended.

'Oh, I'm so glad you came! I hoped you would.' She kissed Agnes on the cheeks, something she had never done before. Agnes responded clumsily.

'Happy birthday,' she said shyly, handing her a neatly wrapped gift.

'Thank you! Oh, Agnes, I'm so glad you came!' Grace sounded sincere and to Agnes's ears it was as though she were trying very hard to make amends. 'Come and say hello to Mummy and Daddy and then we'll go and find you a partner. Which won't be difficult! You look lovely.'

Agnes smiled. She had taken much more trouble with her appearance than usual and had bought her first real evening dress at an exclusive gown shop in Leeds. It was a floral printed grosgrain, ruched and cut low over the bosom. The skirt was a straight sheath and the cut accentuated her slim waist.

Agnes possessed no jewellery, so her chest and neck were bare, but she held her head with a certain poise, and the natural highlights in her chestnut hair gleamed as she turned her head to listen to Grace. Heads turned towards her from the moment she came in.

Grace's parents kissed her warmly.

'We've missed you, dear,' Mrs Calthorpe said, reaching up her hand and looking into Agnes's eyes. 'Was something wrong?'

'I was busy with the election.'

'Of course. Well, I hope we'll see more of you now.'

'I invited Barry Holloway,' Grace said, looking round. 'But I doubt whether he'll come.'

'I think he will.' Agnes smiled at Stephen Hetherington, who appeared from behind Mr Calthorpe.

'Hello, Stephen. How was America?'

'Wonderful! I nearly stayed there.'

'Stephen will look after you,' Grace said, giving him her dazzling smile. 'And then we must have a talk. Auntie, how lovely to see you!' As she bent to kiss one of Mr Calthorpe's sisters, Stephen took Agnes up the stairs of the club into a large room, where a small band was playing 'Here Comes Summer', although it was in fact nearly November.

'May I?' Stephen said, and took her expertly into his arms. 'You look ravishing, Agnes! When's your twenty-first?'

'Next month.'

Agnes was never at ease with Stephen. He spoke standard English with no trace of a Yorkshire accent, and seeing him in his immaculate tails, she felt less in common with him than ever as he led her around the floor. He didn't attempt any further conversation but hummed under his breath, his hand firmly on her waist, his sharp blue eyes darting about.

'Why, look who's there! Your candidate!' Stephen stopped just as the music changed to 'Magic Moments' and Barry, standing in the doorway, raised a hand in greeting.

'Let's go over to him, shall we?'

Agnes nodded, the increased beat of her heart not caused she knew, by exertion.

'I nearly didn't come,' Barry said, shaking hands with Stephen.

'Enemy territory, I suppose.'

'Yes.' He laughed and then looked at Agnes. 'You look lovely, Agnes.'

'Doesn't she just?' Stephen said enthusiastically. 'And have you seen Grace? My word!'

'Have I not!' Barry laughed. 'I don't know why these girls don't go in for modelling.'

'Why should we go in for modelling?' Agnes knew her tone was curt.

'Use your looks. Or would you think it demeaning?'

'Yes, I would.'

'Well, I'm sure Grace wouldn't. I can just see her on the cover of *Vogue*.'

'That sounds very degenerate.' Stephen put his arm round Agnes again. 'I wonder that a chap like you even knows such things exist.'

'Oh, I'm all tuned in.' Barry backed away, smiling. 'Could I have the next dance, Agnes?'

As she nodded, he turned and found himself looking straight into the face of Rose Munday.

Mrs Munday had been one of the last to arrive and was feeling very nervous. Henry had told her approximately what time to arrive so that she missed the receiving line and spared him the embarrassment of having to introduce her to his wife and daughter and sisters and brothers-in-law.

Rose was there, largely because she had insisted. She was tired of being the mistress tucked away on the far side of town and had told Henry she wanted to integrate herself more into Beckersleigh society. There was no reason why she shouldn't, she had argued. Henry, with some doubts, had been forced to concur.

Rose had taken hours over her appearance, had dieted strictly for a week beforehand, had visited the hairdresser and the beautician on that same day and had had tantrums all by herself in the house as she had decided the dress she had chosen so carefully for the occasion was perhaps rather on the tarty side. It had been a dream of multicoloured chiffon drapes and fluttering veils floating to the floor; but she discarded it in favour of a clever, expensive affair of black lace over stiff taffeta, sleeveless but with a high neckline. With this she wore silver stiletto-heeled evening shoes and carried a silver bag, with a sable wrap (an early present from Henry) draped over one arm. The effect was breathtaking, and the concourse broke ranks to gaze at her as Henry nervously, but with some pride, steered her through it to the bar, his wife having safely departed.

Rose had seen Barry as soon as he came through the door. She drifted over to him as Henry paused to talk to a deferential group of Calthorpe employees, all dressed in their best.

'I wondered when you'd notice me,' Rose said, with a thin, high laugh, gazing after Agnes as she took to the floor with Stephen. 'She's a pretty girl, isn't she?'

'One of my former students,' Barry said offhandedly. 'How on earth did you get here?'

'Same as you, I expect. By car.'

'But why didn't you tell me you were coming?'

'Why should I? You never mentioned it to me.'

'But I never dreamed . . .'

'I'll go, if you don't like it.'

'Don't be silly! Let's dance, Rose.'

He drew her into his arms, realising it was the first time he had ever been with her out of her house except for the first time they had met. Yet their familiarity with each other was obvious as they fell into step.

'He wanted me to come,' she said confidentially, looking up at him. 'I didn't like to refuse, to tell the truth. He said it would give him courage, he was that nervous. He needs me a lot, you know – more and more.' Rose lied quite easily, deceiving even herself.

'Are you trying to make me jealous?' Barry moved closer. Her dress was tight-fitting and he could feel her thighs through his trousers. She looked stunning; next to Grace and Agnes she must have been one of the most attractive women in the room – but a mature woman, a woman of experience: a woman who had lived. 'I'm thinking of you with your thighs apart,' he whispered and saw her blush beneath her skilfully applied make-up.

'Get away with you!' she whispered sharply. 'If old Calthorpe heard I'd be out on my ear!'

'I'd marry you.'

'You would?' She almost missed her step and stopped dancing.

'Did you think I didn't want to?'

'I thought you were ambitious.'

'I am, but I want you too.'

The music changed again and they moved closer together.

'I'm nearly forty.' She smiled at him. 'I'm also very greedy ...'

'Your age doesn't matter. Your greed does. I couldn't promise to keep you as you like, but if Calthorpe ever dispensed with you and you were hard up, you could rely on me.'

'You know, I believe I could.' Rose leaned back and smiled brilliantly into his eyes. 'We're real friends, Barry, aren't we?'

'For life,' he said. 'I shall always want you.'

'I didn't know you knew Mrs Munday.' The jovial tones of Henry Calthorpe interrupted them as the dance sequence ended and the band took a rest. Barry had escorted her to the bar, handing her a large gin and tonic just as Henry Calthorpe came up with Grace.

'Oh, we're old friends,' Barry said. 'Mrs Munday is a relation of my first landlady.'

Calthorpe looked relieved.

'I see. May I introduce my daughter, Grace? Mrs Munday is an old acquaintance, my dear. A friend of mutual friends.' Henry had decided beforehand to be as vague as he could but not to lie deliberately to his daughter.

'Oh?' Grace smiled at Rose, the curiosity remaining in her eyes. She had noticed Mrs Munday come in – who wouldn't notice such an attractive woman? – and observed how her presence seemed to agitate her father. 'I'm pleased to meet you, Mrs Munday.'

Her father beckoned to someone who was standing behind Barry.

'Mr Winchester – Keith! Over here.'

'I was just looking for you.' Keith Winchester took Grace's hand. 'A very happy birthday.'

'Thank you – and thank you for the lovely flowers.'

'I'm glad they arrived safely.'

Mr Calthorpe threw back his head, showing a mouthful of gold-capped teeth. 'Flowers! I never saw so many flowers. She must have had two dozen bunches – and as for arrangements . . .'

'They're all lovely,' Grace said. 'Daddy, don't make people feel awkward.'

Mr Calthorpe pointed a finger at his chest in astonishment. 'Me!' He turned and saw Stephen and Agnes. 'Agnes, you look gorgeous tonight.' He drew her to him and then took her arm. 'Mrs Munday, this is a very good friend of Grace's, Agnes Rivington. They were inseparable at school.'

'I can see why – they're both so lovely.' Rose shook her hand and looked from one to the other. 'And what do you do now, Agnes?'

'I work for Mr Calthorpe,' Agnes said quietly.

'Really? Aren't you lucky having such a pretty girl working in your office, Henry?'

Henry shook his head. 'She works for Mr Coldfield, the Production Manager. *He's* the lucky man.'

Agnes felt that there was an undercurrent here that she couldn't quite understand. Everyone seemed over-excited, as though they had all had too much to drink. She looked at Barry.

'Wasn't this our dance?'

'Of course. I didn't even hear the music start. Excuse us.' Barry smiled at the company in general and swept Agnes on to the dance floor.

'She's a very attractive woman.' Agnes's voice was slightly questioning.

'Who?'

'Mrs Munday.'

'Oh, her! I've known her for years.'

'That doesn't mean she's not good-looking.'

'Yes, she is, come to think of it. But a bit old for me!'

'Don't be so ungallant!'

'Well, she is!' Barry protested. 'She must be at least forty.' They danced in silence for a moment, then: 'Look, I'd like to take you out some time, Agnes. Do you think your father would allow it?'

'Why shouldn't he?'

'I don't think he approves of me.'

'He did once warn me against you.'

'Oh?' Barry held her back and looked at her. Agnes felt elated and smiled at him.

'He only likes men from the working class.'

'Does he like Jeff Orchard?'

'Yes.'

'He would! Jeff's no danger, is he?'

'What do you mean?'

'You know what I mean, young woman.' He pulled her closer than ever and the power and strength of his body, his animal vitality, were almost overwhelming.

Without any official prompting, there was a general movement to Mr Calthorpe's supper table. Apart from himself and his daughter, he was joined by his great friends the Hetheringtons, with their two sons Stephen and James and their daughter Mary, who was in her last year at school. There were Agnes and Barry, with whom she was still dancing when the supper interval came, and naturally there was Rose Munday, and Mr and Mrs Parsoe. Lastly there was Keith Winchester, who happened to be dancing with Grace.

In the centre of the table was a large birthday cake which Grace proceeded to cut to the accompaniment of 'Happy Birthday'. Champagne corks popped as the cake was cut into pieces by a chef and carried round.

Agnes found herself sitting opposite Grace. Next to Grace was her father and next to him Mrs Parsoe, the Chairman of the Orphanage Committee, who had asked various awkward questions when Mr Calthorpe surprisingly had put forward Mrs Munday's name to fill a vacancy.

Mrs Munday was a person of some mystery in Beckersleigh. All people knew was that she was a war widow and that some tenuous connection with a brother of her late husband's had first brought her to Beckersleigh. She was known to have money, a good dress sense and to play a fair game of bridge. Beyond that, she kept herself to herself and seldom entertained. It was supposed, again very vaguely, that Mr Calthorpe must have some connection with Mrs Munday's late husband, or his brother.

Mr Parsoe was the Calthorpe lawyer. His grandfather had helped to finance the founder of Calthorpe Carpets and there had been a strong link ever since. He sat next to Mrs Munday, and next to her was Keith Winchester. His thin strands of blond hair had obviously been draped across his pate with great care, but with the heat of the room and the exertion of dancing they now fell back over the left side of his head where they sprouted and where his hair was still plentiful, even thick. Keith Winchester was one of those men whom a bald head suited. It made him look older than he was, and distinguished. He had a big head and bushy eyebrows, and cheerful smiling blue eyes, but his lips were thin and bloodless; his was a firm set mouth that rarely broke into laughter. It was then that, if you looked at his eyes, you saw their apparent cheerfulness was deceptive. He was constantly weighing up, observing, calculating – a cautious, rather cunning man; one who would not easily be taken for a ride.

As he talked to Rose Munday, he looked at her appraisingly and she fluttered her beringed hands and laughed a lot as though his presence, his earnest gaze made her rather nervous.

'Can't stand that Labour fellow on the other side of you,' Mr Parsoe whispered loudly to Agnes. 'Can't think why Henry invited him.'

'Grace invited him,' Agnes corrected. 'He's a friend of hers.'

'Really?' Charles Parsoe's protruding eyes grew even more prominent. 'Can't think how she came to meet someone like that.'

As Mr Parsoe droned on, Agnes watched Grace, who seemed as bored with Stephen as she was with Charles Parsoe. James Hetherington, Stephen's elder brother, caught Agnes's eye and smiled. As soon as the dancing started again, he stood up and held out his hand.

'Dance, Agnes?'

Agnes got up gladly. She knew very little about James Hetherington except that he lived in London and had come up specially for the party.

'I hate this sort of do,' he said, grinning. 'Don't you?'

'I haven't been to one before.'

'Really? You're lucky. I seem to go to them all the time.'

'What do you do?' Agnes asked, genuinely interested.

'I'm in publishing. Very low down in the editorial hierarchy but I like it. What about you?'

'I work at Calthorpes.'

'Of course, I heard. You and Grace were such friends at school, weren't you? The two Graces.'

She wondered how long people would go on remembering that. 'I also study creative writing at the Poly,' she said.

'Really? What do you write?'

'Only stories,' she said deprecatingly. 'Romances, that kind of thing.'

'Well, that's what people want to read. You should let me see your stuff sometime. Have you heard of Catherine Cookson?'

'No.'

'Well, you will. She's becoming very well known. She writes novels set in the North East, Tyneside.'

'I write about the South Seas! Who wants to read about Beckersleigh?!' Agnes laughed.

'You should write about what you know. The golden rule. Look, I mean what I say – I'll give you my address and you can send me some stuff.'

The music stopped and James took out a card and wrote something on it. 'And I'll give you a meal if you ever come to London!' He smiled at her. 'I must dance with my sister now. She looks such a wallflower.'

Barry's tongue flicked out and licked Grace's ear. In her white evening dress she looked at the same time very chaste and rather wanton, a most fetching combination in Barry's eyes. He was aware of her large breasts and could see the deep cleavage without any difficulty every time he glanced down. He let his hand travel over her buttock and she put back her head and looked at him.

'You mustn't be too familiar, you know.' She was smiling at him teasingly and he smiled back, feeling that they understood each other. Barry knew Rose's eyes were probably on him, but he didn't care.

'So Agnes came after all,' he murmured after they had danced in companionable silence for a while. 'I thought you two weren't talking?'

She looked at him with surprise. 'You *do* know a lot, don't you?'

'I only know you don't see so much of each other. Does she bore you?'

'Agnes? Of course not! She's my best friend. But last summer I was horribly rude to her. I meant to apologise but I could never bring myself to. I despised myself so much I couldn't face her. That's why I asked her tonight, to try and make up.' She grimaced. 'Oh-oh, Daddy wants me. He's terrified I'll fall for you. He hates socialists!'

She left him abruptly with a dazzling smile. He shrugged. She was very brittle and rather cool. But he found her very intriguing ...

On the dance floor, Henry Calthorpe was trembling at the close proximity of Rose in front of all these people. He saw the eyes of some of the men gazing speculatively at her and felt proud but at the same time terrified of people knowing. Yet, maybe because they were in such a public place, he also wanted her passionately.

'I'm glad you came,' he said feverishly, pressing her back with the palm of his hand.

'I'm so pleased, Henry,' she murmured, aware of his desire. 'I didn't embarrass you, then?'

'Not at all!'

'Good. I didn't want to. But I do want ... to get about a bit more, Henry. Not to be so cut off. I'm quite a sociable creature, you know.'

'I know, my dear, I know. And you're quite right. I'll make sure you're invited on to more committees and things. You'd like that, wouldn't you?' He went on, seeing Rose nod; 'And you'd do it well. I really need you, you know,' he whispered into her ear. She was aware of his hot, almost scalding breath on her cheek.

Just then a waiter came up and murmured something to Henry who stopped dancing, murmured something back and then guided Rose in the direction of the top table, mopping his brow. He held out a chair for Rose, who sat down, ignoring Barry who was sitting there.

'Hope you're enjoying yourself,' Henry said with forced heartiness. 'No pretty girls around?'

'You've got the prettiest,' Barry said gallantly. He saw Rose frown.

Henry didn't know what to make of this remark. 'You mean Grace or Rose?' he said.

'Both.'

Henry lit a cigarette. His hand trembled as he put it to his mouth. 'Have you seen Agnes Rivington?'

'She's dancing with Keith. Why?'

'Her father's downstairs waiting for her. I just had a message.'

'Oh, ask him to come up,' Grace said. She and Stephen had heard her father's remark.

'I already have. But I shouldn't think he will.'

'Oh, Dad. It's terribly early for Agnes to have to go. She's enjoying herself! I'll go and tell him we'll take her home.'

Grace disappeared through the crowd while Henry gesticulated towards Agnes. She came running over.

'Your father's here for you.'

'Oh dear, I forgot' Dismayed, Agnes looked at the clock on the wall.

'Don't worry, Grace has told him we'll take you home.'

After several minutes Grace appeared, shrugging her shoulders.

'It's no good, he's quite adamant. He's got a taxi waiting and he refuses to come up for a drink. Oh Agnes, what a pity!'

'I'll go down and see if I can reason with him,' Barry said. 'I can easily take you home – it's on my way.'

'I'd better come with you.' Agnes looked round for her bag. 'If I don't come back, thank you for a lovely party.'

Grace took her hands and kissed her cheek.

'Do come back. Please,' she said. 'It won't be the same without you.'

In the large hall Albert Rivington stood looking up anxiously towards the stairs, clearly feeling acutely out of place. When he saw Agnes he put his cap on and made for the door.

'Dad! Wait!'

He turned as she and Barry reached the same level and stared at Barry with a look of outright hostility.

'What do you want?'

'Albert, Agnes is having such a good time. We wondered if she could stay? I'll see her home.'

'I've come to take my daughter home, Mr Holloway.' Albert Rivington's voice was cold. 'Have you got yout coat, Agnes?'

'*Please*, Dad.' She joined her hands almost supplicatingly and leaned towards him. 'I'm nearly twenty-one too.'

'I said you've got to come home now, Agnes. There's no point in arguing.'

'I think you're being a bit unreasonable, Albert.' Barry lit a cigarette, as if preparing for a long argument.

'I'll thank you to mind your own business, Mr Holloway! I've put myself out to come and get Agnes – *and* I've paid the money for a taxi.'

'I'll refund gladly.' Barry reached in his pocket, but before he knew it he was reeling as Albert Rivington reached up and hit him across the jaw.

'Don't you ever dare talk to me like that, young man! Insinuating that I can't afford to take my own daughter home!' Albert was shaking with rage.

'I did no such thing!' Barry rubbed his jaw, then stooped to retrieve his cigarette, knocked from out of his mouth on to the floor. 'You're a sensitive bastard, Albert Rivington, and I pity Agnes having a father like you. Now, *I* say she stays here and *I* drive her home. You go home by yourself and pay for your own blasted taxi and realise your daughter is a young woman – it's high time she lived her own life.'

They glared at each other, so concerned with their own hostility that they hadn't noticed that Agnes had disappeared. Now she came from the cloakroom, pulling on her coat. She was very pale and her eyes were luminous with tears.

'Thank you, Barry, but I'll go with Dad. I'm sorry he hit you. I think he's had one or two at the pub, haven't you, Dad?'

Albert Rivington shook his head and wiped his mouth on the back of his hand. 'I'll thank that young man ...'

'Come on, Dad! It's lucky there was no one here to see this carry-on or they'd have sent for the police by now.'

She steered her father towards the door, and just before they went through it, she turned round to wave to Barry. But he was already halfway up the stairs and never looked round.

CHAPTER EIGHT

CONNIE SHILTON HAD BEEN AT Calthorpes since she was fifteen. She had a neglectful father who drank heavily, and her mother was burdened beneath a family of eight children. Connie came somewhere in the middle. But she was a cheerful girl and she bore her parents no grudges. She accepted her place in the family for what it was; but she longed to better her lot in society. She burned fiercely with indignation about all the injustices she saw around her, and the hazards of the nuclear bomb had become an obsession with her. Connie was two years older than Agnes, so that in the spring of 1960 she was nearly twenty-four.

Unlike Agnes, Connie had never had special privileges at Calthorpes and had never learned shorthand and typing; but she was good with figures and had for many years enjoyed a niche in the Export Department as a clerk. When she first began to talk to her fellow employees about being unionised, the suggestion was received with some horror; Calthorpes, after all, was a family firm. Then Connie obtained some figures about the wages received in comparable industries that had been unionised, and the workforce began to see how low their wages really were.

In April a preliminary meeting to discuss affiliation with a union was attended by more than half the workforce. The press were there in strength and the *Beckersleigh Chronicle* gave it banner headlines: 'STRIKE THREATENED AT CALTHORPES!'

In fact, no strike was threatened at all, but the meeting struck terror into the hearts of Mr Calthorpe and his senior managers. They were of the opinion that unionisation had done untold damage in other industries and felt that the cotton industry partly owed its decline to the influence of the trades unions, preferring to blame the unions rather than the fact of cheap imported foreign goods.

It was difficult for Henry Calthorpe to believe that a girl of twenty-four, whom he had known since she was a child, could be advocating such a dangerous course – was, indeed, the leader of the committee that had been formed. Henry Calthorpe took it personally. He sent for her alone and pleaded with her, more like a sorrowing father than an angry boss. He even promised her a small increase in wages for herself. All of which showed that he didn't really know Connie. She read him a lecture on social injustice and gave notice of a meeting by the committee to seek talks with the relevant trades unions.

Agnes, meanwhile, was in a dilemma. She felt sorry for Mr Calthorpe, but she felt the committee had justice on its side. However, she decided not to attend the meeting and sit on the fence and see what happened. Maybe everything would come right.

But everything was far from coming right. Mr Calthorpe called in his lawyers and tried to threaten the committee with legal action unless it stopped its activities. He could hardly have been more badly advised.

At this point the national press stepped in, and Connie Shilton became a sort of Grace Darling of the trades union movement, her picture constantly in the news.

It was just as things were getting out of hand at Calthorpes that Mrs Calthorpe died. Whether her husband's distress hastened her death, no one could say for sure. But Henry was in no doubt: he blamed his workforce for it – especially Connie Shilton. The day after Mrs Calthorpe's funeral he felt strong enough to act. He called Connie Shilton to his office and personally gave her the sack, handing her an envelope with her cards, a month's wages in lieu of notice and a letter saying that because of her outside activities her work had become unsatisfactory. He never even asked her to sit down.

Connie had just returned from the second Aldermaston March in which 100,000 people had gathered in Trafalgar Square. It was true that she had a few days off for this but these she had taken as part of her paid holiday entitlement. Mr Calthorpe seized on her absence to blame her for the falling off in her work.

Connie now made the front page of the *Daily Mail*: 'WORKER SACKED FOR HER BELIEFS'. The committee called to discuss negotiations about trade unionism gave notice of its intention to call the workforce out on strike unless Connie were reinstated.

Agnes had never seen anyone lose their beauty so suddenly. Grace looked about thirty and her hair had lost its lustre. She had also shed a stone in weight and her eyes burned as though she had a fever.

Agnes had moved in to stay with her when her mother died. Although they had not seen very much of each other since the twenty-first birthday dance, their relationship had subtly improved – even if they still were not fully back to the heyday of the two Graces.

'If you ask me, this business will kill Daddy,' Grace said, folding her mother's cardigans into a box. 'Can't you do anything, Agnes?'

'If I could, I'd have done it a long time ago.'

'Connie seems to think she's some sort of Joan of Arc.'

'No!' Agnes leaned against the windowsill and looked at Grace, who held the cardigan crushed up against her cheek like a baby cuddling a beloved blanket for comfort. 'No, she doesn't. She doesn't think she's a heroine and she hates this publicity. In fact, she looks quite ill. She really believes she's right.'

'And after all Daddy's done for her! When her mother was ill he paid for that huge family of hers to go to Fleetwood. That's gratitude for you.'

'Your father's a very kind man,' Agnes said, 'there's no doubt of that, and all this has upset him terribly. He doesn't understand it.'

'Well, why should he?' Grace looked at the cardigan as though looking for her lost mother. 'He's always been a good man, a good employer. Why should he have all the trouble they have in other mills? This country's in ruins because of the trades unions.'

'I can see your father's point,' Agnes said gently, 'but I can see theirs, too. You see, there's no structure here for the workers to bargain for pay increases. Your father just gives them a rise when he feels like it.'

'Well, that's fair, according to how much profit he makes.'

'It isn't always fair. There are all sorts of things that employers can hide to disguise profits, so that they don't have to pay too much tax.'

'Daddy would never do a thing like that!'

'All businesses do it. There's nothing dishonest about it, or at least, they don't think there is. It's what their accountants tell them to do. But that's why we need unions – to protect the workers against dodges like that.'

'Sometimes I wonder whose side you're on!' Grace said furiously, narrowing her eyes. 'Ours or theirs! Daddy has been very good to you, especially to you.'

Agnes turned and faced the garden. She didn't want an argument with Grace.

'I'm not on any side,' Agnes insisted. 'It's been very hard for me. Father keeps on asking why I haven't got my picture beside Connie Shilton. He thinks I've been weak. I'm going to leave Calthorpes because it's too much of a struggle for me. I'll even be blamed for that! They'll say I'm deserting. But I can't strike against your father.'

Grace came over to Agnes and put her arm around her. 'Then you *are* on our side.'

'Of course I'm on your side! It's just that I don't want to see you unhappy and your father ill.'

'Oh, I'm so glad.' Grace squeezed her arm. 'Will you get another job easily?'

'I suppose so. I'll get something. Come on, let's go for a walk. This room is depressing.'

'It stinks of death,' Grace said. 'Yet it reminds me all the time of Mummy; but I agree, let's get out.'

It was a blustery day, so they put on raincoats and boots and headed for the moors, arms linked as when they were girls. They stood at the top, the wind bringing some colour back into Grace's face.

'Oh Agnes, I so want to leave Beckersleigh, but I'm still trapped!'

'Why? Your mother was your only reason for staying.'

'But I can't leave Daddy, especially with all this going on. He needs me more than ever. I think I might marry Stephen Hetherington ...' Grace turned and looked into Agnes's face, a little half-smile on her lips. 'Surprised? He asked me the other day. I like him, I really do.'

'I know you like him; but is that enough?'

'The Hetheringtons are like family. I'd be near Daddy. I think I'll go mad if I just carry on as I am.'

'But how can you marry someone you don't love?'

'I *like* him,' Grace insisted. 'It's a sort of love, isn't it? He's potty about me and his family like me. I want to be married. I'd have a nice house and a couple of children. I'd be like my mother. Mummy always told me not to wait too long until I was married. We'll be twenty-two this year.'

'Oh yes – completely over the hill!' Agnes laughed; but deep down she felt disturbed. Was she jealous, or was she really concerned that her friend could contemplate marrying someone for motives that seemed so calculated, so unspontaneous?

'You should marry, too,' Grace said. 'If you leave Calthorpes, what else can you do?'

'Marriage isn't the only way out.'

'What else is there?'

'I think it's wrong.'

'Jeff Orchard's keen on you, isn't he?'

'Oh, I could never marry him!'

'Why not?' Grace gave a malicious little smile.

'I don't fancy him,' Agnes said.

'You mean physically?'

'Yes.'

'Well, I don't fancy Stephen physically, either. I mean he's not repulsive like Jeff, but I don't find him at all sexy.'

'Then I don't think you should marry him.'

Grace ignored her. 'You still yearn for Barry, don't you?'

'Barry would never marry me! Especially after my father hit him!'

'Yes, that was terrible.' Agnes had told Grace about the scene some time after the party. 'I remember he came into the room looking very angry and left soon after. He gave that Mrs Munday a lift, which Daddy seemed very annoyed about. I often wondered if Daddy fancied Mrs Munday. I must say, I thought she was a horribly vulgar little woman.'

'I'm sure he didn't. But you could see she appealed to the men. They all liked her – even Keith Winchester. She has sex appeal, that's what.'

'But Barry spoke to you again, didn't he?'

'Yes. He said he'd ask me out, but he never did. I see him at LP Headquarters from time to time, but that's all.'

'Let's go home,' Grace said suddenly. 'I'm getting cold,' and she started to run down the hill.

'I was terribly sorry to hear about your mother.' Keith Winchester got up as Grace and Agnes came into the room. 'I've been abroad and only heard yesterday. I hope you don't mind me calling.'

'It's good of you to come. You remember Agnes?'

Keith took Agnes's hand and smiled. 'Of course. You both look terrific. Have you been out walking?'

'Mm. On the moors.'

'This business at Calthorpes! It's terrible.'

'Isn't it? It killed my mother, and if it doesn't end soon it'll kill my father too.'

'How does it affect you at Calthorpes, Agnes?'

Grace spoke for her. 'She's going to leave.'

'Oh, then you're against it?'

'I'm against upsetting Mr Calthorpe and Grace. I'm much too fond of them to want that. But I'm a Labour Party member and that makes it all difficult. So I'm leaving.'

'Do they know?'

'Not yet. I wanted to talk to Grace first.'

'Why don't you stay for dinner, Keith?' Grace went casually to the bell to summon the maid. 'You'd cheer us all up.'

'That's very kind.' Keith looked pleased. 'If you mean it, I'd be delighted.'

'Of course I mean it.' Grace glanced at him. 'I never say anything I don't mean.'

Agnes saw Keith Winchester suddenly look at Grace as though seeing her in a completely new way.

Mr Calthorpe was delighted to find a guest for dinner.

'And how's the swimming pool coming on?' he asked Keith jovially.

Keith looked at his host apologetically.

'I'm afraid I've had too many other things on my plate. The swimming pool's largely voluntary, so it's had to be put at the bottom of the pile, I'm afraid ...'

'A swimming pool?' Grace queried.

'Next to the sports complex. It's crying out for one.'

'But it's all built up round there.' Agnes sipped at her wine and decided she didn't like it; but it felt sophisticated to go on sipping and pretending that one did. Grace would approve.

'Yes, it'll all have to come down. The people will all be rehoused on the fine new Wirrall estate.'

'I thought the Wirrall estate was having a lot of opposition?' Agnes began to feel uncomfortable. Her father was one of those most vehemently opposed to the development, which involved moving people out of their homes and rehousing them in tall blocks.

'Oh, we've got friends in high places.' Keith Winchester

laughed. 'We'll gradually get rid of the opposition.'

'I don't think we should really discuss it at table.' Mr Calthorpe looked nervously at Agnes. 'It's very confidential. But I'm sure that if it does get going – and I think it will – the people of this town will benefit all round. Though God knows if they'll ever show any gratitude.' He coughed on his wine, and Agnes saw that tears had come into his eyes. She cleared her throat.

'Mr Calthorpe, there's something I should tell you.'

'What's that, dear?'

She thought Mr Calthorpe looked apprehensive as he passed his plate for Grace to serve him with another helping of meat.

'I'm going to leave Calthorpes. I can't bear the conflict of loyalties any longer.'

Mr Calthorpe sat back, shocked.

'What sort of conflict, Agnes?'

'Between my loyalty to you and my belief in trade unions.'

'But we've trained you! We've spent a lot of money.'

'And she's repaid you, Dad,' Grace said firmly. 'I agree with Agnes. I think she's doing the right thing.'

'I hardly call it grateful when my best people leave me just when I need them! I'd have thought she'd want to be there beside us, giving support to the few, the very few, who still defy the union tyranny. Because it *is* a form of tyranny, whatever you like to say. These people are just as tyrannical as any medieval baron.'

Agnes put her knife and fork together. 'I think I should go home tonight, Mr Calthorpe. I can see you're upset and I don't want to add to your worries.'

'But you have! Can't you see that? You're not loyal! You're disloyal. After all my family's done for you ...'

'Oh Daddy, that's very unfair ...' Grace reached out and took her father's hand. 'I want Agnes here with me. Please, Dad. She won't resign if you don't want her to. Will you, Agnes?'

Agnes got up, looking pale and very confused. 'I don't feel well,' she said. 'Please excuse me.' And she ran all the way to the bathroom and was sick. Afterwards, feeling utterly miserable, she sat for a while on the floor trying to compose herself.

When she came back to the drawing room, coffee was being served. Mr Calthorpe and Keith were drinking large brandies, and Grace's father was looking at her rather sheepishly. Grace had come to the bathroom and persuaded Agnes into going back. 'Daddy feels differently now,' she had said. 'He's very sorry.'

'I do apologise, love.' Mr Calthorpe gestured her over to sit next to him. 'I think we're all upset.'

Agnes sat down nervously. 'I'd still like to go home tonight. I want to talk to my Dad, anyway. I'll come back tomorrow.'

'Come back and have a talk with me too, dear,' Mr Calthorpe said. 'We'll work something out.'

'I'll give you a lift.' Keith Winchester glanced at the slim gold watch on his wrist. 'It's time I was going.'

'Do stay and have another brandy.' Agnes saw that Grace looked annoyed.

'No. I must go,' he said getting up. 'I've been away in the Middle East as you know, and I've got a lot of work to catch up on.'

'What's happening with those Arabs, then?' Henry Calthorpe asked, expansive now that Grace had soothed him.

'Oh, that's where the money is. In my opinion a lot's going to happen out there.'

'In what way?'

'I think one day, when they realise they've got a monopoly of oil, they'll put such a squeeze on the West that we won't know what's happening to us. They'll become rich, and then they'll want to improve their standard of living, which is wretched. And I plan to be out there, helping them improve it.'

'In what way?' Agnes was interested.

'Building, of course.'

'Oh, I think you're wrong about the Middle East.' Henry Calthorpe refilled his guest's glass. 'It'll always be poor and backward. Those Arabs are different from us, you know.' Henry tapped his head. 'Besides, there's so much oil about they could never charge too much for it. That's why we're running down our coal industry.'

'You mark my words.' Keith Winchester nodded solemnly. 'We could be doing the wrong thing.' He got up and turned to Agnes. 'Ready?'

'Yes, thanks. I'll just go up and get my case.'

Agnes noticed that he hadn't touched the brandy he'd said he didn't want. She realised he was a man who meant what he said.

Keith drove his large Jaguar very fast through the main streets of Beckersleigh. In the centre of the town he drew the car into the kerbside and looked at his watch.

'Time for a nightcap? The pubs are still open.'

'I think I should get back.'

'Come on. Just a quick one. I want to talk to you about something. It might be to your advantage, as they say.'

Agnes was intrigued.

The Clarence Arms was a large, well-appointed pub which prided itself on the exclusive quality of its clientele. By keeping its prices high, it ensured that only the best people would drink there. Agnes had only been into the Clarence a couple of times, both of them with Grace and her friends. It went without saying that her father had never been there in his life. Keith told her to take a seat and asked her what she would like to drink.

'A gin and bitter lemon, please.'

Keith came back with the gin and a pint of beer and sat down next to Agnes. He wore a camel-haired coat and suede shoes and underneath a well-cut grey suit made of best worsted. The effect was tasteful but a trifle flashy. A gold name bracelet round his right wrist added to this impression.

'I bet you wonder what all this is about?'

Agnes tasted her drink and then put it down carefully in front of her. She half-expected he was going to ask her for a date; if he did, she was going to refuse, because she felt that Grace had rather fancied him. She didn't want more conflict with the Calthorpes.

'I wondered, if you're serious about leaving Calthorpes, if you'd like to work for me?' he said. 'I'm opening an office here.'

Agnes was taken aback.

'*Work* for you?' she asked.

'I need a good secretary. Someone to run the office. There'd be just you and me to start with, and maybe someone to do the accounts. You could help find the offices and furnish them as you like ...'

'But how do you know I'd be any good? I don't know a thing about building!'

'You'd learn very quickly. I asked Henry Calthorpe what you were like when you were out of the room. He said you were first-class. Oh, and I tried to explain your problem.'

'I thought someone must have spoken to him.' Agnes sipped her drink again. 'He was so different when I came back.'

'Oh, it wasn't me! Grace pitched into him. Said you were her best friend and if he upset you she'd leave home! She really is quite a girl.'

Keith paused, his eyes gleaming in admiration.

'And did you tell him you were going to offer me a job?'

'Oh no! I wanted to see what you'd say. I'm careful, you see. I wouldn't want to be snubbed.'

Agnes smiled. 'I wouldn't snub you. I just don't know if I'd be right for the job.' She hesitated. 'And I don't know what my father would say.'

'What do you mean?' Keith selected a cigar from a long leather case.

'Well, building is mixed up with politics now, as you know. A lot of people are against the Wirrall development and that sort of thing.'

'But only a small portion of my business is in Beckersleigh. I'm a public benefactor! I'm going to build swimming pools and nice places for people to live in – flats with lots of light and central heating, bathrooms – things they've never had before! I've never previously had an office because I've always travelled about so much; but I've decided to come and live in Beckersleigh and make this the centre of my operations. I like the place and the people, and it's very convenient for me, with Leeds airport only a few miles away. Anyway, how would you like to go to Persia? Or Saudi Arabia?'

'Travel there myself?'

'Why not? The job is what you make it. So think about it, Agnes. I won't press you for an answer tonight. But I'd like to know in about a week's time. I'm staying at the Grand – just drop me a note or leave a message. If you want to talk about it in the meantime, please do – I'll tell you anything you want to know. But I hope you accept. I think you'd do well.' Keith looked at his watch and drained his beer. 'You'd better be getting home to that dad of yours now. Sounds as though he keeps an eye on you!'

Mrs Rivington hardly ever cried; tears were as much strangers to her as kisses and hugs; but the way Albert had pitched into Agnes was too much for her. She put her apron to her eyes and only then did she burst into tears. Albert was so astonished that he stopped his diatribe in mid-sentence and stared at her.

'What's up, love?'

'Oh, give over,' Kathleen Rivington begged. 'I can't bear all this. She's only been offered a *job*. She's not changing her way of life!'

'But that's where you're wrong, Kathleen,' Albert said patiently. 'She *is* changing her way of life. Besides, that man's a scoundrel, a confidence trickster. He'll end up in prison.'

'Oh Dad, just because you don't like the swimming pool plan.'

'But I do like it, love.' Albert protested reasonably, packing tobacco into the bowl of his pipe. 'I just don't like it there in Swallow Street. People have lived there all their lives and their fathers before them. It's their home. They don't want to go and live on the fourteenth floor of one of them skyscrapers on the Wirrall.'

'You don't know that for sure, Dad.'

'I do! That's the point. I do know. I know the people and I know how they feel.'

'But the town needs a swimming pool. It isn't even having to pay for it. All the money's being donated by people like ...'

'People like Calthorpe and Hetherington and Parsoe and their cronies. Charity! That money should have come from the rates. But no. There'll be the Calthorpe Pool and the Hetherington Pool, the Parsoe Shower and Christ knows what – and every time anyone takes a dip they'll be expected to be grateful!' Albert's voice was passionate. 'And in order to build that, they're putting people out of their homes! If we didn't have a Tory Council as well as a Tory Government it would never be allowed. A nice ally your pal Barry Holloway is. He always sides with the Tories. Next time I see him I'll ask him when he's changing sides.'

'He isn't my pal any more,' Agnes said stonily, 'thanks to you.'

'Good. I don't like him and his sort and, although I've never clapped eyes on the man, I don't like Mr Winchester either, from what I've heard of him. And I'm not having you working for him.'

His wife began weeping again and Agnes went over to her and sat on the arm of her chair.

'There, Mum. Don't take on.'

'But what are you going to do, love?' Mrs Rivington put her arm round her daughter's waist. 'You'll have no job. Oh, I wish our Paul were here. He'd know what to do.'

'*I* know what to do, Mum.' Agnes straightened up and pushed the hair back from her eyes, staring boldly at her father. 'I've had enough of Dad telling me what to do – when to leave school, who to see and where to work. A lot of the girls I was at school with have got husbands and children by now. I'm sick of being treated like a child by Dad. I'm going to work for Mr Winchester whatever he says. I shall tell him tomorrow I've made up my mind.'

'I tell you I forbid it!' Albert lifted a finger and shook it at her. 'If you do, you're no daughter of mine.'

'I am your daughter, Dad. Nothing can change that,' Agnes said. 'But if you don't like it, I don't have to live here.'

'Oh, go on'. Albert turned testily to the fire and lit a spill for his pipe. 'You've said that before.'

'I said it before and I meant it! You were the one who gave in, not me. I said that if I couldn't work for Mr Calthorpe I'd leave home, and you gave in.'

'Well, I'm not giving in this time.'

'Then I'm leaving home,' Agnes said and, kissing her mother on the cheek, she ran swiftly up to her room and flung herself on her bed.

But she didn't cry. For some moments she lay on her face, listening to the pounding of her heart and then, as it quietened, she turned over on her back and looked at the ceiling, bathed in the orange light of the street lamp. How familiar that sight was; the light shining through the lace curtains and, in the distance, the glow of the lights over at the pit, where work continued twenty-four hours a day. How often she would lie in her little room in the narrow bed which almost filled it, gazing at the ceiling and dreaming, listening to the sounds outside and, when she was small, Mum and Dad coming up to bed. In those days she used to hear strange sounds coming from their room when they were in bed; but by the time she was old enough to understand their meaning, she realised they had ceased.

She wondered when her mother and father finally stopped making love. Or did they do it so quietly now that she never heard the bed squeak or her father grunt? She had never heard her mother make a sound, either of enjoyment or fear; but there was always a great big grunt, almost a groan, from Dad and after that the bed was still and there was silence ... She hadn't heard the grunt for years.

Hers was the smallest room in the house. As the eldest, and the boy, Paul had been given the room next to his parents. Yet now that he was grown up and away from home, it was Agnes who needed the larger room, not Paul. But Agnes loved her room with its view over the street and towards the moors, and never suggested she should change. It may not have been pretty and chintzy like Grace's; but it, too, contained objects and memories of childhood.

It was a narrow room with lino on the floor and a rag rug by the side of the bed. The end of the bed nearly reached to the window, leaving just enough room for a chair, a desk and a chest of drawers, on which stood a mirror in a wooden frame that swung over at the lightest touch.

Agnes was very neat. All her possessions were tucked away out of sight. Over her bed she had a cupboard where she kept her writing paper, notebooks, the few letters she received, mostly from Paul, and various other personal mementoes. Along the side of the bed was a shelf with her books; mainly novels by her favourite nineteenth-century authors – Thackeray, Dickens and George Eliot – but a few works on modern political economy and European history as well.

The top of the chest of drawers gleamed, and the mats on it were clean and often changed. One of Agnes's elderly aunts had embroidered them, and the stitches were simple little flowers that looked like the first attempts at embroidery that children make at school. On top of the chest were brushes, a hand mirror and a porcelain trinket box. There were two candles which were never lit, whose white wicks were slightly grimy through being exposed to the air for so long. But they weren't dirty. Nothing in the room, or in the house was dirty. Underneath the beds there was not a speck of dust. The floors were swept regularly, and the lino, which was in all the rooms, shone with polish.

Agnes's wall had a light, pretty wallpaper of pink-and-white Regency stripes on a primrose background, which she had chosen and hung herself, and which made the room look bigger than it was. The ceiling was painted primrose too, and on the walls were pictures that Agnes had collected over the years; mostly scenes of the countryside around Beckersleigh, but one or two early prints of the Lake District as well.

There were no trophies, shields or pennants of her schooldays; no group photographs of classes or hockey teams – nothing to remind Agnes, or anyone else, that she had once been such an adornment of Beckersleigh Grammar School for Girls ...

This room was her life. She had slept in it ever since her mother had brought her home from the hospital where she was born. She had had tantrums in it, cried in it, been ill in it – lovely days then, when Mother came home at lunchtime to see she was all right, and Aunt Annie, who lived next door but one, popped in several times a

103

day, bringing comics and good cheer. In those days Agnes had been content to dream. She had always known that life was good to her and that she was clever and pretty. She had never thought it would change.

Well, she was still clever and pretty, but life, she knew now, was not always good. It was not quite what you expected when you were a child. She knew, however, that the challenges it offered had to be faced up to; and she would never do that as long as she stayed in this room that she loved, living under her father's roof ...

Part Two

CHAPTER NINE

THE WINDOW OF AGNES'S OFFICE faced onto the market place, but she rarely had a chance to look out and see what was going on. Sometimes she couldn't have said with any honesty what sort of day it had been, rainy or sunny, hot or cold. She worked with her back to the window, and when she wasn't at her desk she was in the next room with Keith or in the large room which now housed five people: two secretaries, a clerk, a bookkeeper and an accountant.

The building, greatly modernised, was one of the few really old buildings in Beckersleigh, and Keith had leased the whole of the second floor from the council. The ground, first and third floors contained municipal offices. The name 'Winchester' didn't appear on any of the brass plaques outside the main front door, and the activities relating to his various business interests went under a variety of names: Global, Universal, Century, Axis, etc.

Agnes flicked the intercom switch on her desk and spoke into it. 'Yes, Frances?'

'Miss Calthorpe's in the waiting room, Miss Rivington. She wondered if you could spare a moment.'

Agnes frowned slightly. 'Of course. Please show her in.'

Agnes got up as Grace walked into the room breathlessly, as though she had been running.

'Grace!'

'Agnes, I hope you don't mind. I should have rung.' Her face was strained and unsmiling.

'Thank you, Frances,' Agnes said with a nod to the receptionist. 'Could you bring in two cups of coffee? And keep any telephone calls for me. Say I'll ring back.'

'Yes, Miss Rivington.' Frances almost curtsied, so much in awe was she of the boss's personal assistant. The fascination Agnes had exercised at school continued to hold sway among the personally selected staff of Keith Winchester's enterprises. All three girls wanted to be like her and tried to imitate her, and the two men, the bookkeeper and the accountant, indulged in all kinds of fantasies involving Agnes in some sort of dominant sexual role.

Grace sat down without being asked and took out a cigarette.

'I've had a terrible shock,' she said abruptly. 'Daddy's going to marry that awful Munday woman! And – he – he's been having an affair with her for nearly ten years!' Grace choked and lit the cigarette with a gold Ronson lighter.

Agnes could think of absolutely nothing to say.

'He tried to explain it all to me last night,' Grace continued bitterly. 'What she meant to him, how he depended on her. He said it wasn't primarily a physical relationship, though he and Mummy hadn't had sex for years and years. It started that way, but apparently it's different now, it's primarily companionship. He says she's very kind and warm and ... supportive.'

'And what did you say?'

'I said I thought she was common, and he was furious. Then he calmed down and asked me if I'd meet her again. I said of course I would, but I couldn't guarantee to like her. That's how we left it.'

Frances came in with the coffee – a silver pot, sugar bowl and milk jug and two dainty porcelain cups on a silver tray.

'I'll see to it now, thanks, Frances.' Agnes smiled and Frances went to the door, a worshipful look on her face. Grace raised her eyebrows.

'I see you've got them all trained to wait on you like the lower fourth!'

'So what are you going to do, Grace?'

'I'm going to make the best of it. If Daddy gets married, he won't need me – and I want to go and live in Paris.'

'Does Stephen know?'

'Not yet. He asked me to marry him again last week. Maybe I'll get engaged and go to Paris and have a good time. I couldn't possibly live in the house with that woman!'

'You know,' Agnes said cautiously, pouring coffee, 'I rather liked what I saw of her. She seemed warm ... Maybe you took a dislike to her because you sensed your father's interest.'

'Oh, *very* psychological!' Grace said scathingly. Then she grimaced. 'Maybe you're right, though. Yes, Dad *was* looking at her all that evening and I resented it because it was my party. But I can't believe it, Agnes! Ten years. That means I was twelve when it began. Dad must have told her everything; the stripping, Switzerland, the lot!' Grace stopped abruptly. 'Supposing they have children?' The thought seemed to appall her.

'Surely that's unlikely?'

'She's forty-one. Daddy's fifty-four. It's possible. And Daddy always regretted not having a son. Just think, if I have a little brother at the age of twenty-three or twenty-four ...' Suddenly struck by the humour of the situation, Grace began to giggle. 'Sharing it with you has helped, Agnes. You always make things seem so normal.'

Agnes hardly ever smoked, but right now she felt the need of a cigarette and took one from the cedar-wood box on her desk which she normally kept for clients.

'You know, when Dad and I had that row about me working for Keith and I decided to leave home, I thought it was the end of the world. I depended so much on Dad and what he thought. I feel that what happened to me is happening to you now. You've been your father's only child – and now that he's going to remarry, the love he gave to you or shared with your mother will be shared with someone else. It's bound to make a change. Your home will really no longer be your home. But we've got our own lives to lead – lives that don't have to be dependent on men.'

Grace looked at her oddly. 'Why do you say that?'

'Well.' Agnes paused for a moment to draw on her cigarette. 'I think we both depended heavily on our fathers – I much more than you, because I let him completely dominate me. We started to ask ourselves why didn't we get married, you to Stephen and me to Jeff, when we didn't even love them. Maybe we felt we should be dependent on them instead of our fathers.'

'But I think life's like that,' Grace said, puzzled. 'I mean, women *are* dependent on men, whether they like it or not.'

'But they shouldn't be!' Agnes said vehemently. 'Even now you're talking about marrying Stephen – and it's all because your father is marrying someone else and virtually throwing you out.'

'But he isn't! He said it'll always be my home.'

'But you know it won't. You'll feel like a guest there, whatever he says. You're not a little girl, you're a grown woman, a rival to Rose Munday. The point I'm trying to make is that now you've got the chance of doing what you say you wanted to do: go abroad, travel. You're not short of money. Instead of which, here you are talking about getting engaged to Stephen, even though you know you don't really want to marry him. You want to belong to him instead of your father.'

When Agnes paused, Grace was silent too, looking thoughtful. Keith Winchester put his head around the communicating door.

'Oh, sorry, Agnes. I didn't know ... Why, it's Grace! Grace, how are you?' Hand outstretched, Keith went over to her, bending to kiss her cheek as she took his hand. 'May I?'

'Of course.' She glanced up at him and Agnes saw that at once her demeanour began to change. She fastened her jacket, subconsciously emphasising her bosom, and stealthily put on the shoe she had eased off while she and Agnes had relaxed and chatted. 'I haven't seen you for a long time, stranger.'

'You're the stranger. I haven't seen you since your mother died.' Keith drew up a chair and seated himself next to Grace. 'How's your father?'

'Oh, he's fine.' Grace smiled and glanced at Agnes. 'And contemplating matrimony!'

'Really? Someone he met abroad?'

'No, someone he met here. Mrs Munday. You remember her, don't you?'

'Of course I remember. I sat next to her at your twenty-first birthday party. A very sexy piece. Good for Dad.'

'Fancy her yourself, did you?' Agnes smiled.

'Well, she's not really my type.'

Agnes had already begun to wonder what his type was. So far he had never made a pass at her or any of the girls, although all of them had been selected for their looks as well as their ability. Keith liked to surround himself with beautiful things: good-looking women, fine furniture and the very best that Calthorpes had to offer in the way of carpets. There had been one or two calls from a woman in London which he always took in his office, and Agnes had her suspicions that the two of them were close. But otherwise she knew nothing about his private life.

'Well, she's Daddy's type,' Grace said, 'and Agnes has been giving me some very sound advice.'

Keith joined his hands and studied Grace. He had given up trying to train longer strands of hair to cover his head and, except for a very fine baby-like down, he was now bald on top. He was slightly flabby, because he liked his food and never had time for exercise, but at thirty-one he was still an attractive man. Suddenly Agnes could see him and Grace together; they were very much of a pair, self-centred, full of charm, ambitious. Exactly what Grace was ambitious for was hard to define, since she never made any use of her talents; but, even so, she gave the impression that she was full of ability and bursting to get somewhere. She and Keith even looked rather alike, though without seeming to share any one definite feature.

'What sort of advice?' Keith said at last.

'She said I shouldn't be too dependent on men.'

'And do you think that's good advice?'

Grace returned his gaze unflinchingly. 'Yes. Don't you?'

In Rose Munday's wide experience she had found that men were more receptive to news, good or bad, when they were replete, drained of sexual energy and preferably rested after the act. So she chose the moment Barry Holloway woke up from his post-coital slumber to tell him that she was getting married to Henry Calthorpe.

'It won't make any difference to us,' she finished.

'Of course it'll make a difference!' he said, groping for his cigarettes on the bedside table. 'How can I come up to your house now, for God's sake?'

'Oh, we'll think of something. I thought maybe we could meet in your flat.'

Barry lit a cigarette and frowned at the ceiling. There would be no tasty little meals waiting for him at his flat – just a pile of dirty dishes and an unmade bed.

'It won't be the same,' he said, stubbornly.

'But you do understand, don't you, Barry? It's a chance for me. A wonderful chance.'

'To be Mrs Calthorpe?' Barry gave a derisive laugh. 'You've got to be joking!'

'You know it's true. Imagine, to have the security I've always lacked. You never have security as a mistress, you know. And without Henry Calthorpe I have nothing.'

'How old is Henry Calthorpe?'

'Fifty-four.'

'He looks older,' Barry said sullenly.

'Oh, I agree. He acts older too. Not like you.'

She gave him a sexy smile and ran a teasing finger down his broad, 'hairy chest. He sat up and glared at her.

'You're always trying to make out he's some sort of sexual nincompoop – but I bet he screws you just as well as I do!'

'You know he doesn't,' she said, leaning back with a satisfied smile on her face. 'That's why we've lasted so long, you and I.'

'Then why have you and he lasted so long?'

'Because he needs me. His wife leaned on him, and he leans on me. He needs a strong woman and I *am* strong. He knows I can run his home well. The only trouble is, will those toffee-nosed friends of his accept me?'

'Oh, that kind of snobbery is a thing of the past, Rose.'

'Oh, no it isn't! Not in Beckersleigh. Maybe in the big cities, but not here. Henry Calthorpe's a wealthy, respected man and no one knows anything about me. I don't intend to let them find out, either.'

'But you can tell me, surely? You've never told me much about your past, you know …'

'Haven't I?' Rose looked at him and moistened her lips. Much as it might scandalise many of the wealthy citizens of Beckersleigh, she was rather proud of her past – or at least, proud of having put it behind her so successfully. 'Well, I suppose I can trust you not to let on. You've too much to lose.'

'My father was a butcher in Blackpool. He didn't own a shop or anything, but he worked in an abattoir. He always came home at night smelling of blood; but he was a kind man, a mild man. He died when I was twelve, killed crossing the road one morning on his way to work. My mother brought me and my brother up by taking in lodgers – lodgers in every sense. I suppose you could say she ran a little brothel in the backstreets of Blackpool. And she did well. She kept us clean and respectable, and it wasn't until I was quite old that I realised what she did and why people came and went at all hours of the night. She never admitted it to me and still doesn't; but I know.'

'Is she still at it?'

'Well, she still lives in Blackpool and she's still got the same house, but she's well over sixty now. I don't see her much. We were never that close. She adored my brother and he went to the bad; ran off to London and even got sent to prison for something or other. I think he went to Australia in the end. We were never what you'd call a united family. When I was fifteen I left school and I worked in various jobs. Then, at the beginning of the war, I was working in a fish and chip shop when I met my husband – it was just after he'd joined up. We got married almost at once and had a year together – well, a few weeks together in that year. Then he was killed.'

'So how did you come to Beckersleigh?'

Barry lit another cigarette. He felt very peaceful and calm, and very close to this warm, courageous, undemanding woman. She had been his mistress for seven years, but she had never asked anything more of him than a good time in bed.

'My husband had a sister who worked here – Maisie Munday.'

'Maisie Munday!' Barry chortled.

'Don't you be funny!' She dug him playfully in the ribs. 'She was very nice, Maisie was. She worked at Shottons, the woollen mill. She had a boyfriend who worked at Hetheringtons and she wanted to be near him. Maisie shaired a flat with a girl called Doris Nicholson and I came to stay with them and look around. I had no ties in Blackpool. I didn't even like it very much and without Ted, my husband, I wanted to get away.'

'Ted Munday!' Barry chuckled again. 'It really is a ridiculous name. Munday!'

'Well, I'm about to change it!' Rose showed her irritation in her voice.

'I'm sorry.' Barry reached up and stroked her cheek. 'You know I'm only teasing. Go on with your life story. How did you meet Henry?'

'I met him in a pub. Maisie and I had gone to the Clarence Arms to have a drink and survey the local talent. Maisie told me she'd met a lot of nice fellows at the Clarence.'

'What about her boyfriend?'

'Oh, he worked nights!' Rose giggled. 'She was a bit of a one, was Maisie.'

'She sounds it.'

'Well, that's where I met Henry. He'd gone in for a quiet drink with a friend, and I could see him eyeing me. Then he bought me a drink. That's how it all began. I was just about to go home to Blackpool too, because there wasn't much work here.'

'And did he set you up at once?'

'Not quite. We went back to Maisie's that evening.'

'Straight away?'

'Well, yes, if you must know – straight away. He didn't get much with Mrs Calthorpe. In fact I doubt if he got anything. And was he

eager! We got on, anyway, and he asked to see me again.' Rose
shrugged. 'You know how it is. I never thought it would last. But when
I said I was going to Blackpool he said he'd buy me a house and keep
me if I agreed to become his mistress. The rest you know.'

'Just like that?'

'Just like that.' Rose smiled at Barry.

'And you lived happily ever after?'

'More happily than ever if I'm his wife!'

'But imagine him in ten years. He'll be ga-ga.'

'Oh no, he won't! He's tired now. He's had a very difficult time
with his daughter, his wife and that trouble at the works. But since
he came back from France he's been looking much better – and when
I said I'd marry him, he looked better still.'

'You mean he thought you wouldn't?'

'Well –' Rose looked rather offended. 'He wasn't *sure*. You never
are about that sort of thing, are you?'

'I'd have thought he'd be sure with you. I mean, he must know
how you long to get your paws on his money.'

'Barry, please don't be nasty.' Rose moved further towards the
edge of her side of the bed. 'You know it's not all about money. It's
about security, position. If you'd been somebody's mistress tucked
away in a backstreet for years, you'd know what I mean. Now I'll
entertain and I'll be entertained. You know I'm a good cook.
Henry's looking forward to having a hostess again to give dinner
parties.'

'And what about Miss Calthorpe, the one with the exhibitionist
tendencies?'

'Well, she's not too pleased, of course. But I gather she's going to
get married herself.'

'Oh. Who's the lucky man?'

'Stephen Hetherington. He's a very nice boy, just right for
Grace.'

Agnes saw the announcement in the papers before she heard it from
Grace. It appeared in the *Yorkshire Post* about three weeks after their
talk. She was staring incredulously at the column when Grace rang.

'I'm sorry, I should have told you first. But we've been so busy and
Daddy was so eager to get it in. Look, we're having a little party on
Saturday and we hope you'll come. Just a small gathering here at the
house – and Mrs Munday is to be introduced to everyone too.'

'A sort of double engagement party?'

'If you like; but Daddy's not announcing it officially. They're just going to have a quiet registry office wedding in a few weeks.'

'Have you had your official meeting?'

'Yes.' Grace's tone changed.

'How was it?'

'All right. Luckily Stephen was there. We all had dinner together, and he helped a lot. That was the night I decided to marry him. He's all right, you know. He's the sort of man you can lean on, and Agnes, I do need to lean ... so say you want me to be happy, and that you understand.'

'Of course I want you to be happy, but I'm not sure I understand.' She glanced at the door as it opened from Keith's room. 'I must go. See you on Saturday.'

'Oh, ask Keith, by the way. Daddy likes him.'

'All right, I'll ask him.'

She smiled as Keith brought over some papers to her desk.

'Agnes, there's a terrible rumpus going on at Halifax over that new block of flats. Would you ... hello, you look pleased with yourself. What was that?'

'Grace. I'm not particularly pleased with myself, but I'm pleased for her. She's got engaged.'

Keith put the papers down and she felt the change in him without looking up.

'She's engaged to Stephen Hetherington,' Agnes went on. 'She's—'

'I'm not really interested,' Keith said. 'I hardly know the girl. Would you ring the Town Planning Officer in Halifax and say ...'

'She wants you to come to the party.' Agnes took the papers and glanced at them.

'I'll think about it.' Keith's voice sounded deliberately vague. 'When is it?'

'Saturday.'

'I think I'll be away.'

CHAPTER TEN

IT WAS ONLY IN THE prejudiced eyes of someone like Grace that Rose Munday could possibly be described as vulgar. She was a petite woman, inclined to plumpness, who had kept her figure firmly in control by dint of strict dieting. The two men present on the night of Grace's engagement party who had seen her naked would probably have described her differently: for Barry, she was the personification of female sexuality, erotic and Rubenesque; for Henry Calthorpe, even after the lapse of time, she evoked memories of his mother, a warm, comforting person given to loving embraces and the protective folds of maternity.

It was one of the rare warm nights in what had so far been a cold May, and the French doors of the large white-and-gold drawing room opened onto the garden. There were tables set out on the paved terrace and just inside the doors was a long buffet table set with delicious food and wine.

'We only ever seem to meet at parties these days,' Barry Holloway said, coming over to Agnes as soon as he arrived. 'You look absolutely ravishing.'

'Thank you.' She smiled at him, vaguely embarrassed by his effusive compliment and the fact that she could think of nothing to say in return. She thought he looked rather good himself, his hair brushed back, his beard trimmed and gleaming. Evening dress suited him, and she thought he'd lost weight.

'How are things with you, Agnes? I hear you're working for Winchester.'

'Yes.'

'It must be very different from Calthorpes.'

'It is, and I like it.'

'You'll be turning into a capitalist.'

She smiled. 'No. Never. Anyway, a lot of what we're doing is corporation work.'

'I'll be seeing more of you, then. I might be Chairman of the Town Planning Committee on the new Council. Is Keith Winchester coming tonight?' Barry looked round and waved at Grace.

'I'm not sure. He didn't seem to know himself.'

Grace had just come in through the French windows, arm in arm with Stephen and heading towards them.

'Have you met my fiancé, Barry?'

'Yes I have, quite a few times.' He shook hands and gave him a clap on the shoulder. 'Congratulations. You're a very lucky man.'

'I know,' Stephen pressed Grace's arm, 'and a very happy one.'

'When's the wedding to be?'

'Quite soon. We don't believe in long engagements, do we, darling?'

'As soon as we've found a house,' Grace said practically.

'Oh, there's Keith.' Spotting him standing on the threshold, Agnes waved. When he saw her his face relaxed and he came straight over.

'I looked round and didn't see a soul I knew. Hello, Grace. This is great news, isn't it? And such a surprise!'

As he bent and kissed Grace on the cheek, she slightly turned her face so that their mouths nearly touched. For a fleeting moment they looked into each other's eyes.

'It was a surprise for me too,' Grace said shakily, and clutched Stephen's hand.

'You can hardly say that, darling! I've been asking you for years.'

'Yes, but it was a surprise when I accepted. That's what I mean.'

Everyone laughed, but Grace avoided looking at Keith and Agnes noticed that suddenly she seemed nervous and ill at ease.

'Ah, there you are, my dear!' Henry Calthorpe put his hands on Grace's hips and kissed her in a fatherly gesture from behind. 'Now that everyone's here I think we should make our little announcement, don't you?'

'What announcement, Daddy? Oh –' Grace looked past him towards Rose Munday who stood in the background. 'You're actually going to announce it?'

'I think so. That was the idea.' Henry, who looked and spoke as though he had had quite a lot to drink, stood up straight and beat his chest with both fists. 'Everyone's asking me as it is.'

'All right, Daddy. Do it now.'

She smiled at Stephen, and Agnes saw her grasp his hand and draw him closer to her as her father clapped his hands for silence and cleared his throat.

'Ladies and gentlemen, I have an announcement to make. I wonder if you'd call the people in from outside?' He looked towards the guests standing by the French windows and cleared his throat again, looking encouragingly at Rose who, perfectly gowned and coiffeured, her blonde hair gleaming, stood on her very high-heeled gold sandals, trying to conceal her nervousness behind a warm, relaxed smile. In contrast to the previous year, when she had worn black to meet Henry's family and friends, Rose had chosen scarlet for her engagement night. A scarlet chiffon handkerchief was tucked into the large bracelet of pearls on her wrist, an engagement present from Henry.

When everyone was assembled, Henry again broke into the babble of voices by clapping his hands.

'Ladies and gentlemen, please! I don't want to spoil your evening by a long speech ...' Someone cried 'Hear, hear!' and Henry gave him an indulgent smile. 'But I would just like to thank you all for being here for what, though most of you don't know it, is a double celebration. The first –' Henry gestured towards Grace and Stephen and drew them closer to him with an arm round Grace's shoulder, '– is the engagement of my darling, only daughter Grace to this fine young man, Stephen Hetherington. There's no one I would rather have as a son-in-law.'

'Hear, hear! Hear, hear!' cried several voices.

'And the second thing, the second thing, my dear friends, is that I, too, am being given another chance at happiness.' He looked towards Rose. The crowd became very still as he put his arm round her and hugged her. 'This lovely lady, who many of you already know, Rose Munday, has agreed to be my wife, and I want to share my happiness and good fortune tonight with you. Thank you.'

After a perceptible silence, loud clapping broke out and then, impulsively, Henry put both arms round Rose and kissed her firmly on the mouth. Tears welled up in her eyes and, as people began to crowd round her and Henry, they slowly rolled down her cheeks, ruining the make-up she had taken so long to apply.

Barry found himself clapping slowly behind everyone else, and everyone started to sing 'For they are jolly good fellows'. Then Mr Hetherington made a very long and emotional speech, with one or two rather tasteless allusions to the purity or otherwise of both newly engaged couples.

'I think he must know about Grace's reputation,' Barry said *sotto voce* when a rather uneasy applause broke out at the end.

'Have you heard of anything detrimental to her reputation?' Agnes said crisply.

'Not recently.'

'You're not still talking about what happened so many years ago?'

'They say that a leopard never changes its spots.'

'That's ridiculous! Grace was very young.'

'Oh, Agnes!' Barry put both his hands on her shoulders and looked straight into her eyes. 'Don't let's argue. Come and have something to eat before those speeches start again!'

'Oh, all right,' she said with an exasperated laugh.

At the buffet table, Barry could hardly have crammed another morsel onto his plate, and Agnes marvelled as he began to shovel the food into his mouth in great forkfuls. They had taken their plates to one of the tables on the terrace.

'It's quite chilly tonight,' Barry murmured, between mouthfuls. 'What a lousy month it's been. What do you think of Wedgwood Benn winning in Bristol?'

'I don't suppose he'll be allowed into the Commons,' Agnes said. 'But I admire him for trying. I'm much more concerned about our wanting to join the Common Market.'

'You're against it?'

'Of course! Aren't you?'

'No, I'm not. I'm a convinced European.'

'I hope I'm not intruding.' Keith Winchester appeared with a full plate and a glass of wine balanced precariously on the side. 'I feel a bit out of it in there. I hardly know a soul.'

'They only really asked close friends.' Agnes moved up to make room for him.

'Then why me?'

'I'm not a close friend of the family, either.' Barry nodded at Keith. 'So why me?'

'They had to have some younger people. The average age seems about fifty.'

'Yes, Grace doesn't seem to have many friends her own age. I'm surprised.' Keith took a sip of his wine.

'She has, but they haven't been asked. Well, one or two are

younger – the Cardales are our age. They were married last month. Stephen and Grace are talking to them now.'

Barry and Keith turned their heads and then Keith said, 'Now Barry, I hear you're going to be Chairman of the Town Planning Committee.'

'Yes, probably from next month.'

'Good, because there are one or two projects I need to talk to you about. You know that the Wirrall project is still being held up by the Labour intransigents? I've got a very good idea ...'

Seeing them sitting apart with their heads bent together, Grace wished she was with them. Or rather she wished she was with Keith. Wherever he went, her eyes followed him ...

'What's the matter, darling?' Stephen looked at her with concern.

'I think I'm getting a headache. Let's sit down with Agnes and Barry.'

'That Winchester fellow is with them,' Stephen objected. 'I can't stand him.'

'Why ever not?'

'I just don't like him – he's so brash. Let's go and talk to your father and Mrs Munday. I must say, she seems to be enjoying herself.'

'She's terribly nervous really.'

'Well, she's certainly hiding it well.'

Henry Calthorpe and Rose were at a table full of Henry's friends. Rose had a high colour on her face and her eyes darted about nervously.

'Move up,' Grace said, sitting down next to her and leaving Stephen standing behind her. 'Are you enjoying yourself, Mrs Munday?'

'Oh, very much thanks, dear, and I wish you'd call me Rose. Everyone's being so nice. How about you?'

'Yes, very much.'

'You look so pretty, Grace. And that Agnes *is* a pretty girl, isn't she?' Rose's eyes strayed anxiously to where Agnes was sitting with Barry and Keith. 'Do you think she's interested in Barry Holloway? She's been with him all evening.'

'I think she is. He once taught her at evening school.'

'Oh, did he?' Rose felt a pang of jealousy. 'Do they go out, then?'

'I think she'd like to.'

'Is that why he was invited?'

'No, my father likes him because he helped settle the dispute at Calthorpes by working out a compromise. He thinks he's good for the town. You'll probably see quite a lot of him when you're married.'

'I think I'd like a breath of air. I'm so hot.' Rose fanned herself furiously with her chiffon hankie. 'Would you like a breath of air, Henry? You look all red in the face, dear. And I do think you've had quite enough to drink for one evening.'

Henry smiled and squeezed her round the waist. 'But this is our engagement party!'

Rose took his hand away, looking nervously at Grace. She wanted Henry's daughter to like her, and she was aware that so far Grace had been polite rather than genuinely friendly. 'I know, but you'll feel awful in the morning – won't he, Grace?' She got up and smoothed her dress over her hips, holding out her hand. 'Come on, Henry. Are you coming too, Grace?'

Grace shook her head, then changed her mind. 'All right. We'll come with you. I haven't talked to Agnes all evening. Stephen?'

The four strolled through the French windows to the table, where Barry and Keith were polishing their plates with their French bread.

Henry gently steered Rose forward. 'Have you met my fiancée, Keith?'

'Yes, indeed – at Grace's twenty-first.'

'Of course.'

'Please sit down.' Keith went to the next table for chairs, helped by Stephen.

'Have *you* met my fiancée, Barry?' Henry leaned across Agnes and looked into Barry's face.

'Yes, I have, Mr Calthorpe, several times. Evening, Mrs Munday.' He nodded briefly at Rose, whose lips cracked into a frosty smile.

'You'll have to come and have dinner with us when we're married. She's a very good cook, aren't you, my love?' Henry slapped her knee and a flush of irritation passed across Rose's carefully controlled features.

'When's the wedding to be, Mr Calthorpe?'

'Call me Henry, Barry. I feel quite a young man, you know, having this wonderful lady promise to marry me.'

'So when are you getting married?'

'Very soon; but not before Grace and Stephen. Grace must have her own home first; at the moment we're doing all we can to find them one. By the way, Keith, there's someone I want you to meet. Councillor Barnes from Wetherby. He's got a very interesting idea ...' Putting his arm around Keith, Henry steered him back into the room.

'I think Daddy *is* drinking too much,' Grace said. 'I'll go after him.' Grace got up and Stephen started to rise, but she said sharply, 'Don't follow me around like a little dog, Steve! Talk to Agnes.'

Stephen flushed and sat back awkwardly on his chair, turning to Agnes in some embarrassment. 'I think she's worried about her father. Would you like a stroll in the garden?'

Agnes got up and smiled at Barry and Rose. 'Excuse me.' Then she linked arms with Stephen and strolled with him into the garden. Barry gazed after them, but Rose's eyes were on him, bright and glittering with hostility.

'Why did you come?' she said.

'Henry asked me.'

'You could have said "no".'

'But why should I?' His hand stole under the table and groped for her knee.

'And take your hands *off*!'

'No one will see.'

'They might! You never know who's looking. I haven't enjoyed the evening at all because of you.'

'But that's silly, love. I know you're going to marry Henry Calthorpe whether I came tonight or not, and I accept it. Besides, he and I see quite a lot of each other. You're just going to have to face it.'

'I don't see why you should have anything to do with each other at all.'

'Municipal things, the Council. He's deeply involved in the baths project. He's got a finger in any number of pies, and he's grateful for what I did to help smooth out that industrial trouble at his factory. Look, Rose, we've got to be grown up and sensible about this if we're going to stay friends.'

'What do you mean *if*?' She had a moment of panic at the thought of losing him.

'Well, if you want to, that is.'

'Of course I want to! I'm marrying Henry for security, not sex. Talking of which, you've been all evening with that Agnes girl.'

'But I've known her a long time. I used to teach her ...'

'Oh, don't give me all that waffle. You've got your eye on her.'

'So what if I have?' Barry gazed at her unsmilingly. 'I'm never allowed to look at another woman, yet you're free to marry whom you like – is that it?'

'I thought your mind was on your career.'

'It is, don't worry about that. Now calm down, your future husband's on his way back.'

Rose broke into a artificially welcoming smile as Henry plomped down beside her, yet another full glass of whisky in his hands.

Inside, someone put on the gramophone and turned down the lights and a few couples began dancing smoochily in the corner, Keith and Grace among them. Keith held Grace very tightly to him and she could feel all the contours of his body through her thin dress. She began to struggle against him.

'What's the matter?' He looked down at her.

'If my fiancé sees you, he'll kill you!'

'Oh, I think I can deal with him. Why are you going to marry him, anyway?'

'Why not?' Her voice faltered and she lowered her eyes.

'He's not strong enough for you.'

'He's devoted to me.'

'But that isn't enough, is it? A woman like you needs strength.'

Grace was silent and leaned against him. They danced silently for some time and then he lowered his head and murmured: 'Will you have lunch with me tomorrow?'

'Tomorrow's Sunday.'

'Well?'

'We're having a family lunch with the Hetheringtons.'

'I'm going away on Monday. Can't you break it?'

'I can't possibly.'

'I'll ring you when I get back. We'll have lunch then.'

'All right.'

He held her close again and they danced in silence, until the record finished and he took her back to her fiancé who was anxiously searching for her.

Barry drove silently through the deserted streets of Beckersleigh.

He glanced at Agnes, who was sitting next to him, gazing blankly ahead. 'Penny for them.'

'I don't think she's in love with Stephen,' Agnes said at last.

'I'm sure she's not.'

'Stephen knows she doesn't love him. He practically wept in the garden.'

'Is that what he wanted to talk about?'

'Yes. He adores her so. He doesn't want to lose her. He asked me what I thought.'

'And what did you say?'

'I said he should talk to Grace.'

'Have they been to bed together?'

'I don't know.'

'Wouldn't she tell you, her best friend?'

'No. And it's none of my business.'

He smiled at her, the lights on the dashboard casting a muted glow over his face. 'Your father's changed, hasn't he?'

'How do you mean?'

Barry glanced at his watch. 'Nearly two o'clock and you're not home.'

Agnes put her hand to her mouth. 'Oh, I never said! I don't live there any more.' She gave him her new address.

'When did you leave home?'

'A year ago.'

'What made you do it?'

'Dad.'

'You mean he threw you out?'

She laughed. 'Not quite. I wanted to work for Keith and he said no; so I said I'd leave home, and I did.'

'That was very brave. Have you made it up now?'

'Only just. He still thinks I'm a fallen woman because I live with Connie Shilton.'

'Connie Shilton! How did that come about?'

'Well, you know she left Calthorpes – you arranged it in fact, didn't you?'

'I suggested it as part of the compromise. She resigned and got a fairly substantial sum by way of compensation, and the workers were then free to form themselves into a union. Calthorpe thought she'd be too provocative. I agree with him. She's a menace – just the sort of mindless militant the Party can do without.'

'That's not fair!' Agnes said spiritedly. 'She's far from mindless – she's a very thoughtful person. She thinks you took against her for personal reasons.'

'Well, don't let's quarrel about what happened a long time ago,' Barry said gently. 'I assure you I had no personal grudge against Connie. But it intrigues me to know how you come to be sharing with her.'

'She got engaged to Mike Orchard just when the Calthorpes thing blew up. They decided to live together and she needed help with the rent.'

'But she didn't get married to him?'

'No. They're having a trial marriage.'

'Very sensible.' They had reached Agnes's new home, and Barry parked.

Agnes was silent, and he looked at her. Then he leaned over and gently kissed her cheek.

'It needn't give you ideas,' she said.

'I've had them for a long time.' He put his hand on her chin and turned it towards him, gazing into her luminous eyes and then at her mouth.

'Well, why didn't you make a move?'

'I was frightened of your father. If you'd told me you were living on your own a year ago we might have come a long way by now.' He held her chin firmly, and she saw clearly the outline of his mouth between his beard and moustache as it came nearer to hers.

His lips were very cool and firm and the thrust of his tongue was warm and welcome, not nauseating as Jeff's kisses had been. He slipped his hand through her low-cut dress and grasped her breast, kneading it gently. She felt the warmth rise up from her belly to her chest and then her face, and when his hand left her breast and slid under her skirt she let him touch her there too.

She would have let him do anything just then; but instead he gently disengaged himself and looked at her.

'Is Connie at home tonight?' he said.

When Agnes woke in the morning it was to find bright sunlight shining right in her face. Then she remembered: in their haste, they hadn't even bothered to draw the curtains. From its position she knew the sun was high in the sky, and when she realised she was naked and saw the back of the man beside her, she felt a momentary sense of shock. But it was quickly succeeded by pleasure. She put her arm around him and the sharp contact of their skin, her breasts almost flat against his back, awoke in her urgent memories of the fierce passion and desire of the night before. At that moment Barry also stirred, turned and opened his eyes in surprise.

'It's me,' Agnes said, smiling.

'I know it's you, silly.' He kissed her gently, a soft caress on the lips, and then he closed his eyes and appeared to fall asleep again, his broad hand still on her hip. His long lashes curled up from his cheeks and his mouth was slightly open. He looked vulnerable and almost beautiful, so different from the creature of power and force he had been the night before. She stretched her naked limbs beside him, then gently crept out of bed, not wanting to disturb him.

Agnes looked frankly at herself in the bathroom mirror and felt no shame or remorse. Her face was shiny and pink and her breasts seemed to have swollen; *surely* they were larger than the day before? Or was it that she had never looked at them in quite the same way before? Women's breasts. Feeling slightly tender, she drew a bath and soaked in the comfort of the warm water. When she went back into the bedroom, Barry was awake. He moved over for her, leaving an arm lying across the bed to encircle her body. He kissed her shoulder tenderly, fondling her breasts.

'All right?'

'Yes.'

'I didn't realise you were a virgin, Agnes.'

'Was it as obvious as all that?' She felt rather shy now that he was looking at her in the daylight.

'I'd never have known, but there's a bit of blood on the sheet.'

'Oh.' She moved quickly away and drew back the bedclothes to look at the undersheet. She saw his frown. 'We really should have taken precautions, shouldn't we?'

'Of course we should have. We just got too carried away. I should know better at my age.' It was Rose who took the precautions, naturally, so he had never given much thought to the matter before.

'Well, I'm not sorry right now. I must have been the last virgin of my age left in Beckersleigh!'

Barry laughed and groped for his cigarette. 'Saving yourself for the right man, were you?'

'No. I just didn't fancy anyone.'

'You're a funny girl, Agnes. A funny mixture. I don't really understand you.' Barry blew the smoke towards the ceiling. 'I don't understand how you can work for a man like Keith Winchester for a start.'

'Why not?'

'He's such a crooked bastard!'

'He's not really dishonest,' Agnes protested. 'Is he?'

'I wouldn't like to say what he was. I thought you might have been to bed with him. I thought maybe that was the attraction.'

'He's never even made a pass at me. I think he's got some woman in London.'

'He's a raving Tory.'

'We never talk politics. When I left Calthorpes, I needed a job very badly. He gave me a break. I seized it and I have no regrets. Nothing dishonest goes on that *I* know of. He pays me a good wage and gives me lots of responsibility. He's often away, and frankly I don't know the half of what he does – I just run the office. I like the job.'

'Just as well you don't know what he does.' Barry ground out his cigarette. 'Mind you, I do admire him in some respects. Some of his schemes are very sound, but if you really think he does it because he has a social conscience, you're fooling yourself. Excuse me a moment.'

He kissed her and jumped out of bed, and she realised with a slight shock that it was the first time she had seen a man upright and in the nude – someone who had made love to her, penetrated her . . .

Was it true that men didn't respect girls who gave in too easily? Was she destined to be thrown on the heap, like so many others she knew in Beckersleigh who had reputations as 'easy lays'? She began to wonder how he would look at her when he came back in.

But when he returned he didn't look at her at all; instead, he went straight to the window, threw it open and started breathing deeply, thumping his chest.

'I didn't know you were an exercise fanatic,' Agnes said, trying to sound amused, but feeling a little nervous. Barry thumped his chest again and then shut the window, momentarily shivering and hugging himself. He took a flying leap right on to the bed, half smothering her. Agnes gave a little cry as he entwined his legs with hers and she felt his body pressing down again on that slightly sore place. His face was an inch from hers and she could see the pore marks on his cheeks, a slight scar by the corner of his right eye.

'You look like a pirate.' The words came out in a gasp – his weight on her was quite considerable. He was gently rubbing her groin with his hand, and to her surprise it seemed to make the soreness go away. All she was conscious of was the over-whelming sensation of needing Barry, wanting him to be part of her again. He entered her gently and tenderly, kissing her, loving her, wanting, too, to be one with her.

'This is going to be a wonderful affair,' he murmured softly, his mouth pressed close to her ear as though he had something very secret he wanted to tell her. 'And it won't just be for today or tomorrow ...'

Agnes caught her breath, but she couldn't answer. She opened her arms and drew him into them, clasping her hands tightly behind his back. She hugged him with love, with joy untinged by any apprehension about what today or tomorrow, or the day after tomorrow would bring ...

CHAPTER ELEVEN

THE HOUSE WAS NEO-GEORGIAN, built in the last thirty years, but with such skill that it could almost have deceived an expert in eighteenth-century architecture. It was an imposing property and stood in the village of Whitley, about three miles from Beckersleigh on the Keighley road. But it was badly in need of repair.

'It's got enormous potential,' Agnes gazed at the high ceilings, 'and I can see why you love it; but it'll take ages to do up.'

'No, it won't.' Stephen said, perched on a window ledge. 'The builders can promise it in three months. They're starting work on Monday. So,' Stephen ticked off his fingers. 'This is June. The wedding is at the beginning of October, just to be sure. We've arranged the date: October 4.'

'And we'd like you to be our chief bridesmaid,' Grace said. 'We're having Mary, and Stephen's cousin Frances and three little pages, also cousins. Won't it be sweet?'

'It's going to be a really big do, then?'

'Of course! The wedding of the year in Beckersleigh.' Grace put her arm round Stephen and he leaned down and kissed her. Maybe Grace was in love, after all.

They went upstairs and explored four large bedrooms, two smaller ones, and a separate flat which could house a maid or be converted into a nursery. They lingered in the master bedroom, which had windows all round with magnificent views of the countryside. Grace described exactly where the furniture was going.

'And the bed there,' she pointed, glancing at Stephen. 'A huge one.'

'King size,' Stephen said, meaningfully.

When they had finished their inspection, Grace said: 'I'm popping into that antiquated loo. See you downstairs.'

Agnes and Stephen went slowly downstairs and through the front door on to the porch. Stephen stuck his hands deep into his pockets and slumped his head on his chest.

'Agnes, you remember that talk we had the night of our engagement party?'

'Yes.' She could feel his embarrassment.

'I want you to forget it ever happened.'

'I already have,' she said gently.

'Good. You see she does love me. You can see it now, can't you?' He looked at her appealingly.

'Without any doubt.'

His face relaxed and he smiled. 'I was so anxious for her to love me that I made myself a bit of a pest. But Grace likes a man to be firm and tough. Things are much better now ...'

After that, the girls met frequently for shopping expeditions to Leeds and Bradford to buy fabrics, furniture and carpets. Grace threw herself into the business of becoming a married lady with great enthusiasm and was in the habit of popping into the office at all hours to consult Agnes on this thing or that. One day she said, in the middle of showing Agnes some new material: 'I never see Keith these days. Where is he?'

'In Saudi Arabia.'

'He said he'd take me out to lunch.'

'When?'

'At my engagement party. That was six weeks ago.'

'Well, he hasn't been here much since then. Grace, do you really think that you ought to go if he asks you?'

Grace flushed slightly. 'Why ever not?'

'Well, you're getting married soon.'

'So? Can't I ever see another man?' She lit a cigarette and blew smoke between herself and Agnes.

'Grace – don't see Keith. Not until after you're married.'

'Oh. Will it be all right then?' Her voice shook with rage. 'Look, Agnes, what are you trying to say?'

Agnes looked at the floor. 'Every time I see you with Keith you're a different person. I noticed it the first time we met him. I remember the way you looked at him ...'

'Well, he's good-looking, isn't he? What's wrong in merely looking at a man?'

'... And at your twenty-first and your engagement party too. He makes you behave differently,' Agnes said insistently.

'Listen, I like him, but I'm not going to marry him. I'm marrying Stephen. And that's a deliberate decision, Agnes – you know that, don't you?'

'You mean you don't really love Stephen?'

Grace flicked ash into the large glass ashtray on Agnes's desk. 'I think it's a good thing for Stephen and me to get married. It's a family thing. Our parents have known one another for ages; we grew up together. Stephen's a nice boy. He'll look after me, take care of me, protect me. Of course I'm going to love him! But that doesn't mean I'm never going to be attracted by someone else!'

'You're "going" to love him?'

Grace nodded her head vigorously.

'Yes, I'm "going" to love him. I am "going" to make him a good wife. I am "going" to make him happy, because he loves me so much already. It is "going" to be a good, sensible marriage. What more could you want?'

'I hope it works then.' Agnes decided to say no more on the subject.

'I can't bear these things,' Barry said, attempting to fit a condom. Because he was clumsy and impatient, this one flew off like a balloon with the air suddenly let out of it. 'Oh hell!' he said, 'I'll come outside,' and he quickly entered Agnes, who had been watching the performance with such anxiety that her own desire had quite ebbed. He came out abruptly, giving loud grunts, then he flopped the length of her body and lay panting.

'Did you manage to come at all?' he gasped, raising his head and looking at her.

'No, and your body's terribly heavy.' Her voice was slightly aggrieved.

'Sorry!' He rolled off and drew the sheets over his shoulder. 'We'll really have to do better than this.'

'What did you do before?'

'What do you mean "before"?' He rolled round and looked at her.

'Before me?'

'In my experience, it's the woman who always takes the precautions.'

'*Always*?'

'Yes.'

'Were they *always* experienced women?'

'Yes – and there weren't *so* many, Agnes.'

'Well, you seem to imply there were quite a few.'

'Over the years. I am twenty-nine, remember.'

She looked at him thoughtfully. 'Barry, was there ever really a great passion in your life? I mean, have you ever *really* been in love?'

'I wish women wouldn't talk so much after making love. They always want to babble. All a man wants to do is sleep.' He closed his eyes, leaving her question unanswered.

When he woke up he lay and looked at her for a long time, turning towards her so that their bodies touched.

'I'm sorry,' he said. 'I've had a hell of a day and I didn't think I'd make it at all. Now I have a committee.'

'Sorry for what?'

'I know I was brusque.'

'Well, you were right. We can't go on like this. I'll find out what women do.'

'They usually have a cap fitted. It ...'

'Oh, I know what it does. I just don't like the idea.'

'Unfortunately,' Barry sighed patiently, 'when the Almighty ordained these things, he made the sexual act very difficult to control, both in its emotional and physical consequences. We're impelled to have sex, however much we reject it logically, as ridiculous or unnecessary, and we have the greatest trouble preventing the results, because of our anatomical constructions, especially women's. Once the cap is in, it's invisible, comfortable and it prevents you having a child you don't want.'

'You obviously know all about it.'

'You wouldn't like a man who didn't, would you?' He glanced at his watch and jumped out of bed. 'Christ! The meeting starts in ten minutes.'

She lay and watched him as he dressed. He was detached from her and the things in the room, as though he were already mentally somewhere else. He straightened his tie in the mirror, smoothed his hair with his fingers and came over to the bed where she lay on her back, the sheet half draped over her. He pulled it right back and looked at her, and suddenly she felt excited by the admiration in his eyes.

'You're very beautiful, Agnes,' he said gently, still gazing. 'I'm really falling in love with you ...'

Agnes was in her dressing-gown making a late supper in the kitchen, when Connie and Mike came home.

'Was it good?' Agnes asked.

'The film? Not bad.'

'I'm going to go to bed,' Mike said. 'I've got a headache.'

'I'll bring you a cup of tea in bed, love.' Connie smiled at him fondly.

'Night, Agnes.'

'Night, Mike.'

Connie, heating the pot, looked at Agnes. 'You seem tired, love.'

'I am a bit.'

'You work too hard in the office.'

Connie was a large girl, very overweight but with a pretty face and a beatific expression. Although she seemed to lack the temperament one would associate with a revolutionary, since she had left Calthorpes she had been more dedicated than ever to the overthrow of capitalism. She now worked full time in Leeds, organising the Peace Movement in the North West.

She had, however, a most bourgeois devotion to her man and refused to let him do a thing in the flat. She washed his shirts, darned his socks, cooked for him and brought him cups of tea in bed in the morning, never seeing the slightest conflict between being a domesticated woman and a revolutionary.

When she had taken Mike his tea that night, she came back to the kitchen in her dressing gown and poured herself some tea. As she sat down, her gown flopped open, showing her huge, bare breasts.

'Oops, sorry,' she said, fastening the gown. 'Nasty sight.'

'Not for some.' Agnes smiled.

'I can never see why men get so fixated on breasts, can you?'

'Yes, I can,' Agnes said. She sat back and took a deep breath. 'I wanted to ask you about contraception, Connie. Do you use something or does Mike?'

'Well, you know that new contraceptive pill they're experimenting with?' Connie said. 'I'm using that.'

'But they don't know anything about it yet!' Agnes protested.

'Oh, they've been trying it out in America for years – mostly with the poor blacks, needless to say. I feel I owe it to my sisters to support them. Besides, it's very convenient. You just pop it into your mouth every night and forget about it.'

'And you don't feel any ill-effects?'

'No, it's fine.'

'Where do you get it?'

'There's a Family Planning Clinic in Leeds.'

'Do you have to be married to go?'

'Well, you're supposed to be, but if you're shy you can just call yourself "Mrs". They don't ask questions. Now, who's the lucky man?' Connie asked eagerly.

'I can't tell you yet,' Agnes said, getting up and taking her cups to the sink. 'It's only just begun and I'm not sure.'

'But you can tell me, love. I won't tell a soul.'

Agnes suddenly had an urge to confide. She had been bottling up all her feelings about Barry for so long, and she had never felt able to talk to Grace about him, because Grace was too full of her own affairs to listen. She doubted if Grace would even be interested.

'You mustn't tell a soul. Not even Mike.'

Connie shrugged dramatically. 'All right.'

'It's Barry Holloway.'

Connie paused in the act of raising her cup to her lips. 'Well – you *do* surprise me. I thought you were going to say it was Keith Winchester.'

'Keith! I'd never sleep with a man I worked for.'

'Well, I'm glad about that. You know he's supposed to have bribed Councillor Willis to try and get the Enderby Street development going?'

Agnes's mouth opened wide. '*What?*'

'They say he's bribed the Tories right, left and centre. I heard that Councillor Willis went on a holiday with his wife to Majorca, and Winchester paid for it.'

'But Keith's never been to Majorca!'

'No, but he paid for the Willises to go there – or so they say. Apparently Willis would have resigned as Chairman of the Town Planning Committee if the Tories hadn't lost the elections.'

'I don't believe a word of it!'

'Well,' Connie yawned, 'I'm just telling you what they say.'

'Who's they?' Agnes leaned over the table.

'Oh, you know what people are. Rumours. I hear them mostly in Leeds.'

'Among the CND?'

'Well, don't just dismiss us as a bunch of loonies.'

'Yes, but it's too left wing. Look, Connie, there are any number of projects all over England and overseas that Keith's involved in. He's done well. He's keen, ambitious and clever. He wouldn't need to bribe anyone, I'm sure of it. And if you hear any more rumours, you should sit on them. Anyway, Barry's the Chairman of the Town Planning Committee now.'

'Then let's hope he keeps his nose clean. I don't trust politicians. If you've got to have a man. I'd rather you had him than Winchester.'

Agnes was about to reply, but decided against it. She didn't want a full-scale row with Connie. On the whole they got on well and she was fond of her. She felt relaxed in the flat, and the last thing she wanted was to have to start looking for somewhere else to live. She went to her room and for a long time she lay on her bed, thinking of all those long hours that Keith and his accountant spent together, of the way some projects didn't seem to get started and then suddenly did.

But if he was bribing people, where did all the money come from? He would have to have thousands and thousands of pounds to bribe people on the scale that Connie was suggesting. Surely she would have known if such a thing was happening. If it was only small-scale bribes, Councillor Willis's holiday for instance, it would only cost a few hundred. But what was the point? Those municipal projects always went through public scrutiny. You couldn't *possibly* bribe someone on the Council.

That at least was what Agnes told herself. But despite this comforting thought it was a long time before she finally got to sleep.

The Huntsman's Lodge was a glorified Country Club, about fifteen miles from Beckersleigh, going towards the Dales. It had a large golf course, indoor squash courts and a swimming pool and, needless to say, you could only go there if you were a member or a member's guest. There was a waiting list to join and the dining room was full every day for lunch and dinner.

Grace doubted whether anyone would recognise her as far out of town as this. It was mostly patronised by wealthy businessmen from Harrogate or York. Anyway, even if she were recognised it wouldn't be the end of the world. After all, all she was going to do was eat lunch with Keith Winchester.

She sat in the elegant foyer, turning over the pages of *Brides Magazine*, her large emerald and diamond engagement ring shining on her finger. She knew that a lot of men were looking at her as they went by, drinks in hand, passing from the bar to the dining room. For a moment she regretted she had come.

'There you are,' he said quietly and she looked up at him. He was very tanned and wore a cream suit, which set it off rather well. 'Have you been waiting long?'

'About ten minutes.'

'I am sorry. I drove from Newcastle.'

'All that way?'

'I'd drive from John o'Groats to have lunch with you.'

As she laughed he bent down and took her arm, gently drawing her to her feet. 'Let's have a drink first. You look absolutely marvellous.'

'You're very brown. Did you get that tan in Saudi Arabia?'

'Oh no. Majorca. But don't tell Agnes – she's not supposed to know. She thinks I'm working.'

'I thought she knew everything?'

'Oh no. Only some things.'

'Then why did you tell me?'

They sat at the high chrome bar and he looked at her. 'Because I hope to take you there one day.'

'I'm getting married in two months ...'

'I'll have to do it quickly then, won't I?'

She smiled and studied the menu. But even though she felt he was teasing, there was a dangerous undercurrent of exhilaration that made her sure she shouldn't have come, but glad that she had. His presence excited her as Stephen's never did, and later, in the dining room, when she felt his knee press against hers, she made no move to withdraw.

'I find you very good company, Grace.' He put a hand lightly on hers.

'It's a pity you didn't find it out sooner!' she said lightly. There was no doubt but that she was going to marry Stephen Hetherington on October 4. This was just an amusing adventure ...

'I did, but I didn't realise you were going to get married so quickly.'

'Anyone would think you'd been trying to date me for years!'

'Well, I've been too busy building up my business. I got a shock when I learned you were engaged. Truly.'

'Keith, what are you trying to say?' Grace tilted her head and looked at him, eyes merry under the large brim of her hat.

'I don't want you to marry Stephen Hetherington.'

'Are you proposing to me?'

'Would you marry me if I asked you?'

She studied his eyes which now met hers, and a smile flickered on her lips. 'We're playing games, aren't we? This is a sort of sophisticated snakes and ladders.'

'No. I'm not playing, Grace.' He took her hand again.

'But you've just been on holiday! You hardly act like a man who's trying to prevent me marrying someone else.'

'That was part business really.'

'In Majorca?'

He nodded. 'Sure. I never really have time for holidays. This is the first moment I've had to see you since your party.'

'Well,' she shrugged, 'I'm sorry, but it's too late now.'

The grasp on her hand tightened. 'But will you have lunch with me again?'

'No!'

In the next few weeks, Keith Winchester and Grace met nearly every day, either for lunch at the Huntsman's or further afield up the Great North Road. They were careful never to be seen together in Beckersleigh. Grace, going to and fro from the house in Whitley, found it easy to explain her absences. Although she pretended to regard it all as an amusing, rather naughty little game, when Keith was away for several days at a time she secretly missed him desperately.

But her flirtation with Keith never took her mind off her wedding. Just after the first fitting for her wedding dress she spent half of their lunch telling him about it.

'... and the train is six feet long and it's going to be carried by three pages.'

Keith suddenly leaned over to her and said: 'I've booked a room here for tonight.'

'What on earth for?'

'Can't you guess?'

'But Keith, we can't ...'

'But Grace, we *can*. We must!' His hand closed urgently on hers.

'No, Keith. No, I can't ...'

'I've ordered coffee to be sent up there,' he said. 'The waiter's just been signalled. You go up in the lift and I'll go up the stairs. It's on the second floor.'

'I thought you said you'd booked a room for the night?'

'Beginning from noon ...'

Grace stood with her back to the long ornate mirror on the wall so that he could see her back as well as her front. She raised her arms like a dancer and started a graceful pirouette. As she slowly turned, he saw the exquisite lift of her breasts, the curve of her thighs ...

Grace had started to strip soon after the waiter had left the coffee. Keith had started to pour and when he looked up, her dress had been laid neatly on the bed and she was already pulling her petticoat over her head.

He watched, mesmerised, as she undid her bra and revealed her naked bosom with all the drama and expertise of a night club stripper. She threw the bra on the bed with a flourish, then stepped delicately out of her lace pants, leaving on only a frilled belt, its long suspenders fastened to the tops of her stockings. Standing there in her high-heeled sandals, she was the most provocative thing he could imagine. Almost sick with desire, he reached for her, but she held up her hand in a gesture of warning.

'You mustn't come near,' she said. 'Stand back.'

He sat on the bed as she completed the strip and then, with a playful laugh, began the pirouette.

Keith started to undo his shirt, his hands fumbling feverishly at the buttons.

'Keith, don't get the wrong idea,' Grace said suddenly, as though his movements surprised her. 'This is just for looking.'

'What do you mean "just looking"?'

'You can look, but nothing else. Not yet.'

'When then? When?'

'When we're married,' she said, reaching for the discarded stocking and beginning to dress again.

'You want to marry me and not Stephen?'

'Well, what's all this been for? You just want an affair, do you?'

'I'm crazy about you, Grace.' He sank on to the bed, aching with frustrated desire.

'Yes. But that's what all this is about, isn't it? An affair.'

'I don't know.'

'Well, *I* do. I want to marry someone. I want to get married, and it's either you or Stephen.'

'You really don't care which?' He stared at her in amazement.

'Yes, of course I care.' Grace put on everything except her dress and came and sat by him. In her white petticoat and high heels she was the embodiment of every man's erotic dream. He reached for her, longing just to touch her. 'I'd rather it was you. It must be marriage, though; that or nothing.'

He leaned over and kissed her. Her lips were very cool and she opened her mouth just a little, then pushed him away.

'Let's not get passionate, Keith. If I marry Stephen I'm never going to see you again, because I haven't the slightest intention of carrying on an affair with you. You can be quite, quite sure of that. I'll be loyal to Stephen.'

'But you don't love him!'

She shrugged. 'He loves me enough for both of us. I may grow to love him – they say one can.' She looked dubiously at him.

'Do you love me?'

Grace slowly nodded her head. 'I want you very much. But I want you in marriage, Keith. I think we'd make a good team.'

Keith knelt on the floor beside her, and embracing her knees, leaned his head against them.

CHAPTER TWELVE

THE CANCELLATION OF GRACE'S ENGAGEMENT to Stephen Hetherington and her almost immediate re-engagement to Keith Winchester caused a scandal that kept Beckersleigh on the boil for most of the summer of 1961. But everyone seemed to agree that Grace had done the best thing. You couldn't marry someone you didn't love, and she lost no time at all in telling everyone that she had never really loved Stephen. It was merely family pressure that had brought the whole thing about.

The wedding was postponed for six months, because it seemed rather cruel, even to Grace, to keep the same date and plans but to take someone different to the altar. But when it did take place, everything was almost as exactly as it would have been, had it taken place on October 4: the church was the same, the reception was the same, the bride was the same, and the guests were more or less the same. Even the house that the bridal pair were to move into was the same; after all, it had been the father's gift to the bride. Grace had no qualms over the fact that Stephen had planned the alterations with her. It was enough that Keith approved of these, too.

The best man, naturally, was different, but the bridesmaids were the same except for Agnes, who felt too close to both the people concerned to attend Grace.

Agnes had received the news with mixed feelings. She was in no doubt that Grace had never loved Stephen; but at the same time she wasn't sure that she loved Keith. She wondered in her heart if Grace was in love with marriage itself, in which case almost any suitable candidate would do. But even she had to admit as they stood at the high table in the Conservative Club to cut the cake – pretty laughing bride and handsome smiling groom – that they looked well suited.

'They certainly seem a good match,' she whispered to Barry.

'A perfect pair,' he murmured. Out of the corner of his eye he could see Rose observing him from time to time, and he felt uncomfortable, conscious of being caught between the Scylla and Charybdis of his emotional life. Would Rose's marriage resolve it? What stopped him from marrying Agnes, when in so many ways she was the perfect mate for him? Although Grace looked gorgeous today, the radiant bride of tradition, he thought her looks pallid when compared to Agnes.

'I'll take you out to dinner afterwards,' he whispered. 'So don't eat too many cakes. There's a nice place called the Huntsman's Lodge. Do you know it?'

Agnes nodded. 'But you have to be a member.'

'I am.'

Agnes looked surprised, but said nothing.

The cake was cut, the bridal couple embraced and the speeches began. Barry was Keith's best man and made the best speech – short, succinct and funny. Mr Calthorpe spoke emotionally and at great length, referring often to his own forthcoming nuptials. When it was all over, the bride and groom led the dancing. Mr Calthorpe took Rose onto the floor and Barry took Agnes.

He leaned his cheek against hers at once and held her tightly in his arms.

'It was almost a year ago we started our affair,' he murmured.

'Eleven months.' She smiled. 'I'm surprised you remember.'

'You're very cynical, Agnes,' he protested.

'Realistic.'

'About what?' He held her at arm's length and looked at her.

'You. You give nine tenths of your life to work and one tenth to me. I fill in the gaps.' There was no resentment in her. She loved Barry – and that meant loving his commitment to his work, as well as the joy of sharing a bed with him when time allowed. 'I'm surprised you belong to a place like the Huntsman's, though.'

'Why?'

'It's so Tory. Did Keith take you there?'

'Yes. He goes a lot.'

'I know. It's where he seduced Grace.'

'Really?' His arm around her tightened. 'Sounds like a good omen!'

In the end, Keith and Grace, Barry and Agnes left together as Barry was to drive the bride and groom to the airport at Leeds.

Everyone wanted to touch the bride and groom, as they made

their way slowly down the broad staircase and out of the door, ducking under handfuls of confetti and rice raining down on them from all sides. Barry had disappeared through the back exit to bring his car round, and Agnes kept well out of the way until the last moment, when she sprinted for the car.

Grace lingered in the drive, hugging her father and finally giving a little peck on the cheek to Rose. Then she embraced her father again and with tears in her eyes took Keith's hand and got into the car.

'Oh dear,' she said, sinking back. 'I'm exhausted already.'

Barry started the car and edged carefully forward. A uniformed commissionaire at the gate saluted smartly, then they were accelerating away on the road to Leeds.

Grace, getting out her compact and lipstick, started to repair the ravages that all the kissing and crying had done to her make-up.

'I look such a mess!'

Agnes glanced at her from the front. 'You look pretty good to me,' she said, and saw Keith bend forward to kiss his new wife. Grace made a little gesture of irritation and moved towards the window.

'Oh, darling, don't! Save all that for later.'

Keith sat back, still smiling, while Agnes reflected that if he wasn't careful, he would soon be reduced to the same servile state that had finished Stephen's chances.

'Is the honeymoon destination still secret?' Agnes asked.

'We may as well tell you now – it's Majorca. That's how we first got involved. Keith said he wanted to take me to Majorca.'

Agnes frowned. 'Why Majorca?'

'He likes it so much.'

'I didn't know he'd ever been there.'

'Everyone's been to Majorca at some time or other,' Keith said, and frowned at Grace and shook his head.

Barry saw the little exchange in the car mirror, but could read no significance into it at the time. But much later, after they had seen them to the plane and waved them off, he remembered it and said: 'Why all the secrecy about Majorca?'

Dinner was at an end at the Huntsman's and he was drinking brandy while Agnes finished her wine.

'Majorca?'

'Keith and Grace going to Majorca. He frowned at her in the car when it was mentioned.'

She shrugged. 'Don't ask me.' Then she paused. 'Oh, I've just remembered something. It's to do with business. But maybe I shouldn't say ...'

'Tell me.' Barry leaned forward, his familiar face inviting confidences. After all, he was her lover, the one person in the whole world she knew intimately ...

'Well, a long time ago, Connie told me of a rumour that Keith had paid for Councillor Willis to have a holiday in Majorca when he was Chairman of the Town Planning Committee. That was just before the local elections last year.'

'Well, it didn't do him much good, did it?'

'Who?'

'Keith. Willis never co-operated in any of his schemes. I co-operate much more and he hasn't given me a thing.'

'But do you believe it?'

'You should know.'

'I don't. Keith keeps a lot of the business separate from me.' Agnes frowned.

'I don't think it's important anyway. It was all such a long time ago.' Barry moved his chair back from the table and stretched. 'How d'you feel about spending the night here? There's a spare room if we want it.'

'But we've no things!'

'We don't need them ...' His eyes sparkled with laughter and desire.

'I'd like to,' she said.

Barry leaned forward eagerly and took her hand, playing with her fingers. 'That's wonderful. I'll arrange for the room and you stay here.'

While he was away, she looked around the room at the tables of parties, at the dozen or so couples' heads bent over their tables, hands sometimes touching. How many of them were going to spend the night together, too?

Then she saw him beckoning to her in the doorway. As she got up, he turned suddenly towards a crowd of people who had appeared in the foyer. She could hear laughter and see Barry's head bent forward as he shook hands. Agnes grasped her purse and went slowly to the door. Just as she got there, he turned, looking for her, and took her arm.

'Look who's here, Agnes!' The note of pleasure in his voice rang false. Henry Calthorpe, his face red and beaming, stood there with his fiancée and half a dozen couples from the wedding party. He wagged a finger at her as she came into the foyer.

'Caught! So this is where you hurried off to, is it? We thought you'd be dining with the other two at Yeadon.'

'Oh no, they wanted to get to London.'

'Well, stay and have a drink with us.'

'We're just on our way,' Barry said. 'We've eaten.'

'So early?' Rose Munday's smile was insinuating, slightly malevolent.

Agnes realised now that she rather disliked Mrs Munday and didn't blame Grace at all for wanting to marry and get away from her.

The Willises were there, the Thorpes, the Parsoes and a couple that Agnes didn't know. They all made their way towards a table which Agnes had noticed being set for a party. Henry was looking anxiously towards his guests, his hand on Rose's back.

'If you're sure you won't join us ...?'

'Sure.' Barry said. 'Agnes wants to get back. She's on her own in the office now.'

'Of course. Early night.' Henry winked and kissed her on the cheek. Rose Munday, she noticed, had gone right on without saying another word to either of them.

'We'd better go out of the door,' Barry said, 'and then come back.'

Agnes had never seen Barry so flustered, so ill at ease. 'I don't mind. If it upsets you we can go home.'

'Don't be silly!' He looked irritated. 'I've fixed up for the room now. Let's go right up.'

It was one of the most luxurious rooms she had ever seen, with honey-coloured furniture, a profusion of small lights on the dressing table and a large bed in the centre. The counterpane had been removed and the beige sheets turned down.

Barry locked the door and threw the key on the bed. Then he took off his jacket and sat down in one of the large easy chairs.

'Seeing them has put you right off, hasn't it, Barry?'

'It's put us both off, let's be honest. We didn't expect to find them here and we like keeping ourselves to ourselves. Look, let's forget about them.' He began to ease her straps off her shoulder. 'This is a very pretty dress, but I'd much rather see it off.' He kissed her neck

144

and slid the dress right down to her waist. 'No bra, too. I thought you weren't wearing one. I've been trying to figure it out all evening.'

Agnes laughed and buried her face in his chest. He began to massage each nipple with his finger, gently drawing them out. She raised her head and sought his mouth, and soon the long, satisfying kiss made her forget about the people downstairs and think only about Barry. He took her in his arms, one arm under her knees and, getting up with an effort, carried her to the bed.

'You're quite a weight, young woman!'

As she lay on the bed, looking up at him, he bent down and turned her on her face and undid the dress completely, drawing it down over her hips, taking her petticoat with it. Kneeling on the floor, he undid the suspenders, drawing off each stocking, and finally removing her elasticated belt. Then he turned her over on her back and took off her pants.

'Just stay like that,' he said. 'Don't move.' He quickly shed his clothes, leaving them in a heap beside hers.

They lay together on top of the bed, embracing each other, touching. She opened her eyes and saw that his were open, that he was looking very intently at her. Then she looked down the length of their bodies, ready to be joined.

'I do love you, you know,' Barry said, and he pushed her gently over and began to straddle her.

'Oh God!' Agnes suddenly wriggled free. 'I haven't got my cap.'

'I'll come outside,' Barry said impatiently, easing her down again on the bed. 'Come on, relax. Don't worry.'

She put all thoughts, all worry out of her mind and clasped both hands around his back, drawing him on to her.

Grace was very brown, her blonde hair bleached by the sun, and she wore a light summer dress and sandals. She stood by Agnes's desk, thoughtfully studying the papers she had brought in from Keith's office. Then she put them down and groped in her bag for a cigarette.

'Keith reckons the time is just right to go ahead with all these plans. He thinks the Labour landslide at the Council elections is a definite mandate.'

'Yes, but you can't just pull the whole town down and leave piles of rubble all over the place!' Agnes said, clipping the papers together and putting them in a neat buff file.

'Well, it's been going on long enough. I agree with him. Sweeping reform is needed. Oh, by the way, we want you and Barry to have dinner with us next week. You'll be our first guests.'

'Can you cook?' Agnes asked, trying to hide her irritation. Grace had been into the office almost every day since she returned from her honeymoon, poking her nose into everything, staying for hours and making work impossible. This was the last thing Agnes had expected.

'Since when did you care about cooking?'

'Oh, I know I'm deficient. But then I don't suppose I'll ever get married.'

'That's rubbish! Of course you'll get married – and quite soon. Daddy told me he saw you and Barry together the night of our wedding.'

'That doesn't mean to say we'll get married!' Agnes laughed. For the moment it was enough to love and be loved, to have passion without the day-to-day grind that seemed to mar almost every marriage she knew.

Grace sat on the edge of the desk and swung her elegant foot, exhaling clouds of smoke.

'Keith thinks you're very suited, and so do I. We're going to fix it.'

'Oh, are you?' Agnes smiled and looked at the document she was copying.

'I can recommend marriage,' Grace said, touching her hair complacently.

'I should hope so.'

Grace stubbed out her cigarette. 'You're very cynical, Agnes.'

Agnes started to type. 'No, I'm not.' She held her hands over the keys. 'If you can't recommend it at the beginning, it's a poor outlook, isn't it?'

'If you ask me, you're jealous.' Grace put her cigarettes back in her bag and draped it over her arm. 'Keith and I are going for lunch and he'd like that surveyor's report copied by the time he gets back.'

She left the room without looking back, and Agnes, furious, slammed her fingers down on the keys.

CHAPTER THIRTEEN

THE LITTLE SEMI-DETACHED HOUSE in which Rose Munday had lived for so many years now had a FOR SALE notice outside. In fact it was already sold. Inside, half the furniture had already gone to the salerooms. Rose was taking hardly anything except a few treasured pieces of bric-à-brac to her new home.

'It was all cheap stuff,' she said, standing with Barry in the hall.

'But I thought Henry only bought you the best?'

'Henry gave me money. I saved on furniture to buy nice clothes instead. I shan't miss any of it.'

'You're not very sentimental, Rose, are you?' Barry put an arm affectionately round her shoulders.

'Only about some things. Come and have a drink.' She smiled at him and drew him into the sitting room, where, since it was summer, the table was laid as usual by the window.

'Our last meal together in his house,' he said, sitting down in an armchair. 'I can't believe it.'

'Are you really that sorry, love?'

'Of course I'm sorry. A good, happy part of my life.'

'But it isn't over.'

'That's what you say. But it can never be the same.'

'I'll come to your flat. I've never been there, you know.'

Barry grimaced. 'It's horrible. It's only one large room and a kitchen, and I share a bathroom with the neighbours. Anyway, it might all be pulled down if any of these various plans come off. It's right on the site for the projected swimming pool.'

'You've been talking about those plans for years.'

'Yes, but with Labour firmly in control of the council they stop being speculation and become reality. We're going to make this the most beautiful town in the North.'

Rose laughed and got up. 'I'll believe it when I see it. Come and have your dinner, Barry. It's only cold, I'm afraid, because the gas has been disconnected.'

He came to the table and kissed her neck before he sat down.

'You should get yourself somewhere nice to live, Barry. If you're elected at the next election – and everyone says you will be – you want to have a nice place.'

'Do you think I should get married?' Barry asked with a smile.

'Well, I wouldn't say you *need* to get married to live in a nice place,' Rose said, trying to sound reasonable, 'but I suppose you want children and that sort of thing, don't you?'

'No.' Barry looked at her seriously. 'I've never had a fatherly urge.'

'Well, then. There's no reason to get yourself wed, is there? I shouldn't think you'd make a woman very happy, anyway.'

'Oh? Why not?' Barry was offended.

'Well, you wouldn't have time for her, would you? She'd be on her own all the time, while you went out and about on your various activities.'

'Yes, but a lot of men have busy professional or commercial lives and still have a home and family.'

Rose looked at him through her thickly mascara-ed lashes. 'Well, if that's what you want, then it's all right. Most men want a home and a family. Henry Calthorpe is a man like that. But I don't think you are. That's why this situation has suited you for so long. Most people wouldn't have put up with it. You've put up with it for such a long time, you must actually like it.'

'Yes, well, it has been very comfortable.' Barry sat back, crossing his legs.

'And it'll go on being very comfortable, dear, you'll see.' She reached over and patted his hands. 'You just get yourself a nice flat in one of those new prestige blocks they're building over the North side, and I'll come and see you often. Now, would you like trifle?'

'No thanks.' Barry lit a cigarette. 'I'd like to go to bed.'

Rose had her face to the pillow and seemed to be sobbing.

'Are you all right?' he said into her ear. He lifted himself off her and sat on the side of the bed, his hand on her back. 'Is there something wrong, Rose?' He put his fingers on her cheek and found it was wet. 'Rose, what is it, love? Did I hurt you?'

She shook her head and turned on her side, reaching for his hand.

He had never seen her weep, never seen the mascara make runnels down her cheeks as it did now. She had always been so poised and happy and willing, in bed and out of it.

She let go his hand and groped under the pillow for a handkerchief. Then she sat up and, as always, modestly pulled the bedclothes over her body, as though drawing a curtain on something rather unseemly. There was a certain rather puritanical streak in Rose. Agnes was wanton, but Rose was careful. He always felt that as soon as Agnes began to make love, she forgot who she was; Rose never did. And when she was Mrs Henry Calthorpe, she certainly wouldn't.

'Oh, I must have got my make-up in a shocking mess.' She tried to smile. 'You've never seen me like this, have you, Barry?'

'No.' He touched her face again. 'But I wish you'd tell me what happened.'

'I can't.' Rose pulled the sheets up to her chin and lay back on the pillow.

'Did I hurt you?'

'No, don't be silly, love.' She touched his hand and drew aside the sheet for him to get in beside her again. 'You've never hurt me. Not like Henry – he's never quite sure if you're ready for him and doesn't care much, either! But then he knows very little about what makes ladies tick. You do.' She looked at him and kissed his shoulder. 'That's why I cried, Barry. I felt so close to you and I shall miss you so much. I wish you could stay, this last night.'

'I wish I could too,' he said. 'But Rose, you've always said that nothing will change ...'

'Well, it will. We're kidding ourselves if we say it won't. What I'm really afraid of is how you'll change, what's going to happen to you.'

'But nothing's going to happen to me!' He looked at her with surprise.

'Henry says you're practically engaged to Agnes Rivington. That's what I was on about before dinner.'

'Oh, I see.' Barry looked thoughtfully out of the window. 'Well, I've no plans to marry her, I can put your mind at rest there.'

'But you see a lot of her, don't you?'

'We see each other from time to time. We get sort of thrown together, mostly by Grace and Keith. We've been invited to dinner there next week – me as Chairman of the Town Planning

Committee, and Agnes as Keith's assistant.'

'Do you go to bed with her?'

Barry had been prepared for this and as he glanced at her, his expression was unchanged. 'Of course not!'

'Well, whenever I've seen you together, you always look like lovers. Especially at Grace's wedding. I reckon you slept with her at the Huntsman's Arms.'

'Why do you say that?'

'Just a feeling. I have no proof.'

'You're just jealous, Rose.'

'Of course I'm jealous! She's young and very pretty. If she was plain I wouldn't mind so much.'

'But I wouldn't be attracted to someone who was plain!'

'Then you *are* attracted to Agnes?'

Barry turned on his side and clasped her on the shoulder. He saw the creases in her breasts, saw the signs of age, reluctantly comparing her with Agnes's taut, firm skin. Rose was nearly forty.

'Look, love.' He stroked her cheek. 'Agnes is a young and pretty girl. I can't say I don't like her; but that's not to say I'm going to marry her. You're the one who's getting married, not me! You've always had two men. I've always been faithful to you. Now you're getting wed, and you seem to be afraid I might do the same.'

'It isn't that I don't want you to get married, Barry. It isn't that at all! If you were to marry a wealthy older woman – or even a wealthy younger woman – I'd know that there was a reason for it. I think marrying for money, for security, is sensible. It would be daft for me to have refused Henry. Henry's like an investment; if he goes, I go. You can't compare my feeling for Henry Calthorpe and my feeling for you.'

'Ideally, I suppose if Henry snuffs it in a few years, you can marry me.' Barry chuckled and pressed her arm.

Rose sniffed. 'It would make sense, I agree. Of course he'd leave a lot to Grace, but there'd still be plenty for me.'

Barry didn't answer. Inwardly he was slightly appalled at Rose's serious consideration of her future husband's demise.

'How are you and Grace getting on?'

'All right. I don't think she likes me, and I don't much care for her; but there it is – we're to be related and I must make the best of it. Thank goodness she's married and has a life of her own!'

'I don't really see why you don't get on. You seem to have a lot in common.'

'*Us*! A lot in common!' Rose looked genuinely affronted. 'How can you possibly say that?'

'I mean,' Barry corrected himself, 'that you're both practical women with plenty of common sense.' He didn't add 'self-seeking', which was the term that initially sprang to mind.

'Well, I think she's capricious and spiteful, and I hope I'm not at all like that.'

'Of course you aren't; but she knew what she was doing when she ditched Stephen and married Keith. And you know what you're doing by preferring Henry to me.'

'There's no question of preferring. I much prefer you; but marriage has never been a possibility for us two. You've no money and neither have I.'

Barry was looking at his watch and interrupted her.

'Rose, I really have to go. I hate this moment, but it had to come. One last kiss?'

She started to cry again, and he gently kissed her lids, licking the salty tears as they came from underneath. He wanted to make love to her again, if only because he didn't know when the next occasion would be. But he had no time. He didn't have time for one woman, never mind two.

He left her silently weeping.

The doctor said it was too early to tell, but Agnes knew. She had never missed her period altogether; besides, she felt heavy and lethargic and frequently a little sick, sometimes in the morning or last thing at night. They were ghastly days, and the worst of it was that she had no one to share them with. She didn't want to tell Connie and she couldn't tell Grace, because Grace was causing problems of her own. Grace was practically taking over the office, and Agnes bitterly resented it.

Now she spent much time at the kitchen table, writing. For many years Agnes had written stories or short articles which she had read and then put away. She was too unsure of her work to show it to anybody. She liked a thing when she was writing it, but when she had finished it she invariably thought it was awful. But now she remembered what James Hetherington had said, and concentrated on local stories about the sort of places and people she knew. Writing had become a kind of release for her. It relaxed her and helped her to sort through her own emotions by considering those of other people whom she had created.

She had retreated into her fictional world one night, when Connie came home alone. Connie was frequently away these days, usually on CND business. Mike, who resented her absences, had gone back to live with his parents, saying he couldn't go on living in a house where half the time he was alone with another girl. This, however, was simply an excuse. In fact he liked someone to cook for him and look after him, and now that Connie was so busy with politics, his mother was a more reliable bet. Connie had gone quite thin with all her activities and the break with Mike had upset her more than she cared to say.

She put her bag on the floor and sat down opposite Agnes.

'You seem to be writing more than ever these days.'

'Yes, I'm really interested.' Agnes half looked at her, one eye reading over what she had just written. 'One day I may have to make a living out of it.'

'Get on! Are you serious?'

Agnes threw down her pencil. 'No, not really. But I'm sick of working for Keith. It's changed entirely since they were married.'

'Grace interfering?'

'The whole time. She comes in to work with him now. She's out inspecting sites and entertaining clients to lunch. It's the last thing I expected. I'm reduced to being the office dogsbody – not that I ever went out much. He promised me trips to the Middle East, but I've yet to get as far as London.'

'And what does Keith think of it?'

'He's pleased. Says she's got good business sense.'

'And has she?'

Agnes folded her arms and sat back, kicking off her slippers. If she talked, wrote and worked, she could stop thinking about the baby; but suddenly it came vividly to her now as she thought of the difference between her circumstances and Grace's. Maybe she resented Grace at work the more because she envied her.

'She has. Grace seems to have found her vocation – not in marriage, though I suppose marriage helped her find it. I just don't like working with her, that's all.'

'You could easily get another job if you left Keith. I don't see what you're worrying about.'

Agnes was worrying abut what was going on inside her. She would be high and dry, with no job, no husband, no money – and a baby.

'Well, I won't worry then.' She smiled at Connie and got up to make a pot of tea.

'Have you seen Barry at all?' Connie's tone changed, but Agnes didn't notice.

'No, but we're going to have dinner with the Winchesters next week. They postponed it from last month because they went to London. Why?'

'I haven't seen him about much, that's all.'

'Well, you never see all that much of him anyway, do you?' Agnes looked round enquiringly at Connie. Suddenly, seeing the look on the other girl's face, she felt a rush of fear. Goose pimples had risen on her arms, making all the hairs stand up so that she could almost count them.

'Do you know something I don't know?' Agnes tried to keep her tone of voice light to hide the panic.

'I'm afraid I do and I think it will rather shock you, Agnes. But I think you should know.' Connie reached for her hand, but Agnes didn't take hers and sat down clasping the teapot in her lap.

'Go on, then,' she said. Connie cleared her throat.

'My Aunt Dorothy has lived in Elm Road for any number of years. She lives next door to Rose Munday, the woman who's just married Mr Calthorpe. You know it was in the papers.'

'Of course I know – I know her.'

'Well, over the years Aunt Dorothy has often seen Barry Holloway going into Mrs Munday's house or leaving it, sometimes early in the morning. You see what I mean?'

'I can see what you mean.' Agnes's voice trembled. '"Over the years", she said?'

'Yes, for ever so long.'

'And why did she tell you?'

'Because we were reading about the wedding in the paper together at Mum's last night, and Aunt Dorothy was there. She came right out with it. "She already had a fellow", Aunt Dorothy said with some envy, she was widowed in the war. "Some people never know their luck".'

'Had she seen Mr Calthorpe, too?'

'She doesn't know him. She goes to work and of course she's only there at night and in the morning. But she knows Barry from his picture.'

'And she's never said anything before?'

'She's not a gossip, my Aunt Dorothy. She just came out with it at Mother's because she kind of envied Mrs Munday. I never even knew they lived next door, to tell you the truth. You see, so all this time he *has* had somebody else, which is what I sometimes thought because he was so cagey with you.'

'But she's married Henry Calthorpe! They've been engaged for over a year. Do you mean to say he's been seeing her *and* me?' Agnes's voice shook with rage.

Connie nodded unhappily. 'It looks like it. My aunt said he was there only last week. She saw him leave one evening just as she was coming home from work. It was just before Mrs Munday moved...'

Agnes thought that Grace showed remarkable accomplishment as a hostess for one who had only been married such a short time. The dinner was perfect and, considering that she'd been in the office most of the day, her poise and timing were remarkable.

They took their coffee into the garden after dinner. Like the rest of the house, the garden was impressive and immaculately maintained.

Agnes had come straight from the office with Keith. She could hardly bear to look at Barry and avoided his eyes all evening. When she had to look at someone she looked at Keith or Grace.

'... So,' Keith concluded, lighting his cigar, 'we're pressing ahead for the Wirral development, the swimming baths and Phase Three of the Enderby Road project.'

'I'd like to get at those slags, too.' Barry pulled on his own cigar, examining the red tip with satisfaction.

'What about the slags?' Agnes said sharply.

'Well, they'll all have to come down; they're a danger.'

'You mean all Enderby Road and those on our side are to come down, too?'

'Eventually.' Barry smiled at her. 'Not for a few years; but eventually we want to clear the slums completely.'

'Well, I don't regard my home as a slum, thank you.' Agnes's tone was openly aggressive.

Barry studied the contents of his brandy glass. 'Well, a lot of others do, love – and that slag is an eyesore.'

'But the kids like playing there!'

'Imagine, they could have nice well-planned, landscaped playgrounds.'

It wouldn't be the same and Agnes knew it; but how could you explain the attraction of the slag to Barry, or Keith, or Grace?

'It's a tremendous development,' Barry said with enthusiasm. 'It's a socialist's dream.'

'And you'll get a lot of the credit for it, Barry, if it comes off. Your vision, your drive.' Keith refilled Barry's glass.

'Mind you, I'm going to have difficulty with some of the boys,' Barry said. 'Some of them feel like Agnes, here. Harry Earnshaw still lives in Enderby Road near Agnes. He thinks it's lovely.'

'Well, if you need any help, let me know,' Keith said expansively.

'What do you mean, "help"?' Agnes twisted in her seat.

'You know the sort of thing. The odd lunch at the Huntsman's, bottle of gin.' Keith smiled at her oddly.

'But that's bribery!'

Both Barry and Keith laughed, and even Grace sniggered.

'No, love!' Barry reached for her hand, but she snatched it away. 'It's just good business. It's common sense.'

'And I suppose giving Councillor and Mrs Willis a holiday in Majorca was common sense, too?'

Keith looked sharply at Agnes and then at Grace. 'Who said anything about Councillor Willis?'

'It was a rumour I heard some time ago. A lot of people called that bribery.'

'*If* it was true!' Barry said, frowning at Agnes.

'Did you hear it, Barry?' Keith put an arm round Grace.

'Only from Agnes. I said I was sure it wasn't true and she should forget about it. Old Willis never did anything towards slum clearance and development that I know.'

'He certainly didn't!' Keith laughed bitterly. 'I had plans on his table for six months and he never so much as looked at them.'

'In that case I'm sorry.' Agnes bit her lip. 'I just got angry about the whole thing.'

'You're not yourself, you know, Agnes,' Keith said with concern. 'I've noticed it recently. You're tired and out of sorts. Why don't you take a holiday?'

'Yes, maybe I will,' Agnes said shortly. 'Maybe I'll take a trip to Blackpool.'

'I was thinking of somewhere further afield, like Italy or the South of France. You need some sun. And it *won't* be a bribe if I offer to foot the bill.'

'It's a fringe benefit,' Barry said awkwardly, looking at Agnes, 'and it's very generous of you, Keith. Think about it, Agnes.' He reached for her hand, but again she held back.

'Blackpool's about as far as my thoughts go,' Agnes said ungraciously. 'The wind there is awfully good for you.'

'Yes, but I still think Antibes is nicer,' Keith said, 'or Portofino. Think about it. The offer's there.'

Barry looked at his watch and stood up. 'I think you should apologise, Agnes.'

'I can't understand why you work for Keith,' Grace added bitterly, 'if you think *that* about him.'

Agnes now felt nauseous and as she got to her feet she started to perspire. 'I'm awfully sorry if you mistook my meaning. I didn't really mean ...'

She jumped out of her chair, propelled by desperation to the edge of the garden, where she was violently sick. Finally she knelt on the grass and shakily wiped her face with a handkerchief.

Grace came up to her and put an arm round her waist. 'Agnes, I feel so awful, you looked bad all evening but I never knew ...'

Placing an arm round her shoulders, Grace led her into the house and took her upstairs to the bathroom, which was *en suite* to the main bedroom. There were twin basins, a large bath, a bidet, a handsome pedestal lavatory and towels embroidered with 'His' and 'Hers' and the initials KW and GW. The walls and the floor were tiled with terracotta tiles from Italy. The bedroom was all white.

Grace made Agnes lie down for a while on the bed after giving her a towelling robe and taking her dress from her.

'I'll send this to the laundry and lend you one of mine. But stay the night here.'

'Oh no! I'm fine. I just feel so terrible about it.'

'I hope it wasn't my cooking!'

'I felt queasy all day. I think it's some bug.'

'Keith's right; you did look pale. I don't think you've been looking too good for some time. Is it Barry?'

'Why should it be Barry?' Agnes closed her eyes and breathed deeply. Soon it would have to come out, but not just yet.

'I think he's playing hard to get.'

Agnes laughed mirthlessly.

'Isn't he the man you want, Agnes? Barry?' Grace sat by her side and sponged her forehead with a soft light blue sponge.

'No!' Agnes shook her head from side to side. 'No, no, no ...'

'Well, it seemed so obvious to me. You seemed crazy about him.'

Agnes opened her eyes and looked straight at Grace. 'But does he seem crazy about me?' When she saw Grace hesitate, she repeated, 'Does he? Does he? What he feels for me is nothing compared to what I feel for him. He doesn't love me at all.'

'You are in a bad way, aren't you?' Grace said, gently massaging the small of Agnes's back.

'Yes.' Agnes was angry now. 'I feel so stupid, so ashamed of myself. Why can't I be detached and sophisticated? Why do I have to care so much?'

'I should have thought it was quite normal. There's nothing wrong with being in love or falling in love. There's nothing weak about it. Barry is very suitable, *and* very sexy. In fact, I think you'd be rather abnormal not to fall in love with him, particularly if he pays you attention – and he does. But they say the woman makes the running, you know – you must plan your strategy.'

'Strategy?' Agnes blew her nose on her crumpled handkerchief and looked at her friend. She knew her face was red and moist and that she looked like a little girl, soft and vulnerable. She couldn't help feeling that no man would ever reduce Grace to that state.

'Strategy,' Grace said briskly, getting up and fetching a fresh handkerchief from the neatly laundered pile in her top drawer. 'If you ask me, Barry's the kind of man who needs to be pushed. A lot of men are, you know. I had to push Keith.'

Agnes looked interested. 'Really? How?'

'Wouldn't you like to know!' Grace flicked her tongue over her lips and gave a naughty little smile. 'I had to make him mad with desire for me.'

'And how did you do that?'

'Not by having an affair with him. Oh no. I'll tell you what I did.' Grace took two dresses from the wardrobe and put them over chairs for Agnes to look at. Then she came back to the bed and sat on it again, her arms folded. 'I stripped off, just like I used to do. Remember?'

Agnes tried to hide her astonishment.

'I saw, then, how it got the men. Drove them mad. Keith would have been quite happy running his business and being the bachelor gay. All he wanted to do was sleep with me. But I wanted to marry him. So ...'

'You stripped off?'

'Just as I used to.' Grace made a rather Gallic gesture with her hands. 'And it worked.'

'You took your clothes off, but wouldn't let him sleep with you?'

'*Sleep* with me? I wouldn't let him *touch* me.'

'Not until you were married?'

'Well, I'd let him kiss and that – but nothing else until this was firmly on my finger.' Grace pointed to her gleaming band. 'Then he had his evil way, as they say. But by that time I'd got what I wanted, so I didn't mind.' She laughed, but there was a note of seriousness that Agnes couldn't mistake.

'You didn't "mind"? Don't you like it?'

'Sex?' Grace gesticulated again. 'I can take it or leave it. Sometimes I think I'd rather leave it. But it's what men want and we have to give it to them in order to get what *we* want. But you mark my words: if you want Barry, don't go to bed with him.' Grace looked at her suddenly. 'That is, unless you have already?'

Agnes turned her face so that Grace couldn't see into her eyes. 'I think I'll wear the blue one with the collar,' she said, avoiding the question.

'Are you sure you feel all right?' Grace looked at her anxiously.

'Perfectly all right. I think maybe the heat ... One thing and another.'

'It's that man,' Grace said ominously.

Barry stopped outside the house and took his keys out of the ignition.

'I'm not asking you in,' Agnes said.

'But I thought Connie was away demonstrating in London?'

'Yes, she is. But I don't want to go to bed with you again.'

'What have I done?' Barry's voice was slightly amused. 'Or has Grace upset you? Was she getting at you in the bedroom?'

'No. Grace didn't upset me.'

Barry frowned. 'You were funny all evening. I can't think what I did – unless you're just tired of the whole thing!'

She pounced on his remark. 'Yes, that's it. I'm tired.'

'Look, Agnes, couldn't we talk about it sensibly? Not now, if you're not feeling well, but over dinner tomorrow or the next day? You know I don't want to finish with you. I don't want marriage, either, right now – I'm not sure why ...'

'Is that what you used to tell Mrs Munday?' Agnes asked bitterly. 'Mrs Calthorpe, as she now is.'

Barry groaned. 'I knew there was something ...'

'But it never occurred to you it might be her?'

'Look –' Barry swallowed. 'It was over a long time ago. Christ, she was ten years older than me. She never wanted to marry me.'

'How long ago did it all end?'

'Ages! She's been carrying on with Calthorpe for years.'

'Ten or eleven years. I remember when Grace first found out she told me that. Didn't you know about him?'

'Not at first.'

'But when you did, did you go on with her?'

'For a time. How did you find out?'

'You slept with her, *knowing* she was sleeping with another man?' Agnes's voice rose.

Barry cleared his throat. 'Well, it was a business thing.'

'*What*? With you or with him?'

Barry thumped the steering wheel. 'With him, for Christ's sake! Look, Agnes, I don't have to explain my behaviour to you or anyone else!'

'I think you do.' Agnes put a hand on the latch of the door. 'It's my business because it concerns *me*. You don't mind having sex with a woman, even though you *know* she has it with another man. Did he know about you?'

'Good God, no!' Barry looked shocked.

'You hope, you *think*. Oh Barry, I know it didn't finish ages ago! In the year you've been carrying on with me you've been screwing Mrs Munday, too! You were seen coming from her house just before she got married!'

Barry made a helpless gesture. 'Agnes, I – I felt I had an obligation to Rose. You can't just finish with someone suddenly because you fancy someone else.'

'Well, *I* think you can!' Agnes got out and stood on the pavement, leaning through the open door. 'I can and I am! I haven't got anybody else, but I don't fancy you any more. Goodnight!'

Slamming the door, she ran into the house and all the way upstairs. Then she threw herself on her bed, aware of the hammering of her heart, the lump in her throat, the pain in her belly.

If God was good, He would let her lose this baby.

CHAPTER FOURTEEN

CONNIE WAS THE FIRST PERSON Agnes told about her condition. By this time she was more than three months pregnant, so an abortion would have been difficult even if it were possible, which is wasn't. Abortions were illegal; if they could be come by, they were expensive, and if they were cheap they were dangerous.

It was August by the time Connie learned about it and she had just returned from a successful foray to London to demonstrate against the National Socialist Movement in Trafalgar Square. She reported with glee how someone had knocked down Sir Oswald Mosley and, although Agnes listened appreciatively, she seemed preoccupied.

'You look peaky, love. Is everything all right?' Connie interrupted her account of the trip to gaze anxiously at her friend.

'I'm pregnant,' Agnes said, surprising herself by blurting it out.

'Oh God!' Connie lit a cigarette. 'I was afraid this would happen. I never trusted that cap. Him?'

Agnes nodded.

Connie put a comforting arm round her shoulder. 'Have you told him?'

'No. I haven't seen him for ages – not since I told him I knew about Rose.'

'I wish I hadn't told you now!' Connie said.

'I'm glad you did. At least I know where I stand.'

'But you've *got* to tell him,' Connie insisted. 'It's his responsibility.'

'I suppose he'll have to know eventually.'

'I'll tell him, if no one else does.'

'Please Connie, don't. I'd hate that. Anyway, it's as much my fault as his. I believe in sharing the responsibility for this kind of thing.'

'I think you're too generous,' Connie said bitterly. 'Well, at least you've got me – I'll stick by you. You know that, don't you?'

Agnes nodded. There was absolutely no doubt about Connie's goodness and reliability. If only she could have felt the same about Grace.

There was no more talk about Antibes or Portofino, and in late August Agnes went to Blackpool for two weeks to think about her future and try and make some decisions. She returned to Beckersleigh with all sorts of plans and resolutions. She would tell her parents, then Grace and Keith. She would stay with Connie and work for as long as she could, and she wouldn't tell Barry. Whatever else, she wouldn't do that. She still loved him, even though he'd lied to her; loved him too much to force him into a marriage he didn't want.

Agnes always arrived at the office early. The first thing she noticed on her first morning back was that her desk was in a different position and that there were now two easy chairs instead of one. There was also an additional filing cabinet, and the top of her desk had been swept bare of everything except In and Out trays.

When she opened her drawers she found none of her papers inside, and on a small table was a large, beautifully arranged, vase of flowers. She was sitting surveying the scene, still rather puzzled, when she heard the outside door open and Frances and Stella, the two typists, enter. She got up and went to the door, a wide smile on her face.

'Hello, I'm back. I see there've been some changes going on here.'

Frances and Stella looked at her and then at each other.

'Did you have a nice holiday, Miss Rivington?'

'Lovely! And good weather too. Tell me, who's been shifting the furniture around in my room?'

'Mrs Winchester,' Frances said, not looking directly at her. 'Mrs Winchester's made all the changes. You're in with us now.'

'What do you mean, I'm in with you?' Agnes sat on the edge of one of the desks and tried to keep calm.

'Mrs Winchester has taken your office. She thinks ...'

'Agnes! Good to see you. Did you have a nice time?'

'Lovely, thanks, Keith.'

He stood in the doorway, his briefcase in one hand, his other extended in welcome. 'Good! Come in. Come in.' He pointed towards his room, ushering her in. 'Coffee, please, girls,' he said over his shoulder, and shut the door of his office behind him and Agnes.

'Keith, what's going on?'

'I knew you wouldn't like it.' Keith said unhappily. 'I tried to get in before you.'

'You mean I've been kicked out of my office?' Agnes began.

Keith intervened quickly. 'Nothing like that! Grace has simply rationalised the whole place. She thinks it's best that the secretarial side are all together – you and the two girls. Ken and John are now also together in the smaller office next door.'

'But what business is it of Grace's?' Agnes was cold with fury, but she kept her tone level.

'Grace is coming in as a partner. Now I must say, I think it's an excellent idea. She can take a lot of work off my shoulders, leave me more time to ...'

'I'm leaving, Keith!' Agnes clasped her hands together to stop them from trembling.

'Oh, nonsense!' Keith leaned forward in his chair. 'I knew you wouldn't be pleased and I wanted Grace to wait ...'

'I've only been gone two weeks ...'

'Look, Agnes, don't make it difficult for me. I didn't agree, but Grace has a mind of her own.'

'A mind that obviously controls yours!' Agnes retorted, and then stopped as Stella crept in with a tray and two cups of coffee on it. 'Thank you, Stella.' She waited until the girl had gone out. 'How could you possibly imagine that I'd tolerate this? I've built up this office from the day you and I shared one desk in this room. It was the only piece of furniture we had. Do you remember? There was no carpet on the floor and the telephone ...'

'Yes, yes, I remember.' Keith held up a hand. 'And don't think I'm not grateful – I am. And I don't want you to leave. We'll rearrange it all when Grace gets in.'

'We'll rearrange it now,' Agnes said forcefully.

'Agnes, be reasonable ...' He put out a hand and came over to her.

'I think I'm being remarkably reasonable,' Agnes said slowly, rising to her feet, 'when you think that your wife has the nerve to throw me out of my office and rearrange my life the moment my back was turned. She could only have done it like this because she wanted me to go.'

'Of course she doesn't want you to go!'

'I find that hard to believe, Keith. I know Grace. She likes things her way. We've never seen eye to eye ever since she started coming in.'

'She said you resented her ...'

'Well, there you are! And Grace is a partner ...'

'Henry's putting a lot of money into the business.'

'Ah, so that's it, is it?'

Keith sat at his desk and lowered his head, the picture of dejection. 'The cash flow hasn't been too healthy lately, and Henry's got access to all kinds of finance. He's going to be a partner, too. We're restructuring the business. Grace and Henry could – ah, here's Grace. You see – we'll soon sort it out!' Relief flooded over him.

Agnes could see Grace's shadow poised on the other side of the door. Keith almost ran towards it and flung it open.

'Here you are, darling! I've just been explaining things to Agnes.'

Grace, cool and summery in a white linen suit, walked calmly into the room, smiling brightly – too brightly, Agnes thought.

'Did you have a nice time, Agnes?'

'Lovely, thanks,' Agnes said, crossing her legs and leaning back, determined to appear every bit as calm and capable as Grace.

'You look very well, I must say. Thanks for your card.'

'I'm just explaining about the changes,' Keith began. But Grace held up her hand.

'Don't rush me, darling. I told you I wanted to tell Agnes all about it myself.'

'But I said she got in early.'

Grace consulted her small gold watch, a little frown on her face. 'Good Lord, it's only five past nine! Whatever ungodly hour did you arrive, Agnes?'

'Eight-thirty!' Agnes said coolly.

'You've been here since eight-thirty?' Grace pursed her mouth and sat down opposite Agnes, taking her hat off. 'Now look, I can see that you're not too pleased ...'

'You wouldn't expect me to be, would you?'

Grace held up a hand again, like a teacher silencing a recalcitrant child. 'Please, Agnes, don't think it was done to annoy you. We just thought that under the circumstances it was best to rearrange things as quickly as possible. Did Keith tell you that Daddy's investing in the business?'

'Yes.'

'Well, we'll be getting bigger all the time. We're going to try and take over some more rooms here, and then perhaps you could have an office to yourself again.' She smiled condescendingly. 'It's obviously a matter of status with you. I'm sorry – I just didn't realise it meant so much.'

'I think you did,' Agnes said. 'You knew perfectly well how I would react. You're not stupid, Grace, and you know me. It's nothing to do with status. It's to do with you walking in here and interfering. All right, you're Keith's wife and you're a partner now; but I've been in this business since the day Keith got these offices. In fact, I found them. I expect to be consulted about what I'm going to do and where I'm going to sit, whatever the new arrangements are.'

'Well, you will be from now on.' Grace looked pointedly at her watch. 'Look – I'm afraid we've got to go up to the factory and sign some papers with Daddy's solicitor now, so let's have a little chat later, shall we?'

Albert Rivington stood by the fireplace, filling his pipe. He seemed to have been filling it for hours. Agnes could see that his fingers were trembling and that he was pressing them very hard into the bowl to try and stop them. She felt relief now that she had told the family, and as she sat back in the chair at last, she felt calm and quite relaxed.

Her mother had accepted the news with the kind of stoicism that working women of her class adopted in situations to do with life and death. Birth and death were familiar things; but women going to work and defying men, as Agnes had done eighteen months ago – that was something different; that had made her cry. But unmarried daughters giving birth was nothing new to women like Kathleen Rivington, much as they hoped it would never happen to them.

'It's just the sort of thing I'd have expected from him!' her father said at last.

'Dad, it was me as well!'

'It was him. He needn't think he's getting away with it, either. He'll have to marry you. He ...'

Agnes stood up and went over to her father, taking his arm. 'Dad, I don't want to marry him! Don't you understand? I'm going through with this on my own.'

'Oh no, you're not! Not my daughter. How do you think it'll affect your brother and his career; have you thought of that? Have you thought of us? Of your mother? They'll all say we should have known better. Our Agnes, having a baby without a husband? No!' He shook his head vehemently.

'You're just as bad as Mr Calthorpe in that case. That's just the sort of thing he'd say.'

'Don't mention Calthorpes to me! I don't want any comparisons with them. Letting you leave your job in this condition ...'

'But it was nothing to do with them! They didn't know. It was just unfortunate it all happened at the same time.'

'She was supposed to be your friend! And who do you think's going to keep you now? Me, I suppose?'

'No, Dad. I'm doing typing for the CND, and when the baby's born I'll get another job.'

'And who'll look after it? Or do you mean to have it adopted?'

'I'd have thought you knew our Agnes better than to say that, Albert.' Kathleen looked at him reproachfully. 'She wouldn't go through all this just to have the child adopted. I know her.'

'I know her, too!' Albert said. 'None of this would ever have happened if you hadn't gone to the Grammar. You'd be properly wed by now, married and respectable. It's associating with people above you that's got you into this fix. Well, I'm going to see Mr Bloody Holloway and I'm going to ...'

'Dad, please! Please ... How can your pride let you do such a thing?'

'Oh, it can, girl, it can!' Albert put his unlit pipe in his pocket, went to the sideboard and slapped his cap on his head.

'Dad, *please* ...'

As Albert banged the door behind him, Kathleen came over and took Agnes's arm. Agnes threw herself against her mother's bosom.

'Oh Mum, I never thought he'd do this. I'd never have said a word if I'd thought ...'

'Then that shows how little you know your father,' Kathleen said softly, patting her shoulder. 'I think it's better that your father tells Mr Holloway. He's got to know sometime, love. You couldn't have kept it from him for ever, you know.'

Barry, now elected MP, put out his hand, but Albert Rivington pushed past him through the door. It was the end of the constituency surgery, and he'd been waiting for an hour.

'I've not come about niceties, nor to mince words with you, Mr Holloway, nor to discuss politics, neither.' Albert turned and faced him as Barry shut the door of his small office.

'Sit down, Albert.'

'I'd prefer to stand, to say what I have to say.'

Barry shrugged and sat down behind his desk. 'Say it, then.'

'It's about my daughter – our Agnes,' Albert began.

Barry sat up, his expression changed. 'Is she all right? I heard she'd left Winchesters.'

'She's going to have a baby,' Albert went on, as though Barry hadn't spoken. 'Yours.'

Barry pointed a finger at himself. '*My* baby?'

'Yes.'

'But we haven't been together for months!'

Albert's voice was scathing. 'She's nearly five months gone. And, foolish though she may be, my daughter isn't the sort of girl to sleep around.'

Barry suddenly thought of the night at the Huntsman's Arms and groaned inwardly. Albert continued remorselessly.

'Now look here, Mr Holloway, I may be a working-class man with no education. I may not speak like you and have all your knowledge, but I'm every bit as good as you and your kind. I regret the day my daughter ever set eyes on you, but what's done is done. You've got Agnes into this trouble, and it's your responsibility. I'm not having an unwed daughter with a baby when I've worked so hard to give my son a good education. He's a doctor now, a proper medical doctor with a degree. He's called Dr Rivington. *Doctor*. What do you think of that?'

'Yes, that's splendid, Albert –'

'He's brought great joy to me, has my son, whatever my daughter's done. He's going to be a surgeon and have a string of letters after his name, and I'm not having him disgraced by his sister. I'm not letting her drag his name in the mud. He's worked very hard to be respectable and do well. What's he going to say when folks find out he's got a sister with a baby and no husband?'

'I've only met him once, but he seemed a fine fellow –' Barry began, but Albert, cap still on his head, went over and banged the table, raising his fist to within an inch of Barry's chin.

'He *is* a fine fellow, a very fine fellow. Now, Mr Holloway, I don't like you much and God knows I don't want you as a son-in-law, but I've no option. Either you make an honest woman of my Agnes, or I'll make sure your career in Beckersleigh is ruined. I'll blacken your name in every part of Beckersleigh and beyond. I'll make sure you're never adopted anywhere else and that everyone knows what you've done. I'll have your name in all the papers, and I'll ...'

Barry got up and came from behind the desk, his face menacing. He caught Albert's raised fist and gripped it in his hand.

'Now you look here, Albert Rivington! Shut up, do you hear me? *Shut up*! I'm sick of your bullying, your insults and threats, and if you hounded me to John o'Groats, I'd never submit to blackmail from you or anyone else. I'll marry your daughter all right, but because I *want* to, do you hear? I want to! I love her and I want to. I had no idea she was pregnant and if she'd told me, as she should have, none of this misery would have happened. We had a terrible row and now I know why. She'd been sick that night and she was unwell and upset. I should have realised something was wrong. I'm going straight over to see her – but you remember this: what you've said to me has got nothing to do with it. You'd have done better to tell me the facts and say nothing.' Barry grabbed his coat and flung it on. 'Where is she?'

'At our house,' Albert said. For the first time in his life he hung his head as he slowly followed Barry out of the door. But there was no one there to see it.

Beyond the slag was a path wide enough for a motor car, but cars seldom passed that way. Picknickers sometimes went along it, or lovers, because it led to an escarpment overlooking the town, a softly undulating patch of green before the moor proper began. Agnes and Barry were the only ones there, because it was nearly dark now and too cold for lovers. The two of them seemed to have been talking for hours – and always saying the same thing.

'Of course, I love you,' Barry said for the tenth time. 'It didn't need your father to persuade me. I wish you'd realise that.'

'Well, you didn't behave like a man in love,' Agnes said slowly. 'Apart from one or two phone calls, I didn't hear a word.'

'But I didn't know what was happening, did I? I thought you were just being proud and angry about Rose and that we'd get together again when you felt better. I didn't know you were pregnant. I had no idea. How could I?'

'I'm not blaming you for that. I just don't see how we can get married when we've had this break. It's all of five months.' She looked at her stomach. 'It's beginning to show.'

'Well, what do you want me to do?' Barry said irritably. 'Leave you to have the baby on your own? Will that make you feel better?'

'Of course not. But I'd rather do that than get married to you for no other reason than because I have to,' Agnes said sullenly.

'But I *want* to marry you. You know I do.'

'No, I don't.'

'That's because you're so bloody stubborn.'

'What about Mrs Calthorpe, then?' Agnes turned and stared at him, her eyes accusing.

Barry sighed deeply. 'I knew she'd come up.'

'Barry, she was the cause of our break.'

'But it was unnecessary,' Barry said. 'She and I were finished with a long time ago. That's what you don't understand.'

'But you were still seeing her, weren't you? Right up until she got married. Someone saw you at her house.'

'But we were old friends. Lovers once, yes; but it had turned into friendship long ago. I just used to call and have a drink or a meal.'

'I find that hard to believe.' Agnes turned round and looked out of the windscreen over the town. The lights were all on now, shining brightly against the encroaching dark. The glow from the blast furnace merged with the red tincture of the evening sky, creating a sudden patch of light, like a firework. 'Whenever we were together, I always felt she was following you about with her eyes. She always looked jealous to me.'

'Oh, she couldn't have been! She had her eyes on Henry for years— she knew his wife was ill.'

'Do you see her now?'

'Since she was married? Of course not! I mean, we might meet at the odd social function, but I never go and see her.'

'But why not, if you were such friends?'

'Because ...' Barry groped for words and gave up. 'Oh, Agnes, you're just tormenting yourself. I love you, *only* you. Can't you understand that? I'd have got round to marriage eventually – so what does it matter if it's sooner, rather than later? I love you, you stupid bitch! Love you!'

Suddenly she was crying, sobbing as if her heart would break. For the first time since she had known she was pregnant she felt part of the real world again. Barry loved her – he was telling her so, over and over again. She simply had to believe him ...

The night before the wedding, they drove over to the new flat. It looked bare and impersonal, because Barry had only moved in a week before. Agnes packed a small case, taking the things that she wanted from the two large cases which she had brought over from Connie's place the day before. She did things slowly, because she felt heavy even though she wasn't very big. She didn't set out to hide her pregnancy, but it was fairly easy to conceal it. In spite of that, they were getting married in a registry office in Leeds so as to keep it as quiet as possible. After all, as her father pointed out, you didn't want to advertise the thing.

When she had finished packing, Agnes went into the sitting room, where Barry stood drinking whisky before the electric fire. He held out a hand and she went up to him, nestling close to him. His arm curled round her and he hugged her.

'Have you got the tickets?' she asked. He patted his pocket. 'Do you think we were right to accept them?'

'It's a wedding present. It's a personal gift from them – nothing to do with business.' He kissed her hand. 'You're a funny girl, Agnes. You know they're as sorry for everything that went on before as I was. They didn't know you were pregnant any more than I did.'

'You think Grace might not have moved me out of the office if she'd known?'

Barry shook his head. 'I don't know. The main thing is, they're trying to make amends. It worked out for the best, didn't it? I wouldn't have wanted you to go on working, with the baby.'

'But what about me?' Agnes said, raising her head to get a good look at the man she was about to marry. Sometimes it was very difficult to tell whether he was joking or serious. Like all politicians, he had a habit of giving the answers he judged his listeners wanted to hear.

'What do you mean?'

'My feelings.'

'Well, you wouldn't have wanted to go on working, would you? It's not as though working as a secretary in a property office, you were giving up an important career, is it?'

'You think a woman should stay at home?'

'Of course I do, if she has children.' Barry released her for a moment and raised his glass to his lips. 'She can choose what she wants to do, can't she? She can either marry and have children, or stay single and work. That seems perfectly fair to me.'

'Except that you don't always have a choice,' Agnes said unhappily.

Barry put his arm round her again and held her tight. 'I'm not getting at you, darling. But most women *do* have the choice. I believe very strongly that when a mother has young children, she should give up whatever work or career she has and stay at home and look after them – and her husband. She can resume work when she's older, if she wants to. All the psychologists say it's for the best. It's her place.'

He bent down and put a finger on her lips as though to keep her silent, and smiled into her eyes – a warm, loving smile. Agnes wondered if he could really believe that a woman's place was in the home? An enlightened socialist like Barry – a man who cared about slums and poverty, Soviet missiles in Cuba and the unemployed?

She decided, for that night at least, to hold her peace, as her mother had advised her to. 'You should compromise more, Agnes,' she had told her in one of their frequent little talks recently. 'If you keep on arguing and rebelling, you'll only make life more difficult for yourself. I think you're lucky. Barry's marrying you, and everything's turned out right. Don't throw it all away. It's the woman who must make the sacrifice, always has been. Look at me and your father. It hasn't always been easy for me, but we're happy. Because I've compromised.'

Barry took away his finger and, turning her towards him, kissed her lips. Agnes put both her arms around him and responded with all her heart, closing her mind to difficulties, suspending judgment, casting out criticism – compromising ...

Part Three

CHAPTER FIFTEEN

'Isn't it time we put the television on, Daddy?' Grace looked across at her father, who glanced at his watch.

'It isn't time yet, love.'

'I didn't realise you were so interested in politics, Grace.' Rose wiped her mouth carefully on her napkin. Despite the fact that she had so firmly and successfully established herself as Henry's wife, Grace still made her uneasy.

'Of course I'm interested in politics!' Grace said sharply. 'Aren't we all? Besides, I want to see how Barry gets on.'

'Everyone says he'll get in again,' Ruth Blackstone looked at her husband, 'and with a large majority, too.'

'He is a good MP.' Henry Calthorpe cut a bunch of grapes with fruit scissors. 'Though I don't doubt Malcolm Longley would be good too, and we've always been Tory. If they get in again, Labour will nationalise steel. They haven't had a large enough majority in the last eighteen months to force it through, but if they get one this time ...'

John Blackstone, the President of the local Chamber of Commerce and an old friend of Henry's, followed Henry's example and cut the grapes very carefully. Ever since Henry had married Rose, the Calthorpe table had been the object of some envy among their friends, both as to the quality of the food served and the manner of its presentation.

'Steel nationalisation will be disastrous,' remarked Blackstone, 'along with all the other schemes the Labour Party has in mind. Look at Rhodesia! What a mess they've made of that.'

'Do you mind if we turn the television on, Rose?' Grace looked at her stepmother and put her napkin on the table.

'Of course not, dear. We've all finished, I think, and we can have coffee in the drawing room. Henry?' She rang a little bell and Henry obediently swallowed his last grape.

The living-in maid entered. She had become a fixture in the house since the death of Mrs Calthorpe. Rose had quickly adapted herself to the stylish life.

'We'll have coffee in the living room, Sadie.'

'Yes, Mrs Calthorpe.'

'Are the twins all right, Sadie?'

'Not a peep out of them, Mrs Calthorpe.'

Rose got up, smiling at her husband. The birth of twin boys two years before had set the seal on what was, by any standards, a highly satisfactory marriage.

To be able to produce a pair of fine boys with the minimum of difficulty at her advanced age had given Rose's self-esteem a much-needed boost: she was a Calthorpe, breeding Calthorpes. Henry, who had always wanted sons, never ceased to be grateful. To have got two advanced his good opinion of himself even further.

'Did you pop up and see the boys when you came in, Grace?' Rose enquired casually.

'No,' Grace said shortly. 'I trust they're well?'

'Oh, beautiful!' Rose's face glowed with maternal pride. 'And do you know what little Robert did yesterday ...'

'I hope he's never called Bob,' Grace said crushingly, cutting the rest of the story short.

'Oh, he's never likely to be that!'

Rose's equanimity was not in the least disturbed. She had her own views about Grace's attitude to her half-brothers: she called it jealousy.

On the television screen, the pundits were conjecturing the outcome of the election, but as yet there were no results to indicate a trend. It was a few minutes after ten and the polls had only just closed. Grace slumped into a chair with her coffee. Henry came round, offering liqueurs.

'Keith?'

'Brandy, thanks.' Keith also looked moodily at the small screen. He had attempted very little conversation at dinner and was at a loss to understand why his father-in-law had invited John Blackstone and his boring wife, who was a local magistrate and spent hours voicing bigoted opinions on the misdeeds of the young. Henry finished serving the drinks and drew up a chair next to Keith.

'I suppose Barry will get in?' he said.

'I suppose so.' Keith's eyes didn't leave the screen.

'You do want him to, don't you? The baths are nearly ready, the Wirrall has more skyscrapers and the bulldozer is almost up to Enderby Road. I think we've done very well in four years.'

'There's a lot of opposition, though. Agnes Holloway actually opposes Barry on the question of clearing the slag; she says the kids like to play there. I'd like to know how she'd like her two running in and out of bits of coal all day. People forget very quickly.' Keith's lips curled. 'With her nice little house and garden it's all very well for her to talk about the privations of others. "Let them keep the slag," she says. "You go and live there," I say.'

'And what does she say to that?'

'What can she say? An MP can't live in the Enderby area; he's got to have his position in society, whatever his party. But Agnes was always much more left wing than Barry. I think she's got worse since they were married.'

'They're happy enough though, aren't they?' Henry said, casually getting up and fetching the brandy bottle.

'Oh, I think so. We don't see too much of them. Grace is always busy, what with the business and the hospital and ...' Keith looked at Henry, who grimaced.

'Aye it's a pity, that. I don't understand it myself.'

'I think she's really getting worried about it now,' Keith lowered his voice. 'It never bothered her much at first, but now she's getting desperate. It's making life rather hard at home.'

Henry nodded and sat back gazing at the ceiling. Grace's predicament worried him, but when you were the recent father of two youngs sons, it was hard to feel genuine sorrow that you might never be a grandfather.

Grace had been watching her husband and father whispering together. By the time they started looking at her, she'd had enough.

'I think we should go,' she said, getting up.

'But aren't you going to stay and see the Beckersleigh result?' Rose looked pained. 'I've made sandwiches, and Henry put some champagne in the fridge.'

Grace shook her head. 'We don't need any more food. Besides, I'm too tired to stay up. Ruth and John will stay on, I'm sure. Do you mind, Keith?'

Keith sprang up, patting his pockets. 'Not at all. Tomorrow's a working day for us, whoever wins the election.'

Grace hardly spoke in the car, but as soon as they got home she ran into the house to switch on the television, while Keith put the car away.

'The Beckersleigh result's expected any minute,' she said as he came in.

'I thought you were tired?'

'I was tired of them – and tired of you and my father gossiping about me. Do you think he really cares about our problems?'

'We weren't gossiping about you!'

'Well, you were talking about me, weren't you? I saw you looking guilty every time I glanced in your direction.'

'That's quite untrue. All I said to him was that you didn't see Agnes very much because you were busy, and that going to the hospital took up a lot of your time.'

'Which he'll relay to Rose. And won't she be thrilled!' Grace sat back, furious. Keith poured himself a drink and sat next to her. He tried to put an arm round her waist, but she pushed him away.

'I'm sure Rose is anything but thrilled, Grace. Why should she be so perverse as to relish the fact that you're having difficulty in conceiving?'

'*We're* having difficulty in conceiving. It's not established it's my fault, you know.'

'I know, darling. I meant that. But why should Rose be pleased?'

'Because she's that sort of spiteful bitch. "*I* can do it easily, but she can't" – that sort of thing. She's forever talking about those twins. You'd think no one had ever had children before.'

'Well, she's certainly pleased and I can understand it. But I don't see why that makes her gloat about us.'

'*I* do. You don't know how she dislikes me.'

'Well, let's stop going there.'

'Don't be stupid. It's my home! Oh, here's Beckersleigh! And look at the smile on Barry's face. He must have won.'

The candidates were standing beside the mayor, who was just about to make the pronouncement. Grace rushed to turn the volume up.

'... results of the General Election of 1966 in Beckersleigh are as follows:

Henry Allinson Carpenter	7,655
Bernard George Holloway	17,547
Malcolm Arthur Longley	14,257

I therefore declare that Bernard Paul Holloway is duly elected as Member of Parliament for the town of Beckersleigh.'

The cheer that went up drowned his final words, and Grace saw Barry hug Agnes, who was standing next to him. Then the picture cut to the studio, where the television pundits immediately began to predict a big swing to Labour.

'Oh God!' Grace got up to turn off the television.

'I thought you'd be pleased. At least we know where we stand with Barry.'

'Yes, but what about the rest of the Party? What about steel? The Hetheringtons must be frantic with worry. Besides, I can't bear that look on Agnes's face; she looks like the cat who's swallowed the cream.'

'I thought she looked a bit as though the cream was sour. She's not finding it easy to cope with two small children, what with Barry away all week.'

'Well, at least she's *got* children. There's *one* thing Barry can do that others apparantly can't.'

Grace went quickly ahead of him and had already undressed by the time he came upstairs. Her things had been flung on to one of the chairs and her shoes kicked off on the floor. She had on her thin nylon nightie and was doing her teeth in the bathroom.

Keith watched her usual nightly routine as he undressed, put his clothes neatly away, unlike Grace, his suit in the wardrobe, his pants and socks in the dirty linen basket in the bathroom where he too brushed his teeth. When he got back to the bedroom, Grace was lying in bed with her hands pillowing her head. Keith put on his pyjamas and clambered in bed beside her.

'Grace, why not give it a break, for once? You've had several goes at me tonight. I knew what the crack meant about Barry being able to do some things that others can't – father children. You never told me you had such a strong desire for children when we were first married. I didn't even think you liked them very much.'

'It's true, I was never that crazy about them before – but that doesn't mean I didn't want any of my own.'

'But if you can't have them, you can't have them – it's no use tormenting yourself. You have the rest of your life to lead.'

She stared at him with hostility tinged with contempt.

'You keep on talking about *me* not being able to have any children.'

'Well, *us* I mean ...'

'No, you mean *me*. You can't believe that it could be you, can you?'

'Well, they don't say it's me. Christ knows, I've had enough tests!'

'But they haven't found anything wrong with me, either, have they? My tubes aren't blocked, my cycle is normal, I ovulate when I should and menstruate when I should. I'm perfectly normal!'

It was true that exhaustive, intimate, embarrassing tests, conducted separately and together had drawn a series of blanks. Keith had his own ideas on the subject and he voiced them now, attempting to put an arm under her back.

'I still think it's because you can't relax and enjoy yourself, you know.

'Oh, that's rubbish! You just say that to protect yourself. It's got nothing to do with it. You don't have to enjoy sex to have a baby. Every schoolgirl who's ever been caught out knows that!'

'Which certainly wasn't you. I thought you were the hottest number I'd ever seen. The way you stripped off in that hotel room, your passionate kisses in the car ...'

'Keith, how many times do we have to go over the same old ground? We've been married nearly four years and you still keep talking about how I didn't fulfil your expectations. Anyone would think I tricked you into marriage.'

'Grace, you know I don't mean that. Look, I've talked to doctors. I've even been to a psychiatrist. I do all I can to make you relax and want me – I don't know what else I can do.'

'You're clumsy, that's your trouble,' Grace said. 'You've got no real technique. You come too quickly. That's why you don't satisfy me. Did you tell them *that*?'

There was no doubt Keith had a problem. He became excited too early, and even though he tried to hold back, he couldn't. But it didn't explain why Grace couldn't conceive. Surely even a miserable sex life was capable of producing a baby?

And Keith loved Grace; he desired her and he admired her. Their social life was a great success, their business was doing phenomenally well. It hadn't been until about a year before that

Grace had started to want children passionately, just after Agnes had had her second baby. After that, it became an obsession with her. Even though she goaded him, made him angry, he still wanted her. He put an arm round her waist and kissed her neck.

'Don't get upset,' he said. 'We should be making love not war.'

'Oh Keith, I'm tired. That prick of yours is so bloody useless, anyone would think you'd try and keep it under control!'

A deep, overwhelming rage suddenly possessed the normally mild Keith. He seized the bedclothes, revealing Grace's shapely form encased in the almost transparent nightie, and pushed her hard in the back with his hand, following with a shove from his feet which propelled her right out of bed and halfway to the window, where she lay spreadeagled on the floor.

Beside himself, Keith jumped out of bed and knelt by her on the floor, his face mottled with rage, a large pulse throbbing on his forehead. As she tried to get up, he tore savagely at the neckline of her nightdress and, seizing her long elegant neck in both hands, started to shake her.

'You fucking stupid bitch!' he yelled. 'You bloody little tramp! You're my wife and you should cleave to me, not goad me and taunt me about my virility, my so-called incapacity to produce children. If I've got problems, so have you. You're frigid and cold and it makes you cruel, frustrated and discontented. You can't bear Rose and you can't bear Agnes, because they're both mothers of young children. Christ knows what sort of mother you'd make! Have you ever thought about that? Have you ever thought that maybe God has stopped you being a mother because he doesn't think you're capable ...'

In a blind rage, he shook her head backwards and forwards. Grace clawed at his hands, her face beginning to bulge, her eyes almost disappearing upwards within their sockets. Suddenly Keith was terrified. The anger left him as abruptly as it had seized him, and he took his hands from her throat, lowering her to the floor. For a moment she lay panting, the red weal from her neck spreading slowly over the breasts he had uncovered when he had torn her nightdress.

'Grace! *Grace!*' he called, squatting beside her and taking her hand to feel for her pulse. But there was no need. He could see it beating at her neck, fast but strongly. He had shaken her, not killed her – probably not even hurt her very much. Her eyelids flickered open and she gazed at him, those blue, translucent eyes almost green with hatred.

'You're a bloody murderer!' she said weakly. 'You'd better call the police.'

'I didn't mean to do it, Grace! You know I never would.' He lay beside her and leaned his head against her breast, listening to the strong beating of her heart, overjoyed that she was vibrant and lived and was his. 'You made me so angry I felt I could kill you; but I never would. I'd kill myself first.' He reached out and stroked her breast, tracing its contours with his fingers, then pulled the torn nightie down to her waist and began to ease it over her thighs. He heard her give a gasp and felt the nipple that he was gently massaging begin to erect and grow beneath his fingers. He felt Grace put a hand around his neck and draw his head up so that she could look into his eyes. He saw her mouth open and the white teeth inside glistening with spittle.

'Oh Grace...' he muttered, and tore the split nightie the rest of the way, but gently, with the tender, demanding impatience of a lover, not the violence and force of a rapist.

It was one of the few bright days of that poor summer, and Paul Rivington sat in an armchair in Agnes's back garden with his one-year-old niece on his lap. He raised his knees with her on top and went 'boo!', then quickly lowered them again and went 'boo!' even louder. Miranda Holloway squealed with delight, begging him to do it again, hands flouncing in the air.

'You'll give her brain damage.' Agnes came out to the line with an armfull of damp clothes.

'You mean I'll rattle her too much?' Paul gazed lovingly into his niece's eyes. 'I think she can stand it.'

Agnes hung the clothes on the line, reaching to the pocket of her large apron for the pegs. Just then, Terry came speeding round the corner of the house on his bicycle and careered straight into her. He looked up, laughing, but Agnes leaned down and smacked him. Terry burst into tears and keeled over on the bike, lying on the ground in the manner of one terribly, perhaps mortally, wounded.

'I can see these kids are a full-time job,' Paul said.

'Aren't they just?'

Paul grinned sympathetically. 'The weary mother syndrome.

Why don't you bring your coffee into the garden and relax?'

'It's easy to say "relax", Paul, but I've a mountain of things to do. Barry's home tonight and he's twice as much work as the kids. I've got to do his typing, correct his articles, listen to his next speech, deal with constituency correspondence, as well as getting his dinner, washing and mending his clothes and doing all the things expected of a good, loyal, obedient wife.'

'Don't sound so cynical.'

Agnes took down the clothes from one end of the line and put them in a basket on the lawn. 'You're right – I am cynical. If you're the wife of an MP you can't be anything else.'

'I thought it was all about idealism?'

'It was.'

'Do I detect a note of bitterness?' Paul asked, keeping his voice light.

'Bitterness about what?'

'Marriage. Barry. Children. Or is it everything?'

'It's a bit of everything,' Agnes said honestly. 'But don't think I'm bitter; I'm not. I'm resigned. This is a woman's lot – she functions as a wife, a bed companion, a mother, a housekeeper and secretary, a nurse and a psychiatrist. She's the lynch pin. Without her, the nation would fall apart and strong men would weep?'

Paul smiled. 'Then she *is* important!'

'Oh, she's very important; but is she appreciated?' Agnes smiled questioningly.

'I'm sure she is. As you say, without you –' Paul gestured broadly towards the house, the children '– everything would fall apart. But you like all this really, don't you?'

Agnes gazed at him gravely, thinking how far apart they'd grown in ten years. She had seen very little of Paul in these years. He'd spent three in the States and the rest of the time in the South of England.

'You mean, do I like the life I lead?'

'Yes. It must be very satisfying to be the wife of a successful man, a Member of Parliament, and the mother of two remarkably beautiful children, surely?'

'But what about hanging out the washing and doing all the chores as well?'

Paul hugged Miranda to him. 'I'd have thought you could afford some help in the house.'

'Well, we can't. Barry gave up his job when he first got into Parliament in '64 and we only have his salary and what he gets from lectures and articles. It's not much.'

'I'm sure it's better than the pay of an assistant registrar!' Paul laughed.

'Yes, but think of your rewards in a few years' time. Consultancy status, perks of all kinds ...'

'And a lot of bloody hard work! I've only to hack someone's leg off by mistake and I've had it.'

'When are you going to get married, Paul?'

'I've no one in mind. Besides, you don't make marriage sound very attractive from the woman's point of view.'

'Don't I?' Agnes reached for Miranda. 'I'm sorry. Monday is washday, and I always get a bit fed up. Barry's been away for a week with this World Cup thing and I know he needs relaxation, but so do I. He calls the World Cup work, but it isn't really. I find the constant companionship of two very young children exhausting. Oh, I know they're fascinating, too; but they're tiring. And even at night when they're in bed, there's the ironing and the typing to do. I do it all year round, non-stop.'

'You read, though, don't you? You see people.'

'Not much; not when Barry's away – and that's most of the year, don't forget.'

'But you share in his work; you like it?'

Terry started riding his bike again and Miranda sat down on her bottom. The clouds scudded across the blue sky above the town of Beckersleigh and the freshly-washed clothes blew vigorously in the wind. The Holloway's back garden faced on to the back gardens of the houses on the other side. Their house was on a new housing estate built specially by private enterprise for the aspiring middle classes – those who could not yet afford the detached villas up the hill where the Calthorpes lived.

Agnes remembered that once there had been fields here, but just after she'd left school this estate had started to sprout and Beckersleigh had begun to spill on to the Leeds road.

Paul, unoffended by her failure to reply, had fallen into a doze, his head slumped in his chest. Agnes felt contrite, knowing that he probably hadn't slept a wink the night before. He had been at Beckersleigh General three months; the next stop was a full Registrar's job at a university hospital. Beckersleigh was just filling in time . . . She looked at him, her head on one side. Did he ever pause to think that it was because of *him* she lead the life she did, and had never lived anywhere but Beckersleigh?

CHAPTER SIXTEEN

BARRY ARRIVED HOME WITH A bottle of wine in his case to celebrate England's victory in the 1966 World Cup.

'Did you see every match?' Agnes asked.

'Almost. The Final was terrific.'

'We saw it on the telly,' Agnes said. 'Even Miranda was excited.'

Barry reached for the baby and held her in his arms, hugging her. 'Were you excited, my little baby?'

Miranda gurgled and Terry, jealous of his sister, tried to climb on to his father's knee.

'I could do with a beer,' Barry said, smiling at Agnes. 'What's for dinner?'

'Steak pie and chips.'

'Good! I'm starving. Oh, did you finish my speech for the Durham miners?'

'*And* rewrote it.' Agnes put cushions on a chair for Terry. 'The English was appalling!'

'Agnes is getting very fussy about my English, Paul.' Barry uncorked the wine. 'She's going to write a novel.'

'Really? I don't know where she'll find the time.' But Paul was obviously impressed.

'Neither do I.' Agnes put the homemade pie through the hatch and brought in a large bowl of chips, nursing it gingerly in an oven cloth. 'Careful, it's hot.'

'What's it about?' Paul asked, interested.

'Oh, stop talking about my novel!'

'I only asked what it was about. Is it pornographic?' Paul smiled conspiratorially at Barry.

'Yes!'

'Ah, that explains all the secrecy.'

'Remember the Hetheringtons?' Barry spoke with his mouth full and reached for the salt.

'Yes.'

'Well, James Hetherington put her up to it. He's a publisher.'

'You mean he's going to publish it?'

'No.' After encouraging Terry to take a few mouthfuls, Agnes finally sat down to her own meal.

Paul, who had finished by now, leaned back. 'I really would like to know about the novel,' he said. 'You never know – I might have a famous sister one day.'

Barry grunted. 'Oh, she'll never be famous.'

'How do you know?' Agnes bridled.

'Well, you said so.' He looked at her in surprise. 'You said it wasn't any good.'

'But she didn't mean you to believe her.' Paul reached out a hand just in time to stop Terry's plate sliding off the table. 'You obviously don't understand women, Barry. Agnes will think it's a masterpiece even if it's a load of rubbish.'

'Thank you!' Agnes was angry, harrassed and overtired. She could feel things slipping and, after looking forward to Barry coming home, she now wished he hadn't bothered. There was a feeling of tension in the pit of her stomach, and her lips felt dry.

'But how did James Hetherington know you were writing at all?'

'I told him years ago.' Agnes took a deep gulp of wine and cleared the hair back from her sticky forehead. 'When Grace and Stephen were engaged. I forget why. Anyway, we met at some door or other. He asked to see my stories and I let him read them.'

'He said they were very good.' Barry belched and lit a cigarette. 'Though I had to take his word for it. She never lets me read them.'

'You're not interested.' By now Agnes's pie was cold and she wasn't hungry any more. Terry started drawing a pattern on his plate where the gravy had been with his finger. The rest of the contents of the plate were partly on the table and partly on the carpet. Agnes no longer felt she cared.

'You're not interested really, are you?'

'Of course I'm interested.' Barry looked at her angrily. 'But I can't force you to show me things if you don't want to. I can't understand people being so coy!'

'I'm not coy –' Agnes began, but Paul leaned over and intervened.

'Let's change the subject. How's Grace Winchester? I haven't seen her for years.'

'Why should you think about her?' Agnes got up and began to stack.

'You mentioned her engagement. What's this fellow like that she's married to?'

Agnes looked at Barry, who shrugged.

'He's all right. He's very fly, and you have to be careful of him in business, but we like him well enough as a person. The trouble is that he lives for business, and every time you meet him socially that's all he talks about. I used to have to watch myself when he was around, but now that I'm no longer Chairman of Town Planning, it's not so bad.'

'I don't understand.'

'Well.' Barry sat, crossing his legs, flicking his ash on the carpet. 'When Agnes and I got married, he gave us a holiday in Marbella in Spain as a wedding present.'

'Very generous.'

'A bit *too* generous – and I was silly to accept it. You see, Agnes had worked for him and – well, it seemed all right at the time, but once we got back, Keith started to put all kinds of pressure on me for contracts for this and that. I said he had to tender like everyone else, and then he started offering me gifts, a new car and so on. I refused everything, and that's when he started reminding me about the holiday. He said if that wasn't a gift, what was it?'

'Really?' Paul, clearly fascinated, glanced from Agnes to Barry.

'It wasn't very pleasant, but Agnes went to see him. She said we'd pay them back for the holiday and she gave him a cheque. He tried to refuse, but she said that I had a position to think of and people might misunderstand about the wedding present. I was away at the time, so it was all quite handy. Since then we've heard a few things about Keith that make us very glad that we put matters straight. Even so he didn't pay the money in for a long time; eventually I said I'd pay it in directly to his bank, so he did. We kept the cheque, just in case.'

'You're not really talking about bribery, are you?' Paul was shocked.

'We don't really know,' Barry said. 'I mean, gifts in business are a fact of life. The trouble is that councillors and various people are quite able to sway committees and so on, and building is always contentious, very competitive. Keith Winchester, as it happens, has a very good reputation for quality, and his prices are keen. He gets the job done. The fact that we're to have a municipal swimming pool is entirely due to him.'

'At the expense of a whole lot of people's homes!' Agnes interrupted sharply.

Barry sighed. 'Agnes and I don't see eye to eye on this, Paul. In fact, sometimes I wonder if we still belong to the same party! Agnes is even against proposals to clear the slag, an eyesore if ever there was one.'

'Why, Agnes?' Paul drank the rest of his wine. 'I agree with Barry – it *is* an eyesore.'

'But think of the fun we used to have! Don't you remember? They want to replace it with a nice little park with swings and plenty of notices saying don't do this and don't do that, just like they have on the Wirrall Estate. No ball games, no cycling, no smoking, no kissing – no excitement of any kind!' Agnes's voice was filled with disgust.

'But that slag isn't only an eyesore, it's a danger,' Barry said angrily. 'Imagine if it started to run down the hill to the town?'

'For goodness' sake, Barry,' Agnes jeered, 'it's been there for years!'

'Well, some people have said it's dangerous. It gets waterlogged and very soft. As for the swimming baths, don't forget I once lived on the site where they're building it. Talk about substandard housing conditions: outside lavatories, rats, cockroaches, the lot.'

'That's because people couldn't be bothered to keep them properly once they knew they were to be condemned.'

'I just don't understand you sometimes.' Barry got up and Terry started to whine, holding up his arms. Immediately Miranda began wailing too and, with a heavy sigh of exasperation Agnes took her in her arms, got up and left the room.

'It's time you were in bed, young man.' Barry took Terry from his chair.

'I wanted to see you, Daddy. Special treat.'

'Mummy let you stay up as a special treat, did she? And have you been a good boy?'

Terry put his arm around his father's neck and hugged him. Side by side, they looked very alike. Terry had dark curly hair, brown eyes and long lashes just like Barry; but he had something of Agnes in him, too.

'I think Agnes is very tired.' Paul turned his chair towards Barry. 'Are you going to have a holiday?'

'We're going to my mother's for a week. She's got a bungalow at Whitby.'

'Can't you and Agnes get away by yourselves?'

'Well, it's not very easy, is it? My mother couldn't cope with the kids on her own.'

'What about my parents? I'm sure they'd have them.'

'Both your parents are working, Paul.'

'Mum could take a holiday.'

Barry shook his head. 'It's out of the question. Besides, I'm not sure that Agnes would want to leave the kids.'

'Did you ever ask her?'

Barry put Terry down and lit a cigarette. 'Go up to Mummy, darling, it's time for bed. Kiss Uncle Paul goodnight.'

Terry ran dutifully to his uncle. There was never any argument with his father. When he had kissed Paul, he climbed on Barry's lap again and gave him a hug. Barry embraced him for a few moments, then walked with him into the hall.

'I suppose we should clear away.' Paul got up and turned to the table.

'Oh, Agnes will do that when she comes down. Come into the sitting room. I've got a bottle of brandy.'

The sitting room was in a state of utter chaos, with the playpen in the middle of the floor and a stack of washing waiting to be ironed in one corner. There were children's toys on all the chairs and a trail of something sticky led from a corner of the playpen to the desk by the window, on which stood a typewriter with paper already in it.

'Just look at this room!' Barry seized the playpen and started roughly to fold it up. 'You'd think she'd try and make it look decent for me to come home to! The place is an absolute tip.' Barry walked over to the typewriter and peered at the paper. 'And this is her bloody novel!' He tore the paper out and started to read:

'For Rachel Culpepper it was a day of decisions. She knew that the situation had been deteriorating to such an extent that she could no longer see it objectively. Around her was the chaos of the home she had lovingly helped to create in the first place...'

'I ask you.' He looked up at Paul. 'She's writing about herself! "Around her was the chaos." Why doesn't she *do* something about it instead of writing about it? I tell you, sometimes I dread bringing people home, because I don't know what I'll find.'

'But Barry – Agnes is overworked.' Paul straightened some cushions and moved a toy fire-engine from the sofa.

'How is she overworked? She doesn't have a thing to do all day except look after the kids and the house.'

'What about all the constituency work she does for you?'

'All? It probably takes about two hours a day, if that. What does she do with the rest of her time? Writes novels about chaos instead of putting the place in order!' Upstairs Terry had started to cry and there was the sound of a loud smack, followed by Agnes's voice raised in anger. 'She can't even control the kids!'

Barry poured brandy into a glass.

'Perhaps we should wash up?' Paul looked at the brandy doubtfully.

'Look, that's her job.' Barry gesticulated at him with the glass. 'You've been at your hospital, saving people's lives. I'm been in London. I'm not doing anything in the house, and Agnes knows it. I never touch a dish. It's not my business.'

Paul looked thoughtfully at his brother-in-law and then drank his brandy.

Barry switched on the television and leaned back in his chair, his eyes half-closed. 'What an exhausting day,' he said.

After Agnes had put the children to bed, cleared the table and washed up, she came wearily into the sitting room, where Paul and Barry were watching a topical play about pit life.

'I hope your father's watching this,' Barry commented.

'My father doesn't have a television,' Agnes said shortly. Then her eyes went to the typewriter. She went over to the desk and looked around it at the papers scattered about.

'Oh, sorry love, here it is. It's very good.'

Barry held up the piece of paper he had taken from the machine. Agnes snatched it from him and tore it up, her face red with anger.

'How *dare* you!'

'Come on, I didn't read much, Rachel Culpepper ...'

Paul looked at his watch and hastily got up. 'Hey, I must get home. I promised Mum I'd be in before she went to bed.'

'My God, how I remember those days,' Barry said, tipping up the brandy bottle. 'Agnes having to get home ...'

'When you knew me *well*, I lived by myself,' Agnes said. 'Unfortunately for me. Otherwise I might never have got into the condition I did.'

'And what do you mean by that?' Barry looked up sharply and put the brandy bottle down rather unsteadily.

'You know damn well what I mean.'

'Oh, you mean I got you pregnant?'

'Well, who else do you think it was?' She seized the bottle. 'Christ! How much of that brandy have you had tonight.'

'Don't change the subject! I thought you wanted children and a husband, no matter what order they came in. Well, you were damn lucky to get both. A lot of men wouldn't ...'

'God,' said Paul. 'I've never heard you two go on at each other like this. I thought you were supposed to be happily married.'

'We are,' Agnes said shortly, 'after our fashion. Barry's had too much to drink. He can't tell the difference between here and the Member's bar at the House.'

'I have *not* had too much to drink. You always say that when you're losing an argument!'

'Well, I don't know what this argument is about.' Agnes closed her eyes and for a moment the room seemed to swim around her.

'You implied that you were happier before you were married to me. "Unfortunately", you said, you got pregnant.'

'Well, maybe it was unfortunate the way it happened.' She looked at him wearily, her face very pale. 'I mean, if you hadn't been forced to marry me, you might occasionally appreciate me more. Instead of which, I'm expected to be perpetually grateful.'

'That's not true!' Barry banged his brandy on a side table and spilt most of it. 'Oh Christ – and the stuff's so expensive. Get a cloth, will you, Agnes?'

'*You* get a cloth!' Agnes yelled and stormed out of the room.

'I'll say goodnight.' Paul quickly shook hands with Barry and followed his sister out of the room. She was already halfway up the stairs. In the hall was a bicycle, a pram, and a shopping basket and a frame with wheels. There were coats over the banister, and a packing case with a collection of books on top that had been there since they moved in. Paul stood looking at his sister and at the chaos around him. He had never seen her and Barry rowing before, and he had never seen her so tired?'

'I told Barry you should try and get away,' he said. 'Both of you; alone, together. There must be someone who can look after the children. Doesn't Barry have a sister?'

'Two. One lives in the South, the other's in Canada. The one in the South is a journalist, who manages to run a husband, five children and a large home with three dogs and two cats with consummate ease – on a large income, of course. But Barry always compares me unfavourably with her.' She grinned, wearily. 'It's

OK, Paul, I'm just tired today. I'll be all right tomorrow.'

Agnes lay in bed, waiting for Barry, her whole body tensed. On nights like this she wished they had separate rooms. She heard him come upstairs and saw the hall light go on outside their room. Then he crept into the bedroom next door which the children shared. After some time she heard him tiptoe in and switch on the light by his side of the bed. He moved around the room, taking off his clothes, putting them on the chair by the window, then went to the bathroom, where he spent quite a long time washing. He was a fastidious man, and he would expect sex after being away for a week.

Expect. What sort of a word was 'expect'? What did it have to do with love, with the brawl they had had that night? What did 'expect' have to do with what she wanted, her own needs and desires? If he didn't feel like sex, they didn't have it; if he did and she didn't, that was too bad.

Barry came back into the bedroom and got into bed beside Agnes. He wasn't wearing pyjamas. He put his arm around her.

'I know you're not asleep,' he whispered in her ear. 'I can see your angry breathing.'

'How can you *see* angry breathing?' Despite herself, Agnes gave a little laugh which made him tighten his arm around her.

'Why do we row, love? Paul will think we hate each other.'

'Paul's a doctor. He knows people.' She turned on her back, and immediately he put a hand up her nightie and stroked her pubic hairs like the fur of a cat. He was stroking her into desire, submission. If he could arouse an erotic response, and he knew he could, she wouldn't try and fight him off. She turned on her side so that they faced each other. His beard tickled her mouth and she could feel his warm breath on her face. It smelt of cigarettes and brandy.

'I was angry all day,' Agnes admitted. 'I don't know why I should feel angry all the time, but sometimes I do. I just feel that my life is so *futile*. Oh, I can't explain it.'

He kissed her gently and put a hand on her breast. She knew that whatever her mind said, her body needed him badly. Sometimes, she thought the whole point of sex was the comfort it gave: the way it could change how you felt, banish all your anger, disappointment and unease. For a time, anyway.

'Your life isn't futile at all, idiot. It's very necessary and important. If you organised things a bit better you might find it easier to cope.'

She drew away from him, a cold indignation suddenly extinguishing her rising passion.

'It's easy for you to say that! Miranda's got a tooth coming through and she's perpetually out of sorts. *And* she's got a sore bottom, which kids sometimes have when they're teething. Terry's so aggressive and undisciplined. He's driving me mad, Barry! I'll *have* to get him into a nursery school. On top of that ...' Agnes paused, because she hadn't intended to tell him just yet. 'I think I'm pregnant again.'

'Oh Christ!' Barry stopped stroking her and sat up, putting on the light. 'How the hell did that happen?'

'I always thought when you were feeding a baby you couldn't conceive.'

'But I thought you'd stopped feeding her?'

'No, I was still feeding her occasionally. And my periods are very irregular.'

'Oh God, Agnes! It's so irresponsible to take chances!'

'But you knew I wasn't using the cap. I don't even know where it is.'

'Then you must go on the Pill or something. Christ, if I'd have known ...'

'I'm sorry, Barry.' Why did she apologise? He could have used something. Still, she did feel guilty. She felt responsible.

'I'm sorry, too,' Barry said, reaching for a cigarette. 'I think two kids are quite enough.' He looked at her, frowning. 'How about an abortion under the new Act?'

'Are you serious?'

'Of course I am! That's what it's for.'

'But there's no danger to me if we have a third – no social hardship.'

'I think there is. I think you'll go under.' Suddenly his face changed. He extinguished his cigarette, put out the light again and snuggled down, tugging at her nightie. 'Come on! Get it off. If you're pregnant at least you're safe.'

'Oh, Barry.' Agnes wasn't sure whether she wanted to laugh or cry ...

Mr Robart sat back. 'Well, there's no doubt you're pregnant, Mrs

Holloway. A healthy, normal pregnancy, I'd say. You're a bit anaemic, a bit run-down maybe, but otherwise a very healthy woman for ... let me see, how old are you?' He adjusted his spectacles and looked at her card.

'I'm nearly twenty-eight. But Mr Robart, I don't want the baby!'

His eyes flickered. 'So you're talking about a termination?'

'Yes. That's what I *told* you.'

'Mmmmmm.' Mr Robert gazed at her card and stroked his chin. 'Of course, the Act is very new and it has a number of important provisions. It's not abortion on demand, you know.'

'I know that.' Agnes began to feel angry. Robart had been recommended to her because he was supposed to be enlightened. 'But it's easier to have an abortion now – and I want one.'

'Does your husband want it, too?'

'Yes. We don't feel I can cope with more than two children.'

'Two children isn't very many compared to what some people have, Mrs Holloway.' Mr Robart began to sound quite indignant about the whole thing. 'I know some women who ...'

'Yes, I do too, Mr Robart. I know some women who have ten and fifteen. But I don't envy them, and I don't want to be like them.'

'But what about contraception? Surely you used some form of contraception?'

Agnes looked at her hands, which were clutching her rather shabby leather handbag. 'I didn't, no; but that's in the past. In the future I will always use contraception – after I've had the abortion.'

'You seem quite determined, Mrs Holloway.'

'Yes, I am.'

The intercom on his desk buzzed and he moved a switch. 'Yes?'

'Mrs Winchester is in the waiting room, sir.'

'I shan't be a minute.' Mr Robart looked at Agnes's card recollecting his thoughts. 'I'll have a word with one of my colleagues. You have to have two signatures for an abortion, you know.'

'Can it be soon?' Agnes stood up nervously.

'I'll be in touch, Mrs Holloway.' His voice was cold. 'You're not the only one, you know. Everyone's trying to leap on the bandwagon with this new Act.'

'I'd hardly call it a bandwagon,' Agnes said as he ushered her to the door. 'I'd call it a trail of pain.'

Mr Robart shut the door behind her, not even bothering to shake her hand.

Even the receptionist seemed mildly disapproving, and as she ushered Agnes to the outer door, her smile was distinctly frosty.

'Goodbye, Mrs Holloway.'

Agnes nodded and made her way along the corridor to the waiting room where she had left her coat. There were three occupants in the room waiting to see the various specialists who shared the house in Park Square. They all looked up as Agnes came in.

'Agnes!'

Agnes turned, and there in the corner sat Grace.

'Grace! I heard the receptionist say Mrs Winchester. Somehow it didn't register.'

'Mrs Winchester, please.' The receptionist stood at the door and Grace, looking very nervous, got up.

'Let's have lunch after?'

'Shall I wait for you here?'

Grace shook her head. 'I don't know how long I'll be. Let's meet at Bernardos in an hour – you know, the little Italian place?' Agnes nodded. 'Then if I'm late you can have a drink of something.'

Agnes put on her coat and watched Grace going along the corridor. She didn't envy her meeting with Mr Robart; but then, Grace probably didn't have her problems.

After ringing the babysitter to make sure all was well at home, Agnes set out with an almost thrilling sense of freedom to do some shopping in Leeds. It was so strange not to be either pushing a pushchair or tugging a reluctant, squalling toddler along by the arm, The thought of yet another pram filled her with horror ...

Grace passed the menu across the table with a flourish. 'I'm picking up the tab, so choose what you like.'

'No!' Agnes protested.

'Yes! I invited you. But what a coincidence!'

'How did you like him?' Agnes asked as she glanced at the menu.

'I've seen him before. He's all right. There's nothing wrong, is there, Agnes?' Grace looked at her anxiously.

Agnes lowered the menu. 'With me? Why should there be?'

'Seeing Robart ...'

'Oh, I see what you mean. No, I'm pregnant.' She looked at the menu again.

'Oh, how wonderful!'

Agnes looked up and saw the most extraordinary expression on Grace's face. She looked envious; no, she looked bitterly jealous. Yet her face was creased in smiles and her eyes were shining.

'Wonderful? You must be joking!'

'You mean you don't *want* it?'

Agnes began to suspect the reason for the expression. She passed the menu to Grace. 'I'll just have an omelette.'

'Oh, go on – have something exotic. The veal here is very good.'

'No thanks, Grace. I have a meal at six with the children.'

'Go on. Have *vitello con limone*. It's their speciality.'

'All right.' Useless to say she was too nervous to feel hungry.

The waiter came up, and Grace ordered with precision and authority. The waiter obviously knew her and gave her his deferential attention.

'Yes, Mrs Winchester.'

'And a bottle of Verdicchio, please.' She smiled and handed back the menu. The waiter bowed. 'I like this place,' Grace said, lighting a cigarette with a slim gold lighter. Then she anxiously blew the smoke away from Agnes's face. 'Oh, I hope this doesn't upset you?'

'No. Barry smokes all the time.'

'He shouldn't, you know. Keith's given up.'

'I know he shouldn't, but he does. He puts it all down to nervous tension and having an angry, irritable wife.'

It was ages since they'd been together. They frequently saw each other, but they hardly ever had the chance to speak intimately. They met at dinners, at cocktail parties, at functions to do with the corporation, the council, political parties, or the many associations and organisations that MPs and important businessmen expected to have to attend with their wives.

'We haven't had a chat for ages,' Grace said, as if echoing her thoughts. 'And I feel I owe you an apology. I behaved very badly about the office.'

'Oh, but that was years ago!' Agnes said, astonished.

'Yes, but I think it put a brake on our friendship. We were never so close after that.'

'Well, I got married and almost immediately had Terry, and you were busy turning yourself into a career woman. And how well you've done, Grace. I'm always hearing people sing your praises.'

'Really?' Grace put her head on one side and smiled. Suddenly Agnes was acutely conscious of the age of her coat, the length of her dress, the shabbiness of her shoes and the fact that she hadn't been to the hairdresser for months; occasionally she even cut it herself when she did Terry's. Grace was wearing a beautifully cut sleeveless dress that came down well over her knees, with a row of pearls round her neck. She wore black patent leather shoes and carried an expensive-looking black patent leather handbag.

The hairstyle that had been her mark since girlhood remained the same; it was drawn back from her brow and coiled at the back in a large chignon. It suited her; suited her face and her *persona*, giving her a somehow pre-Raphaelite look: withdrawn, unattainable, infinitely alluring, infinitely mysterious and desirable.

'Everyone says you know all there is to know about the property market in the North.'

'*And* the Middle East,' Grace said with pride, smiling as the waiter brought the wine. 'Thank you. Pour it, Franco, will you?'

'Only half a glass for me, please.' Agnes looked at him with a smile.

'Oh, go on. Be mad.'

'I don't know about mad, but I'll be sick,' Agnes said. 'I can't really drink when I'm pregnant.'

Grace looked embarrassed and moved her wine glass backwards and forwards nervously in a little half-circle in front of her.

'You don't know how lucky you are.'

'To be *sick*?'

'To be pregnant.'

Agnes looked at Grace uneasily, then decided the best thing in this case was the direct approach.

'Grace, is it that you *can't* have children or you don't *want* to?'

'You mean you don't know?' She paused and looked at Agnes, who remained silent. Grace continued hesitantly. 'At first, of course, we didn't want children ... but after a year or so we decided we'd like to start a family. I stopped taking the Pill and waited and waited. I thought you could conceive quite easily; most women I know seem to.'

'Too easily at times,' Agnes said thoughtfully, watching a succession of emotions register on her friend's face.

'After a while I saw the doctor; then Keith saw the doctor, and then the whole thing began: specialists, hospitals, tests. Tests, tests, tests!' Grace sighed deeply. 'They couldn't find anything wrong with either of us. I ovulate properly and my tubes are clear; Keith has a normal sperm count. Apparently, some couples are just incompatible – they don't know why. We spent a year on all this and then we stopped. But I couldn't get it out of my mind, so I've started the round again. The same doctors with different methods, new doctors with methods you've tried before. It's very wearing.'

'I can see that,' Agnes said, as the waiters brought their food and with a great deal of ceremony started to serve it. 'I had no idea ...'

'Well, it's not the sort of thing you broadcast. We've told very few people. Like you, they assume I'm all set to be a career woman. Yet there's nothing in the world I'd like more at this moment than to be in your shoes. Keith says it's an obsession with me, and I know it worries him. Of course, I see a psychiatrist too.'

'What does he do?'

'It's a she. She tries to uncork all my mental blockages about sex. I suppose it must seem strange to you, seeing I was always considered so fast, but, do you know I've never had an orgasm?' She shrugged. 'I enjoy all the preliminaries of sex, taking off my clothes and so forth, but I don't enjoy the act itself. Technically, I'm supposed to be frigid.'

'But it doesn't explain why there's no baby, does it?' Agnes said quickly, almost at a loss for words.

'No. But Dr Walters, my psychiatrist, says that at least she can try to help me enjoy sex, even if I never conceive. Oh, Agnes, I feel that if I don't have a child of my own, I'll *never* be fulfilled. I envy other women with children so much I find the only solution is to avoid them. That's why I've avoided you. I'm always saying "I must ring Agnes" or "I must ask them round"; but every time I ask someone else instead – someone who doesn't know as much about me as you do. Someone who won't see how unhappy I am and know the reason ...' Grace's voice was trembling now.

'I'm very sorry, Grace. I'm terribly sorry. But you know, the joys of motherhood are pretty humdrum. I won't say I'd rather *not* have had my children, but sometimes I feel such a drone, a boring housebound woman, a nag, a shrew. Barry has his life in London and his work, and all he ever gets from me is complaint. I know he stays away a lot more than he needs. He doesn't find me really very interesting any more – if he ever did.'

'Oh, I can't believe that!'

'It's true.' Agnes looked into Grace's blue eyes and smiled. 'The fact that Barry and I were forced to get married has always been a barrier between us. I won't say that we haven't been happy. Miranda was planned, and we both love the kids. We love each other too, I'm sure of that; but I'm increasingly resentful of my life and jealous of Barry. I've always felt peripheral to Barry's life, and I still do. I'm not sure he really needs me, and I know I don't make the best of myself. But Grace, I started to write a novel and he found it and started ribbing me. He still does.'

'That's not very nice, is it?'

Agnes shook her head, but didn't answer. She put her knife and fork together. 'I can't eat any more, and I really should be getting home.'

'I'll take you,' Grace said, summoning the waiter. 'I'm going back to Beckersleigh anyway.' Grace leaned over the table, looking earnestly at Agnes. 'Agnes, let's be friends again – yes? I've missed our friendship so much. I've never talked so openly to anyone, not even Keith.'

'Nor me,' Agnes said shyly. 'I've never told this to a soul.'

'We can talk now,' Grace pressed her arm, 'and help each other. You must come round a lot more often. You can bring the children, and when the baby ...'

Agnes avoided looking at Grace, keeping her eyes on the red check tablecloth.

'Grace, I'm going to have an abortion. That's what I came to see Robart about. I ...' She looked up and saw the shock and pain in Grace's eyes; shock and pain and bitter resentment. 'Oh, I know it must sound terrible to you, but I simply can't go through with having another baby. Miranda's only just twelve months old. This baby was a mistake, it wasn't planned. I don't want it!'

'If you knew how I felt ...' Grace whispered.

'I do know how you feel, Grace. Because there are things that I want that I just can't have. I'd love a career, I'd love to feel worthwhile and important. I'd love ...'

But Grace was looking over Agnes's shoulder. Agnes turned and saw James Hetherington taking a seat in the corner of the restaurant with another man. At that moment James saw her too and came over, hand outstretched.

'Well, if it isn't the two Graces! Fancy seeing you girls together.'

Grace laughed delightedly and put her cheek up to be kissed. 'Fancy you remembering that, James!'

'And still as beautiful as ever. Even *more* beautiful, I think.' He stooped and kissed Agnes, looking into her eyes. 'And how's my budding author?'

'Not authoring,' Agnes said. 'She's too busy with children and nappies and food.'

'So you know about Agnes's book?' Grace said, looking at him with surprise.

'Know about it? I'm responsible for it! I think she's got great talent. She's a natural writer. I've been telling her that for years.'

'Oh, then the novel is serious?' Grace looked at Agnes.

'No.' Agnes shook her head vigorously.

'But you said you'd begun one and Barry found it.'

'Oh yes, Rachel Culpepper. Well, she's gone.'

'Rachel *Culpepper*!' Grace started to laugh. 'Why Culpepper?'

'Heaven knows.' Agnes smiled suddenly, feeling better. The feeling of camaraderie, of sharing a joke again with Grace, made the years roll away. 'I only saw what a ridiculous name it was when Barry went round the house calling me Rachel Culpepper all day. But I've started a new plot and it's Joan Cartwright now. Of course, Barry still calls me Rachel Culpepper – it's his way of taking the mickey.'

James sat down and crossed his legs, looking solemn. 'Agnes, I can't stay. But I do want you to be serious about all this. Don't let Barry laugh at you and talk you out of it. Husbands get jealous of working wives; they want them in the home. Barry has a career, and what you want to do is perfectly compatible with being a wife and mother. You stick to it. I'll ring you up soon to see how you're getting on.' He got up. 'It's been lovely seeing you girls again.'

'You must come round for dinner, James.' Grace looked at him. 'I'll ask Agnes and Barry, too.'

CHAPTER SEVENTEEN

WINNING THE WORLD CUP WAS one of the few good things that happened to England in July 1966. After being returned with a majority of ninety-seven the previous March, the Labour government lost a by-election at Carmarthen. There was a wages freeze. Sterling was weak. George Brown offered to resign. And in Vietnam, the Americans bombed Hanoi and Haiphong, and there was a rebellion in the Labour Party because of it.

'The Americans have no place in Vietnam,' Agnes said angrily to Barry, shortly after her visit to the specialist. 'They should get out.'

'They can't just leave!' Barry shouted back. 'They've got a duty to the civilised world.'

'Civilised world, my foot!'

'I can tell Connie Shilton's been getting at you again!'

'I've *always* agreed with Connie about this!'

They sat cramped together at the table in the dining room, Terry on his cushioned chair, Miranda on her mother's lap. Barry was redecorating the sitting room in fits and starts, and most of the furniture had been moved out into the dining room or the hall. There were smudges of paint everywhere – on the furniture, the children, and a lot on Barry. He was not at his best as a decorator, and hated it; but there was no money to pay someone to do it and the job badly needed doing. Even the thought of redecorating as he lay in bed in the mornings was enough to put Barry in a bad mood for the whole day.

Barry had the evening paper spread out across the dinner table and shook it angrily whenever he spotted some outrage perpetrated by a group he didn't approve of.

'Of course, Jeff Orchard's leading the march in Leeds. He ought to be sent out to Vietnam – then perhaps he'd see how those Communists really fought the war!'

'Well, you can't forcibly send him to Vietnam!'

'I wish I could. People like him are splitting the Labour Party down the middle.'

'I should have thought it was split already. Clause 4, unilateralism – what more?'

'Wilson's got a far stronger hand on the Party than Gaitskell had.' Barry spread jam on his bread. 'In my opinion, anyway. I like him.'

'Maybe he'll give you a job, and then we'll get a bit more money.'

'That's all you ever think of, Agnes, isn't it?'

'Well, we haven't got enough, have we? And now we've got to scrape together the money for this abortion.'

'Oh, you'll get the money for the bloody abortion. I thought the whole point was that you'd have it on the National Health.'

'Robart will only do it privately, and even then it's dodgy. He said I'd never get away with it on the National Health. As far as they're concerned, I'm fit, healthy and quite able to have a child, so there's no danger to me or it.' Barry didn't appear to be listening. She got up and snatched the paper away from him. 'Did you hear me, Barry?' she shouted. 'No danger to me or it!'

Barry tried to grab back the paper and tore it in half. Miranda, still in Agnes's arms, thought it was a game and made her contribution by grabbing what she could and tearing some more. Terry wasn't so sure it was funny and started to cry.

Just as Barry got up and threw the rest of the paper on the floor, the doorbell rang; but it was only half heard through the noise that was going on in the dining room – the shouting, the laughing, the crying.

'Was that the bell?' Barry looked at Agnes.

'I think so. Go and see who it is.' Agnes bent down to pick up the paper and hastily tried to put it out of sight. She stood up just as Grace came into the room, followed by an apologetic and still angry-looking Barry, who gesticulated helplessly across the room.

'Grace, I'm sorry about this tip. I'm redecorating.'

'It's a tip even when he's not.' Agnes, white-faced, didn't smile. 'Do sit down, Grace.' She swept a small pile of ironing off the chair next to her. Suddenly, in her mind's eye, she saw the elegance of Grace's home and knew how she must be comparing the two. Agnes had been sick in the morning and felt sick all day; her breasts ached and her belly seemed distended, even though is wasn't; the fact of the abortion was continually on her mind – she wanted it and yet she dreaded it.

'Obviously I've come at a most awkward time,' Grace said. 'I tried to ring, but you're always engaged.'

'The phone never stops ringing.' Agnes sat down next to Grace. 'You try being married to an MP. That's what comes of living in the constituency.'

'If we didn't live in the constituency, I wouldn't get in,' Barry snapped.

Grace smiled nervously at Agnes.

'May I smoke?'

'Of course.'

'Look, I've come about something rather important,' Grace said, exhaling. 'Do you think we could talk?' She looked at the children, smiling in the rather diffident way some childless people do, as though unsure of how to address this curious alien species.

'Just you and me, or Barry as well?'

'Oh, Barry too. It concerns him. I wondered if the children ...' She looked at Barry, who gestured towards Agnes.

'Take them to Marjorie's nextdoor, Agnes. They hardly understand a thing, but it'll give us some peace.' He turned to Grace, his manner suddenly smooth and charming. 'Grace, you look absolutely marvellous. Tell me what you've been up to?'

'Come on, Terry,' Agnes wiped his mouth and tried to get him off his chair.

'Don't want to!'

'Terry, I said get up! This instant!'

Terry deliberately pushed himself back from the table and his chair, overbalanced, and fell on the floor. Agnes, who still held the wriggling Miranda, put her down and knelt by the bawling Terry. She couldn't be sure whether or not he had hurt himself, but she decided that he hadn't – that he was crying with rage. She looked at him anxiously, then took an arm and tried to help him up, but he resisted. She could see that he was deliberately trying to drive himself into a frenzy, so she seized his arms and dragged him up. But he only cried all the more and started stamping his feet on the ground.

'Barry, can't you help me.' She looked desperately over her shoulder. He was talking to Grace as though not even aware of the commotion around him. Barry got up and bodily picked Terry off the ground. Terry immediately stopped crying and put both arms around his father's neck.

'He's terribly sweet,' Grace said, smiling up at him and giving a little wave. 'Hello!'

'Oh Barry, *you* take him next door!' Agnes said. 'And I'll bring Miranda. We won't be a moment, Grace.'

'That's OK.'

Agnes was sorry they had to leave her even for a second, because it would give her even more opportunity to survey the chaos in the house.

When they got back Barry smiled deprecatingly. 'Grace, let me get you a drink.'

'We've only got sherry.' Agnes took off her apron to try and make herself feel a little more on Grace's level. But it was impossible. Her jeans were stained, her shirt was torn at one side, and her hands were grubby, in spite of the fact that only shortly before she had sat down at table for a meal. To complete the picture, she was sweating and her hair hadn't been touched since the morning.

Grace gazed at her, thinking her the embodiment of fecundity with her large breasts, rather flabby stomach and big hips. Because of her height she managed to avoid looking fat, and looked matronly instead – a quality Grace envied. With her face freckled and slightly sweaty and her curly hair dishevelled, Agnes looked healthy and vital and alive. And, absurd as it would have seemed to Agnes, seeing this chaotic household of screaming children, with her and Barry obviously at the end of their tether, Grace was filled with a bitter, all-consuming envy.

'Sherry would be lovely.' As Barry went off to pick his way through the ladders and paint pots in the sitting room, Grace turned to Agnes. 'How I envy you.'

'Envy *me*?' Agnes nearly choked. 'I was just envying *you*.'

'There you are, you see.' Grace smiled and made a gesture with her long manicured hands. 'We each want something that the other has got.'

'It's only Cyprus sherry.' Barry apologetically showed her the half-empty bottle, producing three glasses.

He held out the glass and she took it, toasting them both. 'Agnes?'

'No thanks.'

'Agnes is pregnant,' Barry said. 'Again.' He emphasised the word as though it were something completely outside his control.

'I know. We met the other day at the gynaecologist's.'

'Oh? You didn't tell me.' Barry's eyes narrowed as he looked at Agnes.

'I forgot. It was the day before you started to redecorate the house. I had paint and things on my mind.'

Grace was grateful to Agnes for keeping their confidence and smiled at her; Agnes seemed to understand.

'I'm sorry there's nowhere else to sit, Grace.'

'That's all right.' She hesitated. 'You must wonder why I've come ...'

'Is it something to do with Keith?'

'In a way ... But it's not business.' Grace crossed her shapely legs, aware of Barry's eyes travelling from her thighs right down to her ankles. She was glad she still had her figure. 'It's about Agnes's baby.'

'Miranda?' Barry's eyes moved from her legs to her bust. She had good breasts, too. The old story about Grace suddenly came to his mind, filling it with erotic thoughts. If only she'd take off her clothes for him some day ...

'No.' Grace pointed at Agnes's stomach. 'The one in there, Barry. Agnes obviously didn't tell you that I'm unable to conceive.'

Barry shook his head. 'She didn't say a word. I'm sorry, Grace; the idea of an abortion must make you angry, but you see, we've already got two.'

'It does make me angry,' Grace agreed. 'The Abortion Act makes me livid, and I'm sorry you supported it in Parliament, Barry. You don't know what it's like to think of thousands of women deliberately getting rid of what I'd give my eyes to have!'

'If you've come to ask me not to have an abortion, I'm sorry ...' Agnes began, but Grace held up a hand.

'I haven't come just to ask you. I've come to plead with you. I want you to have the baby and let me adopt it.'

The silence in the room was all the more uneasy after the din that usually pervaded the house from morning to night. Agnes could hear the sound of her own heart beating slowly, steadily in her breast.

'It may sound strange, even bizarre,' Grace went on nervously, 'but I mean it. I've talked it over with Keith and he agrees, if you're willing. We'd love to have your baby and bring it up as ours. Because it's your child, Agnes. And we'd know it was from good, solid stock.'

'Working-class,' Agnes said, without emotion, looking straight into Grace's eyes.

'That's not what I meant. Good genes is what I meant.' Absently, Grace held out her glass. 'May I have another sherry, Barry? It's not easy ...'

Barry, grateful for the chance to do something, refilled his own glass and Grace's. Then he looked directly at Agnes.

'The answer is no, Grace,' Agnes said flatly. 'I can't do it.'

'But you can have it aborted?' Grace's voice began to rise.

'It's not the same thing! This is just a foetus. It doesn't have any meaning for me ... well, not much. But the longer I go on, the worse it gets. I couldn't possibly go to full term and give away my baby. Not even to you.'

Grace lit a fresh cigarette from the stub of her old one. 'But isn't it better than killing?' Grace pleaded.

'I don't believe abortion *is* killing, not at this stage.'

'If I'm honest, I have to admit I believe it's killing at any stage,' Barry said. 'But sometimes it has to be done all the same.'

'Can you really go through with it?' Grace looked at Agnes, her eyes furious with longing. 'When I'm offering to take the child, give it a loving home? Give it every chance in life? I want a baby. I don't want anyone's baby.' Tears were streaming down Grace's cheeks. 'We've always been friends, Agnes, we have a – a bond. Can't you do this for me? For our friendship?'

'No,' Agnes shook her head. 'I can't. If I had that baby, I'd keep it. I could never, ever give it to you.'

Grace put her face in her hands and rocked in the agony of her grief.

Barry had taken the children to Whitby and the house was silent. It was also tidy. The sitting room had at last been repainted and given a spring clean. It was amazing how much you could throw out when you put your mind to it, Agnes thought.

She wandered round the house, looking at each object, familiar and unfamiliar. She was wearing her best dress; her coat was ready and her bag was packed. She even had new shoes on. Connie, the only other person to share the secret apart from Grace, was going to take her to the nursing home in Leeds and then to the train for Whitby after it was all over. Neither Barry nor Agnes pretended it was a happy occasion, and Barry for one was glad to be let off the hook.

The children had gone off the day before and she'd slept badly, alone in her bed. Maybe they would give her a sleeping pill tonight, before the operation the next day. *Operation.* She thought she had felt a quickening during the night but she couldn't have, it was much too early. It must have been just nerves, imagination. She went back into the sitting room and gazed at the pictures of Terry and Miranda as babies. Then she turned them towards the wall and started, quite unexpectedly, to weep.

'Anyone at home?'

Connie called again and then came along the hall and into the sitting room.

'Hey, Agnes ...' Connie put an arm round her and turned to face her. 'Why are you crying, love? Are you that nervous?'

'I'm that sad,' Agnes said, and threw herself against Connie, weeping helplessly. Connie, perplexed, stood stroking her shoulders.

'I don't understand, love.'

'Neither do I. I don't want the baby ...'

'Well, then. It won't take long. You won't feel a thing. This time tomorrow it'll all be over. My goodness, I've never seen such tears.' Connie sat on the floor by Agnes's side. 'Whatever brought all this on? ... You wait; tomorrow ...'

'It's Grace,' Agnes said, staring wide-eyed at Connie.

'Grace?' Connie was bewildered.

'Grace wanted the baby.'

'What? *Your* baby?'

Agnes nodded. 'She can't have her own and she wanted this one.'

'Well, I've never heard of anything so daft!' Connie folded her hands on her lap and looked indignant. 'What's it to do with her anyway?'

'Nothing at all.' Agnes felt calmer. 'But I understand it. I feel it in my heart, because I know how she feels, too.'

'I think you love Grace,' Connie said, slowly.

'No, not physically.' Agnes shook her head positively. 'But in another way. Not sexually, not like a sister or a mother, but something else ...'

Agnes knew they would be at the Sandgate end of the beach at Whitby, and she made her way there after leaving her case at the bungalow. She walked along the front, down past the caravan park and the refreshment huts and then on to the main Sandgate road. She could see them far over by the rocks at the bottom of the cliff. Her mother-in-law sat under a large sun umbrella, and Barry was covered to the waist with sand, his long legs looking like a burial mound.

As she got nearer, she could see Terry shovelling enthusiastically with his spade and Miranda toddling about, half-filling a bucket and emptying it over Barry. Agnes stood outside the shop that sold crab sandwiches and looked at them, waving. Barry saw her and held up an arm. He seemed to say something to Terry and got slowly to his feet, shaking off the sand.

She saw him take Miranda in his arms and hold out his hand for Terry, and slowly they came towards her, her family, eager and excited to see her – the children, at least. She went down the steps towards them and sat on the last one, taking off her shoes. Terry reached her first and threw himself into her arms. She kissed him, feeling his hard, warm little body. Then Barry stood in front of her, his great shadow falling across her. She looked up slowly, following the line of his brown hairy legs, his brief bathing trunks, the fine hair that went to his navel before spreading like a tree over his chest.

'I never realised you were such a hairy man,' she said, gazing up at him.

'Perhaps you've never looked at me from that angle.'

Miranda was leaning down making noises, and Agnes stood up and took her from Barry, hugging her too. She felt the tears come into her eyes again and buried her face in Miranda's long curly hair.

'How was it?' Barry asked, putting a hand on her arm and bending to kiss her cheek. His attitude was tender and his voice sounded loving. 'I didn't expect you so soon.'

Agnes drew her face away from Miranda. She had never felt so close to her family, so thankful for the gift of maternity that she had always taken for granted; thankful, too, for a few days of summer – for who knew what the winter would bring?

'I'm afraid we're going to be a family of five after all,' she said, avoiding Barry's eyes. 'Grace won.'

The sight on the television of the rubble pouring down on Aberfan was terrible, almost unbearable to watch. But more heartbreaking still were the reports of people, most of them children, trying to escape as the avalanche of wet sludge poured down streets, through schoolroom windows, trapping everyone in its path.

Sludge? Mere *sludge*? Was it possible? Agnes ran to the door and looked at the slag, towering over the town in the distance. Could it, after days of rain, start sliding down over Enderby, the fine wet coal pouring through the windows of the council school halfway up the hill – the school from which she had won a scolarship to the Grammar?

'It must come down', she said to herself, and she scooped Terry up as he came after her, kissing, hugging him close, so close, tears in her eyes. In the sitting room, Miranda lay asleep in her pram – the pram that would now have to be saved for the new baby – her black lashes curled up over her white cheeks, her lips twitching into a smile as she dreamed some happy dream.

The slag would have to come down. But what a monstrous thing to have happened in the tiny Welsh village of Aberfan!

When Barry came home, Agnes was slumped on the couch, hardly seeing the television, her eyes full of tears.

'Did you see?' she said, without looking up.

'I saw the early news. My God, what a terrible thing.'

'Over a hundred children ... Why did it have to fall on the *school*?' Her voice was anguished.

Barry sat down beside her, putting his arms on his knees, his hands cradling his cheeks. He still had his coat on.

'I was so wrong about the slag, Barry.'

'Now you say it!' Barry laughed grimly. 'Let's just thank our lucky stars it wasn't us! Is Terry in bed?' Barry got up and started to undo his coat.

'Yes.'

'Has he been good?'

'No; but I think the nursery school will take him. I saw the head teacher today and I explained I was pregnant ...'

'Did she ask why you were having more children when you couldn't cope with two you've got?' Barry's tone was sarcastic.

'No, as a matter of fact she didn't.' Agnes got up, smoothing her maternity dress and keeping her voice even. 'She may have wondered it, but she didn't say it. Have you eaten?'

'I had a pie and chips in the cafe after the ward meeting. Jeff Orchard was there and Connie Shilton. An unholy pair, if you ask me.'

'I don't see what's unholy about them. Jeff I haven't seen for years; but Connie's a kind person. Look what she did for me.'

She gathered up his coat where he had thrown it on the chair, hung it up in the hall and went into the kitchen. She hadn't yet washed up the tea things, and they lay under a congealing film of egg, tomato sauce and chip fat in the sink. The cooking pans still stood on the stove. Agnes leaned up against the sink and her stomach started to churn. Suddenly she leaned forward and vomited on top of the dirty dishes.

'Christ, what on earth's the matter?' Barry stood in the doorway, but he didn't come near her. He asked her again, but she couldn't answer; still gripping the edge of the sink, she slid down the side and lay on the floor. 'Agnes, what *is* the matter?' His tone was cross, impatient rather than anxious.

She looked up at him, his sturdy shoes, the bottoms of his tweed trousers, the hard edge of his jacket, the beginnings of his beard, the personification of maleness, of proud uncaring masculinity. Instead of bending down or kneeling by her side as she would if he had collapsed on the floor, he leaned over the sink and ran the water, exclaiming at the mess as he did so.

Agnes sat up and put her head in her hands. Barry had turned off the tap and was looking at her again, his face rigid with disapproval.

'No wonder you don't feel well! This whole place would sicken me if I lived here all day. God knows what effect it has on the kids.'

'I was so upset about Aberfan,' she protested. 'It's not usually as bad as this.'

'It is, Agnes,' he said despairingly. 'It is.'

'You know half the time I don't feel well.' Agnes got to her feet unsteadily and sat on the chair by the kitchen table. 'Neither of my other pregnancies were as bad as this.'

'Then you should have got rid of it when you had the chance, shouldn't you?' he said. 'It's too late now, though – and I blame Connie Shilton.'

'Connie Shilton had nothing to do with it! How many times do I have to tell you?'

Barry got a bottle of beer from the pantry floor and took off the top, tipping it into a glass. He poured it very carefully, his eyes fixed in concentration. Then he put it to his mouth and drank, the foam clinging to his upper lip.

'All I know, Agnes, is that when I left on the Sunday you were going into the clinic for an abortion. There was no doubt in your mind. You wanted it, and so did I. Two days later you arrived in Whitby, not having had an abortion, saying it was all because of Grace!'

'But it was true! I thought, how can I get rid of a baby if Grace can't conceive?'

'Christ, Agnes, thousands, millions for all I know, can't conceive! Are you atoning for all of them by having a baby neither you nor I want?'

'I do ...'

'You *what*?' He looked at her incredulously. 'You can't honestly say you want it?'

'Yes, I can. I feel it moving about inside me. It's *mine*, Barry!'

'That's a load of women's nonsense.' His eyes were filled with distaste.

'To you it is. Barry, why can't you just accept it and give me some support, like you used to?' Instinctively Agnes raised her hands to him, appealing.

'Look, Agnes.' Barry drank deeply from his glass. 'I've got a thousand things on my mind. I'm busy, overworked and hard up. You don't even do as much typing for me as you used to. I have to put some of it out and pay extra for it. Yet here you are, all caught up with yourself and your own body, not living in the outside world at all. I can't understand it. I want to, but I can't. All you can say by way of justification is that you're having a baby you didn't want and you're doing it for Grace. Well, let Grace have it! If you love her that much, give her the baby!'

'It isn't "love" in that sense.'

'Then I don't know in what sense it is. There's something unnatural between you and Grace, if you ask me.'

'There's nothing unnatural between us, and you know it. We're just very close friends.'

'But you hardly ever see each other.'

'That doesn't mean we can't be close.'

'I can't imagine myself doing something like that for another man.'

'Sometimes I can't imagine you doing anything for anybody!' Agnes snapped. 'For instance, I don't suppose you could make me a cup of tea, could you?'

Barry thumped his glass on the table. 'Now that's something I really take objection to, Agnes! What the *hell* do you mean I never do "anything for anybody"? My whole life is spent doing things for other people. I travel backwards and forwards to London every week because of other people. For years I've been appealing for the removal of that slag because of other people's children. "Oh no," says Agnes Holloway. "It's so nice to have the slag to play on. Let's keep it like that for old times' sake".'

'Oh, don't mention the slag – please!' The appalling pictures swam in front of her eyes again: the roof of the school appearing over the sea of mud and slush ...

'You don't like to hear it mentioned *now*, do you?' Barry took up his beer again and put it to his lips with an air of righteousness. 'As for not doing anything for other people ... I take strong objection to that remark.'

'I'm sorry,' she said wearily. 'You always provoke me and then misunderstand me.'

'You get your own blasted tea!' Barry strode out of the kitchen and slammed the door behind him.

Agnes went slowly to the sink and squeezed some washing-up liquid over the mess, then ran the water and watched as it swirled over the crocks, obliterating everything in a lovely green foam. She thought of the sea, of the way it washed over the rocks, of the white foamy crest on the edge of breakers as they rolled in from the Atlantic.

Sometimes she wished that it would wash all over her and take her away forever ...

CHAPTER EIGHTEEN

SPECIAL LIGHTS HAD BEEN RIGGED up on the ceiling of the baths, which were causing such a bright reflection in the water that the swimmers were complaining they could hardly see. But the television people insisted that the lights were essential; and the organisers insisted that television was essential and that the new town needed all the publicity it could get to show off its new amenities. And naturally the local Member of Parliament also wanted the cameras to be there, so that he could show *himself* off and take all the credit.

It was going to be one of *those* days again, Agnes thought as she stood behind the podium. In front of her were the Mayor, Barry, Keith, Mr and Mrs Calthorpe and several other worthies, all of whom were about to officiate at the opening ceremony of the Beckersleigh Municipal Swimming Baths.

Agnes had wanted to leave Terry in the nursery school and Christopher, the baby, with a neighbour, but Barry had insisted that all his children should be present. It was essential for his image – the caring, concerned man of affairs, backed up by his loyal and adoring family. He was hoping he would be offered a place in the Government.

Agnes held the baby in her arms and kept an anxious eye on Miranda, who would never keep still for more than a minute. Every now and then Grace would dart out and pull her back from some hair-raising danger. Terry had decided to be very good because his father was there, and with curly hair brushed and slicked back, he looked a model of good behaviour in his neat flannel suit.

'If he's heavy, I'll hold him,' Grace whispered, but Agnes shook her head. The last thing she wanted was for the TV cameras to catch her passing the baby to Grace just in the middle of Barry's speech. They'd think she couldn't cope.

In fact, the birth of Christopher had marked an interruption in the downward curve of Agnes's life. She had had a miserable pregnancy and a difficult labour. But Christopher was a lovely baby, weighing over eight pounds at birth and with a cheerful disposition that she had no right to expect of him, considering her emotional and physical condition all the time she was carrying him.

Christopher scarcely ever cried unless seriously annoyed or irritated, and he had none of the upsets – the three-month colic, nappy rash or other troubles – that had afflicted her other two children. It was as though Christopher was intent on making up for all the trouble he had unwittingly caused. Even at this moment he was peacefully asleep in the arms of his mother.

Some way at the back of those assembled in the splendid new baths were the Rivingtons, about to be moved to one of the new high-rise flats, because their street was next on the list for demolition. The slag was nearly level, and the whole of Enderby Ward was being turned into a planner's dream: tall, elegant buildings, smooth, green lawns and waving trees. From the tops of some of the buildings you could see as far as Leeds in one direction and almost to the undulating Dales in the other.

Barry Holloway MP came to the end of a stirring speech about the benefits of urban development and, to applause, continued. 'And now it is my duty, my very pleasant duty, to invite Mr Henry Calthorpe to open the baths – a pool has been named after him in recognition of his very generous contribution. In fact, I can say that without Mr Calthorpe, who has been behind this project from the very beginning – and ladies and gentleman, I need not remind you that that goes back a very very long time ...'

'Since we were at school,' Grace whispered to Agnes. 'I remember Dad talking about it even before I left.'

When Barry had finished at last, Henry Calthorpe got solemnly to his feet and launched into an account of the progress of the town for as far back as he could remember it, while the waiting swimmers began slowly turning blue with cold. Finally Henry paused and then proclaimed in a loud, sonorous voice: '... And I name this the Calthorpe Pool!'

He sat down, rather red in the face, and Rose, sitting next to him, led the clapping. The two Calthorpe boys, the same age as Terry, stood on the podium just in front of their father. Henry never lost an opportunity of showing everyone that old as he was – sixty-one last birthday – he had still fathered two splendid sons.

When the clapping died down, Mr Calthorpe stood up again and stepped forward to cut the tape. Simultaneously the swimmers, who had been poised on the side, cast away their towels and dived gracefully into the water, breaking the surface with simultaneous strokes.

There was a fresh burst of applause, and the small daughter of one of the city councillors stepped forward and presented Mrs Calthorpe with a bunch of flowers.

Everyone now took their seats for the gala, and for an hour they watched diving and races of all kinds in all styles, and of all lengths, performed by swimmers ranging from very young children right up to middle-aged ladies and portly gentlemen. All were keen to show the varied and excellent uses to which the baths in general – and the Calthorpe Pool in particular – could be put.

Afterwards the dignitaries went on a tour of the completed baths, the smaller Elizabeth Pool, and the paddling pool. The new building was attached to the adjoining sports complex, and both had been encased in reinforced concrete, to a design many called an eyesore.

Grace stood on the steps of the complex, surrounded by a throng of people, chatting away, interminably, until Agnes thought that she would drop the baby if she had to stand there one minute longer. But most people who knew Grace knew her as well, and after talking to Grace or shaking hands with her, they went up to Agnes peeping at the baby slumbering in her arms and murmuring words of congratulations.

'Isn't it beautiful?'

'Thank you.'

'How old?'

'Six months.'

'Is it a "he" or a "she"?'

'A he. Christopher.'

'Oh my goodness, I'm nearly dropping,' Grace exclaimed at last. 'And I think it's going to rain.' She smiled dazzlingly as Agnes's mother appeared. 'Oh, Mrs Rivington, I do insist that this time you come back to the house for tea.'

Kathleen Rivington smiled and shook her head regretfully. 'We really can't, but thank you, Grace. We're getting packed up, ready to move.'

Kathleen Rivington nervously adjusted the new felt hat she'd bought for the occasion, her eyes appealing to Agnes for help.

'I think Mum's serious, Grace. They're moving at the weekend. They'll be on the fourteenth floor of Park Rise from now on.'

'We couldn't get anything lower,' Mrs Rivington said anxiously. 'They like to give the lower floors to people with children. The very thought of that height makes me nervous.'

'But you'll have a lovely view, Mrs Rivington,' Grace enthused. 'I'll come and see you.'

'Oh, you'd be very welcome, Grace.' Kathleen clutched Miranda, trying to think of something else to say. Then her husband and son came up. 'You remember our Paul, don't you, Grace?' Kathleen turned and took her son's arm. 'Paul, do you remember Agnes's friend, Grace Calthorpe? Mrs Winchester, she is now.'

'*Of course* I remember her. Hello, Grace!' Paul took her hand and shook it warmly. 'I don't think I'd ever have recognised you.'

'Oh, have I changed that much?' Grace laughed and grimaced. 'I try not to feel my years.'

'I don't mean that, Grace.' Paul looked at her with undisguised admiration. 'You're so elegant.'

'After a compliment like that, Paul, I insist that you come to tea, even if your mother can't.' Grace put a hand on his arm in a warm gesture. 'Do say yes.'

Paul smiled faintly. 'How could I refuse? I'll take Mum and Dad home first, though.'

They all went down the steps through the jostling crowd, then at the bottom, Grace, Agnes and the children went one way, Paul and his parents the other.

Terry and Miranda climbed into the back of the car and Grace took Christopher on her knee, sitting next to Agnes. She cradled the baby, and from time to time nuzzled her face against him. 'I still think of him as mine.'

Agnes put the car into gear and laughed. She had undone her coat and taken off her hat and now shook her hair free.

'How I hate hats!'

'I've always rather liked them.' Grace looked at Agnes with approval. 'You look very well, you know.'

Agnes glanced sideways at Grace, noticing the way she cradled the baby, the possessive, protective way her hand curled around his back. 'Chris'll need feeding as soon as we get to your place.'

'Have you brought his bottle?'

'I'm still breastfeeding.'

'You can go into my old room, remember? The den at the top of the house?'

'I'm not likely to forget it. What fun we had there.'

'Yes – and think what's happened to us since.'

Grace gave Christopher a little kiss and breathed the smell of warm baby. She felt tranquil, more adjusted to her life than she had been for some time. Really, Agnes had had the baby for *her*, he was partly *hers*. But for her, he wouldn't exist.

'You make it sound awful,' Agnes said.

'Oh, it's not so bad; but we didn't exactly make our mark on world affairs, did we? I never imagined I'd spend the rest of my life in Beckersleigh.'

'Grace, you're not yet thirty!' Agnes laughed. 'You've got a lot of life ahead of you yet. Who knows where it'll take you.'

'I shan't ever go from here. Keith occasionally talks about London, but he doesn't mean it. You've done more than I have, Agnes. You've had three children and your husband's an MP. Doesn't that make you feel proud?'

'Not particularly. Because, personally, I haven't done very much. I've been a pretty rotten wife, an awful housekeeper ...'

'What happened to your novel?'

Agnes hesitated. 'I finished it, actually.'

'You never told me.'

'In the summer. James Hetherington's got it now.'

'Oh, how exciting!' Grace was really thrilled. 'What's he said about it?'

'I think he rather likes it,' Agnes said modestly.

'What do you mean, you "think"?'

'Well, he *says* he likes it.'

'Agnes, that's wonderful! And you never said a word; I'm hurt.' Grace looked at her reproachfully, beginning to open the car door as Agnes pulled up in the drive of the house.

'I haven't told anyone, not even Barry.'

'You'd have thought that Rose would be home to receive her guests,' Grace said scathingly as she rang the doorbell. 'Always hogging the limelight with the celebrities.'.

'I don't suppose she could get away.'

'I don't suppose she'd want to,' Grace sneered.

* * *

At the head of the procession of the dignitaries heading up to the Calthorpe home for tea was the mayoral Daimler. Behind, Keith's Jaguar bore the Mayor's wife, who was sitting next to him, and at the back, Rose and Barry. Henry and his sons travelled with the Mayor in the official car.

'Grace and Agnes must have gone on ahead.' Rose stared at the back of Keith's head. 'Grace is sure to criticise me for not being at home.'

'Well, you can't help it.' Barry looked Rose full in the face for the first time in years. 'You had your duty to perform.'

'Oh, Grace always finds fault with me as a matter of principle, doesn't she, Keith?'

Keith looked sideways at the Lady Mayoress, who wore the fixed smile of one used to turning a deaf ear to indiscretions from whatever quarter.

'I wouldn't say that, Rose,' Keith murmured. 'Grace thinks very highly of you.'

Rose glanced meaningfully at Barry. Even in the spacious, comfortable car he was so large that his bulk spread over into her part of the seat. She was aware of his thigh next to hers. Had she wanted to remove her leg, she couldn't have done so – but she didn't want to.

Small, sensory waves seemed to pass between them. Rose felt the colour rising from her neck to her cheeks, and turned her head and smiled. Barry winked and a large familiar hand stole quietly into her lap and grasped one of her elegantly gloved ones. Instinctively it curled, clasping his. Then just as quickly she removed it.

When they arrived at the house, the maid and the hired butler were already dispensing drinks, while Agnes kept an anxious eye on Miranda, who had obviously destructive designs on the Calthorpe furniture. As soon as she saw Barry, Agnes called to him to look after her.

'I can't!' he whispered. 'I've got to speak to the Mayor and the other guests.'

'And *I've* got to feed my baby!' She glared at him, holding the screaming child out for him to see. 'You were the one who wanted the children to be at the ceremony, not me; please help look after them!'

'Where's Terry?' Barry looked round in a harassed fashion.

'God knows.'

Agnes turned away, but Barry leapt after her, reaching for her free arm. 'Agnes, it's your *business* to know! Where's Terry?'

Agnes looked round as Rose entered, one hand firmly in Terry's, the other in Robert's. Andrew, licking a lollipop, sauntered a few steps behind. Terry already looked as if he had been in his new clean clothes for at least a week. He had no jacket on, his hair was tousled and he had lost his tie; his shoelaces were loose and his flies open. Andrew and Robert Calthorpe, on the other hand, looked as immaculate as when their nanny had dressed them, wearing neat matching jumpers and shorts, socks well pulled up and shining polished shoes. They'd been dressed more sensibly than Terry anyway, Agnes decided. It was Barry who had wanted him to wear that ridiculous suit. In spite of that, the sight of the well-groomed, beautifully behaved Calthorpe boys made her feel her own and her family's inadequacies all the more.

'Here we are!' Rose carolled cheerfully. 'Nanny's going to take all the children up to the nursery and give them tea.'

'Thank God!' Barry murmured, holding out Miranda.

'Tomato sauce,' Terry said, in a loud voice.

'I beg your pardon, darling?' Rose bent down, smiling, her pretty face a picture of motherly concern.

'Tomato sauce.'

'He means, have you got tomato sauce for tea?' Agnes wished the ground would open and swallow either her or Terry up; she studiously avoided Barry's eyes. 'He has it with everything, I'm afraid.'

'Really, Agnes ...' Barry began, but Rose held up a hand.

'I'll send out for some.'

'No tomato sauce?' Terry looked at Andrew and Robert with amazement tinged with derision.

'No, darling. Robert and Andrew don't have it usually; but if you want it, you shall have it.'

'Really, Rose, it's not necessary ...' Barry looked furiously at Agnes. 'It's high time Terry got used to doing without tomato sauce. Agnes just gives in to him to keep him quiet ...'

'You told me you were brought up on tomato sauce.' Agnes looked accusingly at Barry and tucked Christopher under her arm. But head down, legs in the air, Christopher Holloway now commenced to bawl, in earnest, as though sensing his mother's crushing despair. Grace came rushing over.

'Agnes, everything's ready for you upstairs. If you'd let me take him ...'

Agnes plomped Christopher into Grace's hands as Keith came over. 'Can I help, darling?'

'What do you think *you* can do?' Grace said ungraciously. 'The baby's hungry and Agnes has to feed him. You go and talk to Councillor Smart.'

Rose took Keith's arm. 'Agnes will feed the baby. Nanny will take the children to the nursery and Grace, you, Henry, Barry and I can relax and talk to our guests. I always think of the Winchesters and the Holloways as family.' She tucked her arm firmly into Barry's – it wasn't an intimate gesture – and drew him over to the Lady Mayoress.

'I'll just see Agnes up.' Grace shooed Keith away with her hands. '*Do* make yourself useful, or Rose will complain to Daddy.'

Keith shrugged, stifling the retort which sprang to his lips. Sometimes he came close to taking Grace across his knee and spanking her. But she was a brilliant, difficult woman, and the only way to live in peace with her was to let her have her own way as far as possible and try to avoid being demeaned.

The den was exactly as Agnes remembered it: the bed in the corner, the bookcase along by the window, the dressing table still with the same silver-backed brushes and combs on it that she used to envy. Only the wallpaper, a pleasing pattern of rosebuds, was different and the curtains looked new.

'Is there anything more you need?' Grace asked hovering anxiously.

'No, it's all in here.' Agnes began unbuttoning her blouse and, without embarrassment, drew out a swollen breast. Expertly she cradled Christopher in a comfortable position in her right arm and he grasped the proffered nipple, eagerly beginning to suck. Agnes sank back and smoothed her hair with her left hand. 'Oh, thank God for that. The disadvantage of breastfeeding is that you can't hold it in for ever. The advantage is that it gives you such a feeling of blessed relief. Sometimes I feel it's the only peace I get. Do you mind if I put my feet on the bed?'

'Of course not.' Grace drew out the bed at a convenient angle and helped raise Agnes's feet, easing off her shoes.

'There.' She looked enviously at the full breast and the suckling child, thinking what skinny breasts Agnes used to have compared to her's. 'I suppose I'd better get downstairs. Though doubtless the second Mrs Calthorpe is coping beautifully.'

'You really dislike her, don't you?'

'I do.'

'Surely it's not just because of the boys?'

'Well, I don't like them very much. They're such prissy little kids; butter wouldn't melt in their mouths. Terry on the other hand is adorable, and perfectly normal.'

'Robert and Andrew are perfectly normal, too. They're just kept on rather a tight leash by that stern-looking nanny. My God, what wouldn't I give for a nanny!'

'What wouldn't I give for a husband who can give me children!' Grace sat on the edge of the bed, her intention of going downstairs apparently forgotten.

'Keith's awfully sweet with you, Grace,' Agnes said cautiously, moved by her attitude of dejection. 'He's much nicer to you than Barry is to me. Look how he offered to help you. Barry likes to be seen with the children, but otherwise he makes damn sure he has as little to do with them as possible. At home he does absolutely nothing.'

'But he loves them, surely?' Grace looked shocked.

'Oh, he *loves* them. But he doesn't want to look after them. At home I have the three children to see to entirely by myself. Then he wonders why I've no time to clean the house or type for him.'

Grace got up and glanced at herself in the mirror, patting her smooth chignon. 'Do you think I should cut my hair?'

'Cut your hair? It wouldn't be you with another style. I can't imagine it. Look: you're a very attractive woman, Grace, so don't let any false feelings of inadequacy make you think otherwise. There are plenty of other things besides being a mother.'

Agnes put Christopher over her shoulder and started to bring his wind up. For a moment the two Graces looked at each other; then Grace Winchester suddenly put a hand to her mouth: 'I've just remembered Paul,' she exclaimed. 'He should be here by now.' With a smile and a wave she vanished through the door.

'You've been a long time.' Keith was by the lounge door as Grace came in.

'I've been chatting to Agnes about babies.' Grace glared

witheringly at Keith and looked round. 'Did Paul Rivington come back?'

'Yes, he's in the next room with Barry and Rose. Grace?'

'Yes?'

'You look lovely today. And I love you.'

She clasped him briefly by the hand, not wanting to snub him, yet not wanting to respond in kind, then went through to the dining room, where Paul, Rose and Barry were chatting by the fire to two of the guests and their wives.

'Do I intrude?' Grace said, smiling.

'Of course you don't.' Barry stood back to admit her to the circle. 'Is Agnes OK?'

'She's fine. She's feeding the baby.' Grace put both her hands out towards Paul. 'You promised to come, and you came.'

'I came,' Paul said, smiling, and took her hands.

Grace linked her arm through Paul's and drew him out of the circle.

'You know, Paul, you and I haven't seen each other for years. And yet I quite fancied you when you were a young man, did you know that?'

'Did you?' Paul laughed. 'I wish I'd known!'

'I don't suppose it would have made any difference to you. You were far too busy with your career, too ambitious.' Grace led him towards the sofa. 'Was it worth it, Paul, all that work? How many years of it?'

'About fifteen.' Paul shrugged. 'Yes, it's worth it. Medicine's my life. And I'm about to be a consultant.'

'But no private life, no family?'

'Well, not much. I've had to work very hard. If I'd had a wife, she would have suffered.'

'Like Agnes,' Grace mused.

Paul looked at her gravely. 'Does Agnes suffer?'

'For Barry's career? I think so. Don't you?'

'I don't know.' Paul frowned and folded his arms. 'I sometimes think it's just that they're incompatible.'

'Really? But they appear to have so much in common – politics and ...'

'They *look* well together, if that's what you mean. But it's not a question of looks. I think they're temperamentally incompatible. They don't bring out the best in each other. Have you ever been to their house and heard them row?'

'I know they bicker a lot,' Grace murmured. 'But a lot of couples do that.'

'Yes, but this is more than bickering – this is war. Not all women let their homes go as Agnes does. I think it's deliberate.'

'But why would she deliberately ...' Grace was amazed by Paul's analysis.

'Psychologically she's smashing up her home. She finds it irksome; it deprives her of something else she'd rather be doing. Like her writing.'

'That seems to be a very clever deduction, but a bit far-fetched.'

Paul shrugged and then smiled deprecatingly. Suddenly Grace saw the resemblance between him and Agnes. It wasn't as strong now as it used to be, because Paul looked a lot older than thirty-three, his dark, curly hair greying above his ears. Yet his premature aging gave him an air of distinction that Grace thought would sit well on a consultant surgeon. A patient could trust Paul, confide in him. He wore a well-fitting grey suit and his moccasin shoes were smartly polished. He was at ease with himself and the world, one long, capable hand resting easily on a crossed knee, the other casually in the pocket of his suit, thumb outside, as he sat back looking at her.

She had always intrigued him. If he had an image of the perfect woman, it was Grace who always came to mind. She was attractive, seductive, clever, purposeful – and slightly intimidating. He remembered, years ago, that it was she who said she would ring him; when she didn't, he hadn't dared. He was aware of the difference between the Calthorpes and the Rivingtons, and almost from that day onwards, although he strove to succeed for the sake of his father, he had also, perhaps unconsciously, set out to increase his stature in the eyes of Grace.

But she had been married for years now. He scoffed at himself. Was she happy? Did the expression in her eyes tell him anything? No – but surely the way she sat spelt out her interest in him? A hip was thrust provocatively towards him, her long legs showing almost up to her thighs, unblemished beneath the sheer nylon.

When Grace, for her part, suddenly became aware of Keith standing beside them, she felt half-guilty, as though she'd been caught almost in the act of adultery.

'How long have you been standing there, Keith?' Her voice was slightly shrill.

'Oh, about two minutes.' He smiled easily, showing no sign of jealousy. 'I was never really properly introduced to Dr Rivington.'

'Really?' Grace looked amazed. 'You don't know Agnes's brother?'

'Well, we've met, but only briefly.' Keith stopped and shook hands. 'Barry tells me you're about to set up a brass plate in Harley Street.'

'Harley Street!' Grace said sharply. 'I thought it was Park Square?'

'I haven't quite decided.' Paul smiled slightly. 'I've got the offer of two appointments, one in London and one in Leeds.'

'But you *must* take Leeds! Mustn't he, Keith?'

'I should think he must take the one that offers the best chances.'

'Chances for what?' Grace asked coquettishly and Paul looked at her with a keen eye.

Keith, apparently impervious to the innuendo, replied: 'To further his profession, of course.'

'And this is our bedroom.' Rose threw open the door and Barry crossed the threshold.

'Very nice. This is new, too?'

'Oh yes. She had a lot of good furniture, but I didn't like it. I didn't want bits reminding me of her all over the place. I think that's one of the reasons Grace dislikes me, I had to chuck out quite a lot of her mother's stuff so as to make the place mine.'

Barry looked round the room with approval. It was a large room, and even though there was quite a lot of furniture, it was spacious, not cluttered like his and Agnes's bedroom always was. This was the bedroom of a meticulous, houseproud woman – someone with the leisure to choose furniture, and money to ensure that it was of the best quality.

Although Barry had been inside the Calthorpes' house often enough before, he had never seen much of it; but his main reason for accepting Rose's offer of a guided tour was the chance it afforded for him to be alone with her. Barry gazed at the bed, thinking of Rose lying there night after night with Henry ...

'You've made Henry happy.' He turned to Rose, smiling.

'I think so.' She gave a sigh of satisfaction. He reached out for her hand, but she withdrew to the door, beckoning to him, a warning light in her eyes.

'Come on, you haven't seen everything yet. All the rooms up here have been redecorated and refurnished.'

He left her bedroom with a sense of reluctance and followed as she opened first one door and then another. But the rooms, though beautifully furnished, didn't have the same appeal as the one in which Rose slept. At the end of the corridor, she threw open the last door without pausing and there, in front of her, Barry could see his wife wiping her naked, dripping breasts, while his child lay slumbering on the bed, a little dribble of milk running down from its mouth. Agnes looked up with a start as the door opened, and made an unsuccessful attempt to cover herself.

'Oh, I'm ever so sorry, love.' Rose backed away and tried to close the door. 'I didn't know you were here.'

'That's all right,' Agnes called. 'I've finished.'

Rose slowly opened the door again. Agnes was hastily fastening her blouse, the cloth she had been using to clean her nipples discarded in a bowl of water on the chair by her side.

'I'm just showing Barry the house,' Rose said. 'I've been refurnishing it, you know – decorating it bit by bit.'

'I know, it's lovely. I noticed the wallpaper and curtaining.' Agnes leaned over Christopher and began to undo his nappy. 'I'll just change Chris and then I'll be with you.' She didn't say a word to her husband.

As Agnes began to peel of the soiled nappy, Rose shut the door and went after Barry, who was already walking away down the corridor. 'Oh, I feel awful about that.'

Barry looked at her without smiling. 'Why should you? She's quite happy to do it on the bus.'

'Really?' Rose was shocked.

'Well, she doesn't think it's anything to be ashamed of.'

Barry saw Agnes's breasts so often that they had almost ceased to have any sexual significance for him, especially dripping with milk, or sagging after the baby's feed. But the unexpected sight of them at that moment had caused a slow stirring of erotic thoughts; his memory began to linger on the image of other, familiar breasts, not seen for too long a time.

As they passed Rose's bedroom, he swiftly opened the door and drew her inside.

'What?' she whispered, but he closed the door too quickly for her to resist and then pressed her firmly against it.

224

'Barry, I ...'

'*Shh* ...' He put his hands on her shoulders and kissed her, slowly, longingly.

As she sagged against the door, she put her arms round his waist, drawing him close to her so that he could feel her hard, prominent breasts pressing against his chest.

'Oh Rose ...' At last he drew away and gazed into her eyes. 'It's been a terribly long time.'

'I thought you didn't want ...' She lowered her eyes, but not before he saw that they were moist with tears. 'You said it would never end ...'

'I wanted to give my marriage a chance.'

'I know.' She gazed at him. 'I suppose you were right – but I've never ceased to care for you, Barry, to ...'

'To want me?' Barry drew her to him again, rubbing his hand against her bosom.

'Well, yes, you know that. You might have loved Agnes, but I married Henry for ... all this.' She drew her arms away from him and made a gesture that encompassed the room and all its possessions.

'And the boys. Don't forget the boys.'

'They were part of it. They were a good investment, too.'

'God, you're mercenary, Rose.' He laughed, half admiringly.

'No. Money's a good, solid foundation for marriage.' Rose pushed him away. 'I don't care what anyone says.' A hand went instinctively to smooth her hair. 'We'd better go down, love. If Agnes gets downstairs first she'll wonder where we are.'

'We can't leave it here, Rose.' His voice was pleading.

'You mean you want to ... to pick up where we left off?'

'What do you think?'

'Has your marriage failed, then?'

Barry didn't reply, feeling in his pockets for his cigarettes.

Rose quickly put her hand on his arm. 'Oh, don't smoke in here, love. It'll be a give-away. I'm nervous enough as it is.'

'When can I see you. Is it possible?' Barry's eyes looked earnestly into hers, and it was easy to believe that he wanted her, and only her, very badly indeed.

'Well ... It's possible,' she said doubtfully. 'But is it right?'

'Let's talk about it when we meet. Does Henry still go away? Can we meet here?'

Rose thought quickly.

'It's best during the day, *if* at all.'

'Best for me too. *If* I'm in Beckersleigh.'

'*If* you're in Beckersleigh. But I can see you in London! I often go. I'm going next week. Will you be there, too?'

Barry clasped her hand and brought it to his lips, excitement racing in his veins.

'You've got yourself a date,' he said, looking into her eyes.

CHAPTER NINETEEN

IT WAS MORE LIKE A wake than a celebration, Agnes thought, as they trailed round her parents' new flat, pausing every few moments to gaze at the panoramic view from one or other of the many windows on the fourteenth floor. It was, indeed, spectacular.

The flat had well-proportioned rooms, a bathroom, separate lavatory, central heating and a chute for disposing of the rubbish. There were any number of wall sockets, including one for an electric shaver in the bathroom, although Albert Rivington scorned such conveniences. Barry went round the flat with a proud proprietorial smile on his face that would lead one to suppose he had built it. Indeed, much of the Wirrall Estate owed its existence to him, especially during his early days on the council.

He stood at an east-facing window, looking at the remains of the Enderby Estate and the gradually diminishing slag above it.

'It's all coming down,' he said, pointing triumphantly. 'You won't know this place in five years.'

'I hardly know it now.' Albert Rivington puffed stolidly at his pipe. 'And I'm not saying I like it,' Albert went on. 'It's just different.'

'I think it's worse.' Kathleen, standing behind her husband, folded her arms. 'This height makes me dizzy, and the other day the lift didn't work. Supposing you got stuck in it?'

'There's an emergency alarm.'

'Yes, but how long do they take to get to you? Supposing you were old and had a heart attack?'

'That's being very pessimistic.' Exasperated, Barry stuck a cigarette between his lips. 'I think you've got a lot to be thankful for, Kathleen.'

'We lived in the other house since we got married. Our children were born in it.'

'But it had no bathroom!'

'You can live without a bathroom,' Kathleen said defiantly. 'My children were always brought up clean and well looked after. What you can't live without is comradeship. I don't know a soul on this floor.'

'But you've just moved in. It'll take time.'

Kathleen shrugged sceptically.

Agnes humped Christopher from one arm to the other. 'Well, Mum, you're here. There's no going back now. You'll just have to make the best of it. And the view *is* nice.'

'Who wants to look?' Kathleen said. 'I'll go and put on the kettle.'

She went into the kitchen, where the array of plugs and sockets still confused her. Agnes, carrying the baby, came after her.

'I still think that water's best boiled on gas,' Kathleen said, muttering through her teeth. 'I can't get the hang of this electric thing.'

'It'll take time, Mum.' Agnes sat in a chair, Christopher on her lap. 'You can't expect miracles all at once.'

'But why should I wait for miracles at my time of life?' Kathleen demanded. 'I was happy where I was. I knew everyone in our street. Now they're all over the place. We'll never keep in touch.'

Agnes sighed and went to one of the gleaming formica cupboards to get out the tea things.

'You'd have thought with Barry being an MP, we could have found something better, lower down.'

'He had no say in it, Mum. It's up to the council. But I'll ask him to see what he can do if it really bothers you so much.'

'I can feel it swaying in the wind at night.'

Kathleen gazed gloomily at the electric kettle, waiting for the steam to come out of the spout.

Agnes went to the kitchen window and looked at what was left of the slag, then at the rubble below, that would soon encroach on their old home. She thought of the fun of being a child in Enderby, the games they played in the street, the adventures they had had, climbing over the slag.

Everything about this new place was lovely – except that, like her mother, she wouldn't fancy living here.

'Some people are never satisfied,' Barry said as they drove away.

'You mean my Mum and Dad, don't you?'

'I mean your Mum and Dad.' Barry sighed heavily.

'But they never wanted to move.'

'You can't mean to say they really liked living in that – that hovel.'

Agnes felt herself bridle. 'Yes, they did. It was home. I liked it, too.'

'But it was dark and narrow and ...' Barry shook his head, truly bewildered. 'I don't understand it at all.'

'Yes, but we were used to it. We liked the big black grate and the coal fire, the oven in the living room. It was warm and cosy and welcoming.'

'But what about the winters when your dad had to come downstairs on freezing mornings to light the fire? Now the place will be warm before he even gets up.'

'Well, we liked it the old way,' Agnes said stubbornly.

'I can't understand you, Agnes. I suppose now you'll be lobbying against the further development of the Wirrall Estate.'

'Oh, is there a lobby?'

'Headed by your one-time boyfriend, Jeff Orchard, abetted by another close mate of yours, Connie Shilton, plus their lefty CND gang. They want the council to stop all high-rise building on social grounds. It shows how little they know about the economics of building.'

'Perhaps they care more about people than economics,' Agnes said lightly.

'Don't be so daft! I care about people, too. But economics is about people; how they live, the conditions they live in. You forget all about that.' Barry was getting angry.

'No, I don't; but even in the government there are people who criticise current policy. I'm not sure the government's on the right course, that's all.'

'You mean you're with the Orchards and Shiltons and their like, looking for Utopia?'

'Maybe.'

'Well, you won't get it in this world,' Barry said grimly. 'Never!'

Agnes sat at the back of the hall, anxious not to be recognised. Even so, several people had said 'hello' to her. Jeff Orchard had just finished reading a long indictment of the Beckersleigh Council, outlining folly after folly. Mostly it concerned housing resettlement, but the new baths had come in for a good deal of criticism, too.

'... The cost of keeping the water warm for one day would keep a working-class family in food for a month,' he said, shaking a fist at the ceiling of the Methodist Hall. He went on to castigate both the recent devaluation of Sterling and the futile attempt of England to enter Europe.

Jeff Orchard didn't look a day older, Agnes thought, though it was ten years since he had made those embarrassing attempts to court her. Next to him sat Connie, plump but unsmiling, her chin thrust upwards in an attitude of aggressive determination. There were about eight people on the platform altogether, one or two of whom she knew by sight. The hall was only half-full, but the discussion following the main speakers was lively.

'I see our MP is conspicuous by his absence, Mrs Holloway,' a man next to her turned and spoke to her quietly.

'He's in London.'

'But would he be here, if he weren't?'

Agnes didn't reply. Her neighbour's face was familiar, and she noticed that he kept making notes on a pad in shorthand.

'How do you know my name?' she whispered.

'We've met before, Mrs Holloway. I'm Sam Armstrong, editor of the *Beckersleigh Chronicle*.'

'Oh, of course.' Agnes felt embarrassed. 'I've seen you several times. I didn't recognise you with your collar turned up.'

'I've also got new glasses.' Sam Armstrong smiled. 'But what makes you so interested in this meeting?'

'Barry, my husband, is rather disturbed by the opposition to all the improvement schemes in Beckersleigh ...'

'Oh, so you're here as his spy?'

Heat rose to Agnes's cheeks. 'Not at all!' she exclaimed indignantly. 'He doesn't even know I'm here. It's just that I saw a notice of the meeting – in the *Chronicle* actually – and I thought I'd like to come along. Jeff Orchard and Connie Shilton are old friends of mine.'

'I'm sorry, Mrs Holloway.' Sam Armstrong extended a hand. 'I shouldn't have said what I did.'

'I'm concerned about issues that affect this town,' Agnes went on. 'I'm a local girl, you know, and my parents live on the Wirrall Estate. Housing and facilities for children and the problems of working mothers affect me just as much as anyone else.'

'But you're not a working mother, are you?'

'No, but that doesn't mean I'm satisfied as I am. I know the kind of frustrations suffered by women with small children at home all day. We need more crêches and nursery schools ...'

They were interrupted by a sudden burst of applause, and the chairman, whom Agnes didn't know, brought the meeting to an end with a graceful little speech.

'I can see you're concerned, Mrs Holloway.' Sam Armstrong reached into his pocket and produced a rather tatty-looking card. 'Do you think I could come and interview you? To get your views?'

'For the paper? Oh no!' Agnes was alarmed.

'Why not? They seem interesting and important.'

'I don't think my husband would be very pleased.'

'You mean your views don't coincide with his?'

'Not always.' Agnes smiled. 'Do you and your wife always agree?'

'I haven't got a wife, Mrs Holloway.'

'Oh.'

'I was divorced five years ago. I came to the *Chronicle* from Sheffield, partly to start a new life.'

'I didn't know. I'm sorry.'

'My wife brings up my two sons, and I see them every other weekend. She married again.'

'I see.' She was embarrassed by his openess.

'Agnes!'

Connie advanced on Agnes like a ship in full sail, both hands extended. Behind her was Jeff, gnawing the side of a finger.

'Connie, you were marvellous!' Agnes greeted her. 'I didn't know you were such an accomplished public speaker.'

'I've had lots of practice since I left Calthorpes.' Connie smiled. 'Is Sam Armstrong brainwashing you?'

'Brainwashing me?' Agnes looked at Sam with surprise.

'I support the Liberal Party,' Sam said. 'I suppose that's what Miss Shilton means.'

'A good old-fashioned Liberal,' Connie said derisively. 'Piss on them, I say.'

'Connie!' Jeff exclaimed. 'That's no way to talk to the influential editor of our local paper. Hello, Agnes.'

Jeff stretched out a hand formally, and Agnes took it.

'Hello, Jeff. You spoke very well, too.'

'I'm surprised to see you here, Agnes.'

'That's what Mr Armstrong said. Why?'

'Well, knowing the views of your husband ...'

'You make him sound like a right wing Tory,' Agnes protested indignantly. 'I'll have you know that Barry is a very sound, caring man; a socialist to the core.'

'Then why does he pull down houses when people want to stay in them? There's an old couple holding out in Enderby that have lived there seventy years. On either side of them there's a bloody great bulldozer.'

'Yes, I know. The Dawsons,' Agnes said quietly. 'Barry's been to see them. He says the house is full of damp and unhealthy. He really thinks it's in their best interests to move to better accommodation.'

'Come and have coffee,' Connie said. 'It's lovely to see you again. How's the baby?'

'Oh, he's fine.' Agnes looked anxiously at her watch, 'I'm afraid I told the babysitter I'd be home by ten.'

'That gives us a good hour. Sam?'

'I'd love to, but ...' Sam said hesitantly.

'Oh, do come,' Connie said. 'You can tell us how Jeremy Thorpe's going to convert the country to Liberalism.' Thorpe had succeeded Joe Grimond as Leader of the Liberal Party the year before.

Sam Armstrong frowned: 'Well, I liked Grimond, myself – he was a good, solid fellow. But Thorpe has plenty of good ideas.'

'I think the Liberal Party's a waste of time,' Connie said dismissively. 'Come on, Agnes, you've only got an hour. You can drive me.'

'Where?'

'To our flat. It's only five minutes away. Jeff, are you coming?'

'No thanks,' Jeff said. 'I've got to get back. Nice to see you again, Agnes.'

'And you, Jeff.'

As Jeff turned away, Agnes wondered if he had backed out because of her. Or was it Barry? She shrugged. What did it matter?

The house in which Connie had her flat was in a solitary row, the surrounding streets having been demolished to make way for the swimming pool.

Connie's flat was on the ground floor, and as they went up the steps, Agnes saw that the lights in the flat were on.

'Is Roman at home?'

'Yes, she'll be in now.'

'Why wasn't she at the meeting?'

'She lectures to a women's group in Leeds.'

'A women's group?'

'It's something new. In the States, women are beginning to organise themselves into protest groups. It's grown out of the Civil Rights Movement, really. Have you heard of the National Organisation of Women?'

'No.'

'Well, you will. The same thing'll be happening here soon.' Connie put her key in the door, but it opened almost simultaneously from the inside, and a tall, striking girl put an arm round Connie and embraced her. It wasn't a hug; it was the sort of welcome that a man might give to a woman, finishing with a gentle kiss on the mouth. It made Agnes feel embarrassed, an outsider.

'You're early,' Roman said.

'It was so cold in the hall; but we had a good turn-out. Roman, this is Agnes.'

'Hello, Agnes, I've heard a lot about you.' Roman Payne smiled and shook hands, and Agnes instantly sensed her attraction. She was like a rather good-looking boy, and her man's shirt and jeans enhanced this impression. Her hair was caught back in a pony tail and she wore no make-up. A large man's watch was strapped to her left wrist and she wore a plain gold band on the third finger of her left hand. So did Connie.

'I've heard a lot about you, too,' Agnes said. 'It's strange we haven't met before.'

Since her decision not to go through with the abortion nearly eighteen months ago, Agnes had only seen Connie three or four times. She knew that Connie had set up home with another woman; that she regarded her as a sexual companion rather than merely a friend; and that they had met in London at the end of 1966. Roman Payne was an American.

Roman smiled and pointed along the corridor. 'Come in.'

'Oh, there are more of us,' Connie said. 'Joe Forman, Mary Westbury and Sam Armstrong.'

Agnes went into the sitting room, while Connie stayed at the open front door to welcome the others. The room had the pleasant, rather appealing disorder she recognised from the time she and Connie had shared a flat – books and records and cushions all mixed up with dirty cups and plates. There were several small lights dotted round the room, and a gas fire glared brightly in the chimney embrasure. In spite of the fire it was bitterly cold in the room, and Agnes's teeth had begun to chatter.

'Cold?' Roman glided into the room. She walked with a curious slipping step, as though conscious of her height. She was very tall indeed, with small breasts and slim, boyish waist. 'There's plenty of coffee. I've put the kettle on. Did you eat?'

'Yes, I ate before I left.'

'Is your husband looking after the children?'

'No.' Agnes laughed. 'My husband's in London.'

'Why do you laugh?' Roman knelt before the gas fire and lit a cigarette with a long spill.

'Well, he's in London.'

'Yes, but I thought – forgive me, I may be wrong – I thought you laughed before you said that. It was as though the thought of your husband looking after the children sounded absurd.'

'Well, it isn't a very usual occurrence, I must admit.' Agnes sat down on the low settee. 'Of course, he's very busy.'

'You regard it as your function to look after the children, do you, Agnes?' Roman gazed at her with disconcerting directness.

'Not primarily,' Agnes said guardedly. 'But it works out that way. I haven't a job, and Barry has.'

'Wouldn't you like a job? Connie says you've written a novel.'

'Well, I like writing novels, yes. But I don't know that I'd want a full-time job. My baby isn't quite a year old. Young children need their mothers, you know.'

'Oh, I'm quite aware of that – but they need fathers, too, to help out with the work at home. Don't you agree?'

Agnes smiled uncertainly.

Roman bent towards the stack of books by the fireplace and drew out a hardback book. She passed it to Agnes.

'This is my bible, but I'll lend it to you.' Agnes looked at the spine and saw that it had been published in America: *The Feminine Mystique* by Betty Friedan.

'What Betty says,' Roman went on, 'is that the last war actually set women back. They no longer want to strive and compete with men in a man's world. They've gone back to the home. They've set up an image of themselves as happy housewives, fulfilled in their role as wife, mother, cook and cleaner. But in fact it's an illusion. They're not happy. She calls it the problem that has no name: the problem of frustrated, unhappy women, bored to death by the role that's been imposed on them by men and encouraged by the media – specifically, the women's magazines, which are edited mostly by men.'

Agnes turned over the pages.

'Well, I don't feel very optimistic, but I'll read it.' She rather resented this girl telling her what to do, implicitly criticising the way she ran her home. She let the book drop by her side.

There were voices in the hall; a gust of cold air blew in from the open door, and then Connie came in, followed by the rest of their guests.

'Sam's car broke down and we had to get the bus.'

'Luckily it wasn't far.' Sam came over to the fire, blowing on his hands to warm them. 'What a winter.'

'Do you know Roman Payne, Sam?' Connie put an arm round her friend, who stood up and shook hands with Sam.

'This is Mary Westbury.'

'How do you do?'

'And Joe Forman – he's in the CND.'

'We know each other,' Joe said. 'I'm going to talk about the bomb to one of Roman's groups.'

'Are you full-time in the CND, Joe?' Agnes asked, thinking she had seen him somewhere before. He was a thick-set man of about thirty-five, with almost grey hair and a big black moustache.

'Oh no. Connie's the only full-time person we can afford. I work in the Personnel Department at Hetheringtons.'

'Is the coffee ready, love?' Connie gazed at Roman, who briefly touched her hand.

'I'll go and see.'

As Connie watched her leave the room, Agnes realised with a sense of shock that Roman was Connie's world. She found it difficult to accept the fact of sexual love between two women. To her, sex was her and Barry, a man and a woman ...

'How are Hetheringtons settling down after nationalisation?' Sam lit a pipe and sat in one of the narrow chairs near the fire. He still had his coat on.

'Oh, nothing's changed. I think they were right to keep out of

BSC, though I support nationalisation. I think the whole thing's too big and unwieldly. There'll be trouble in a few years' time, you mark my words.'

'With Hetheringtons or the BSC?'

'Oh, not with Hetheringtons. They make a very special kind of steel that wouldn't have fitted into the BSC framework. No, it's BSC that's too big. I don't think it's been properly thought out. This government's a mess, if you ask me. You can blame me if you like – I voted for it. I don't know that I'll vote for Holloway again.'

'You do know that Agnes is Mrs Holloway, don't you?' Sam pointed quietly to Agnes, who had been sitting on the floor, listening attentively.

'Oh, I'm so sorry.' Joe looked contrite. 'I didn't realise that. I'm ever so sorry, Mrs Holloway.'

'You're free to vote whatever way you like,' Agnes said calmly. 'My husband isn't all that pleased with the party either at the moment. He thinks devaluation was a disastrous move.'

'I think it was inevitable.' Sam shook his head.

'Yes, but it's led to this run on gold. Think of how rich a certain tiny segment of society is getting ...' Connie went to the door as Roman came back, bearing a huge tray.

'Would you get the biscuits, Con?' Roman turned her head. 'I couldn't carry everything.'

Roman put the tray down on the table and started dispensing mugs of coffee.

'You should have called me to carry that,' said Sam, taking a proffered mug and looking up at her.

'Do you think I'm too feeble to carry it myself?'

'No, I don't mean that at all.'

'What do you mean, then?' Roman passed him the sugar and watched, smiling, as he fumbled for words.

'Well, in my view, it's a privilege for a man to help a lady carry a heavy load.'

Mary Westbury laughed and clapped her hands. 'Well said, Sam!'

Agnes couldn't fit Mary into the picture at all. She wondered if she was a girlfriend of Sam's, though she hadn't seen her near him at the meeting. She was a small, quiet girl, rather nondescript in appearance, with lank brown hair and pale, unhealthy-looking complexion.

'I see you're not in the Women's Movement then, Mary,' Sam laughed.

'I certainly am not!'

'It's hardly got going yet.' Roman calmly passed her a mug. 'And it's people like you who are women's worst enemies.'

'Now, don't you quarrel, you two.' Connie brought the biscuits over to the group sitting round the fire. 'They're always at each other's throats.' She shook her head and wagged a finger at them both, then sat down next to Agnes, her hands wrapped round her mug for warmth.

'Why does Mary do?' Agnes asked her.

'Mary teaches at Beckersleigh Infants, and she's very active in the CND; but she's got no time for the Women's Movement that Roman's trying to get going up here.'

'I know.' Agnes held up *The Feminine Mystique*.

'Now that's something you should be interested in, Agnes.'

'Why?' Curious about the edge to her voice, Agnes stared at Connie, but Connie had turned away and pretended to be busy sorting through the biscuits.

'Because of the way you're exploited by your husband.'

'Oh Connie, that's an awful thing to say!' Agnes was furious.

'But it's true!'

'You never liked Barry.'

'I never liked him because I knew what he was like. He's the sort of man that justifies the Women's Movement.'

'But he'd support any movement to do with women's rights! He has a very liberal voting record.'

'Yes, but what sort of record does he have as a husband and father?'

'I really take exception to that!' Agnes got up. 'I can't just stay here and have my husband abused ...'

'Defend him, then ...' Roman's voice from the background was gentle, but it contained a challenge.

'I don't have to defend my husband,' Agnes protested indignantly. 'He's a hard-working man, a good socialist and a good MP. What he's like at home is *my* business.'

'It's your misfortune!' Connie said bitterly.

'I don't honestly think you should go on with this, Connie,' Mary said, looking anxiously at Agnes. 'I don't think it's fair to your friend.'

'I don't either,' Joe Forman said. 'I find it embarrassing – and I don't even know Mr Holloway personally.'

'Well, I think Barry's a male chauvinist and I know him better than most.' Connie slammed the lid back on the biscuit tin. 'His wife's expected to be a slave around the home, and he even criticises her for writing a book!'

Agnes fastened her coat with shaking fingers. Sam Armstrong stood up too.

'Perhaps you could give me a lift?' he said quietly. 'I live quite near you.'

'Yes, I'll give you a lift with pleasure.' She looked at Connie without smiling. 'I really do have to go, Connie. It's nearly ten o'clock.'

'Well, I'm sorry if we got too personal.' She obviously wasn't.

'I think you should be more careful about what you say in public,' Agnes said. 'It really is nobody else's business to know about my married life.'

'I'm sorry,' Connie said. 'But Barry *is* a public person.'

'All the more reason not to talk about his home life. Especially if it's not true.'

Connie was about to make a retort, but seeing the expression on Agnes's face, she changed her mind. 'Still friends, love?' she asked, as Agnes walked to the door.

'Of course.' But Agnes didn't smile. 'Goodnight, everybody.'

'Oh, don't forget this!' Roman held something towards Agnes. 'It's the book that could change your life.'

Agnes tucked *The Feminine Mystique* under her arm. 'Thanks,' she said briefly, still not smiling.

Sam Armstrong slid his tall, gangling frame into the seat next to Agnes. Agnes found it difficult to tell how old he was. He had a narrow face, short, straight brown hair and rather bushy eyebrows. There was an ascetic air about him, and he looked like a man who didn't go much for compromise.

'That was very unfortunate,' he said, as Agnes started the ignition.

'You mean Connie and Barry?' Sam nodded. 'It really doesn't matter. But I admit I was angry.'

'You had every right to be,' Sam said sympathetically. 'Have you known Connie long?'

'She and I used to share a flat years ago.'

'Oh really? When was that?'

'About 1961. Yes. I was married in 1962. My God nearly six years ago. She was living with a man, then.'

'Oh? But she and Roman live together quite openly as a Lesbian couple, don't they?'

'Yes. I rather admire her for it, but I don't pretend to understand it.'

'What made her change?'

'I think it had something to do with the way she was treated by her boyfriend – he was Jeff Orchard's brother. He was a bit of a left-wing layabout. When Connie got involved in all that fuss at Calthorpes and became active politically, he really resented it. She said she found out then what men were really like.'

'Not *all* men,' Sam protested.

'Of course not all men. But on the other hand, I don't know ... maybe most men. I'd like to see what my husband would do if I started being active in the CND and addressing meetings all the time. I think it's normal, actually. Most men would object.' She glanced at him. 'I expect you would.'

'Is that a roundabout way of asking why I got divorced?'

'No, it isn't. It's no business of mine, and I don't particularly want to know.' But she did.

'I'll tell you anyway. My wife left me for another man. I expect I was inadequate as a husband, I don't know. Maybe I was too full of the newspaper world, or maybe I was just lousy in bed. She never really spelled it out. But, to return to what we were saying: do you see much of Connie?'

'Very little. Barry doesn't like her and I really don't have much chance to spend time with her. She's so involved in everything.'

'She's busy opposing Mr Holloway, too. They say they're going to try and flood the GMC with left-wing types and unseat him. Have you heard that?'

Agnes, who was coming to a crossroads, was so alarmed she nearly forgot to stop. 'No!'

'I'm sorry if I rattled you. I thought you might have heard.'

'Does he know?'

'I should think he's bound to know.'

'Well, he's never said anything to me.'

'Maybe he doesn't consider them a threat.' Sam shrugged. 'I don't blame him. They're very disorganised; but they're definitely setting up a new left-wing group right here in Beckersleigh, and I think they mean business. You can drop me off here.' Sam pointed to a small block of flats on the road that led to the estate where the Holloways lived. Agnes slowed down and then stopped. She saw that he was gazing at her in the dim light of the dashboard. 'I'd like to read your novel,' he said. 'It might be most illuminating. Thanks for the lift.'

'You're welcome.'

She watched him disappear into his block and waved; then she drove off, squaring her shoulders to prepare for the reproaches of the babysitter.

CHAPTER TWENTY

BARRY THREW THE PAPER TO the end of the bed and gave a howl of rage.

'Oh, Christ! Look what she's up to now.'

Rose cautiously raised herself on an elbow and gazed at the offending sheet of newsprint.

'What is it, dear?'

'Agnes.' Barry rolled his head from side to side as though in pain, and Rose tentatively groped for the paper and pulled it towards her. 'The end of page two – where it says WIFE OF MP ATTENDS LEFT-WING MEETING.' Barry stabbed at the paper and Rose peered hopefully in the direction indicated by his indignant finger. 'There!':

"Mrs Agnes Holloway, wife of Beckersleigh's MP Barry Holloway, attended a meeting of the Workers' Socialist Party held at the Methodist Church Hall, Beckersleigh on Wednesday last. The Party is thought to be intent on penetrating the Beckersleigh Labour Party in order to secure an eventual change of representative in Westminster. It is known to disagree with the views of Mr Holloway and to be in favour of unilateral disarmament and a greater role for the rank and file members of the party in the selection of candidates, and the eventual election of the leader. It is also very much opposed to the extension of the Wirrall Estate to Enderby, which is now in the final stages of demolition.

"When questioned by our reporter, Mrs Holloway said that her purpose in attending the meeting was not to lend support to its views, but to see what was going on while her husband was in London attending the current Parliamentary session. She also said that she was an old friend of Mr Jeffrey Orchard and Miss Connie Shilton, two of the speakers.

"It will be recalled that some years ago, Miss Shilton figured prominently in an unsuccessful attempt to introduce unionisation at Calthorpes Carpet Factory. Mrs Holloway was also once an employee at the factory, before her marriage.

"In his speech Mr Orchard said ..."

Rose stopped reading and glanced at Barry. 'Well, dear, it

doesn't say anything too dreadful. It explains that she was there to find out what was going on.'

'It also says they're her friends,' Barry shouted. 'Don't you see? It's an attempt to undermine me yet again. Now, even my wife is on their side.'

'Barry, it doesn't say anything about being on their side. On the contrary ...'

'It *implies* it. And there's a picture of her and all.'

'It's a good picture.' Rose examined it. 'But it must have been taken a few years ago, I reckon.'

'But why have a picture at all?'

'Because she's your wife!'

'To draw attention to it!' Barry thumped the eiderdown. 'Otherwise no one would notice all that rubbish at the bottom of the page.'

Rose put the paper down and stared thoughtfully in front of her. She glanced at the clock: it was nearly 2 a.m. Barry had had a late sitting in the House, and she had waited up for him at the hotel; a cold supper from the restaurant had been laid out in her suite, but he had hardly touched it. When at last he had got into bed, he'd decided to start reading the week-old *Beckersleigh Chronicle*.

'You mean they're deliberately trying to undermine you?'

'Of course they are!' He was impatient with her.

'It doesn't say who it's by. It just says Staff Reporter.'

'Sam Armstrong is who it's by, I'll bet you anything. He's friendly with Connie, even though he calls himself a blasted Liberal.'

'And doesn't he like you?'

'No, he doesn't. We've had several rows over various things. We don't see eye to eye at all.'

'You're too strong, that's the trouble with you, Barry.' Obviously it was hopeless expecting sex tonight; she might just as well put the light out and go to sleep. She began to wind up the alarm clock.

'What do you mean, "I'm too strong"?' Barry asked aggressively. 'You want some kind of weakling? You *have* to be strong to represent a town like Beckersleigh with all its conflicting elements.'

'Oh, I know that, love.' Rose put out her light and nestled up to him. 'What I meant was, you don't want to compromise.'

242

'I'm not mealy-mouthed, if that's what you're trying to say.'

'That's it. That's exactly what I'm trying to say. You're not mealy-mouthed at all.'

'And I've got to be strong to cope with that wife of mine, too. She drives me to drink at times. Literally.'

'Yes, you're not getting on, are you?' Rose said cautiously.

'No, we're not! Agnes's intent on needling me. She didn't go to that meeting to find out what was going on; she went in order to annoy me – she knew I'd find out she was there sooner or later. She didn't even mention it to me last weekend.'

'Didn't she? Well, there's a thing.'

Barry glanced at his watch and lit a cigarette.

'What are you going to do, then?'

'What about?' Barry exhaled and looked at her.

'Agnes.'

'Nothing. What can I do? I've got my own life to lead, thank God. Anyway, I couldn't leave Agnes with three young children even if I wanted to. It would be very bad for me politically.' His voice softened. 'Besides, I've got you. You make me very happy, Rose. You're everything she's not – thoughtful, considerate, generous. You know how to please a man. After all, that's what women are for – mainly.'

Rose looked at him with surprise, but decided to say nothing. Besides, if he was getting what he wanted, so was she.

Barry put an arm round her and kissed her tenderly. Rose smiled contentedly. In the six months of their new affair they had been very happy. It worked perfectly, meeting here at this large, discreet hotel in North London, where no one ever queried who they were or what they were doing. She came down about once a month and stayed for three or four days. Barry always joined her for the stay, leaving the room he rented over in Maida Vale.

Rose felt no guilt or remorse. After all, she had known him much longer than Agnes had, and she had been more faithful to him, more loyal and true. She didn't annoy him like Agnes did. She would never go off and attend meetings with his enemies ...

'I don't know what you see in me, but I know what I see in you.' Rose put a hand on his chest and stroked it the way he liked, as though he were a great cat. Her slow, sensual caresses made the little hairs spring up one by one, and she could see his tiny nipples grow tense and hard.

'What *do* you see in me?' Barry stubbed out his cigarette and lay back, surrendering to the gentle, stimulating touch of her hand, his anxious frown being replaced by a sensuous smile.

'Oh, go on – you're fishing for compliments now!' Rose laughed and kissed his mouth. 'It must be obvious what I see in you.'

'You like a bit of prick, don't you?' Barry turned towards her, his expression lustful.

'That as well.'

'You don't get much from old Henry, do you?'

'Oh Barry, don't talk like that.'

'Well, you asked me about Agnes. She's very good in bed actually. If you can ask me about her, I can ask you about Henry.' Rose stopped stroking him and lay stiffly. 'There's no need to go all funny,' Barry continued, still smiling. 'It would be silly to pretend that she doesn't make love well when she does. She enjoys it. Besides, you didn't marry Henry for sex, you married him for money. You said so.'

'And stability,' Rose said virtuously.

'Well , whatever it was, the point is there's very little else in our relationship, mine and Agnes's. Whereas with you.'

He took her chin between his fingers and kissed her hard. She had been wanting it for so long – they hadn't met for three weeks – that her reflexes responded automatically; she wanted him to take her without any preliminaries. She had been ready for him ever since they got into bed, ever since she had seen him come into the room . . .

It was over very quickly, that ecstatic joining of their bodies. He lay heavily on her afterwards, and she knew he wouldn't speak again until morning.

It was after eight when they woke up; or rather, Rose woke up – Barry was dead to the world. Rose got out of bed, donned a fluffy nightgown, and made a pot of tea, then brought it back to the bed.

'Cup of tea, Barry.'

Barry didn't move, and she had to say it again. He looked disagreeable in sleep, she thought – rather bad-tempered, as though the moment he woke up he would say something unpleasant. It was as though when he went to sleep all the cares of the world invaded his unconscious. She stroked his head and kissed his bearded cheek, and slowly he opened his eyes, looking bewildered. Then they focused on Rose and he smiled.

'I wondered where I was for a moment.'

'You're with me, Barry.'

'Thank God!' He sat up and scratched his head. 'I had awful dreams. Did we make love last night?'

'Yes, dear.'

'I should remember, shouldn't I?' He put his hand on the front of her gown. 'We can't do it again, I haven't got time.'

'You said you'd a meeting at the House at ten.'

'Yes, I have. What time is it now?'

'Eight-thirty. Here's your tea.'

'Plenty of time then. Thanks, Rose.' Barry took the tea and lay back on the pillows she had puffed up for him, sighing deeply. 'Yes, awful dreams, about the children. It was something to do with Agnes's parents' flat. You know the one they don't like. All the windows were open and the children . . .' Barry put a hand over his eyes. 'I can't bear to think about it.'

'Don't, love.' Rose pressed his hand. 'They say dreams are always the opposite.'

'Yes. Yes they do.'

Barry put his tea down and drew her close to him. 'I love you, Rose, you know that? I wish that we'd been sensible and got married. There was nothing to stop us, was there?' Rose's eyes filled with tears and she shook her head silently. 'Well, I suppose there was,' Barry went on, almost as though to himself. 'Money . . . you wouldn't have had the nice home you have now, would you?' Barry mussed his hair and pointed to his cup. 'More tea, please, Rose. Oh, and could you run my bath while you're there?'

Rose disappeared into the small kitchen, poured his tea, brought it back and then ran his bath. Barry was demanding, she thought, as the water started to run. He expected to be waited on hand and foot and never argued with. It suited her; but she could see how irksome it could be to someone as high-spirited and independent as Agnes.

'How's Agnes getting on with her book?' Rose perched again on the bed while the bath ran.

Barry shrugged. 'Well, she thinks she's going to get it published. She's already started on another.'

'Really?' Rose was impressed.

'Aye.'

'But will she really get the first one published, do you think?'

'Oh, yes. James Hetherington – you know, Stephen's brother –

he's been trying publishers he knows in London. And one is definitely interested.'

'She must be very excited.'

'Yes, she is.'

'It could make quite a difference to her life.'

'Yes, it could,' Barry said, and swung his feet over the side of the bed.

Rose watched him and pondered as he strode into the bathroom. If Agnes started being successful in her writing things would be more difficult than ever between her and Barry. Barry wanted a wife to be a wife – not a successful author.

Keith Winchester sat slumped in the tubular chair which went with the new tubular desk Grace had bought him. She had given his office a decidedly futuristic look, in keeping with the outlook for their enterprises. But to Keith's dejected eyes the potted plants, the tubular chandelier and occasional lamps looked more like stalactites and stalagmites in some prehistoric cave.

For her own office, Grace had favoured matured wood and well-worn leather. Her desk was rumoured to have belonged to Josiah Wedgwood, but there was no official authentication for this. There was little that was feminine about Grace's room, and indeed, little that was businesslike; but if anyone thought either quality was lacking, they would have been sadly mistaken. Grace was very much female and was turning into a very tough businesswoman indeed.

The Winchesters now offered expensive packages – whole complexes, offices, blocks of flats, ready designed, ready built, even ready furnished in the case of the oil-rich sheiks. They had designed and equipped a hospital for a Middle Eastern state and were now furnishing another palace for its ruler. Grace had just returned from the Middle East with an interior designer and as Keith pored over the evening paper, Grace was examining materials spread on his desk.

'Keith, do say which you like. I think the Princess would prefer this ...'

'For Christ's sake, Grace! A block of flats has fallen down, four people have been killed, and all you can think of are the bloody curtains for the Sultan's palace!'

'Keith, I would ask you to be kind enough to extend to me the courtesy you extend to the Princess when she's about to place £50,000 of business in your greedy little hands. We didn't build the fucking block that's fallen down and you've talked of nothing else all day. Where the hell is Ronan Point anyway?'

'Just outside London.'

'Then what's it got to do with us? I don't understand you.'

Keith didn't reply, but held out his glass. 'Give me another whisky, would you?'

Grace seized the glass from his hand and thumped it on a small occasional table. 'No, I will not. This is not the first occasion that you've spent the whole afternoon drinking, and ...'

'I have *not* spent the afternoon drinking!' Keith got up and went over to the cupboard where the drinks were kept. 'I've had one or two drinks since lunchtime, that's all.'

'And it's now five o'clock. We must go anyway. The Holloways are coming for dinner.'

'Oh, curse the Holloways!'

Keith poured a large tot into his glass and swallowed it at a gulp.

'It was caused by gas apparently.' Barry toyed with the cheese on his plate. 'It was an explosion. It didn't just fall down. It could have happened anywhere.'

'The thing is that the whole building collapsed like a pack of cards! Didn't you see the pictures?' Keith was obviously shocked and worried.

'Yes, I read all the papers on the train coming up.'

'The whole of one side just collapsed – and all because of one explosion in a top-floor flat. What does that say about modern construction?'

'Not much, I agree. But you didn't build it, Keith.' Barry put the entire biscuit, liberally spread with cheese, into his mouth.

'That's what I keep telling him.' Grace watched the biscuit disappear in its entirety. She wondered how Barry could possibly eat as much as he did and still manage to keep his figure. Keith was definitely running to fat, but then, he was drinking a lot, too. Drinking too much ...

'I feel it's a bad omen for the whole business,' Keith said, opening yet another bottle of wine. 'There's heavy opposition to the tower blocks already. Some councils are saying that no more should be built. We've already got schemes on various drawing boards waiting for approval – schemes on which we've already lavished thousands of pounds in the certainty of getting them accepted.'

'But you will,' Barry said. 'Of course you'll get them accepted.'

Keith grasped his glass firmly in his hand, squeezing the stem so tightly that Agnes thought it would break. She'd been watching him with some concern during the meal. When they'd arrived, he'd already looked, and behaved, as though he'd had a few. His conversation was wild and sometimes disconnected, and he seemed obsessed to an extraordinary degree by the Ronan Point disaster.

If we don't, we'll never see that money again. I tell you, I'm fair washed up if something good doesn't happen soon.'

As he thumped the glass on the table the inevitable happened. The stem snapped and the contents poured on to Grace's snowy cloth. Grace didn't say a word. She rang a little bell for the help.

'Bring Mr Winchester a new glass, please. No, on second thoughts, Joan, just bring a cloth.'

'I want some more wine,' Keith said belligerently.

'Bring Mr Winchester another glass, please, Joan.' Grace joined her hands in front of her and smiled dazzlingly at Barry and Agnes. 'Sorry about that.'

'Oh, we have spats, too,' Agnes said.

'And how.' Barry rolled his eyes to the ceiling.

'I guess that's married life,' Grace said. 'Shall we go to the lounge upstairs?'

'I'm having some more wine,' Keith said, tipping up the bottle into a new glass. 'I don't care what anybody says.'

'I'll join you, Keith.' Barry sat down again and passed his glass to Keith.

'We'll just powder our noses.' Grace beckoned to Agnes.

The bedroom had a new decor; pale blue walls with a dark blue carpet and pale teak furniture.

'You've got new furniture.' Agnes looked round with amazement.

'That other stuff was *six* years old!'

'I think we'll have ours for the rest of our lives,' Agnes said ruefully.

'Oh, Agnes, I'm sorry!' Grace was contrite. 'I should have offered you ours. It never occurred to me. It was all done while I was in the Middle East.'

'Oh, don't worry. It wouldn't have fitted anyway. I think we could get our entire house in your bedroom!'

'I only sent it to the sale room. We got peanuts for it.'

'Is it very serious about the business?' Agnes stood behind Grace, studying herself in the mirror and adjusting the belt of the blue silk dress she had bought in Leeds.

'Well, Keith's very depressed by it. This Ronan Point thing has made him turn the corner. But he'll get over it.'

'But how can it affect him, seriously? One isolated instance?'

'It's a culmination, Agnes. Tower blocks have come in for a lot of criticism. You know how your parents hate where they live?' Agnes nodded, and Grace continued: 'Well, multiply that several thousand times over and it adds up to a lot of discontent. And these professional agitators make it worse; all these students marching up and down for this and that. There are three very big schemes, two in the North and one in the Midlands, that we simply can't go ahead on now; there's just too much pressure on the councils concerned. Even Callaghan as Minister of Housing is back-pedalling on them. Keith wines and dines people and gives them expensive presents, but they can only go so far and no further. I think he's trying to have a word with Barry now.'

'But what can Barry do?'

Grace began to pace the room, betraying her own agitation.

'Well, Barry *is* an MP. He knows Callaghan personally, doesn't he?'

'But Barry's not in the government and he's not remotely connected with housing or planning. He also got a lot of stick here over the redevelopment. I don't think there's anything Barry can do.'

'Or wants to do?'

'Oh, Grace, that's *not* true! Barry would do anything he could to help, I'm sure of that.'

'Are you?' Grace looked speculatively at her friend and came and sat beside her. 'Barry's a bit nervous, if you ask me. We weren't even sure whether he'd come tonight. Keith keeps on writing to him and all he gets are evasive replies or acknowledgments from a secretary. He's asked Barry to join several enterprises as a consultant and Barry always declines.'

'Well, he has to be careful. Remember our wedding ...'

Grace gave a brittle laugh. 'Oh, I remember that all right! Keith was personally insulted. Since when are you not allowed to give a wedding present to your best friend?'

'But it was money.'

'It was not: it was a holiday. Keith was terribly offended when you returned it. It took him a long time to get over it.'

'I'm sorry.' Agnes put her hands in her lap and gazed at the floor. 'We certainly didn't mean to be offensive. I think Barry feels out of his depth in high finance. He's really quite a simple person, basically.'

'Oh, I like that!' Grace looked sideways at Agnes. 'I wouldn't call him simple at all. I hear he's a great manipulator in the Palace of Westminster.'

'Where did you hear that?'

Grace shrugged. 'We have lots of friends in high places, inside and outside the Commons.'

'I always seem to be attacked because of Barry. People really don't understand him,' Agnes sighed.

'Do *you*?'

'Me?' Agnes looked at Grace. 'Yes, I understand him quite well.'

'But you say you have awful rows.'

'We do; but we have other things.'

'A satisfactory sex life ...?'

'Yes, that.' Agnes looked quickly at Grace.

'Three children ...'

'Grace, I see you're going to get on your hobby-horse again.'

'Can you blame me?' Grace reached to a box by the bed and fished out a cigarette. 'I say you *don't* understand Barry. I don't understand Keith. So maybe I'm talking about myself. All we have is the business, which up to now has been very successful. But if that fails, we fail. We have absolutely nothing else to keep us together except an interest in the dynamics of the building business, and making money. Also, Keith is starting to drink quite heavily. I can't stand that. I hate to see a person deteriorate.'

'Can't you help him?'

'You saw what happened at dinner. You know how mild he is normally; but after he's had a few, he starts getting abusive. He drinks almost steadily now, begining at lunch and going on all through the afternoon. I'm just waiting for him to start at breakfast. It makes me wild – it's so weak and unnecessary!'

Grace stubbed out her cigarette furiously, as though suddenly gripped by some vital, uncontainable force. 'Oh, I don't know what to do! I'm very worried about the financial basis of our business, about all the bribes Keith has paid ... Who's going to stand by him if it comes to the crunch? I'm worried about my relationship with him, and now his drinking. Sometimes I think it's all going to go up in smoke. If we'd had children, at least we'd have some stability.'

'Did you give up the tests?'

'Oh, yes, eventually. If we'd had kids it would have helped, but I don't want to have them now. I'm *thankful* I haven't any. If anything happens to Keith I can just get out, free.'

'How do you mean?'

For a moment, Grace looked Agnes straight in the eye. 'A lot of things could happen: he could go bankrupt, go to prison or go into a home for alcoholics. Not very nice options, are they?'

Downstairs, Keith and Barry were watching the News.

'Students demonstrating all over the place as usual,' Keith said bitterly. 'I ask you! Most of these layabouts are there on public money. Why the hell don't they round them all up and send them to Siberia, where they belong? Can anyone tell me that? Barry, you're an MP. What do you think about all these people supported by the State, most of them never having done a day's work in their lives, roaming all over the streets, while buildings are collapsing and hard-working men like me are faced with ruin?'

'It's not the same thing ...' Barry began awkwardly, but before he could go on, Grace gestured towards Keith.

'Oh, do be quiet. You'll start on that awful old spiel about being a self-made man any moment ...'

'Well, I am ...'

'I know, I know, I recognise the symptoms. Too much self-pity, too much to drink. Send them all to the mines! You were born in the wrong age, Keith Winchester.' Grace's voice was savage.

'I certainly was,' Keith said with feeling.

'I've got some pleasant news,' Agnes said hurriedly. 'I'm going to have my book published. It's been accepted by a major London publisher.'

Everyone stared at her. Then:

'Oh, that's wonderful!' Grace ran over to Agnes and hugged her. 'Why didn't you say so before? We could have had champagne.'

'We can have champagne now,' Keith said eagerly.

'Well, I didn't say because it seemed selfish to be happy when you're so worried.'

'Isn't she noble?' Barry put his brandy glass to his lips, masking his sarcasm.

'But aren't you thrilled, Barry? I think you deserve a kiss, too.' Grace bent down and touched his brow with her lips.

'I didn't write the bloody thing!'

'You don't sound very pleased.'

'I just don't know where she found the time to do it. She's always grumbling about how much she has to do. I say let her do it – or pay for a nanny with the proceeds from her book.'

'It's not much,' Agnes said bitterly. 'Only a few hundred.'

'A few hundred is enough.'

'Oh, Barry, I think you're being very surly.' Grace gazed at him reprovingly. 'You should be delighted for Agnes. A lifetime's work.'

'It's not a lifetime,' Barry sneered. 'Just a few years.'

'Well, a few years is still a long time.'

'It *is* a long time,' Agnes said grimly. 'And now that I've had some success I feel encouraged to go on.'

'Oh Christ!' Barry put his head exaggeratedly in his hands, shaking it from side to side.

'You're very late, Mr Holloway,' the babysitter said, exactly as they had expected her to do.

'I'm terribly sorry, Sally. We thought we'd be earlier.'

'You always say that.'

'It's difficult to predict.'

'You say that, too.' She held out her hand sullenly as Barry counted the money into it.

'Oh, for Christ's sake, don't come again!' He snapped a final note into her palm. 'Don't do us any favours.'

'If that's the way you feel, Mr Holloway, I won't.' Huffily, Sally put the money in her pocket and went for her coat.

'Oh Sally, please.' Agnes pushed past Barry and took Sally's arm. She was the nineteen-year-old daughter of a near neighbour, and it was very useful to have her.

Sally shook off Agnes's hand. 'No, I'm sorry, Mrs Holloway. I just don't like being taken for granted.'

'But we don't take you for granted!'

'You may not, but your husband does.'

'We're very grateful. What'll I do without you?'

'Get someone else. You're always late back anyway, Mrs Holloway, and my mum's fed up with me coming home at midnight.'

'But you're a big girl now, Sally,' Barry said. 'You should be able to please yourself. Anyway, go now or your mother will be sending for the police.'

'Oh Barry, please ...' Agnes turned to him, but Barry made a dismissive gesture and disappeared in search of a drink.

Sally grabbed her bag, stuck out her tongue at Barry's back and ran from the room, followed by Agnes.

'I'll come and see you –', she began, but Sally had already slammed the front door shut. Upstairs a child, wakened by the commotion, started to wail.

'Oh God,' Agnes said half-aloud. 'Is this really life?'

'Yes, it's life.' Barry came from the sitting room with the whisky bottle in his hand and stood by the door. 'Life in the raw.'

'What the Hell did you have to go and do that for? It's impossible to get babysitters.'

'You just haven't tried hard enough. There are plenty of young girls round here.'

'Yes, and after what she'll tell them ...' Agnes gestured towards the door and glared at him.

'Well, you'll have to use your charm. You've got plenty.'

'I don't know what you mean by that.'

Barry put his glass to his lips. 'I often wonder why James Hetherington goes to all the trouble to help you. Why the heck should he?'

'Pure kindness.'

'Oh yes?'

'Yes! He felt sorry for me, having a husband who couldn't care less what I do as long as the children are fed and the beds made.'

'But they never are, are they?'

'What do you mean by that?' Agnes gripped the bannister, her face white and tense. 'Do you mean to say I don't *feed* my children? Is that what you're saying now?'

'You certainly don't make the beds! You certainly don't look after this house! You're too damn busy trying to become a famous writer ...'

'I don't want to be famous ...'

'Rivalling me, that's what you're up to. "If he can do it, I can". Well, you bloody well can't!'

Barry put his face so close to hers tht she could see the tiny red veins in the whites of his eyes. Agnes almost felt faint with anger. She started to back up the stairs.

'I've no wish to rival you, Barry. I just want to be a person in my own right. I want something outside the home. But I do have three children and they need me. By writing I've found a compromise. You should be happy for me, not jealous.' Her voice was passionate with feeling.

'Jealous?' Barry, enraged, caught her by the arm. 'Me *jealous*? Of you? Christ Almighty, what on earth is there to be jealous about?'

'Well, I think you *are* jealous. You've been horrible about this book. Now you pretend it's James who's the threat. Don't you know he's married, with three children? *And* very happy.'

'I notice you emphasise the "and".'

'I do. Happier than us, I can tell you. And what's more, you're drinking too much. If you're not careful, you'll end up like Keith!'

Agnes turned as a second child started to bawl, and fled up the stairs.

The sun was already flooding into the room, and the local blackbird had started its dawn chorus. Agnes didn't know if she'd slept at all. She felt deathly tired and her body ached. She had tried to see her life in perspective, but found she could not. The small hours of the morning, she knew, was not the time to try. All one could see before the dawn came was blackness and despair. She wondered how much longer she and Barry could exist together like this. For that was all it was: co-existence, nothing more.

Beside her, Barry stirred and she turned and studied his face, noticing the cross, disagreeable expression he always wore when he was sleeping. His mouth was turned down and even his closed eyes looked angry.

Did she still love him? It was something she hadn't asked herself for ages, hardly daring to. If she abandoned the love that she had sacrificed so much for, what would happen to her?

Barry grunted, opened his eyes, then closed them again and ran his hand through his hair.

'What time is it, Rose?' he said.

Agnes stiffened; then the significance of what he'd said seemed to dawn on him too. He opened his eyes wide and sat up. 'What time is it?'

'You said "Rose".'

'Did I?' Barry looked at her in surprise. 'What a crazy thing to do.'

'Maybe you were dreaming of her.'

'Why should I do that? It was all over a long time ago.'

'That's the thing about dreams,' Agnes said, turning the clock round. 'They take you back to the past. It's half past five.'

'Time for a good fuck,' Barry said sexily, snuggling up to her. His arm came up and encircled her hips, his hand intruding between her legs. 'Why do we have these silly rows?' he murmured. 'We should always make love afterwards.'

'Maybe if we didn't have rows, we wouldn't make love.' Agnes turned her face towards him, wanting him, wanting to bridge this awful chasm that was widening between them.

'You know, I think you're right,' he said. His eyes were hooded, amorous. They were fine eyes, and when they were filled with love – or desire, which seemed to amount to the same thing for Barry – Agnes found them beautiful. 'What a dull life that would be.'

'Sometimes I think I'd like it dull.' Agnes twined her legs around him as he gently sank into her, excited by his intrusive, physical presence as she always was, grateful for the wonderful sense of peace and mutual forgiveness that she knew would descend afterwards – for a few hours, at least . . .

Part Four

CHAPTER TWENTY-ONE

IN 1969, THE YEAR THAT saw the first man on the moon, Agnes Holloway had her first novel published, after a gestation almost as long as that needed for the Apollo 11 moonshot. She had started to tackle the business of writing a novel in 1965, three years after her marriage. Four years later the end product appeared – a very slim volume of only 196 octavo pages. Barry scoffed when the copies arrived from her publishers. 'All that work for *this*?'

Copies of the book were now stacked in James Hetherington's lounge, and every guest who arrived for the launch party took a copy and brought it over for Agnes to sign. She felt confused, embarrassed and very shy. James meant so well; the party must have cost a fortune – but she wished it could have been smaller, or given when Barry was in London.

But James Hetherington was proud of his work. He told everyone that he felt like Svengali and put his hand fondly round the shoulders of his Trilby.

'Without me, she'd never have got started.'

'Is that true, Agnes?'

'Yes.'

It was such a good story that the editor of the *Chronicle*, Sam Armstrong, had decided to come along himself with a photographer.

'I hope you'll be kinder to me than last time.' Agnes looked at him gravely.

'What did I do last time?'

'That bit about attending that meeting.'

'That was over a year ago! What was wrong with that?' Sam scratched his head. 'I don't remember being unkind.'

'It caused a heck of a row with my husband.'

'I'm sorry about that.'

'Anyway, I never went to any more.'

'Well, your husband stifled the opposition pretty effectively anyway. He had a gigantic vote of confidence just this year, didn't he?'

'After the huge swings to the Tories in the March by-elections, I think that Beckersleigh Labour Party realised what an asset they had in Barry. They had to close ranks.'

'Well, at least you're honest. Will you sign my copy?'

Sam held it out with the title page open and Agnes inscribed her name underneath the printed one.

'I'll look forward to reading it. Are you writing another?'

'When I've time.'

'Agnes, would you like to write some articles for the paper?'

Agnes's eyes widened. 'What sort of articles?'

'Oh, anything that strikes you. I'd be glad to suggest something to get you started.'

'I'd love to!'

'Thought you might. You'd be paid, of course.'

'Nothing political, though, Sam.'

'We'll see,' Sam said, turning towards a couple who were approaching them. 'I'll keep it in mind. You know Malcolm Longley and his wife, don't you?'

'Of course. We've met several times.' Agnes shook hands with the Conservative candidate and his wife, wondering why they were here.

'I'm dying to read your novel,' Elizabeth Longley said warmly. 'I've started dozens myself without ever finishing one.'

'You must be more persistent,' Malcolm Longley smiled as he shook hands with Agnes, going so far as to kiss her on the cheek. 'Maybe, if I get into Westminster at the next election ...'

'Oh, don't,' Agnes laughed. 'Then I'll never have time to write at all. My husband will be so busy sulking.'

'Doesn't your husband *mind*?' Elizabeth Longley moved close to Agnes as Sam drew her husband away, lowering her voice intimately.

Agnes looked at her. She was a tall, attractive woman, a friend of Grace's. She had something of Grace's urbane elegance, too, her black hair fashionably set in a bouffant style. Her face was carefully made-up, pleasant, but without a lot of expression, as though here was a person who kept herself firmly in control.

'Why should he mind?'

'Oh, Malcolm's *furious* if I do anything which excludes him – except the garden and the housework, of course. Women's things.'

'I'm sure you do that very well.' Agnes glanced around to make sure Barry was out of earshot. 'I can't write and be a good housekeeper. Barry resents that. Do you remember Mrs Longley, Barry?' she said, as Barry came up to her with Rose and Henry Calthorpe.

'Do I not?' Barry said jovially, shaking hands. Obviously, he didn't feel as easy with her as her husband did with Agnes, and didn't kiss her. 'I hope you're not a novelist, Mrs Longley.'

'*Hope*? You should be very proud of your wife.'

'He is really,' Rose reached up and kissed Agnes. 'I'm so pleased for you, Agnes. You must feel very thrilled.'

Agnes never felt quite at ease in the presence of the woman who had once been Barry's mistress. She felt that Rose was always making some mental comparison between them. Did she find her wanting? Rose was now holding out her copy to be signed. Once again she wrote her name on the title page.

'Oh, couldn't you put "To Rose and Henry Calthorpe"? There – you can just squeeze it in.'

Agnes complied with a flourish and Rose took the book and turned to her husband:

'Isn't that thrilling, Henry? Agnes has signed our book!'

Henry made a great point of admiring the signature and kissed Agnes. 'We're both very pleased, Agnes. Is our Grace here yet?'

'I haven't seen her. I hope you like the book, Mr Calthorpe.'

Henry put a hand on her shoulder and patted it. 'Agnes, I've no doubt I shall. I'm proud to have known you since you were a little girl; proud that you're my daughter's best friend and that you've done so well. Your husband's a very lucky man – I hope he realises it!'

Rose saw that Barry wasn't even listening but was questioning Mrs Longley on her own efforts to get her ideas into print. There was no doubt that Barry was jealous of Agnes. She had known Agnes's success would upset him.

'I keep on stopping and starting again with fresh characters,' she could hear Elizabeth saying.

'Agnes did that. This book's taken her nearly four years.'

'Well, at least she finished it.'

'Yes, but it was achieved at no little cost to the peace of our household.'

Malcolm Longley had now rejoined the group and stood listening, his hands in the pockets of his blue striped suit. He was a partner in a leading firm of accountants who looked after most of the major businesses in Beckersleigh, including Calthorpes. He was a man of average height with a rather jolly face, receding hair, bright blue eyes and a snub nose. Although he had an unprepossessing face, he did have considerable presence, and proclaimed his self-confidence by the thrust of his chest, by the aggressive tilt of his chin as he swayed back and forth on his shiny black shoes, whisky in hand.

'That's what I say,' he said at last. 'We've got four children, a large house and three pets. My wife has no time to write books.'

'Agnes, Grace is here ...' Barry whispered as though announcing someone of great importance; before she was pulled away, Elizabeth called after her.

'You must come for tea.'

'I'd love to.'

Grace was alone. For the past few months Agnes had been deeply worried by Grace's appearance. Although apparently her usual capable self, she had, underneath, a worried, anxious air. Today was no exception. Keith was being sued for a huge sum by a large firm of architects, and the construction work in the Middle East had fallen through because of competition from a larger group. Now Keith spent most of his time locked up with a bottle, and Grace was showing the strain. The look on her face turned to relief when she saw Agnes, who had already given her a copy of the book.

'I finished it last night,' she said quietly. 'It really *is* good.'

'Thank you,' Agnes smiled gratefully. 'I'm so glad you were able to come.'

'I *had* to come.' Grace lifted her eyebrows and linked her arm through Agnes's. 'My best friend's publication party!' At her elbow a waiter hovered, and she accepted a glass of champagne.

'What a lovely party. I can see lots of people I know. Wasn't it sweet of James?'

'Very sweet.' Agnes nodded. 'Could Keith not come?'

The customary shadow that always seemed to darken Grace's face when Keith's name was mentioned flickered over it now.

'He's gone to London to see those wretched solicitors. I don't know why he can't have his lawyers here, or in Leeds, like everyone else. He's going back to his roots, I suppose. I wish he'd go back for good sometimes.' Then her face brightened. 'Still, I think we'll pull through. If we contract the business and drastically curtail our activities, we might do it. Malcolm Longley's been an angel. He really is awfully clever. Thank God Keith took Barry's advice about that and made them our accountants. Oh, I see Rose is here, as usual.'

'Of course, she's with your father.'

'*And* Barry. Do you know, I don't think I've ever been at any gathering where Barry and Rose aren't together. Have you noticed that?'

'They were old friends, of course,' Agnes said. 'Don't be bitchy, Grace.'

'*Me*! Bitchy?' Grace pointed a finger at herself in amazement. 'I'm simply commenting, that's all. They were very *good* old friends, if you ask me. I wonder Daddy doesn't get suspicious.'

Agnes avoided Grace's gaze. She had never told her the full story about Barry and Rose.

'Well, if anything did happen, it's dead and buried now.'

Grace looked at her suspiciously. '*Did* something happen?'

'Oh, I often think they'd make a good couple,' Agnes went on, a trace of mockery in her voice. 'Barry likes elegant, experienced women – and Rose is certainly that. She's also very obsequious and defers to men – and Barry likes that, too. Even the way she looks at men seems to put them firmly into the Number One spot. First she lowers her eyes and then she opens them very wide and starts to vamp them – but in the nicest possible way. I mean, no one could take exception to what she does. She does it to everyone, even the waiter!'

Grace seized Agnes's hand, threw back her head and roared with laughter.

'The two Graces giggling together, I see.' James came over and put an arm around each. 'Have you read Agnes's book, Grace?'

'Yes, I finished it last night. It was marvellous. I only hope her mother didn't mind about being portrayed so frankly by her daughter.'

'I don't think she'd recognise herself,' Agnes murmured, 'even if she reads it, which I doubt. More likely she'll put in on the sideboard and dust it every week.'

'Is she here?'

'No, she refused to come, naturally. Dad's over there, though.

Surprisingly enough, he seems to be enjoying himself.'

'I hear Paul's coming to Leeds,' Grace said. 'Didn't he like London?'

'It was only for a year or two. Now he's to be a full consultant. Come and say hello to him.'

Albert Rivington was standing by the window, a pint of beer in one hand and his pipe in the other. He was wearing his best suit, which as usual looked too large for him, a soft white shirt and a stiff collar, through which his wife had with great difficulty threaded a red tie.

'Paul, I haven't seen you for two years!' Grace took him affectionately by the arm.

'Well, you'll see me more often now. I'm going to come and live up here.'

'Then the first thing you must do when you're settled is to come and have dinner with us. Mr Rivington, you look remarkably handsome.' She kissed him on the cheek and he stared at her, unsmiling and unbelieving. 'I hear your bronchitis has been very bad this winter.' Grace's face creased with sympathy. 'I'm so sorry.'

'Worst winter I've ever had. Worse than last – that was the first in the new flat, and that was bad enough. They say central heating cures all ills. Rubbish – it brings 'em on, as I keep on telling my son-in-law ...'

'Oh, please don't get on to property, Mr Rivington.' Grace put a pleading hand on his arm.

'I'm not talking about property, I'm talking about central heating.'

'It's the same thing. It all leads to property. Anyway, there'll be no more tower blocks from now on. I believe that's official council policy?' She looked from Paul to Agnes, who nodded.

'Bit late now,' Mr Rivington said. 'They're now starting to modernise the old houses. I never heard such a bloody carry-on!'

It was true; Enderby Street remained standing after two years, the houses shuttered up, still facing a row of flattened rubble where the new building had come to an abrupt halt. Weeds and even small trees had begun to sprout, and the children from the tower blocks played there now, instead of on the flattened slag.

Albert suddenly pointed towards the door. 'Is that Connie Shilton?'

'Oh, good,' Agnes clasped her hands together. 'I wasn't sure if she'd come.'

'Did James ask her?' Grace said, incredulously. 'With my father here?'

'Oh Grace, all that was so long ago,' Agnes protested.

'He's got a long memory,' Grace said. 'And so have I. That business at the factory killed my mother.'

'Well, try and put it out of your mind now, for me. Please.'

'For you and your book I'll try,' Grace said, but she looked distinctly glacial as Agnes went over to fetch the new arrivals.

'Oh, Agnes, thank goodness you're here.' Connie took Roman's hand. 'We were about to go out again.'

'My father saw you. And Paul's here.'

'I haven't seen your brother since he was at school. Is that him?' Connie pointed to Paul, who came towards her. 'Paul, I'd never have recognised you. You're so tall and so . . . well, quite handsome.'

Paul shook her hand, laughing.

'This is Roman, Paul. Roman Payne, a friend of Connie's.'

'Not friend,' Connie said, unabashed. 'She's my lover.'

'How do you do?'

'This is my father.'

Albert held out a hand, making no attempt to mask the shock Connie's remark had caused him.

'D'ye do.'

'My friend, Grace Winchester.'

Grace, her expression imperturbable, shook Roman's hand and did her best to ignore Connie. 'How nice to meet you. Do I detect an American accent?'

'Yes. I came over in '66 and loved it so much I stayed.'

'You *love* Beckersleigh?' Grace said incredulously.

'I love Connie.' Roman put an arm lightly round the waist of the plump, smiling girl by her side.

'Oh, I see.' Grace with studied unconcern glanced from one to the other. 'Hello, Connie.' .

'I didn't think you'd remember me, Grace.'

'Oh, I remember you all right. As Agnes said, it was a long time ago.' She shook Connie's hand and looked at Roman. 'Is this one of those very sophisticated relationships we read about in *avant garde* papers?'

'If you read the *avant garde* papers,' Roman laughed. 'It's just a purely honest relationship between two people who love each other.'

Agnes began to wish she hadn't asked them. It was not only ridiculous, it was downright rude for people to come to a private party and start talking about their intimate lives. It seemed deliberately calculated to disturb her and spoil her party. But Grace, her head bent intently, was listening with every appearance of interest to whatever Roman was saying and Albert Rivington, having overcome his shock, had relit his pipe and resumed his conversation with Paul.

'I'm dying to read your book,' Connie said. 'So's Roman.'

'Thank you. Look, I wish you wouldn't always go on like this in public, Connie.'

Connie looked at her in surprise. 'What do you mean?'

'About your relationship.'

'But we love each other,' Connie protested.

'So do a lot of people – but they don't go on about it in public all the time. It's not normal. If a heterosexual couple behaved like you, you'd feel irritated too.'

Connie flushed. 'We don't want there to be any misunder-standing – "Just friends", that kind of claptrap.' Connie's expression took Agnes back to the days when she was trying to bring everyone out on strike at Calthorpes. What she lacked, Agnes decided, was a sense of humour.

Grace seemed quite absorbed by Roman who, despite her trouser suit and man's shirt and tie, looked very feminine and alluring. Her fair hair was combed back from her forehead and gathered in a bunch at the back with a rubber band, but her pale lips and arched brows, the curiously enigmatic quality of her smile, made her look strangely exotic.

In a way, she wasn't unlike Grace, Agnes thought. There was something feline about both of them; something slightly boyish that seemed, perversely, to enhance their femininity.

'It's all terribly interesting, you know, Agnes,' Grace said, smiling slightly. 'I do think they're so brave, and so ... *right*, don't you? I mean, to proclaim the relationship.'

'I'm not so sure about proclaiming it at my party,' Agnes said, noticing with concern the rage on Mr Calthorpe's face as he pointed Connie out to his wife.

'You should proclaim it everywhere,' Roman said. 'We have nothing to be ashamed of. I was telling Grace about how the Women's Movement is developing. It's getting quite strong in this country.'

'It's the image of the Women's Movement that puts me off,' Agnes said. 'All that bra-burning nonsense.'

'That was a travesty put about by the press,' Roman riposted. 'It never happened.'

'I thought it happened in a demonstration against the Miss America Contest last year? There were pictures in the papers. Of course it happened,' Agnes snapped.

'It was merely meant to symbolise all that women represent to men – the main sexual focus being a woman's breasts.'

'Then it *did* happen?'

'Maybe once,' Roman admitted, 'but it doesn't happen every day. Feminists are serious, involved people. Did you read *The Feminine Mystique*?'

'Not yet. I'd better give it back to you.'

'You don't want to read it, do you?' Roman challenged.

'I haven't time.'

Agnes was relieved to see Barry coming towards them with a plate of sandwiches.

'Peace offering, Connie?' He passed her the plate. He'd obviously had quite a lot to drink. 'May I kiss you?'

'Don't be daft,' Connie said, snatching a sandwich. 'What a stupid thing to say! Why aren't you in London, governing, like you're supposed to?'

'Oh God, she doesn't change, does she?' Barry said wearily.

'Why should *I* change? It's *you* that needs changing, with your reactionary right-wing views. They're getting you nowhere, are they? The government's in a mess, and now the Tories are going to romp home in the next election.'

Agnes could see Barry struggling to keep his good humour.

'Well, at least as long as you're there, Connie, guiding things in London outside the American Embassy, I can rest assured the country won't go completely to pieces.'

Roman Payne was gazing at Barry, a hand on her hip, a sardonic smile on her face. Agnes could see him watching her even though he was talking to Connie.

'I don't think you've met Roman Payne,' Agnes said. 'A friend of Connie's.' She flashed Connie a warning glance, and Connie visibly bit back what she was going to say.

'How do you do?' Barry shook her hand and then held it in his for a moment. Roman's glance was now flirtatious and the smile provocative.

'How do you do?'

'Are you actually called *Roman*?'

'I'm afraid so. It's Romany really, but even I balk at that.'

'Were your parents gypsies?'

'No, just eccentric.'

'But tell me ...'

As Barry and Roman drew closer together, Agnes whispered to Connie to come and meet James Hetherington; then, with her father and Paul, she took them to the far side of the room.

Agnes noticed that once parted from Roman, Connie became visibly nervous. She kept on glancing at Roman standing opposite Barry, who was leaning towards her, resting his right hand against the wall so that it seemed as if he was about to embrace her. It was a stance of masculine insouciance, casual yet potentially powerful, threatening.

'It's all right, he won't seduce her,' Agnes said, smiling at Connie.

'How do you know?'

'Well, *will* he?' Agnes looked surprised.

'He fancies her, if you ask me,' Connie said sullenly.

'That's not very complimentary to me!'

'Well, you've been married a long time. Seven years, isn't it? The Seven Year Itch, then. Roman had a boyfriend, you know, not so long ago. She does like men. She knows what it's all about.'

'You had a boyfriend, too.'

'That was years ago!' Connie's voice was rising angrily. 'I haven't had a man since. I don't like them! I don't want them! Oh good, Mrs Calthorpe's going to break it up.'

Rose was indeed advancing on Barry and Roman, and as she came up to them, Barry turned and casually put an arm round her shoulder.

'*There's* a tender gesture,' Connie said, insinuatingly.

'Oh really, Connie! You're the second person today who's tried to make out that Barry's interested in Rose.'

'Well, he was. You know that.'

'It was years ago!'

'I wonder ...'

Suddenly, Agnes remembered him addressing Rose when he had woken up one morning, and she knew a moment of apprehension, a passing feeling of doubt and terror. Barry and Rose? It was impossible.

Unfortunately, just as Rose approached Barry and Roman, Henry Calthorpe decided to go looking for his wife, and Connie, unable to bear it any longer, went back to Roman. Agnes's attention had been sidetracked, and the first she knew of the encounter was when she heard raised voices on the other side of the room.

'... You've been nothing but an agitator since you tried to wreck my factory,' Henry was saying, wagging a finger at her.

'I don't call it agitating, Mr Calthorpe. I'm trying to change society.'

'Well, don't change it here! Take your crackpot notions somewhere else.'

'Oh God!' Agnes momentarily covered her face and when she looked again, James was by her side.

'I knew I shouldn't have asked her.' He looked apologetically at Agnes. 'I'm so sorry, Agnes.'

'No, it was silly of me. Oh good, there's Grace. She'll know what to do.'

Grace had taken her father's arm and was talking to him in a low voice, but Henry shrugged her off.

'I'm just telling this young woman what I think of her. I hold her responsible for your mother's death ...'

'But Dad, this isn't the place ...'

'What ever do you mean by *that*, Mr Calthorpe?' Connie took a step nearer to him.

'I mean *you* killed her by the way you disrupted things at the mill. She was a very sick woman already. I haven't forgotten it.'

'And what about all the people who are dying every day in Vietnam? Men, women *and* children ...'

For a moment Henry was completely nonplussed.

'*What*? What the Hell has *Vietnam* got to do with this?'

'You just see your own suffering, Mr Calthorpe. Typical of your class. *I* didn't kill Mrs Calthorpe, far from it; but you and your kind, by your support of the fascist American Government, are undoubtedly killing people in Vietnam every minute, as surely as if you'd pulled the trigger yourself.'

Henry's face turned puce. 'Well, I never heard such nonsense ...'

Now everyone in the room seemed to have stopped talking and slowly converged on the group in the corner. There was a moment's pregnant pause. Then it was Roman who, with poise and decision, stepped between Connie and Henry and took Connie's arm.

'I don't think this is the place either, Connie ...'

'You let me go!' Connie tried to shrug her off, but Roman retained her firm, friendly grip.

'Come on, Henry.' Rose put her arm through his. 'No use upsetting yourself.'

'We should go anyway.' Roman looked at her watch. 'Let's go, Connie.'

'I do think Roman's right, Connie,' Barry said. 'It's spoiling Agnes's party.'

'And when did you care about Agnes?' Connie bawled at him. 'When did you care about anyone other than yourself?'

'Oh my goodness!' James Hetherington moved quickly to Connie's side and held out his hands placatingly.

'*Please*, Miss Shilton. Please don't upset Agnes, or any of us ...'

'But it wasn't me ...' She glared at Henry.

'It *is* time to go,' Roman insisted.

'It's time we went, too,' Elizabeth Longley said in a loud voice. Suddenly it was as if her words were a signal for everyone to begin talking at once.

Connie turned round, looking for Agnes, but Agnes remained where she was. She never wanted to see either her or Roman Payne again.

Agnes drove home, because Barry had had too much to drink and didn't want to give his enemies in Beckersleigh more ammunition by being fined for drunken driving.

'Well, what a carry-on.' He mopped at his forehead with his handkerchief. 'You must have been crazy to invite that girl. She's a fanatic.'

'Look, she just feels very strongly about things, and Henry did provoke her.'

'Maybe, but I blame you for asking Connie.'

'You would.'

'Well, who else asked her? Be reasonable. I don't suppose James wanted to for one minute.'

Agnes fell silent, and Barry, slumped in the seat, appeared to brood. 'You're lacking in judgment, you know, Agnes. It surprises me, because you're such an intelligent woman – a writer of novels, no less. Yet you do such silly things.'

'At least two people said to me this evening that you seemed very fond of Rose.' Agnes had been determined not to bring it up, but it seemed to burst out from inside her.

'I am very fond of Rose,' Barry said. 'As you know, I was friendly with her for a number of years.'

'You looked intimate to me,' Agnes said jealously. 'You put a hand round her neck. Yet you always try to give me the impression you never see Rose at all.'

'Of course I see her! We meet every time we see the Calthorpes, and we see plenty of them. I think Keith's in grave trouble by the way.' Barry was glad to change the subject.

'Oh?'

'Apparently there's going to be an enquiry about some of the work he's been given. Thank God we never got involved.' Barry reached for his cigarettes and lit one, rolling it about in his mouth and half-closing his eyes. 'Who was that Roman somebody?'

'She's Connie's lover.' Agnes smiled to herself.

'Her *what*?'

'They're Lesbians.'

'Oh my God, I might have known Connie Shilton was a Lesbian as well as crazy. But Agnes, she used to have a man when you shared a flat with her.'

'Well, she's a proclaimed and unashamed Lesbian now!'

'And that girl and she ...'

'Yes.' Agnes felt rather pleased with the effect of her announcement.

'But she's so sexy!'

'Fancied her, did you? Well, I suppose people are entitled to their sexual inclinations, homosexual or otherwise.'

'The thought of them in bed together makes me feel sick. Connie Shilton. God.' Barry grimaced.

'Roman says she's crazy about her.' Agnes enjoyed rubbing it in.

Barry closed his eyes and leaned his head against the back of his seat. 'What she needs is a good prick,' he said.

CHAPTER TWENTY-TWO

A Time of Life, even Agnes had to admit, was a very slight story; but it was rich in atmosphere, which was what had appealed to James Hetherington when he first read it.

The story concerned the fortunes of a working woman who married in the Depression, produced three children and lived in a town like Beckersleigh, and it began shortly before the First World War and ended in the present day. This time scheme roughly coincided with the life of Agnes's mother, who had been born in 1912.

As is the custom with first novels for which the publishers do not hold out great commercial hopes, *A Time of Life* received little publicity, and the only review was in the *Beckersleigh Chronicle*. This, of course, was a glowing one, but it did little to sell the novel nationwide. By October 1969, five months after publication, the book had sold only eleven hundred copies, and in Leeds, Beckersleigh and elsewhere it was now unavailable. For a first novelist like Agnes, who knew little about the labyrinthine ways of publishing, it was all very disheartening. Although there had been an exchange of letters with her London editor, expressing mutual regard on both sides, Agnes had had no invitation to go and see him. All he had said was that he looked forward to seeing her next novel.

It all seemed very bleak and unsatisfactory and very much of an anticlimax. Agnes in fact began to wonder whether it was worth going on.

In 1969, the Prime Minister, Harold Wilson, at last decided to recognise the talent of the Member for Beckersleigh and appointed him Parliamentary Private Secretary to a safe and rather obscure Minister. It wasn't much, but Barry considered it a step in the right direction. If he went on agreeing with everything the government proposed and voting the right way, he reckoned he could expect a junior ministry before the next election.

Agnes rejoiced in Barry's good fortune, even though she knew he would be home even less than he was now. In the summer they went to Whitby as usual, and in October he returned to London for the opening of Parliament. As usual he had found the children irritating, the house untidy and Agnes's cooking unpalatable. He even went so far as to buy her a cookery book, saying she might find it useful, but she put in on one side with all the other unread books in the house, including *The Feminine Mystique*, which she had never returned to Roman.

When Barry went back to London a bleakness descended on Agnes. She felt cut off and isolated in her semidetached house, far from her parents, Grace or any of her friends. The crisis in Keith's business was mounting, and writs had begun to fly hither and thither like blossom petals in springtime.

One day, Agnes got out a fresh notebook, sharpened some pencils and wrote the date on the top of the page. Then she drew a line under it and sat there for some time before penning the opening words. Terry and Miranda were both at school now, and Christopher, who had always been the best behaved of her children, was playing quite happily at his mother's feet. It was a productive, happy day and by the time the children came home from school, Agnes felt more relaxed and tranquil than she had for some time.

The first event to mar this unusually carefree mood was when Terry refused to eat his tea and sat listlessly at table, complaining of a headache. She felt his brow and knew that he was feverish. Suddenly all the terror of isolation overwhelmed her. She could have been in a foreign country, on a desert island, on the other side of the world for all the comfort she drew from her all-too-familiar home. Darkness seemed to surround the house like an all-enveloping mist, cutting her off from neighbours and friends. She made a positive attempt to hide her fear, gave Terry a children's aspirin and put him to bed.

But during the night Terry got worse, not better. It was after midnight, and he had already been sick and was now complaining once more of a pain in his head; he also had difficulty moving his neck and kept on shading his eyes from the light. Agnes grew desperate and phoned the doctor, who came within twenty minutes. His diagnosis was almost immediate.

'I think it's meningitis, Mrs Holloway. We must get him to hospital at once.' He dialled there and then for the emergency ambulance. By this time the two other children were awake and crying, and it was impossible for Agnes to leave them to go to the hospital with Terry. She saw the ambulance off with a brave face and dry eyes, but then, weeping, dashed into the house to phone Barry. It was nearly 2 a.m.

In London, Barry's answering machine said he was out, but if the caller would leave name and telephone number he would call back. Agnes listened to the message twice and then phoned the House of Commons. She was told there had been no late-night sitting.

In desperation she called Grace, but there was no reply. She called Barry again, but the answering machine repeated its tiresome message. It was now three o'clock. She called the hospital and was told that Terry was as well as could be expected.

At last she called Connie. Connie said she'd come at once.

Connie arrived with Roman, a packed bag and an expression of sympathetic good humour. When she saw her, Agnes burst into tears. The girls took her inside and made her a cup of tea.

'I called Barry, he's not there. And Grace. Mum's not on the 'phone . . .'

'It's all right, love.' Connie patted her shoulder. 'Roman's going to take you to the hospital and I'll take over here.' She helped Agnes on with her coat and kissed her cheek. 'Stay as long as you like at the hospital. Everything'll be perfectly all right here, you see.'

'I'll send a message to Mum, first thing.'

Roman smiled and drew her into the car. 'What's the quickest way to the hospital?'

'I can't tell you how grateful I am.'

'You don't have to. Women's solidarity.'

'Yes, I suppose it is really, isn't it? When it comes to it, there are so few people you can really call on. I never felt as lonely and isolated in my life as I did tonight.'

Roman put a hand on hers and squeezed it.

By the morning, meningitis was confirmed, but it was thought that Terry was not seriously ill. Paul had come at dawn as soon as Roman arrived with the message, and Kathleen had taken over the house.

By eleven in the morning, Agnes, though desperately tired, was feeling less overwrought. She rang Grace at the office again, but was told that she was away in Manchester for two or three days.

'Why don't you go home and get some rest?' Paul said. 'Terry will be all right.'

'No, I want to be with him. Supposing his brain is affected? They say meningitis can damage the brain.'

'I've seen far worse cases in which the patient's made a complete recovery.' Paul sat on Terry's bed, looking at her. 'You look all in.'

Agnes wearily passed her hand over her face. 'I panicked last night. I felt so cut off, so isolated. I couldn't get you or Mum; Barry didn't answer; Grace was away.'

'What about the neighbours?'

Agnes shrugged. 'I felt I couldn't ask them. We had a row in the summer, because the kids annoyed them by straying into their garden. I've hardly got any friends on our estate. I suppose people think because I'm the wife of the MP, I'm a bit standoffish. I don't mean to be. I'm just so overworked.'

'Well, if you won't go home I'll ask Sister if you can lie down somewhere here.' Paul looked at his watch. 'I've got to get to my hospital. I'll come back tonight.'

'Barry should be here by then,' Agnes said. 'He must've had a dozen calls on his answering machine.'

When Agnes woke up in a small room off the children's ward, Barry was standing over her. She sat up quickly, immediately wide awake.

'What is it? Is Terry ...'

'Oh, he's fine.' Barry sat himself down on the edge of her bed. 'They say he's going to be OK. They seem more worried about you.'

Agnes heaved herself unsteadily off the bed. 'I was just exhausted.'

'You're too emotional! He's obviously not very ill.'

'You didn't see him last night, did you?' Agnes hunted for her bag. 'His temperature was 104 and rising. He was practically unconscious.'

'Kids run up high temperatures very quickly.'

'Oh, thank you, Doctor Spock.' Agnes got up and straightened her skirt. It was very creased, and so was her jumper. She knew she looked a sight, and the critical expression in Barry's eyes confirmed it. 'I was terrified, panic-stricken. I didn't know what he had and I had no one to turn to, nowhere to go.'

'There were your parents ...'

'They're not on the phone. And talking of phones, where were you?'

'There was a late-night sitting at the House. I didn't get home

275

until the small hours, and I was too tired to play back the machine so I left it until the morning.'

'I phoned the House, too. They said there was no late sitting,' she said flatly.

'They don't know everything, you know,' Barry replied gruffly. 'We had a committee that went on until nearly three.'

'The man I spoke to said emphatically that all the MPs had gone home.'

'Well, he was wrong!' Barry's voice began to rise. 'Are you suggesting I'm lying?'

'I don't know,' Agnes said. 'I don't know why you should be lying or what you've got to lie about. I want to go and see Terry.'

She went ahead of Barry into the ward. She felt no comfort at all in having him home, and the worry in her heart had suddenly been replaced by suspicion and doubt.

Keith Winchester sometimes thought – or rather, hoped – that one day he would wake and find that it had all been a bad dream. In his thirty-nine years he had never known real hardship, nor experienced any setbacks serious enough to make him pause and reflect. Until now ...

Henry Calthorpe had been droning on for about half an hour, or so it seemed, and Keith was no longer quite sure when he had begun, or what he was saying. He tipped his cigar ash in the crystal ashtray and studied his empty glass longingly, aware all the time of Grace's cold blue eyes across the table. Malcolm Longley was there, but not Elizabeth. It was a strictly business occasion, although the meal had been up to Rose's usual excellent standard. Shortly after dinner Rose had excused herself to go and visit Terry Holloway in hospital.

'... So Malcolm and I strongly suggest voluntary liquidation.' Henry put the palms of his hands on the sides of the table. 'There's very little that they'll get. When Grace joined the business I made certain provisions to safeguard her just in case something like this happened. Even so I've lost a packet.'

'Liquidation?' Keith started, the wine haze suddenly clearing. 'Did I hear you say liquidation?'

'We see no alternative. If they put you into compulsory liquidation, there's always the danger of an enquiry – and nobody wants that.'

'I'm not afraid of an enquiry!' Keith blustered. 'I've done nothing wrong. Let them liquidate. I'm not going to.'

'Oh, come now, Keith.' Malcolm tipped the brandy decanter into his glass. 'There are lots of little things that would do you no credit if they were generally known. You know that as well as I do. Little holidays, little gifts, that sort of thing.'

'But that's an accepted part of business practice!'

'It depends,' Malcolm said cautiously. 'It *could* be interpreted as attempting to bribe local government officials in order to get business. I think – we *all* think you should lie very low.'

'And what am I supposed to do?'

'Go away. Take a holiday. Make yourself unavailable.'

'In other words, get lost!'

'Exactly.'

Keith's eyes glittered. He grabbed the brandy decanter.

'Keith!' Grace's voice was cold and hard.

Keith glared at his wife. 'You keep out of this! I'm not a child to be told what to do, where to go or what to drink. I am a man of nearly forty years of age, who's fought hard to build a successful business career and made a lot of money. Do you think I'm going to give in? Let you and your father and his precious advisers take over? The Hell I am! I'm keeping all my businesses going and I'm going to run them just like I always did. To do that I want more money – a lot more. And you,' he jabbed a finger at Henry, 'are going to give it to me.'

'Let him speak, Dad.' Grace knew Keith was at the dangerous stage now; he had had enough drink to make him aggressive, but not enough to make him maudlin.

'Yes.' Keith sat back, sensing a captive, if reluctant audience. 'I need a *lot* more money. I want our debts paid off, our bad schemes scrapped and the good ones made viable. It can be done. With money.'

Malcolm shook his head.

'Keith, if you borrow money or are given money, the whole pack of cards is going to come tumbling down. You owe over a million pounds already! Any money you get now will be seized by your creditors. And you *can't* raise that sort of money without word leaking out. They'll all be after you.'

'He can afford it.' Keith jabbed a finger again at Henry.

'Henry has *not* got a million pounds,' Malcolm said. 'Nothing like it.'

'He can lay his hands on it.'

'Keith, I wouldn't let him if he could. He'd be throwing money away. You must take my advice; go into voluntary liquidation, *hope* that you get away without an enquiry, and then start again.'

'I'm not going to do it!' Keith poured himself a large brandy. 'And you can't force me. I'm the boss, and the majority of shares are mine. I can do what I like.'

Grace's voice was smooth as silk.

'You and *I* own the majority of shares, Keith.'

He waved an impatient hand. 'It's the same thing.'

'You're talking of us as one?'

'Of course.' Keith stared at her arrogantly.

'Well, we're not. We're separate identities – married, but two people. I agree with Daddy and Malcolm. It's a complete waste of money to try and save the business as it is. If we're lucky we'll be all right, but we've got a long hard climb ahead of us.'

'You mean you're in *favour* of liquidation?'

'I see no alternative. Luckily, because of the way Daddy and Malcolm arranged things, our personal fortune won't be affected, or rather mine won't be. We have the house, which is in my name, and the offices are only rented. Anyone liquidating the business will find very little in the kitty.'

Keith rose violently and banged the table, spilling his drink. 'I'm *not* going to give up! I don't want my name to smell. Let the Calthorpe name smell; let it stink to high Heaven! You're telling me that your father, one of the richest men in the North of England, let alone fucking Beckersleigh, won't raise a finger to help his own at a time like this? I tell you, that's something that would never happen in the East End where I came from. There everyone would rally round with support, dig into their pockets, mortgage whatever they owned. I tell you, there ...'

'Perhaps you should go back, then,' Grace said coldly. She had always hated Keith to refer to his working class background. 'Maybe looking after a barrow will calm you down for a while ...'

Keith rushed at Grace, but Malcolm Longley, anticipating his move, was there at the same time. Though small, he was strong, and he put his arms round Keith's waist in a wrestler's grip and joined them across his stomach.

'*Stop* it!'

Keith, caught by surprise, shut his eyes and for a moment leaned against Malcolm, his forhead covered with sweat, his breath jerky. Malcolm slowly relaxed his grip. For a long time no one spoke.

'That was a disgraceful display, Keith,' Grace said in the same level tones. 'I hope you'll apologise to Daddy before you go.'

'You shouldn't speak to me like that!'

'You shouldn't provoke me by defaming my family name. I happen to be proud of being a Calthorpe and I'm proud of Daddy and all he's done for me in the years I've been married to you. He's treated us with unstinting generosity and poured money into the business. He introduced you to everyone who was anyone in the North West. I grant you, you're not entirely to blame for the way things turned out. But when you started drinking so heavily, I knew you were finished. It's addling your brain, destroying your judgment. If you don't stop drinking, you'll not only be a failed businessman, but an alcoholic too. In fact, you're probably one already,' she finished wearily.

Keith appeared not to be listening. It was as though he was in shock. Grace continued:

'Now, I'm just saying this, Keith, before we go, in front of Daddy and Malcolm. If you don't do as they suggest, you'll be outvoted at the emergency board meeting which we'll call. Because I shan't vote with you. Without me, you're no longer a majority sharcholder. You and I are *not* one. We're two, thank God – two very different people.' She gazed at him witheringly and then picked up her bag. 'Now, for Christ's sake, let's go home!'

Rose looked at the sleeping child and tears slowly slipped down her cheek.

'He's all right now, Rose.'

'I know,' Rose whispered. 'Thank God.'

'Even if I'd been here, there's nothing I could have done.'

Rose nodded and said nothing.

'Let's go and have a drink,' he murmured. Rose bent and kissed Terry's cheek. Beside the bed was the Action Man she had bought him in London, complete with assorted gear and equipment. Barry steered Rose firmly and quickly out of the ward.

They drove out of Beckersleigh and stopped at a pub well off the main road.

'It isn't very nice,' Barry said, 'but at least we won't see anyone we know.' Rose sighed and got out of the car.

She didn't speak again until she had drunk almost half of her dry Martini.

'It *is* a dingy little place,' she said, shivering and looking round.

'Sorry, love.' Barry downed his beer, then wiped his mouth on the back of his hand. 'Well, he does seem much better. And he'll love that Action Man.'

Rose's lower lip started to tremble. 'I feel so *guilty*, Barry.'

'But why, Rose?' He took her hand and looked into her eyes. 'We couldn't possibly have known.'

'But supposing there had been something badly wrong – an accident ... you know?'

'Look, Rose, Agnes was perfectly able to cope, and anyway, Terry's going to be A1.'

'But the fact that we were *together*, enjoying ourselves. That you had to lie to her.'

'Of course I had to lie to her! That was just common sense. She doesn't know – she couldn't possibly know. Even if I'd been here, what use would I have been?'

'You could have supported Agnes.' Rose looked at him, but he avoided her eyes. 'I know how she'd feel, all by herself; being a mother, I know. You haven't got much of a conscience, have you?'

Barry's face clouded with anger. 'What's that supposed to mean?'

Rose lowered her eyes. 'I suppose neither of us have, if we're truthful. I never really think of it as deceiving Henry and Agnes. I don't know why. But when something happens ... Then ... then I *do* feel it's wrong.'

'Well, it isn't! Don't be so damn silly.' Barry looked at his watch. 'What time is this dinner party finishing?'

'Oh, I don't know. There's something serious afoot. I left them to it. I said I had to go to the hospital. I think they're going to force Keith to liquidate the business.'

Barry pursed his lips. 'Well, if he doesn't, someone else will. The hounds are beginning to bay. I only hope that if there's an enquiry it doesn't affect me.'

'But why should it? You haven't been in on any of his business activities, have you?'

Barry shifted. 'No, but his interests and mine did coincide. I wanted the new pool and the Enderby Estate cleared. The Left are all ganging up on me because of it now. If Keith goes bust and then there's an enquiry, it'd give them just the fuel they need. It could mean my seat if there's an election soon. I just hope Keith goes quietly, that's all.'

CHAPTER TWENTY-THREE

'BUT HOW DID HE MANAGE to lose a *million* pounds?' Agnes said with awe. 'I can't even imagine that sort of sum.'

'Oh, easy!' Grace lifted Christopher on to her lap. 'You have to invest an awful lot of money in large building projects before you get anything back. You have to pay architects, designers and draughtsmen even before you know you've got a deal. Then a lot of graft goes on. Keith's given away a small fortune greasing official palms – that's very confidential, of course, Agnes.

'After the '64 election there was a huge housing programme, but after Ronan Point the special government subsidy for high-rise schemes was withdrawn. Everyone began to ask questions. In the Middle East, the Arabs now want bigger people to build for them – companies that can undertake huge projects which we can't possibly compete for. Keith kept our size down on purpose, thinking we had enough to handle. Now, we're not big enough to compete – or small enough to survive.'

'I'm terribly sorry.' Agnes made a helpless gesture. 'Oh, that sounds such an inadequate thing to say!'

Grace hugged Christopher. Perhaps because she was indirectly responsible for him being born, Grace always felt an especial affinity with this youngest Holloway child, and he with her. She put her cheek against his and kissed him.

'This child's awfully like Barry. Pity!' Grace smiled ruefully. 'I feel he's mine, you know. I really feel you *are* my family. I'm so alienated from Keith. I can't stand Rose, and those horrid kids of hers bore me to death.'

'Rose went over to see Terry the other night and took him a toy. It was kind of her.' Agnes got up and went to the box containing Terry's Action Man. Terry himself was asleep upstairs, released from hospital the day before.

'Oh, she's kind enough,' Grace admitted grudgingly, glancing at the box. 'But how she knew he was ill if she was in London all that time, I don't know.'

'London?' Agnes stared at Grace.

'She bought that in Hamleys – look at the label. She came back from a few days in London last week – she was there while I was in Manchester.'

Agnes stared at the Hamleys label.

'Maybe someone from the house rang and told her.'

'But I didn't ring the house, did you?'

'No. Only yours and your office. Maybe she heard from your office.' Agnes's voice trailed away. 'But I never told your office why I wanted you . . .'

The two Graces looked at each other – the one Grace beautifully dressed, a smart, competent businesswoman, enjoying the role even though she was in the middle of a crisis; the second still beautiful, but more careworn, her face innocent of make-up, beginning to show a few lines.

'We know what we're thinking, don't we?'

Agnes turned towards the window. It was a dank November day and the moisture dripped to the ground from sodden weeds and bedraggled bushes. It was depressing inside as well as out. Everywhere there were piles of clothes, stacks of books, records and children's toys. The furniture was scratched and shabby, and the cloth from the last meal was still on the table.

Grace tried not to feel depressed when she came to Agnes's house, but she always was. Agnes, who was so neat in class, who had run an office so successfully, had been destroyed by Barry. He had warped her, taken the life from her. Yet, in its place, he had given her children. Grace's arms tightened round Christopher.

'You're suggesting that Barry and Rose meet in London?' Agnes turned, her hands in the pockets of her jeans. 'You could be right; they used to be lovers . . .'

'Barry and *Rose*?'

'Yes. I never told you.'

Grace turned in her chair, trying to take in the astonishing revelation. 'Why didn't you tell me?'

'Because of your father.' Agnes shrugged. 'I thought you might tell him.'

'You mean she and Barry . . . while my father was keeping her as his mistress?'

'Yes.'

'What a pair of bloody swines!' Grace said forcefully.

'He said she was good to him, that it was like having a mistress who was married.'

'But she wasn't married to my father then.'

'No; but he kept her.'

'And how long do you think they've been carrying on now?'

'Maybe they never stopped. Barry was pushed into marrying me, after all. Oh, I was passionate about him – but if I'm honest, I know he didn't feel as strongly as I did ...' Agnes slowly went over to the table and started to stack the objects on it as though she wanted something to do. 'If you start badly, you never manage to get things right. I'm always hoping that things will come right; but they never do. The relationship was one-sided from the beginning.'

'Because of Rose?'

'I realised that afterwards, when I knew about her.' Agnes went to the hatch and slid the dishes into the kitchen. 'Then she was going to marry your father, and I became pregnant. It never occurred to me that their affair would continue. Barry assured me that it had finished years before. Of course I *wanted* to believe him, so I did. Rose had Robert and Andrew – and Barry and I always had a good time in bed. It seemed to make up for a lot.'

'Even now?' Grace queried.

'Well ... yes.' Agnes leaned against the hatch. 'Yes, it eases the tension between us for a time. If we make love a lot, we feel better; we don't quarrel so much.'

'And then he goes off to London and screws Rose. Christ!'

'How often does Rose go to London?'

'About once a month, for about four or five days. But look, Agnes, we don't know for sure ... I mean, we could be quite mistaken.'

'I shan't say anything to Barry, anyway,' Agnes said wearily. 'I don't want to have yet another blessed row. He's going off again tomorrow, now that Terry's home. And he's been good, I must say.'

'Then I'd leave it.' Grace got up with Christopher and cradled him in her arms. 'He's getting terribly heavy, my baby.' She held him out to Agnes. 'I still envy you, you know. At least you've got these. Now that the business is on its knees, Keith and I have absolutely nothing to keep us togther, not even mutual respect.'

'But what'll Keith do now?'

'Well, right now he's in London trying to raise money. He won't succeed. When he comes back we'll have a board meeting and he'll be outvoted; so we'll go into voluntary liquidation.'

'And then?'

Grace smiled. 'I have plans,' she said enigmatically. 'I rather fancy business, you know. I think I'm good at it, but not with him round my neck.'

Just as Agnes was seeing Grace to the door, the phone rang. Grace waved goodbye, but Agnes urgently shook the phone at her and signalled to her to stay.

Finally Agnes put the phone down and wrapped both arms round Christopher.

'It's the pool,' she said. 'It's spilling all over Beckersleigh High Street. There's been a crack.'

The crack in Calthorpe Pool caused no immediate danger to anyone, although crowds flocked with amazement and some pleasure to see the spillage, as it leaked from a large crack in the lower wall of the baths and clogged up the gutters in the High Street. The whole complex was closed until further notice.

Grace and Agnes, who had left Christopher with a reluctant neighbour, watched the proceedings from one of the administrative offices in the sports complex. Both inside and outside the building there was chaos.

All those who had been in the bath when it started to leak were interviewed. They gave graphic accounts of how they had been rushed out of the bath by attendants, who seemed to be expecting some kind of massive disaster any moment, which not unnaturally induced a good deal of panic among the bathers. Some embellished their stories and claimed they had felt themselves being steadily sucked under – which was nonsense, but made good copy when it appeared later in the *Chronicle*.

Grace said little during the day, and when her father came to pick her up, Agnes went to collect the children from school. She gave them an early tea and put them to bed, and by the time Barry came home she was making dinner. As usual he was late, and fuming about the way the whole thing had been blown up for the benefit of his political opponents.

'Surely they didn't do it deliberately?' Agnes put his plate before him.

'Who did what deliberately?' He started eating before she sat down.

'Sabotaged your pet project. I was waiting for you to blame Connie and Jeff.'

Barry salted his dinner. 'I wouldn't put it past them.'

Agnes sat down and stared at her plate. Next day he was leaving for London ... She had to know. She wiped her sweaty palms on her knees and looked at the congealing food.

'Barry, are you still having an affair with Rose Calthorpe?'

'Oh Christ!' Barry put down knife and fork with a crash. 'Why on earth do you want to bring that up?'

'Because I want to know!' Her voice was ragged.

'The answer is I'm *not* having an affair. There! Satisfied?' Barry belched and reached for his cigarettes.

'I'd like to think you were telling the truth.'

'Well, I am. I am *not* having an affair with Rose Calthorpe!'

'But you do see her in London?'

She was watching his eyes to see whether they looked at her or avoided her. They avoided her.

'No I don't.'

Agnes got up and produced the Action Man. Barry stared at it, then at Agnes.

'Well?'

'Rose bought this for Terry – in a shop in London.'

'So what?'

'How did she know that Terry was ill?'

'Search me.' He shrugged.

'Because you told her, Barry! It's the only way she could have known. I phoned you and told you in London, and you told Rose.'

'Somebody else could have told her.'

'No.' Agnes shook her head. 'Only you.'

'All right, then, I saw Rose in London.' Barry leaned back and looked at her through a pall of smoke.

'But why?'

'Because we're friends, old friends. You know that – I've never hidden it from you. But an affair? No!'

'I wish I could believe you.'

'*Why* is it so important, Agnes?'

'Because you would have mentioned it before if you hadn't felt guilty. I ...'

To her horror, Agnes felt the tears coming. She was filled with panic, and realised now how badly she had wanted him to deny it. She bent down, but the tears trickled down her face. Through a salty mist she was aware of Barry getting up and coming over to her.

'You deliberately upset yourself, Agnes.' He put a hand on her shoulder and she could feel his warm breath near her face.

'I didn't want to know the truth. I hoped it wasn't true.'

'But you know the truth. I've told you the truth.'

'But why should you want to see her?' She was almost pleading.

'Because I like her. We meet for a chat now and again. I didn't mention it to you because of the past – I knew you'd get the wrong idea. That's all there is to it. Really.'

Suddenly there were no more tears. She felt weak and vulnerable in the face of this implacable, detached man full of self-confidence and charm. The gulf between men and women had never seemed so wide to her as it was now. But tears couldn't help. 'I wish I could believe you,' she said, distantly. 'I really wish I could.'

The crack in the pool seemed to seal the fate of Keith Winchester. There was an immediate demand for an enquiry into how a pool not two years old could crack in this way, and this, of course, involved Winchester and all his enterprises.

Sam Armstrong made it a personal crusade, and his fierce attacks appeared every day in the *Chronicle* under banner headlines.

When, later that week, Keith Winchester arrived in Beckersleigh, reporters followed him all the way home.

It was the worst week of Grace's life, but she knew she would survive it. She was a survivor, and the very awfulness of the situation helped her to discover her own strengths. At the end of the week Grace voted against her husband and for the voluntary liquidation of all his business concerns. Keith left the room before the meeting ended, evaded the waiting reporters and disappeared.

'He's probably buried himself in some pub,' she said to her father. 'And he's taken the car.'

'I'll drive you back, darling.' Henry looked at her anxiously. 'I can ring Rose from your place.'

Grace signed all the papers with a sense of relief. Everything would be taken out of her hands. It was now the concern of the advisers her father had had all his life – solid, practical people who knew just what to do, who would protect the Calthorpe name as far as was possible from the damage wrought by outsiders like Keith Winchester.

Malcolm Longley gave them sherry; then Grace and her father had a meal at a restaurant. Neither was hungry and the meal was soon over. There was still no sign of Keith's car as they drove into the drive at about half-past nine.

'He'll soon be back,' Grace said as she switched on the lamps in the drawing room. 'Sometimes I wish he'd just go for ever.'

Henry Calthorpe helped himself to a whisky and sat down in the seat by the fire. He reached out a hand, and Grace took it in hers.

'I'm sorry, Daddy.'

'*You're* sorry, darling? It isn't your fault. You've got nothing to reproach yourself with.'

'Except, perhaps, marrying Keith Winchester.' Grace let go her father's hand and helped herself to whisky and a cigarette. 'That was my first and greatest mistake.'

'Well I must admit Stephen Hetherington's done well. Since his father died he's run that business magnificently. I knew he was a solid boy.'

'Oh, Dad! Don't rub it in! To me, it was Keith who had all the marks of success, not Stephen. How on earth was I to know he'd be such a failure, both as a husband and a businessman?'

Henry drank his whisky, frowning into it. 'And has he failed you as a husband, Grace?'

'Of course he has failed me as a husband!' Grace blew smoke into the air. 'Our sex life has been terrible. I longed for children, and he couldn't give them to me. I've spent at least half my married life at some clinic or the other.'

'But that's not really Keith's fault, is it, Grace?' her father said diffidently. 'Keith told me he would have liked children, too. He said his dream was to have a successful business, marry a girl like you and have a family. He always wanted to send his sons to Winchester. He had it all planned.'

'He never told me.' Grace sounded surprised. 'Well, he said he'd like children, but nothing about Winchester. I wonder why Winchester?'

'Because of the name, I suppose. Keith talked to me quite a lot, you know, Grace. Before all this, before he started drinking, I liked him. I felt sorry for him because I always thought you were a bit impatient with him, so ratty with him in public. But I couldn't get through to him in the end. And I'm sorry. I'm very sorry it had to end this way. But no doubt you'll both pull through. Would you like me to wait until he gets home?'

'Oh no! He'll be drunk,' she said contemptuously, 'and he'll go to bed and sleep it off. I'll be all right.'

'Come back and stay with me.'

'No, I'll be fine, Dad. I've got to talk to Keith, anyway. There's obviously going to be an enquiry and I think the more open he is the better. After all, we know he hasn't done anything criminal. Stupid, perhaps, but not criminal. He'll just have to face the music.' She lifted her head, looking directly into her father's eyes. 'I think we'll probably get divorced when it's all over, Dad, I might as well warn you. I no longer love Keith – and I don't want to be associated with failure.'

'It makes you sound very hard, Grace.' Henry's voice was soft but unsurprised.

Grace joined her hands in her lap and leaned towards her father. She had on a tweed suit of red and grey check and a pale grey cashmere sweater. Her smooth gold hair gleamed in the light of the sconces on the wall above her head. She looked poised and attractive, a mature woman of great charm.

'You've got to be hard in this world, Daddy. Well, not hard exactly – but tough.'

'But what is it you want?' Henry drew on his cigar and looked at his daughter in bewilderment.

'I want to be successful, Daddy. I want to be someone. I'm a Calthorpe, but I never made much of that when I had the chance. I was bright – I could have gone to University, but I didn't. I had no real interest in men or sex, but I pretended I did because I didn't know what else to do and their interest flattered me. I married Keith because I thought I could bask in his glory; that we'd be wealthy and happy and successful, and that we'd have children quite effortlessly to enhance this image I had of what our life should be like.

'Well, nothing's come out right, has it? I've done the Calthorpe name no good at all. But when all this has blown over, I plan to start again. I intend to start a new business of my own. I've a flair for interior decoration and design, and I'll deal with the rich – with those who can afford to pay. There'll be no risk.' Her eyes were shining with enthusiasm. 'What do you think, Daddy?'

'It's a good idea,' her father said, admiringly. 'I take my hat off to you, Grace. You never admit defeat, do you?'

'Never, Daddy. And I never shall,' Grace said triumphantly, smiling her odd, feline smile.

After her father left, Grace had a leisurely bath and took a long time over her face, massaging cream into her clear skin, glad that it was still firm, supple and youthful. She searched for lines by the side of her eyes and mouth. Agnes had some very deep ones, but she could find none. That pleased her.

By the time she got into bed it was nearly two and she turned on the radio and listened to some light music, half-wishing she had gone to her father's after all. But that would have meant looking helpless in front of Rose, and she didn't want that – not Rose, that scheming bitch who had got what she wanted out of her father while deceiving him on the side. *That* was a bit of information she had carefully stored away and would use as soon as the opportunity presented itself.

She was dozing when she heard the car pull up outside the garage. She listened for the doors to open, but they didn't. He was going to leave the car in the drive. Her throat felt dry and she realised she was tense.

It was a long time before she heard the front door open. Instead of banging it behind him, as she had expected him to, he closed it quite gently. She heard lights go on downstairs and then, to her surprise, the door of the drawing room being shut. Swiftly, Grace got out of bed and put on her robe. She wasn't going to stay up here while Keith spent the night drinking himself into a stupor downstairs.

She found Keith slumped in a chair, glass in hand, the whisky bottle on the floor by his side. Grace scooped up the bottle and put it back in the drinks cabinet. Keith didn't say a word.

'I think you should come to bed, Keith.'

'What for?'

She turned round, and his face shocked her. He seemed to have aged ten years in the space of a few hours. There was a damp stain on his jacket and one lower down on his trousers. She realised he was very drunk.

'A night's sleep will do you good, Keith.' She spoke gently.

'What the Hell do you care?' His voice was quite normal, but she wasn't deceived.

'Of course I care!' Grace sat down opposite him and pulled her robe around her legs, while he stared at her, trying to focus his eyes on her crotch. 'Keith, I know it's been bad, but it's all over now. There's nothing more you can do. We've signed papers giving Malcolm powers of attorney. He'll appoint a liquidator and ...'

'It isn't over!' Keith said harshly. 'Not by a long chalk! They're going to tear me apart; they're going to examine every cheque I ever signed, every bill I ever presented, every piece of work I ever did. How can you say it's over?'

'Keith, if you trust Malcolm ...'

'I don't trust Malcolm!' Keith suddenly got to his feet and went quite steadily over to the bottle. He finished what was in his glass and refilled it. Grace didn't try to stop him, but she noticed with inner alarm that he moved in that awful automatic way that so often preceded violence. 'And I don't trust you or your fucking father. From the day I brought you into my business you've plotted against me. Things started to go wrong from the day you came in.' His voice was rising hysterically.

'That's not true, Keith!' Grace suddenly felt very frightened. 'I wanted to help you. The business expanded after I came in and Daddy put up more capital.'

'But not enough! There was never enough. There was just enough for me to ruin myself!'

'Oh, that's ridiculous!' She lost patience. 'For Christ's sake, stop drinking and come to bed.'

'What will we do in bed? Make love?' Keith slowly came over to her and stood towering over her. 'Is that what you want, Grace, a good screw?'

'Well, I won't get it from you, will I?'

The words sprang to Grace's lips, and she regretted them as soon as they were out of her mouth. He reached over and jerked her to her feet, pulling her close. She could smell the drink on his breath, see the cruel, desperate glimmer in his eyes.

'Keith!' She clawed desperately at his hands. 'Don't let this get out of control. Please!'

'It's already out of control,' Keith said quite calmly. 'Everything's out of control. And I blame you. Before I met you I was successful. I even made love well,' he said conversationally. 'D'you know, I had a woman in London – and she never complained about the way I made love. I even had a child by her. So it *wasn't* my

291

fault we didn't have any, was it? It was *your* fucking fault and yours alone! There was, is, *nothing* wrong with me.'

As Grace opened her mouth, he slapped her across the cheek.

'... But I had to endure all those stupid examinations, just to please you. I knew I was all right. I almost told you, but I didn't know what effect it'd have on you. But there was nothing wrong with me; it was you, all that time. *You, you, you.*' Keith started to shake her in time with each word.

'I never came too quickly, either, with the other woman. It wasn't till I met you that my sexual ability got fouled up. Like my business. I couldn't fuck you properly, and I couldn't make my business succeed. And all because of *you.*'

She opened her mouth again, and once more he hit her. Then he released his grasp, spun her round, taking the robe off as he did so, and caught her again. Holding her by the shoulders, he pulled her to him, his mouth clamping down on hers, his teeth grinding against her clenched ones.

Suddenly Grace opened her mouth and bit his tongue violently. She felt an acrid spurt of blood in her mouth and saw blood trickle on to his chin. Keith gave a cry of pain and let her go, raising a hand to his mouth. His eyes flamed suddenly, and she turned to run towards the door.

'You're going to pay for that, you bitch!' Keith shouted and lurched after her, catching her as she struggled desperately with the door.

'Keith, please, *please*! You'll kill me!' She was terrified, hysterical.

'I don't care if I do!'

Roughly he broke the straps of her nightgown, pulling it down round her ankles. For a moment he backed away from her and his eyes roved lasciviously over her body. His tongue was still bleeding, the blood dripping onto the front of his tan shirt. Slowly he undid his trousers.

'Get on the floor!' he said.

'Keith!' She was weeping, her hands twisting together in despair. 'I beg you ...'

'I said lie on the floor! If you don't, I really will kill you.'

Later, Grace remembered that she had looked round the room as though seeing everything afresh, but for the last time. She lay on the floor, her legs close together, and shut her eyes.

Keith, completely naked now and with blood streaming from his mouth, took hold of Grace's legs, wrenching them so wide apart that he could hear her groin crack, and plunged into her with agonising force.

The people who lived in the house on the other side later claimed they heard a scream. But unable to believe that anything untoward could happen in the Winchesters' home, they went back to sleep again.

Grace got to her father's house shortly before dawn. She couldn't remember the journey, or how she had got into the car. She'd wrapped the torn nightgown round her bruised body, tucking it between her legs to try and staunch the blood; but as she stood on the threshold of the Calthorpe home, it dripped on to the carpet and Rose, who saw her first, almost fainted.

By the time the doctor came, Grace was calmer. She lay in the bed in her old, familiar room, her right cheek bruised, a purple circle forming round her eye. The doctor had had to stitch the outside of her vagina, like a tear in childbirth, and had given her a heavy shot of penicillin.

'He'll have to be arrested, Grace.' Henry could hardly speak for shock and anger. 'We'll have to call the police.'

Doctor Spencer nodded.

Grace lay back and stared at the ceiling. 'This isn't going to the police or anyone else outside this family,' she said quietly, intensely. 'I won't go back to Keith, but I won't take him to Court. You can tell him to leave here or whatever you like, but I don't want to see him again.'

Grace closed her eyes, while Rose carefully, tenderly, drew the sheets up to her chin. For the first time Rose felt close to her stepdaughter. She was a woman, like her. And a man's lust had done this to her.

Later the three of them went to the house: Henry, Rose and Doctor Spencer.

Henry had Grace's key and unlocked the door. It was very still inside, and Rose felt a tremor of fear. From the hall they could see into the drawing room: the chairs knocked over, Keith's scattered clothes, and the large bloodstain on the floor where he had violated his wife. Henry felt surprisingly calm, but the smell of blood and drink was ghastly and made him want to retch.

'Well, he's not here,' he said thankfully.

'He's probably gone to sleep,' Doctor Spencer said. 'Where's the bedroom?'

Henry pointed upstairs. Rose said she would wait while they spoke to Keith.

Dr Spencer told Henry to wait outside the bedroom door; but Henry went in with him. The bedroom was empty and the bed had obviously not been slept in. But the bathroom told a different tale.

Keith Winchester lay across the bath, his head half severed by a barber's razor that had fallen by his side onto the tiled floor. Even after the passage of several hours, the blood still dripped from his head into the bath, as though from a tap with a leak.

CHAPTER TWENTY-FOUR

COUNCILLOR WILLIAM ADAMS, Chairman of the General Management Committee of the Beckersleigh Labour Party, rose to his feet and looked round the packed room. He adjusted his glasses and consulted the document in his hand.

'Comrades,' he said, 'we are here this evening for the purpose of readopting our candidate for the General Election, the Member of Parliament for this constituency, Mr Barry Holloway.' One or two people put their hands together and politely clapped.

It was hardly a storm, Barry thought, raising his head to see who they were. But then, he didn't expect it. The individual Wards of the Beckersleigh Labour Party had been solidly infiltrated by left-wing members – the New Left, as some of them liked to call themselves. All of them were opposed to the politics of Harold Wilson and indirectly, his faithful henchman, Barry Holloway. Even so, the number of hostile faces surprised him.

'This readoption is a mere formality, comrades,' Bill Adams continued, 'but, as you know, we're required to readopt our candidate, who ceases to represent us in Parliament when a General Election is announced and offers himself for re-election. Now, do I have someone to propose that Mr Barry Holloway is adopted as the official Labour Party candidate for Beckersleigh for the election to be held on June the eighteenth?'

Councillor Adams removed his spectacles as a hand shot up. 'Mr Jones? Thank you. Mr Holloway is proposed by Harold Jones of Grafton Ward. Do I have a seconder? Thank you. Seconded by James Shuttleworth of Berryhill Ward. Now, could we proceed to the vote, please? Those in favour ...'

'Point of order, Comrade Chairman!'

Connie Shilton, sitting in the back row, got to her feet.

'I don't think a point of order is in order, Miss Shilton,' Councillor Adams said sternly. 'We're about to take a vote.'

'It's the vote I wish to protest against, Comrade Chairman. I wish to speak to the proposal that Mr Barry Holloway is adopted as our parliamentary candidate.'

Barry glared at Connie Shilton, who was staring at the Chairman with that determined, fanatical little half-smile he knew so well. She looked like a pig, he thought. A pretty pig, because she had a nice face; but still a pig with her fat, uncared-for body. So this was Connie's revenge! This was what was at the back of all the rumours he had heard about plans to unseat him. Only the election had taken everybody by surprise.

The elections to the Greater London Council in April had shown a modest swing to Labour. The Tories had lost control of the Inner London Education Authority and the national opinion polls seemed to suggest that the swing would continue. Wilson had decided to go for a snap election. Which explained why Barry found himself, in May 1970, facing a readoption meeting which was usually a formality.

Connie was still arguing with the Chairman. She had been joined now by several others, also on their feet, and the meeting began to assume the aspect of a minor brawl.

But then a figure who always commanded respect at GMC meetings stood up and made himself heard. Albert Rivington silenced the meeting, and Connie Shilton and several others abruptly sat down.

'Comrade Chairman,' Albert said, pushing his cap to the back of his head. 'May I suggest that, in accordance with our constitution, this meeting is entitled to debate the proposal that Mr Holloway should be adopted as our parliamentary candidate at the next election?' There was a murmur of approval, but Albert held up his hand and looked behind him to Connie. 'But ... *But*, Comrade Chairman, I move that, also in accordance with procedure, the candidate be asked to leave the room while this matter is discussed.'

'That's out of order, Comrade!' Councillor Adams frantically waved the papers in his hands. 'The constitution is quite clear that if there's a debate on the adoption procedure, the candidate should remain in the room.'

'Hear, hear!' voices yelled.

'I second that.'

Bedlam threatened to erupt again. But Albert Rivington remained imperturbable, still keeping his place on the floor, his cap perched on the back of his head, his mouth pursed, waiting for silence.

'May I suggest, *with* respect, Comrade Chairman, that whatever the constitution says or does not say, we of the Beckersleigh Labour Party have the power to do as we think fit and ask the candidate to leave the room?'

'Put it to the vote!' someone shouted. Three-quarters of those present raised their hands. Barry got up and attempted to speak.

'I have the right, Comrades . . .' But Bill Adams pulled him down and whispered:

'Would you leave the room, Barry? It's not an order, and if the vote goes against you we can always refer it to the Party Headquarters. But you see the mood. It might be best. I think Albert's got a card or two up his sleeve.'

Barry wavered. But it was true: if anyone could bring the meeting to order, it was his father-in-law. His own presence seemed to be acting only as an irritant.

'All right, Bill, I'll go; but if you ask me, our comrades from the Left have some cards up their sleeves, too!'

'Don't worry, we'll get shut of them.'

'I'm not worried.'

Barry got to his feet and strolled towards the door, fishing his cigarettes out of his pocket in a leisurely manner, just to show everyone how unruffled he was. Outside, he slumped against the wall and lit his cigarette. He felt far less confident than he hoped he looked.

'Trouble?' There were a few chairs in the corridor outside the committee rooms and one of them was occupied by a girl. Barry vaguely recognised her. She wore jeans and a man's shirt, a long cardigan over her shoulders. Her ash-blonde hair was tied in a thick plait down her back and she wore no make-up. She looked like a boy – an attractive, handsome boy. 'You don't remember me, do you?' she said.

'The face is familiar.' Barry frowned and went over to her. 'Are you a friend of my wife's?'

'Roman Payne.' Roman held out a hand.

'Oh yes! You took Terry to hospital. Thanks very much.'

'That's all right. How is he?'

'Oh, he's fine.' Barry sat down beside her. She looked vaguely like Grace Winchester, he thought. Then he remembered where he'd seen her. 'You were at Agnes's publication party last year.'

'That's right.'

'Yes, I remember now.' Barry exhaled and looked at her consideringly through the smoke. 'We had a long chat.'

'About women's liberation.'

'Oh, Christ! Yes, that.'

'Still don't care for it, Mr Holloway?'

'What? Women's liberation? I don't really think it's necessary. My wife's a very liberated lady. At least, she seems to do just as she pleases.'

'It isn't really about doing as you please. It's about the right of women to be equal with men. In many things they're not. It's about justice.' Her voice was impassioned.

He shrugged. 'I think you go about it the wrong way.'

'You mean we're too strident? People like saying that. Stridency implies masculinity; they enjoy putting us down for that.'

'Well, I agree with them in a way. If you were more subtle ...'

'Subtlety didn't get women the vote in this country or America.'

'No, you've got a point; but I don't really think women are oppressed. Why, Agnes ...'

'Don't let's talk about specifics, Mr Holloway.' Roman uncrossed her legs and felt in her breast pocket for her cigarettes. She had good breasts, Barry thought irrelevantly. The packet she produced was crumpled and she held it out to him. 'Will you have one? As a *sisterly* gesture?' Her mocking eyes suddenly seemed a challenge. Reaching forward, he took a cigarette.

Inside the committee room, Albert listened while Connie Shilton vilified Barry's Westminster record; then he stood, clenched his thin hands together, paused, coughed and thrust his head in the air.

'Comrade Chairman, I haven't spoken before, because Comrade Holloway, whom we're discussing, is not only our candidate but he's my son-in-law, the father of my three grandchildren. But I'm not here to discuss him in that capacity.' Albert paused and glared around him. 'What we've heard today is a scandalous attack on a man who has never shirked in his duty to the people. And it's the more scandalous because it's based on nothing but rumour and innuendo!' Albert consulted a paper on which he had made notes. 'Comrade Holloway is not attacked because of his politics or his voting record in the House of Commons – though that comes into it,

I grant you – but mainly because he is thought – *thought*, mark you – to have been implicated in some scandal involving the late Keith Winchester. Now what is the nature of that scandal?' Albert raised both arms like a biblical prophet and looked about him. 'We're not told. There was an inquest when Mr Winchester died, and his suicide was *thought* to be connected with some irregularities in his business affairs. *Thought* to be. But there was also the suggestion that he and his wife were unhappy together. The verdict was suicide while the balance of the mind of the deceased was disturbed ...'

'What about the enquiry!' someone shouted from the back.

Albert silenced the caller with a glance.

'I'm coming to that. An enquiry has been instituted by the Board of Trade into *supposed* irregularities in the late Keith Winchester's business affairs. But what has come to light?' Albert paused for effect. 'Nothing! Certainly nothing that implicates Mr Holloway, who volunteered to appear before the committee of enquiry. He wasn't summoned, he *volunteered*. Subsequently the committee apologised for taking up his time. Now, that enquiry is still going on; but it has nothing at all to do with Barry Holloway and by suggesting that it has, you, Connie Shilton, are committing a calumny. You are taking away the good name of a man who ...'

'What about nuclear disarmament?' Connie shouted. 'He's sold us out to the Americans!'

'Then so has Harold Wilson and Jim Callaghan and Roy Jenkins. All these men support the official party line on defence. Barry Holloway is a loyal party man. And it's on those grounds that I move he be readopted. Those, and none other. Let smear, innuendo and false accusations be banished from this campaign, and let it be a good and fair one!'

As Albert sat down, coughing, over half the room stood up to applaud. He knew he had won the day.

For all her toughness and determination, Grace often wondered, looking back, how she had managed to survive the six months since Keith's suicide. It was not only the knowledge that her husband had raped her and then killed himself that she had to live with, but also that he was a failure and probably dishonest as well. And thanks to the inquest, her private life was now very much public property.

The coroner, who was a great personal friend of the Calthorpe family, had done his best to conceal the more unsavoury details, but as Keith had left no note, the reasons for his suicide and all the circumstances surrounding it had to be explored. The rape, the mutilation, the fact that Grace had subsequently to enter hospital for further emergency gynaecological surgery, couldn't be hidden. For many weeks the Calthorpe name had hardly been off the front pages of the *Chronicle* or the other Yorkshire papers, including the *Post*. It even made the inner pages of the national press, page three of the *Daily Telegraph* treating its readers to a detailed report of the inquest.

When it was all over, Grace went with Rose and the children to the Canary Islands to rest and recuperate. She would have preferred Agnes as a companion, but Barry sensed that an election was in the offing and refused to let her go. Grace didn't really want Rose or the children to come, but she couldn't bear to be on her own, with only her own thoughts for company.

When she came home, she stayed on with her father and never returned to the house at Whitley again. But being a Calthorpe didn't protect you from those terrible, frightening thoughts and dreams.

Now she was beginning to feel sufficiently recovered to start looking for a flat, for premises for her new business. She also attended Barry's final meeting before the election.

The hall was packed, and Barry had hardly been able to make himself heard above the catcalls and barracking. The campaign hadn't gone well: government policies were attacked time and time again from all quarters, and Malcolm Longley had got all the big guns up from London to speak on behalf of the Conservatives, pressing home the message that a Labour government was disaster for the country and that the Labour Party was too torn by internal divisions to govern.

Agnes was on the platform behind Barry, looking anxious and wincing every time he had to sit down because he couldn't be heard. Grace glanced at Paul, who was sitting next to her.

'I don't think he's going to get in, do you?' she whispered.

Paul grimaced. 'The polls are backing Labour, but I don't know about Barry.'

'Perhaps I shouldn't have come tonight. I should have stayed away,' Grace said unhappily.

'Barry's done nothing wrong!' Paul hissed. 'And neither have you. You've as much right to be here as anyone else.'

A warm, unexpected feeling of gratitude welled up inside Grace. She looked at Paul again, seeming to see a new man – firm and strong and reliable. A decisive man: a surgeon.

Afterwards Paul took his father and mother home, having asked Grace to join him for a drink.

'The Huntsman's Arms?' he suggested.

Grace shivered. 'Oh no. Not that place. It has bad memories for me.'

'I'm sorry. I know, we'll go to The George at Brakely. We might get a sandwich, too. I'm starving.'

Paul put his car into gear while Grace looked up at the block where he had left his parents.

'It looks terribly deserted.'

'Well, people live there, but sometimes you wouldn't think so. I don't even know how the vandals do their work, because no one ever sees anyone else. I'm going to try and buy a house and move my parents there. I think it's making them both ill.'

'Oh Paul, I'm so sorry.' Grace put a hand on his arm and was rewarded by one of his rare, brilliant smiles.

'I've always liked you, you know,' Grace said later, half in banter, as they sat in the bar of The George over sandwiches and a bottle of Beaujolais. She felt she could say something like that to him because she knew him so well; perhaps also because of her relationship with Agnes. 'Do you remember that night we went dancing?'

Paul shook his head apologetically. 'I'm afraid not.'

Grace pouted. 'I'm a bit offended.'

'Oh, don't be offended.' Paul grinned and sat back. 'I thought you were stunning, way out of my class. It isn't that I didn't notice you then – I just don't remember that particular night. I was very shy then, you know. And I knew nothing about girls.' He shrugged deprecatingly. 'I'm afraid I know very little even today – about women, that is.'

His dark hair, thick and curly like Agnes's, was flecked with grey and white at the sides. Yet he could only be about thirty-four or so. He had a thin, ascetic face, but sensual lips ... A tiny frisson went through her.

'You'll have to marry, Paul,' she said lightly.

'Why?' He looked at her directly.

Grace, to her astonishment, found herself blushing. Confused, she put her hands deep into the pockets of her camel-hair coat on the pretext of looking for her cigarettes.

'Well, most people do – for one reason or another.'

'Most of them not very happily,' Paul said gently, lighting the cigarette she had taken from her silver case. 'By the way, you should stop smoking, you know. If you could see the lungs of a lung cancer victim ...'

'Oh don't!' Grace drew on her cigarette and laughed. She had lovely teeth, Paul thought, and the long earrings she wore these days seemed to jangle with merriment. The moment of laughter made them both aware of the special way they were gazing at each other. As he abruptly looked away, Grace stopped smiling and the intimate spell was suddenly broken.

'You were saying "not very happily"?' she queried.

Paul refilled their glasses. 'Well, most people I know don't seem very happily married. Take Agnes ...'

'She looked terrible tonight, I thought.' Grace still felt excited by his glance and nervously stubbed her cigarette out, realising that she wanted to please him.

'Yes, but that was because Barry was having a bad time at the meeting. What'll they do if he loses?'

'I suppose go on living,' Grace said, looking at Paul. 'I have.'

She had a hand in her lap and he wanted to touch it, to press it and reassure her that she was still a beautiful woman, that she would still love and be loved despite what she had been through; but it was too early, too fragile a beginning. He looked at her hand and she followed his glance. She opened her palm and he took it; her fingers closed over his.

'You've had a terrible time, Grace,' he said softly. 'I shouldn't have said what I did about marriage.'

'I know you didn't mean me; but it was bad all the same. If only it hadn't ended like that ...' Grace's eyes filled with horror, and Paul brought her hand to his lips.

'I know. Don't talk about it.'

'But talking helps! I can't complain that I've lacked friends, though. Agnes was wonderful – she was there every day at the inquest. Even Rose has grown on me; she couldn't have given more support to me and Daddy, and she was marvellous when I arrived on the doorstep after ... it happened. Did you know I'm starting a new business?' Raising her voice to simulate gaiety, Grace let her hand fall to her lap, still entwined in his. 'Grace Calthorpe Designs Ltd.'

'Calthorpe?' Paul looked at her in surprise.

'Calthorpe.' Grace nodded her head. 'I always think of myself as a Calthorpe, you know. The "Calthorpe girl" they used to call me, whatever they had to say – good or bad. "The Calthorpe girl is brainy", "the Calthorpe girl is scatty", or whatever.'

'The Calthorpe girl strips off,' Paul thought, but he said nothing.

'Besides,' Grace continued, 'I want to banish everything to do with Winchester. That part of my life is over now, and I want to bury it.'

'Can you completely bury the past?' Paul tightened his grip on her hand.

'I think you can try. Changing your name is one way.'

Paul nodded. 'Was it always so unhappy? Your marriage, I mean.' He studied her eyes as she weighed her reply.

'Well, not at the beginning. We had quite a lot of happiness really, until about two years ago, when Ronan Point happened. Our marriage was so tied up with the business and when that went ...' She shook her head. 'Anyway, the important thing is that I'm starting again. I'm taking the lease of a shop on the High Street, and it's going to be *terribly* elegant – just a yard or two of cloth and an urn.'

'It sounds like a funeral parlour!' Paul laughed, and Grace responded instantly. She couldn't believe how happy this man made her, how joyful.

Malcolm Longley, who had fought a good and honest campaign, won by over three thousand votes, almost the same margin that Barry had had in the previous election.

It was a devastating setback for Barry. It was so unexpected – and so unnecessary, because Barry had been convinced that the election was a mistake in the first place. He felt a deep bitterness about it – against Wilson, against the voters, but most of all against Connie Shilton, Jeff Orchard and their friends, who he felt had deliberately undermined him throughout his campaign. Whatever was said, or carefully not said, Barry was convinced that the Winchester business had been dragged into the election and had obscured the real issues.

In the mood of bitterness and recrimination that possessed him during the bleak days after the election, he blamed not only the Calthorpes, the Winchesters and the Left of the Labour Party, but also Sam Armstrong, who had been blatantly prejudiced against him and whose daily column in the *Chronicle* had constantly urged the citizens of Beckersleigh that it was time for a change.

But worst of all, like so many unseated candidates, Barry was at a total loss to know what to do. He had no job; all he was entitled to was three months' parliamentary pay, and after that, the dole. As a result he was constantly around the house, under Agnes's feet, and criticising her more than ever.

'How you can write, God only knows,' he exclaimed one day, coming into their room to find Agnes bent over her exercise book. She was sitting at the small desk in the corner which she tried to keep as her own. Now that he had no place at the House of Commons, Barry had taken over the rest of the house; his papers were everywhere, his books and documents strewn all over the sitting room, the dining room and even the kitchen.

'What do you expect me to do?' She put her pencil down and cupped her chin in her hands. Her eyes were smudged from lack of sleep and the premature lines on either side of her mouth more deeply etched than ever.

'Work! Look after the house.' Barry threw his arms in the air. 'Have you seen the kitchen today, for Christ's sake? I just don't know how you can *sit* here when the place is in such a state of chaos.'

'I didn't think you'd be back until later,' she said coolly. 'I thought you were going to the Poly to see about a job.'

'That's beside the point, Agnes.' Barry sat down heavily on the bed. 'Whether I came back or not has got nothing to do with it. This place should be clean and tidy and well run. You've got three children and me. God, you've got me!' Barry looked at the ceiling again and ground his teeth.

As she studied him, it suddenly occurred to Agnes that Barry could have done rather well as an actor. Certainly his histrionics would be put to better use on the stage than in the home, now that he could no longer perform in the House of Commons. He seemed to notice her air of apartness and turned to her accusingly.

'You don't really care, do you?'

'Of course I care!' Agnes got up and stretched. 'But I can't see that shouting helps. Look, I hate housework, Barry, I always have.'

'You'd think you'd have some pride ...'

'I have pride.' Agnes glanced at her closed exercise book. 'I have pride in my work – in the fact that, despite you, I've managed to produce a novel and have it published. But that was a year ago. I haven't even completed a quarter of my new one. It'll take me another four years at this rate, maybe longer. This is me, Barry, *me* – Agnes Holloway, the real me. This is what *I* want to do. In the same way that you want to be an MP, I don't want to do housework.'

'Then you should have said so!' Barry said truculently, looking at his wife's long, slim form. She was leaning against the wardrobe, and he could see her buttocks in the mirror, the jeans stretched tightly over them. She was a good-looking woman, a desirable one, despite her moods. He reached up his arms for her and moved over on the bed, but she ignored his sexual signals.

'I don't know what you mean by that. I *have* said so.'

'I mean, before we got married; you should have told me that you wanted a career.'

'I had no choice, did I? I had to get married because I was having a baby. Now I regret it, but then, in 1962, it seemed the only thing to do, the only course to take.'

'You *regret* it?' Barry sat up on the bed. 'What do you mean, you regret it?'

'I regret that I got married.' She shrugged. 'I wish I'd been strong enough to resist my father and you. I wish I'd said "No, I'll have this baby and bring it up myself, and be my own woman. I won't do what's expected of me just for the sake of it." People have, and I wish I had. I think I'd have been more proud of myself than I am now. Because I compromised. I was too frightened. I'm ashamed of that, now that I look back on it.'

'I'd like to see you now if you had!' Barry said, laughing mirthlessly. 'You'd probably be living in a Lesbian commune with Connie Shilton and her pals and arguing about women's rights all day long!'

'Well, women do have rights; and if they want to love each other as well, let them.'

'No one's stopping them.'

'I know; but you're laughing at them, aren't you? You're doing exactly what a male chauvinist pig is expected to do – make a joke of Lesbians, just like you make a joke of me.'

'I don't make a joke of you!' he blustered.

'Of my writing, you do. You think it's hilarious. "Oh, Agnes *writes*," you say in your amused, tolerant "isn't-she-a-scream?" sort of way. You don't think it's in the least bit important; what *you* think is important is cleaning and cooking and making beds. Talking of which, Barry, why don't *you* make them for a change? And wash up, and cook and clean and wash the children's clothes? Did it ever occur to you that you could make yourself useful in other ways, besides looking for a job and moaning about being banished from the House of Commons?' Her voice was even, unexcited.

'Don't be absurd.' Barry's tone was tetchy. 'I wouldn't know how to start. A woman's meant to know about domestic things...'

'Why?'

'Because she always has. Don't try and tell me you don't know your history. From the very earliest days men fought and caught the food and women cooked it, cleaned and bore the kids. I'm not saying they can't be clever and talented as well. I admire women like that – like you. But don't expect me to start choring at my age. Leave that to the next generation.'

'But will the next generation be any better? Will Terry be any better?'

'You'd better teach him, then, hadn't you?'

Barry leaned back. He loved the fire that came into her face when she was angry; and the sight of her bosom heaving and stretching against her shirt never failed to excite him.

'Oh, Agnes, talking of beds – come to bed now. I've got a terrific desire to fuck you. You may say some silly things, but you're one hell of a woman. Come on –' his voice grew wheedling '– come to bed with me now and let's forget all this nonsense. I'm beginning to think *you* should be in the House of Commons.' He patted the place beside him. 'Come on, be a sport.'

Agnes looked at him and the bed. She was tempted. It was odd how losing one's temper made one feel sexy. But she *had* to resist Barry, resist her own desires. With the problems that she and Barry had now, it wasn't going to solve anything; it was going to prolong them.

Barry put his arms under his head, waiting for her to join him, confident that she would lie down next to him and unzip his flies and begin all those nice, intimate things she was so good at. He let a little smile of anticipation play on his lips. But to his surprise, Agnes wiped her hands on the back of her jeans and went swiftly from the bedroom to the chaos of the kitchen downstairs: the woman's place.

CHAPTER TWENTY-FIVE

IN THE DIM HALF-LIGHT of early afternoon, with the curtains drawn, Barry lay very still. He felt at peace. The spaciousness and order of the room, its tranquillity, seemed a part of her, part of Rose. The wide bed with its printed sheets, soft pillows and neat coverlets; the antique furniture, the soft mauve carpet on the floor – they were all such a contrast to the disorder he had left behind. Barry sighed and Rose stirred beside him.

'What are you thinking, love?'

'About all this.'

Rose turned over. Even after making love, hardly a hair of her head was out of place. Her make-up was still fresh, and surrounding her was that faint fragrance of expensive perfume that had always been inseparable from Rose ever since he had known her. They hadn't made love since the summer and Barry's last visit to Westminster, which fortunately coincided with one of Rose's trips to London. Now it was November. It wasn't so much that he had ached for her sexually, but he had ached for this: this order, symmetry, harmony, conformity, opulence, restrained luxury. This aura of space and air and light. *Peace*. Rose was looking about her too, as though pleased with what she saw.

'You should see our bedroom,' Barry said. 'You can cross from the bed to the door in one step, but even then you fall over the kids' toys.'

'It's a very small house, Barry, you can't help that.'

'It's not what I want, though, is it?' He looked at her, saw the puzzled frown on her face. 'You know, Rose, I've gone down in the world, not up.'

'It's a pity they couldn't give you your old job back in the Poly.'

'They didn't want to. Nothing fails like failure. You know that.'

'Oh Barry, you're *not* a failure. You've just been unlucky.'

'It's the same as failing. You're unlucky because you fail and you fail because you're unlucky; one feeds on the other. The funny thing is that as a lecturer and a councillor I was a success. I was on the way up. But now, because of the election and the Winchester business, I'm down, right down.'

'That was very unfortunate about Keith.'

'Unfortunate? It was a disaster! And I had absolutely nothing to do with his sordid business affairs. He paid for my honeymoon, but I paid him back. I never answered his blasted letters asking me to become involved in this and that. Yet all his letters to me were produced at the enquiry. Christ Almighty, it's as though I *knew* what was going to happen, but he dragged me down anyway, like some great bloodsucking insect.'

'It's not as bad as that,' Rose protested.

'It *is* as bad as that! Rumour is much worse than fact. This town has fed on the rumours, because somewhere along the line they've decided not to like me; to ditch me. Because I'm a foreigner, not from Beckersleigh at all.'

'I'm a foreigner, too,' Rose said.

'Yes, you're not like them!' Barry snorted. 'Thank God! Grace practically murdered the poor bugger, but who dares say a word against her? She's a Calthorpe, she's from Beckersleigh. *And* resuming her name, just to show everyone.'

'I was annoyed about that, I'll admit,' Rose said. 'Now there are *two* Mrs Calthorpes. I don't like that.'

'But you quite like her now, don't you?' Barry fumbled for his cigarettes.

'Well, when she was really down, she needed me – I couldn't help but feel sorry for her. Now she's up again, and I have to mind my Ps and Qs where she's concerned. She's found a flat now, thank God. But to say that Grace murdered Keith – oh no, Barry. He killed himself with his drinking and his remorse ... If you could have seen her that morning as I did!' Rose closed her eyes. 'My God, it was a terrible sight. The doctor told me privately he'd never seen anything like it. No, I don't think Grace murdered Keith. Far from it! I can't be sorry he died, after knowing what he did to her, or the way he died, too. I can't be sorry.'

Barry lit his cigarette. 'Well, I didn't see her, of course – but I did see the way she treated him in public. She taunted him, you know – especially when things started to go wrong. Mind you, she was the same with her first fiancé. Did you ever meet him?'

'Stephen? Of course I did. Henry and I got engaged at the same time.'

'Well, enough about the Winchesters.' Barry turned to Rose and kissed the tip of her nose. '*You* make me happy; only you. I wish you were my wife, Rose. If I hadn't got you, I don't know what I'd do.'

Rose drew his face to her and kissed him tenderly. She felt she understood him better than anyone in the world: he was her lover and her baby, but not her friend or her master; he needed her too badly.

Grace, pausing outside Rose's room, stopped and sniffed. Smoke! Yet Rose didn't smoke – and, as far as she knew, her father was in Newcastle. She tapped on the door.

'Rose?' she called.

No answer.

Grace was suddenly filled with fear and foreboding and gripped the door handle; but it wouldn't yield.

'Rose, Rose,' she called. 'Are you there? Are you all right?'

Inside, Rose looked at Barry. They both lay stiff and petrified in the bed.

'She's smelt the smoke,' Rose whispered. 'For God's sake, put your cigarette out!' Barry quickly did as he was told.

'Yes, I'm all right, love,' she called.

'Could you open the door a minute?'

Rose got out of bed and tiptoed towards the door. Barry followed her naked body with his eyes, as frightened as she was.

'What is it you want, Grace?' Rose put her mouth to the door.

'I smelt smoke – it made me anxious.'

'There's no smoke here, Grace. I'm just doing a facial, love, and I really can't open the door. I look such a sight! I'll see you in a few minutes.'

'I'm going out,' Grace replied. 'I'll see you later.'

Rose waited until she heard Grace's high heels tapping down the elegant wooden staircase, then she stole back to bed and wrapped herself in Barry's arms. For minutes they lay together, giggling like children.

Grace went into the hall. She *had* smelt smoke, and Rose didn't smoke. There was no one else in the house. She knew Rose was lying.

'She's gone!' Rose said. She had peeped through the closed curtains and seen Grace drive away from the house. 'Thank God for that!' She went to her dressing table and looked at her face in the mirror. 'I feel I've aged ten years.'

'Didn't you know she'd be here?'

'I thought she'd be spending the day in the flat she's hoping to buy. She told me she would be.' Rose put on her robe and came over and sat on the bed. 'You'd better go now, Barry, just in case she decides to come back. Where did you leave your car?'

'In the town centre. I walked. But Rose, she'll never believe you.'

'Well, what's it matter? There's nothing she can do. Grace isn't the sort to go telling tales to Henry. If she does, I'll say I was smoking one of Henry's, to see what it was like. I know she won't, though. I know Grace very well by now.'

Barry still looked disturbed. 'We can't carry on like this, though, Rose, can we?'

'Of course we can, dear.' She leaned over and took his hand. 'Grace won't be living here any more after next month, and Henry's very regular in his habits. He's *always* away for a day or two each week on business. It'll be just like old times, Barry. Just as it used to be.'

Barry got out of bed and sat on the edge, gazing at the floor.

'Rose, you can't put the clock back. And I may get a job in Scotland anyway.'

Rose's heart gave a lurch. 'Scotland?'

'Aberdeen. They have a College of Further Education there.'

'Does it – does it have to be so far away? Isn't there anything nearer?'

'It's a good job. Head of the Department of Government.'

'What does Agnes say?'

'She's not keen. But I want to get away, Rose. Not from you, God knows – but from here. I want to start again. There was something going in Leeds, but I don't want to stay in this part of the North. I want to get right away.'

'I can understand that. But what about the constituency? Will you give it up?'

'It depends,' Barry said. 'I know they'll try and get rid of me. If they succeed, that's it – I'll go.'

Grace parked up the road, well out of sight of the house, turning the car round so that she could see whoever came out of the gate or went in. She waited there for an hour, with the engine running occasionally to keep herself warm. In the end she almost missed him when he came out, because she was fiddling with the ignition and looking at the dial on the radio. But there was no mistaking the bulky figure with the turned-up collar. She put the car in gear and cruised down the hill.

'Can I give you a life, Mr Holloway?' she said, drawing alongside him.

Barry looked back towards the house, then opened the car door and climbed in beside Grace, breathing fast as if he had been running.

'It is cold, isn't it?' Grace said conversationally, and accelerated. 'Where to?'

'You can drop me in the centre of the town.'

'Is that where you left your car?'

Barry didn't reply, but looked ahead, frowning.

'You smoke a very distinctive brand of cigarette, Mr Holloway.'

'Oh, shut up with this "Mr Holloway" business. You've been waiting for me, haven't you?' Barry stared accusingly at her, as though she was the one who'd done something wrong.

'Yes.' It was difficult to keep the satisfaction out of her voice, yet she couldn't have said exactly why she felt so pleased. Rose had helped to betray her father and her best friend. It was so sordid. Rose was her stepmother, the mother of her half-brothers. There was a blood link, like it or not.

'Well, you should feel pleased, then. You certainly sound it.'

'I'm not! How could I be pleased?'

'Then try not to crow.'

'You're very grumpy, aren't you, Barry?'

'What the Hell do you expect? You think I'm happy to be spotted coming out of your father's house? You must be barmy.'

'So you don't deny you've been to see Rose?'

'What's the point?' He got out his cigarettes and shoved the packet under Grace's nose. '*This* is the brand I smoke, for your information.'

Grace nodded, but kept her eyes on the road. 'I see. No, I won't have one now, thank you. I suppose you're going to ask me what I'm going to do?'

'Well, what are you going to do?' Barry lit his cigarette, lowered the window and threw out the match.

'I haven't thought. It's all rather sudden, you know – even though I learned some time ago that you were an old flame of my father's wife. I was pretty disgusted then but, like Agnes, I thought and hoped it was all over.'

'Oh, when did you two girls discuss all this?' In the past Barry had hardly ever felt uncomfortable because of the double life he led; but he did now.

'About a year ago. We discussed the toy Rose had bought for Terry at Hamleys.'

'Oh, that was you, was it? I might have known!'

'Did she say anything to you?'

'And how!'

'She said she wouldn't. I think she would have preferred not to know.'

'Well, I lied to her. I was thinking of her, Grace. What point was there in Agnes knowing?'

'Oh, you men!' Grace stopped at traffic lights and looked at him angrily. 'Why do you have to do this? You know how intelligent Agnes is. Why do you have to deceive her?'

'Sex has nothing to do with intelligence – or maybe it has …' Barry looked thoughtful. 'Maybe I only like intelligent women. Both Rose and Agnes are very clever and intelligent. I like them both in different ways. I don't want to give either up. Why should I?'

'I would have thought the guilt would be unbearable.'

'I don't feel guilty.' Barry looked surprised. 'I've known Rose for so many years. It's a different sort of relationship; not as intense as with Agnes, but nice. I can't explain it to you.'

'Please don't try,' Grace said coldly. 'Obviously my stepmother won't get hurt – she's too much of a cold-hearted bitch for that – but Agnes might.'

'I won't hurt Agnes,' Barry said seriously. 'You'll be the one who'll hurt her if you tell her about this.'

'I won't tell her,' Grace said wearily. 'Far be it from me; but one day she's bound to find out. You know she will.'

Barry turned to her, and for the first time she saw how tired he looked. But Barry was the sort of self-confident, cocky type it was very hard to pity, even when they were down. The lights turned to green and Grace drove into the High Street.

'Which car park?'

'By the baths.'

'Right.' Grace drove into the park and stopped behind a row of cars.

'Will this do?'

'Yes, thanks very much.' Barry made to unfasten the door.

'So you're quite happy leaving things as they are, Barry?'

He stopped and turned. 'What do you mean?'

'Like this. Just running away.'

'I'm not running away! But I don't see the point of going on. Look, Grace, sex isn't the main thing with me and Rose; it's more a question of companionship. Agnes isn't a companion to me, but she *is* a good lover. Agnes and I have so many blasted rows, it's a pleasant change to spend some time with someone like Rose. Rose and I have never had a row in all the time we've known each other.'

'Why didn't you marry her then?' Grace was curious to know.

'Well, there was the difference in our ages, but it wasn't primarily that. She had your father when I met her, and I was poor, with no prospects.'

'I see. That wouldn't have suited Rose!'

'Well, she's made your father happy, hasn't she?' Barry said rather defensively.

'He wouldn't be quite so happy if he knew about you. But yes, up to a point, I suppose she has.'

'There you are. Agnes thinks all men are rivals, constantly trying to stop her doing things she wants to do. I feel that Agnes resents me – positively resents me. I feel she was even quite happy when I wasn't re-elected, because that made us more equal.'

'Oh, that's not true!' Grace intervened angrily.

'Well, maybe I'm wrong about that: but I've never felt easy with Agnes. You can't relax with her. You're being inspected the whole time.'

'Paul said a long time ago that he thought you were simply incompatible,' Grace murmured. 'I think that's what we're talking about: incompatibility.' She looked at her watch and made an exclamation. 'I must go! I'm sorry I gave you such a shock, Barry; but I wanted to know, and I felt it would be dishonest not to let you know I knew. I'm not going to say anything to Dad or Agnes. But I hope you'll try and sort out your life – for your sake and Agnes's. I'm not awfully concerned about you, because you're a survivor, like me. But I'd be terribly sorry to see her suffer. In a way, purely platonic and all that rot, Agnes and I love each other, you know.'

'I know,' Barry said, unfastening the door. 'Christ, how I know!'

Paul said: 'It's a very nice flat.'

'Do you think I should take it?'

'I don't see why not.' He moved to the window and looked out. 'It's got a lovely view from this side, and the other side isn't too bad.'

Inwardly Paul didn't want her to take this flat; but what could he say? How could he know whether or not she was ready? He dreaded the thought of ruining everything by being precipitate, but to him this year had seemed interminable. He'd realised that he loved Grace a long time ago, just after he had come North. He'd gone back to London primarily to be away from her and away from temptation. Today he'd cancelled all his afternoon consultations, something he had never done before – and all because he wanted to be with her. Suddenly he put a hand on her shoulder, his eyes on her breasts. He could see the outline of her nipples quite clearly, hard and erect.

'Grace,' he said, and placed the other hand on her other shoulder so that she was forced to look at him. 'Do you really want this flat?'

'I don't know. That's why I asked you. I thought I'd let you decide.'

'Why me?' He swallowed.

'Well, if I take it, it's a long lease. I think it's sixty-six years. Isn't that a long time?'

'A very long time.' Caution went to the winds. 'Grace, I love you. I love you very much. I know it's not a year since ... but ...'

Grace closed her eyes, not wanting him to see the exultation in them. She had been afraid that she would have to ask *him*, and that would have unbalanced the relationship because she didn't want to have to take the lead. If she took the lead in this marriage, it would end up like the last one. Paul was strong, but she wanted him to show his strength first, before she showed hers. She let out a deep sigh and felt his lips on her cheek.

But that wasn't what she wanted. She wanted *him*, not physical contact. The feel of his lips on her cheek made her shudder, and blunted the sensation of joy. She opened her eyes and put her hands against his chest, pushing him gently away.

'Not yet, Paul,' she begged. 'I'm not ready ... Oh, don't misunderstand me! It's just that I'm not ready for the physical thing.

314

I *am* ready for you. I love you – I want you. But not physically, not yet...'

At once he realised what she was trying to say. 'My God, I'm a doctor – I should have known how much you suffered; *of course* I understand. But Grace, I love you so much. I promise I'll do everything I can do to make you really well again and happy again. I promise.'

He folded her very gently into his arms as though she were a precious, frightened child, and gently kissed the top of her shining gold head.

Part Five

CHAPTER TWENTY-SIX

ON 15TH FEBRUARY, 1971, away went shillings and old pence, and in came new pence – two-and-a-half old pence equalling one new penny. On the same day two-and-a-half old Agnes Holloways equalled one new one – or so it seemed, fancifully, to her.

15th February was also the day Barry told her he had decided to take the job in Aberdeen. Agnes immediately told him that she didn't want to go with him, and nor did the children, and that they wanted to stay in Beckersleigh. Of course, she had known about Aberdeen for some time, but at this stage it was far too late even to discuss the matter, since the appointment had now been confirmed. Perhaps that was what made her so mad – not only had he not told her he was going to accept, but he had actually gone ahead and done it.

'It's not what you'd call consultation between husband and wife, is it?' Agnes said, letting her book fall on the bed. 'And why do you tell me last thing at night? It's the worst time.'

'I think it's the best time.' Barry put the letter on the dressing table. 'Then if you're angry, I can make love to you and soothe you.'

'But it doesn't solve the problem, Barry, does it?' Agnes said wearily. 'Making love solves nothing. You're still going to go to Aberdeen!'

'Why do you always resist sex?' Barry said, getting into bed beside her. 'Because you really like it so much. Why do you pretend you don't?'

'I don't pretend. I *do* like it. But I don't like it when it always covers up what's wrong between us! You think you can stroke me and make love to me and everything'll be all right. Well, it won't. Tomorrow I still won't want to go to Aberdeen.'

'But you'll feel more relaxed now,' Barry said, putting his hand under her nightie. 'And then we can talk about it again tomorrow.'

Agnes seized the book on the bed cover and held it before his eyes. It had a picture of a naked Venus on the cover.

'What in Christ's name is that? It looks like Venus with no clothes on.'

'Don't look at the picture. Look at the title.'

Barry screwed up his eyes. '*The Feminine Mystique* by Betty Friedan. Who the Hell's she?'

'She's an American psychologist, and she's written a book about the passivity of women in modern society – the myth that requires them to be passive, receptive and feminine; to stay at home, bear kids and look after their families.'

'But she's perfectly right,' Barry said, trying to brush the book to one side. 'Thank God someone's said something sensible at last.' He had hitched her nightie right up over her breasts now, and she knew that she wanted what he wanted too – but for different reasons. She wanted sex because she felt sexy; because she liked him baring her body and looking at it, caressing it and entering it. She knew that afterwards she would feel better and she would sleep well, and that in the morning this mood would continue even if Christopher was bawling, Miranda wouldn't eat her breakfast and Terry refused to go to school. The happiness engendered tonight, she knew, would reach over until tomorrow; but during the day it would slowly ebb away, until she felt as she did now – tense, frustrated and angry.

But tonight, as she relaxed for Barry, letting *The Feminine Mystique* fall on the floor, and entwined herself around him, clinging to him, she wondered how long they would continue to make love like this, how much time remained to them. Because she knew that she would not, under any circumstances, leave Beckersleigh and go to Aberdeen.

Albert Rivington was propped upright in bed so that the fluid drained from his lungs – or what was left of them. He could now breathe only with a tremendous effort, and the sounds that emerged were pitiful, like a rickety, old-fashioned bellows.

Paul gazed down at his father and then sat beside him, taking his pulse lightly between finger and thumb. Albert smiled wryly.

'Am I still alive?'

'I think you'll see us out, Dad.' Paul joked.

'I doubt it. I doubt it.' Albert shook his head. 'I doubt if I'll ever get back to work, will I?'

'Perhaps not, Dad.'

Albert hadn't worked since the summer, when a first attack of emphysema had accelerated the deterioration of his already badly damaged lungs. 'I wish we were back in Enderby Street,' Albert said suddenly. 'I don't want to die here.'

'You're not going to die, Dad. It's just a question of getting you better.'

'I won't get better here. Neither of us has been well since we came to this place.'

It was true, Paul reflected. His father's lungs had worsened – though admittedly that might have happened anyway – and his mother had suffered from frequent bouts of depression.

'Are you still looking for a house, Paul?' The old man's eyes fluttered hopefully. Paul had told his parents that when he found somewhere, they could come and live with him; what he hadn't told them was that he was going to marry Grace Calthorpe and that, so far, the question of his parents living with them had not yet been discussed.

The door opened and Agnes came in, her face flushed as though she had been hurrying.

'How are you today, Dad?'

'About the same, love.' He smiled at her, but she wasn't deceived. She looked anxiously at Paul.

'I was asking Paul about his house,' her father said. 'He said when he got a house we could go and live with him. I wish he'd get one soon ...'

Paul got off the bed and went and looked out of the window. It had been a fairly mild, dry February and the day was almost springlike. The view from here really was spectacular; dales and moorland as far as the eye could see.

'Dad, I've got to tell you and Agnes something – and I might as well tell you both now. I'll just go and get Mum.'

Paul went towards the door at the moment his mother came in, carrying a tray with cups and a plate of biscuits.

'I've brought you some tea. Do you feel up to a cup of tea, Albert?'

'Yes, I'll try a cup, love.'

'Having his children with him does him the world of good,' Kathleen said; but she herself looked tired and drawn. Agnes knew that most nights she was up with Albert, making sure he didn't slip down the bed and drown in the fluid from his lungs.

'Paul was about to say something, Mum. He's got some news.' Agnes took the tray from her mother and handed out the cups of tea.

'Well, Paul, what is it?' Wearily Kathleen sat down on a chair and stirred her tea. 'Something to cheer us all up, I hope. Is it about the house?'

'Well, I hope it will cheer you up, Mum. It's something that's made *me* very happy.' As he spoke, he knew it wasn't going to make them happy at all, but it had to be done. 'I'm going to marry Grace – Grace Calthorpe.'

His mother choked on her tea.

'You mean you're actually going to *marry* her?' Kathleen's face still wore the half-hopeful expression that she might have heard wrongly.

'Yes, Mum.'

'I didn't even know you were seeing Grace, Paul! Did you, Agnes?'

'Well, I knew they were going out, but I didn't think there was anything to it. I'm very happy for you, Paul.' Agnes didn't even attempt to smile; but her tone was polite, perfunctory.

'Thank you, Agnes. Dad?'

'I'm wondering if I heard you right, Paul. You're going to marry Grace Calthorpe? Grace?' The expression on his face was one of utter incredulity.

'Yes, Dad.'

'But, *why*?'

Paul smiled. Even Agnes grinned.

'Because I love her.' There was no mistaking the feeling in his voice. 'In a way I've loved Grace ever since I was a schoolboy. Then I was so tongue-tied in her presence I could hardly look at her. Did you guess that, Agnes?'

'No – I had no idea.'

'Well, it's true. I knew she was way beyond me, and that was that; but I never fell in love with anyone else, and every time I came home and saw her, even caught a glimpse of her, I felt more attracted to her than ever.'

Paul sighed, but with happiness; nothing could make him unhappy now – even his family's disapproval.

'A couple of years ago I had the choice of a job in Leeds or London, remember? I met Grace at a party and she said she hoped I'd choose Leeds. I knew then I loved her and I also knew I couldn't be near her without wanting her. So I chose London because she was still married. But when the Leeds post came up again I had to take it; it was an important step forward in my career. Then, as you know, a year ago Grace's circumstances changed dramatically.'

Agnes was filled with amazement; it seemed so extraordinary that Paul, whom she knew so well, was so close to, had never once, in all these years, confided to her his true feelings.

'Just after Christmas I asked her to marry me,' Paul went on. 'Last week she told me that she would. That's why I haven't bought the house, because it depended on what Grace felt about me. I can't tell you how happy I am.'

His father sighed. 'So we'll just have to stop here, I reckon.'

'If you feel so strongly, Dad, I'm sure we could get you a transfer on health grounds.' Agnes felt sorry for Paul.

'It'll take time,' her father said, looking at her pathetically. 'I don't feel I've got much left. I thought Paul would be in that house by now. He's been talking about it for over a year.'

'I *was* looking at houses, Dad; but when Keith died I knew that one day I'd ask Grace to marry me.'

'And you couldn't have your old parents living in your house then, could you?' Albert said bitterly. 'Oh, the mighty Miss Calthorpe wouldn't like that, would she?'

Please don't talk about her like that, Dad,' Paul said quietly. 'I'm sure she would have accepted, for my sake, whatever the situation was.'

Albert snorted with disbelief.

'I don't really think you could start your married life living with your parents, Paul,' Kathleen said firmly. 'Especially as we're not the same sort of people as Grace. I can see it wouldn't do at all.'

'It's not that, Mum!' Paul looked angry. 'Grace isn't in the least like that. Agnes is her best friend, after all. It's an idea you've always had about Grace and the Calthorpes, and it's totally wrong.'

'Well, be that as it may, that's how we feel,' Albert said loftily. 'I don't like her, and I don't like her father. I was sorry that Grace ever had the influence she did on our Agnes, because I think a lot of what happened to Agnes – having to get married, and that – was *her* fault. I'm sorry, more than sorry, that you intend to wed her.'

Albert stopped, panting, and Agnes hurried over to pass him his invalid cup.

'Don't upset yourself, Dad. Have you taken your pills?'

Albert nodded and sipped the water. Agnes carefully put the cup by the side of his bed and sat down beside him, taking his hand.

'You can't blame Grace for all my ills, Dad – certainly not having to get married! You see, I've got some news for you, too – I don't know whether it's good news or bad, but it might as well all come out now. Certainly, it's no fault of Grace's.' Agnes stuck out her chin to give herself courage and looked at her mother.

A little tremor passed over Kathleen's face. 'What is it, Agnes?'

'Barry's accepted a job in Aberdeen. He's to be head of a department at the Technical College there. It's a very good job.'

Her mother's hand flew to her mouth. 'Oh *Agnes!*'

'I'm not going with him,' she said flatly. 'I've told him I don't want to.'

'You're not *going* with your husband?' Albert said, his tone once more strong and authoritative.

'No, Dad. I didn't want to go to Aberdeen. He didn't ask me before he accepted – and I don't want to go.'

'You mean he didn't want you to go with him?' Her mother started to fan her face with her hand.

'Of course he wants me to go with him! But he didn't ask me before accepting the job. He just took it and thought I would go. Well, I'm not going to.'

'But Agnes, it's your duty to go.'

'I don't think it is, Dad. I think Barry should have consulted me and taken my wishes into account.'

'Do you mean you're splitting up?' Paul asked, anxiously.

'No, not exactly, Paul. Barry will commute – not as much as he did in London – but he'll come home for the holidays.'

'It seems an odd sort of marriage to me, that,' Albert said. 'Very modern. If you ask me, my girl, your duty is to stay by your husband's side.'

Agnes smiled and gripped his hand. 'I was sure you'd say that, Dad. But it occurs to me now that when Barry goes, you and Mum could move in with me. You can have our room, and I'll sleep with Miranda. It'll be nice to have you, and I can't tell you how much I'd appreciate some help in the house and the odd bit of baby-sitting! That's if you'd like it.'

'But what about Barry?' Kathleen said. 'Where will he go when he comes home?'

'Oh, we'll think of something, Mum,' Agnes said lightly. 'I shouldn't think he'd be there long anyway, knowing him. he'd be like a visitor ...'

*   *   *

324

Paul was silent for a while as he drove Agnes home. Barry almost always had the car now, and Agnes went everywhere by bus; when Barry left, she wouldn't have the use of the car at all, because they certainly couldn't afford two.

'Are you sure you're not splitting up?' Paul drove towards Enderby Street meaning to take the moorland road to her home. Then he planned to go and see Grace.

'No, I'm not sure,' Agnes said honestly. 'We haven't been getting on for some time. I feel increasingly used by Barry. I'm a sort of cross between a hotel-keeper and a mistress. He loafs about, goes all over the place looking for jobs; often he doesn't even tell me when he's coming back.'

'He must be very unsettled and unhappy.'

'Yes, he is. But I'm unsettled and unhappy too, Paul. Would you drop me off at the *Chron* offices? I want to talk to Sam.'

'Sam?'

'Sam Armstrong, the editor. He once asked me to write for the paper. I want to see if he still wants me to. We're very short of money.'

'I can imagine.' He glanced at her. 'I can help there, you know.'

'Not if you're going to marry Mrs Grace Calthorpe! She's an expensive lady.'

'That sounds cruel, Agnes – not like you. I was hoping you'd be happy for us.'

He stopped the car just before they came to Enderby Sreet, where they used to live.

'Oh, Grace is my friend, Paul, but I have very mixed feelings, to be honest. I wish you'd talked it over with me first. I don't mean asked my permission, but just discussed it with me. In the first place I had no idea you had this obsession with Grace. That staggered me.'

'It was hard to talk about.' Paul laughed slightly.

'I can imagine! It's like something out of the Knights of the Round Table – very romantic, but is it sensible?'

'Sensible? I don't understand.'

'Grace is very beautiful and very clever. I can see she makes a most desirable propqsition. But she's not easy to live with, you know. As her friend, I can say that from experience.'

'I haven't found her at all difficult. On the contrary.'

'Well, she is. She's got a very nasty tongue, with men especially, and she can be quite cruel.' She hesitated, then: 'Have you been to bed with her?'

'Agnes!' Paul was shocked.

'I'm your sister, Paul,' she said impatiently, 'and this is 1971. A few years ago, when I first married, people didn't talk so freely about sex; things are different now. Look, Grace hasn't had children – I wondered if you'd thought of that, if you wanted them.'

'Well, I'd like them, of course.'

'But have you talked to her about it?' Agnes insisted.

'You mean Grace doesn't want children?'

'She wants, or wanted them, desperately, but she can't have them. She had a lot of examinations.'

'She told me it was all inconclusive. That they couldn't really find a reason.'

'Oh, so you have talked about it?'

Agnes stared ahead, across the rubble which was gradually becoming a landmark in the town. Some thought it had its own particular charm, especially the children who played on it. She wondered if she should tell Paul what else she knew about Grace; what Grace had once told her, long ago, about her attitude to sex, about her frigidity. But looking at her brother, a consultant surgeon, a man of the world, no longer a gauche schoolboy, she decided against it. It wasn't her business to tell him. She hadn't the right.

Paul was gazing over the wheel, shielding his eyes against the sun high in the sky. It was nearly noon.

'Can you see some sort of demonstration over there?'

Agnes followed his gaze, looking towards Enderby Street. There appeared to be an unusual number of people thronging the normally deserted street.

'I can see banners or something. Let's go and look.'

Paul switched on the ignition and his Rover rolled gently forward. They stopped just at the bottom of the hill where they used to live.

'Let's walk up.'

The street was full of people; mainly women, many children and a lot of excited dogs. One of the houses looked as though it had been prepared for some sort of gala: a banner hung right across it and flags had been hung out of the windows. Heads were poking out on each storey and hands waved. The atmosphere was definitely very festive.

Agnes and Paul stood in front of the house, which was about five along the road from their old home, and read the banner:

'WOMEN'S RIGHTS SQUAT TO SAVE ENDERBY STREET. MAKE OLD HOUSES FIT FOR HABITATION'

'My God, it's a squat!' Agnes exclaimed. 'They've had them in London, but I hadn't heard of any up here! People occupying buildings to get something done.'

'But surely they're not intending to live here?'

'Yes. They squat with blankets, cooking materials and things. There's a real housing problem in Beckersleigh, Paul, partly because the high-rise blocks are so unpopular. No one wants to live there.'

Other banners said: 'TEAR DOWN THE TOWER BLOCKS AND BUILD REAL HOMES.' 'HEATH OUT, WILSON IN.' 'WHERE IN THE WORLD ARE WE GOING? WHERE, OH WHERE?'

'Have you come to stare at us, Agnes, or sit in?'

Agnes turned, hearing the familiar voice. 'Connie! We've only just seen it. We've been visiting my parents.'

'How's your Dad? He hasn't been to ward meetings for weeks.'

'Not too grand, I'm afraid. Oh Connie, it *is* good to see you!' Agnes clasped Connie and kissed her cheek. Connie put down the bags she was carrying, full of food and supplies, and returned the hug.

'Have you forgiven me?' she asked rather shyly.

Agnes laughed. 'I have, but I don't think Barry has. In fact I don't think he ever will.'

'I'm not worried about *him*. It's you I was worried about. I missed you.'

They hadn't seen each other since Connie had tried to get Barry turned down as candidate. But, with time, her indignation at Connie's behaviour had inevitably cooled.

'You look very well, Connie. I think you've lost weight.'

'I've been busy with women's rights. We're going to organise a workshop here in Beckersleigh. And I went to the first National Conference of Women in March of last year. There's going to be a big women's movement in the country – and this is only the start.' Connie pointed proudly to the house. 'We're going to occupy *all* these houses, until someone does something about them. One by one, we'll put homeless families in them and clothe them and feed them. All done by women to help women. We need money, of course.' Connie smiled sweetly, rather guilefully, at Paul. 'I hear you're a wealthy surgeon these days, Paul.'

'Not wealthy! I'm partly in the Health Service – but I'll help.' He gave Connie a fiver.

'Thanks, Paul.' Connie picked up her bags and sighed. 'These are bloody heavy.'

'Did you carry them all the way from the town?' Agnes enquired.

'Yes. Good for my figure.'

'Are you still with Roman? I've never forgotten the pair of you and Terry, you know. Whatever happened afterwards never made me forget that.'

'That was nothing. Nothing compared to this. Yes, Roman's inside. She went to London to get first-hand experience of squatting and now she's in charge here. She'll be very pleased to see you.'

'I'll be back,' Agnes said, looking at Paul. 'We've got to go now, but I promise I'll come back.'

'And *help!*' Connie called after her.

All the way down the hill Agnes thought about her laughing, eager face, almost unchanged in ten years. Causes, no matter what or where, kept Connie youthful. There was no doubt about that.

Sam Armstrong got up from behind his desk and came over to greet her.

'Agnes, this is a pleasure!'

'Thank you, Sam.' She let him kiss her on the cheek.

'All forgiven, I hope?' He looked into her eyes, and for a moment she didn't know what he was talking about.

'Oh, you mean Barry?' She shrugged. 'It wasn't very nice the way you attacked him.'

'It wasn't personal, Agnes.'

'I think it was a bit personal, Sam. You got your tune from the GMC meeting. There were hints that Barry wasn't quite honest. He's never forgiven you for that.'

'I didn't mean to give that impression. Maybe you read too much into it.'

'Well, it was what a lot of people thought. Anyway, Sam,' Agnes clasped her hands together and looked at him. 'I haven't come about that. It happens that I need a job, and I wondered if you still wanted me to write articles for the paper?'

'You *need* a job, or you *want* one?'

'Both.'

'I suppose Barry had a hard time after the election? I am sorry; but I couldn't support him, you know. Mind you, I didn't support Longley either.'

'So I noticed. Let's hope he doesn't get involved in any scandal.'

'Well, he dealt very competently with the last one. That final Board of Trade report on the Winchester business was a masterpiece of whitewash.'

'What else could they do? Keith was dead, and Grace certainly made nothing from the business. She was as clean as a whistle.'

The final report, which had been issued just after Christmas, had been something of a damp squib, and had left many people dissatisfied. No names were named, and the Commissioners seemed to be unable to do anything more than hint darkly at unsavoury goings-on. No one could pay up, since there was no money in the kitty. Keith Winchester had covered his tracks well.'

'Yes, but it was Calthorpes protecting Calthorpe interests, no doubt about that. You know, the interesting thing is that now it's as though Winchester never existed. Grace changing her name back to Calthorpe helped. It was a shrewd move.'

'Well, she's changing it again now. She's going to marry my brother.'

'Paul? You surprise me. Or maybe I'm not so surprised. A surgeon would suit Grace very nicely. Nothing sordid and commercial about that, is there? On the contrary, terribly respectable.'

'I think you're being rather cynical, Sam,' Agnes said, with some spirit. 'Maybe I should come and talk to you another day. Grace Calthorpe is *still* my best friend and Paul's my brother.'

'I'm sorry, Agnes.' He ran his fingers through his hair. 'I'm being very clumsy today, and believe me, I don't mean to be. Look, I'll make up for it. You can write me some articles about women's rights. And you can begin with the squat.'

'Are you serious?' She was delighted.

'Perfectly serious. I was just going there to see for myself. You know Connie Shilton and all that lot behind it; I think you'd be ideal.'

'I don't know what Barry would say,' Agnes said doubtfully.

'Don't ask him,' Sam said. 'Just do it. I think you'll do a terrific job. And it could open all sorts of doors for you.'

Agnes didn't feel she had any choice. She could be in the position one day – quite soon, maybe – of having to support herself, and her children; but, like the camel, she didn't like to look that far ahead.

CHAPTER TWENTY-SEVEN

FROM THE END OF FEBRUARY onwards, Agnes wrote a weekly article in the *Chronicle* about women's rights and the progress of the Enderby Street squat. Partly as a result of her coverage the other houses in the street soon began to fill up with the discontented, the dispossessed, and the dissatisfied and their assorted children, pets and possessions.

The Enderby Street saga, fanned by the writings of Agnes Holloway, became a *cause célèbre*, and the town of Beckersleigh once again made the national press – though *The Guardian* was more enthusiastic about the issue than the *Daily Telegraph*, which gave it little space. Such was Agnes's sudden rise to prominence that her publisher even wrote to enquire about the progress of her second novel – though at the same time informing her regretfully that they had now remaindered the first.

None of which improved the relationship between Agnes and Barry.

'It won't do you any good, you know,' he said, thrusting her latest article under her nose.

'I know, I've read it,' Agnes said brusquely, removing the paper from her place at the breakfast table.

'I know you've read it! You wrote the bloody thing!'

'Then why show it to me?' Agnes removed Miranda's hand from the jam pot and smacked Christopher, who had dipped his finger in the tomato sauce and was drawing with it on the tablecloth.

'Blood,' he said, licking his lips.

'I'll give you blood! Barry, if Terry and Miranda are to get to school on time you must be off.'

'I'm really not up to it this morning,' Barry said sullenly. 'I'm not sleeping at all well. Could you take them?'

'If you stay in and keep an eye on Chris.'

'When's he starting school, for Christ's sake?'

'September,' Agnes said shortly and got up. 'You could also do the breakfast things, if you don't mind. While I've got the car, I may as well go on to the *Chron*, too.'

'What for?'

'To discuss my next piece.' She looked at him sharply. 'We need the money, you know, Barry.'

'Don't I just.' Barry sat back and picked up the *Chron* again, staring at it as though it was the last hope for mankind.

Terry, now eight, had turned into a bright, well-behaved child. He, more than the others, had sensed the change in the relationship between his parents; but it seemed to have made him reflective rather than anxious. He was careful not to take sides, and would often question one or other of them about things he had heard them discuss in public. As a result he soon became aware that his parents could hold sharply divergent views of the same event or issue.

'Are we poor, Mummy?' Terry enquired in the car on the way to school.

'Not poor, darling. But we have to be careful.'

'Is that why Daddy's at home all day?'

'It has something to do with it, but he'll be taking a job soon. He may go away for a while.'

'Don't you and Daddy like each other any more, Mummy?' enquired the perceptive Miranda who, at six, was as sharp and almost as mature as her brother.

'Of course we do. Why shouldn't we?'

'You don't talk very nicely to each other.'

Agnes immediately felt guilty. 'We're both a bit worried at the moment, that's all.'

'Jack Alderson in my class saw his father hit his mother,' Terry said, his eyes glinting with envy.

'Well, at least we don't do that.' Agnes turned with relief into the road where the school was. 'We like each other really, but mummies and daddies do sometimes find living together a strain.'

'If Daddy hit you, there could be a fight.' Terry was warming to his theme. 'And I ...'

'Would rush in and save me.' Agnes laughed. 'I don't think it's likely, Terry. Sorry to disappoint you.'

She drew up by the school and let them out, watching them scamper off through the gates and into the playground; then she drove towards the *Chronicle* offices.

On the way, passing the Calthorpes' house she saw Grace's car in the drive. She slowed down and, as she did so, the door opened and Grace appeared, dressed for the road. Agnes pulled up and gave her a toot.

'Hi!' Grace called. 'What are you doing here?' She came over and leaned through the window.

'I'm going into town. I've just taken the children to school. I'm going to the *Chron.*'

'Look, give me a lift? I'll leave the car here and then I can walk back. Paul says I don't get enough exercise.'

Without waiting for a reply, she jumped into the car and Agnes started off down the hill.

'It's unusual for you to take the children to school, isn't it?'

'Yes. But today Barry's staying at home looking after the baby and doing the dishes!' Agnes grinned.

'Get away!' Grace laughed disbelievingly.

'Well, in theory anyway. When I get back, Christopher will have hopefully escaped electrocution and other serious injuries by a hair's breadth and Barry will be slumped on the bed. I must say he does seem depressed.'

'Doesn't he work at all?'

'He does the odd lecturing job, writes the odd article. He could have got a part-time job quite easily if he wanted; but nothing was good enough.'

'I can believe that. Paul's taking me to see a house today.'

'Oh lovely. Where?' Agnes glanced quickly at Grace. She found it difficult to get used to the fact that they were to be sisters-in-law, especially as they had scarcely had a chance to speak alone since the engagement.

'Near Ilkley, so it's quite a long way away; but it's a gorgeous house.'

'You've seen it, then?'

'I saw a picture. Paul's very keen. It's midway between here and Leeds, so we can both commute. Actually, I might move my business to Ilkley. It's a very elegant little town.'

'Oh Grace, I'd miss you! Don't leave Beckersleigh – especially as I might be on my own.'

'Barry's definitely taking the job?'

'Yes, unless there's a selection committee before and he's chosen. Then he'd take a job in Leeds or Bradford.'

'Do you think he would be chosen?'

'I've no idea.'

Grace looked out of the window. 'Paul thinks your father should be in hospital.'

'I think so, too; but you know how mother would hate being in that flat on her own.'

They came in sight of the *Chronicle* office and Agnes turned down a side street where she could park. 'Is this OK?'

'Fine. Have we got time for a coffee?'

Agnes looked at her watch. 'Yes. Let's go into the bar opposite the front entrance.'

From the bar Agnes could keep an eye on the main door and see when Sam went in. She didn't want to be too late home and annoy Barry. She stirred her coffee and took a sip.

'You look terribly pale, Agnes. Are you sure you're all right?'

Agnes smiled at her friend. 'Oh, I'm all right. It's just that we're terribly short of money. Do you know, a man came the other day to cut off the electricity!'

'God! What happened?'

'We gave him a cheque, but it was rather humiliating. Everyone knows Barry, and in a place like this people gossip.'

'I seem to remember Paul offered to help, but you were too proud to accept.'

'Of course we couldn't accept! I'm getting quite well paid for my articles and Barry gets various lecture fees. Then we have our savings. By the time we've come to the end of them, Barry will be in full-time employment again. Besides, Paul will need all the money he's got if you're to live in style – and obviously he wants that.'

'It's not just for my sake,' Grace said hastily. 'I mean, as an up-and-coming surgeon, he naturally wants to be seen to live well.'

Agnes finished her coffee and looked at her watch. If Paul wanted to live well, she thought, it was more likely to be for Grace's sake than his own. He had never been one to care about his creature comforts.

'Agnes, you *are* pleased, aren't you?' Grace leaned over, whispering, so that the few people in the bar wouldn't hear. 'Pleased about us?'

'Well, I am pleased of course,' Agnes began cautiously, 'because Paul loves you very much. I never saw him so happy; but ...'

'Yes?'

'Do *you* love him?'

'Of course I love him! What a thing to ask.' Grace was indignant.

'He's a very gentle man, you know, Grace. Very different from Keith and Barry.'

'Oh, *very* different – thank God! Paul's a gentleman, something I can say neither of my late husband nor yours, if you'll forgive me.'

Agnes sat back and toyed with her spoon. 'I didn't realise you disliked Barry so much.'

'Well, I do.' Grace sipped her coffee. 'I don't think he's been good to you – or for you. He's a selfish, self-opinionated lout, if you ask me. I'll be jolly glad to see the back of him. There, I've said it!'

'We're not getting divorced, you know,' Agnes protested.

'Well, you should think about it. If Barry does go to Aberdeen, you'll have all the disadvantages of being tied to someone and none of the advantages of marriage, you mark my words. Now, I must go to Bentons and look at materials. Paul's coming to the house for lunch. Why don't you join us?'

'No, I must get home, thanks. Really. Have you fixed the date for the wedding?'

'Probably September. I think Paul wants to see how your father fares.'

Suddenly Agnes felt anxious. 'Does Paul think Dad might *die*?'

Grace reached out and covered Agnes's hand with hers. 'It's a possibility. You know, Agnes, I'm quite prepared to have your parents to live with us. That's why Paul is looking for a big house – so that they can have their own separate apartment. I don't mind at all, really.'

'*Really*? Honestly and truly?'

'Honestly and truly.'

'It's very kind of you, Grace. I'm impressed.' And she was.

'You think I'm selfish, don't you, Agnes?'

'Well, you like to have your own way. You're used to it and you've never had to think very much about other people. Starting married life living with your in-laws isn't easy, you know – especially if one of them's an invalid.' Agnes hesitated a moment and then leaned over towards Grace. 'Grace, can I ask you something terribly personal?'

Grace's eyes glinted, the expression on her face changing. She shook her head. 'If it's about me and Paul, no. That's *my* territory. *Our* territory. I know what you're going to bring up, Agnes, but that was years and years ago. It's all quite different now.'

Agnes leaned back and gave a shy smile.

'I'm sorry, Grace. I shouldn't have brought it up, but that's what I wanted to know. That things are all right now.'

'Paul's a very different man from Keith. I'm beginning a new life.' As she spoke, Grace's face softened.

Agnes looked through the door and saw Sam hurrying up the steps opposite.

'There's Sam – I must go. I'm so glad we had this talk.'

'I'll pay,' Grace said. 'You go.'

'Thanks.'

Agnes ran to the door, trying her hardest to put the doubt she still felt about Grace out of her mind.

'You want me to sit in with the squat?' Agnes exclaimed, her voice shrill with astonishment. 'To *live* there?'

'To get the atmosphere,' Sam said enthusiastically. 'You realise we're syndicating your articles throughout the North West and further? I think you've discovered your genius, Agnes. Journalism – an ability to identify with other people. It's a rare gift, you know.'

'It isn't only identifying with them,' Agnes said. 'It's helping me to find myself. It really makes me think. Do you know, I wanted to sign a hire purchase agreement the other day, and I wasn't allowed to without my husband's consent? In this day and age! 1971! And at the moment, I'm earning more than he is. But *he's* the head of the house. Head of the house – I ask you.'

'You're beginning to despise him, aren't you?' Sam looked at her keenly.

'No, I'm not. I'm just angry. Angry for all that women have endured in the last two hundred years, in fact throughout history – but especially since the suppression of women began in earnest in the nineteenth century.'

Agnes had spent hours in the library researching the history of the Women's Movement in Britain and America. Why, after the suffrage, had women not pressed on to secure their newly-gained advantages? Why, had there been such a wide-scale retreat to hearth and home on the part of well-educated women? Because they were afraid, according to Friedan and others – afraid of being stereotyped as bitter spinsters. For the sake of so-called self-fulfilment in their roles as wives and mothers, women gave up any chance of promising careers. Home and a happy sex life were the ultimate feminine goals, and no woman who lacked these things could possibly consider herself fulfilled. Sometimes Agnes saw herself among the ranks of these women – unrecognised, perhaps, but there. She couldn't be accused of embracing matrimony, home and children willingly; but nonetheless, in her fear, in her dread of not conforming, she had sacrificed much of herself that was important and that she was now discovering.

'I've heard rumours that you and Barry are splitting up.' Sam looked at his typewriter passing his fingers over the keys.

'Well, we're not! Barry may take a job in Aberdeen, but we're not breaking up our home here, in case he doesn't like it.'

'Would you go later?'

'I might.'

'I see.' She saw Sam didn't believe her.

'People love making up rumours,' Agnes said. 'Look, if Barry's selected again as Labour candidate he may not go at all. It's much too early to tell what's going to happen in the future. Meanwhile I'm glad of this work. Thank you.'

'I don't think you'll have any trouble getting work in future. I might even take you on the staff – that's if you want it.'

'Let's see what happens, Sam.' Agnes stifled the feeling of excitement inside her. 'And you really want me to go and squat? God knows what Barry will say!'

Sam grinned evilly. 'If he didn't intend to leave you before, he might do now! The best of British when you tell him.'

'I really think it's the end!' Barry said. 'What's going to happen to the children while you squat, for Christ's sake?'

'Mum said she'd look after them if you don't mind having her here. She can look after you, too. You don't exactly seem to thrive on the household routine.' Now it was Agnes's turn to look contemptuously round the dining room. Everything was as it had been when she left home: beds unmade, table littered with crockery, dishes still waiting to be washed up. Barry had even dumped Christopher on a neighbour, and Agnes knew that he'd gone back to bed again as soon as she had left.

'I tell you, I don't feel well,' Barry said, noticing her expression. 'I've got the 'flu coming or something. Well, I suppose it's all right, if your mother doesn't mind. But what about your father?'

'He's going into hospital for a while to have his lungs cleared. Mum will be glad of a chance to get out of the flat, and I think she'd enjoy it here. It would give us all a break.'

'You mean you're going to *enjoy* squatting?'

Agnes looked at him, unsmiling. 'I'm just climbing out of the rut, Barry, can't you see that? Can't you see that I'm not happy as I am and that I want to do something else?'

'Oh, I can see *that* all right.' Barry glanced around the room with a gesture that wasn't lost on Agnes. 'In fact I'd say that it's your sluttish, unhousewifely habits that have destroyed our marriage!'

Agnes sat down, gripping the arms of the chair, staring up at him, white-faced.

'How can you say that? Do you really think it's true?'

'Yes.' Barry tilted his chin defensively. 'That, and our inability to understand each other.'

'I'd have thought that came first. I once said that I was sorry I'd married you, Barry. That wasn't strictly true. I loved you and I did want to marry you. What I regretted, and what I think I was trying to say, was that I don't think you ever really loved me as much – or maybe loved me at all. I think you've always suffered from the feeling that you did me a favour – and that's what soured our marriage, not my failings as a housewife. You've just picked on them to express your discontent.'

'That's not true!' Barry said tetchily. 'I did love you, and I still do. Why, our love life ...'

Agnes held up a hand. 'I'm not talking about that. How two incompatible people can enjoy such sexual harmony, I don't know, but that part's always been great.'

'Let's go to bed now, then.' Barry's expression rapidly altered and he held out a beckoning hand. But Agnes stood her ground.

'You still think sex can settle everything, don't you?'

'It settles a lot. And if you're going squatting, we mightn't have it for a bit ...'

'There's always Rose,' Agnes said suddenly. 'Oh, of course, you never see her now, do you? Or do you?'

'No, I don't,' Barry said firmly – virtuous, because for once he was telling the truth. 'I don't see Rose and I don't sleep with her, so please don't resurrect that old red herring. Throw it away, forget about it, leave it alone. And for goodness' sake don't tittle-tattle with Grace! She causes all the trouble around here; she and Connie Shilton.'

338

'Why bring Grace into it?' Agnes asked, surprised.

'Because you talk to her about me,' Barry said defensively. 'You talk to her about our sex life, don't you? You can't keep anything to yourself. Women! That's why they're inferior; they can't resist a gossip.'

Agnes got furious despite herself. 'Oh, for God's sake! Grace and I gossip very little about intimate matters, if you want to know.' She paused and looked at him. 'I don't know how *you'd* know anyway.'

Barry got up and went hurriedly towards the door. 'Stop being so complicated. Christ, I shan't be sorry when this squat begins.'

Barry stumpd out of the room, leaving Agnes sitting thoughtfully in her chair, looking after him.

From the window of her old room, Agnes looked out across the rubble. She could see as far as the high-rise flats where her parents lived. It was certainly lighter indoors now than it was then, but she wasn't so sure things had improved in other ways. In the old days there used to be a row of houses opposite just like hers, where the Barnes's lived. She wondered what had happened to them, and to all the Barnes children she used to go to school with. She could remember the names of all the people who once lived in Enderby Street, on both sides. When Enderby had gone, a community had been broken up.

'It's a sight for sore eyes, isn't it?' Jenny Wallace standing next to her, stuck out her head. 'What a waste! If only we'd known about squats then.'

'You think we'd have saved it?'

'Oh, yes. If we'd have made a fuss like this.'

Agnes shared this room with Jenny Wallace and her four children. The baby screamed constantly and the nights seemed interminable; there was no electric light, and if you wanted anything or had to do anything, you had to grope around for matches in the dark and light a candle.

'People have learned they can get things changed if they make enough fuss. The Women's Movement's made them stronger.'

Jenny looked sceptical. She was a thin, nervous woman with dyed blonde hair and an emaciated figure.

'Don't give me that, Agnes! The Women's Movement's just composed of middle-class types like you. They don't really get anything done. They just talk or write. It's the women *here*, the real working class of this country, who get things done.'

Jenny jerked a hand behind her back and bent down to slap three-year-old Nicky, who wanted her, not unreasonably, to pick him up. Jenny did a lot of hitting, and it got on Agnes's nerves.

This was her fifth day on the squat, and already she had sensed hostility towards herself and other helpers. Roman Payne was particularly unpopular. The one woman most accepted was Connie; at least she spoke the same language.

'But *I'm* working-class, Jenny,' Agnes said angrily. 'I lived in this very house until I got married, and my father worked in the pit with his hands. You can't get more working-class than that!'

'But that was your parents,' Jenny said pointedly. 'You married a Member of bloody Parliament! You write for the papers. I wouldn't call you working-class now – not with that accent, I wouldn't.'

Agnes found her own accent hard to place; but Paul now had only the very slightest Yorkshire intonation. She supposed she must sound the same.

'I consider I'm working-class, and I identify with you women completely. By writing I can help you, and help us all to try and change things.'

Jenny giggled. 'Well, if you can get me a decent flat, that'll do to be getting on with. A flat and a nice new husband, so I don't have to go out to work.'

Jenny's husband was in prison. His criminal activities had given her a nervous breakdown, and the children had been taken into care. When she recovered she refused to be rehoused in a tower block, and the alternative had been to put the children back into care again. So Jenny had joined the squat.

From next door came the sound of banging, and a child started screaming. Agnes dashed through the door into the room that had belonged to her parents, and found it full of children. One had got hold of a hammer and was banging the bare boards. Accidentally he had hit the hand of his brother. Agnes scooped up the injured child.

'We'll have to put this under the tap. Where's your mum?'

'Downstairs.'

'Come on, then. Jenny, can you take that hammer from Alfred?'

Downstairs, the women were gathered in the kitchen and what had once been the Rivingtons' sitting room. The downstairs windows were boarded up and the atmosphere was dark and gloomy. Candles guttered in the saucers, and in a corner was a paraffin lamp. But there was much noise and laughter coming from the kitchen, where a cheerful group were trying to prepare a communal meal on a portable calor gas stove.

'Is Clive's mother here?'

A small, neat woman with a frying pan in her hand turned round. 'What is it, love?'

'Alfred's banged Clive on the hand.'

Clive began to bawl again at the sight of his mother, and Agnes went over to the bucket of water by the side of the door, which had been left open to get rid of the smell of cooking. There was no running water since everything had been cut off by the council when it had been planned to demolish the house. The Squatters' Committee had tried to get the services restored – at least, light and water – but instead had been threatened with a repossession order.

The squat wasn't yet two months old, and already tempers on the council were very frayed, especially as local elections were looming and the fuss in Beckersleigh was bad for the Tory image. It had been agreed that if the women would move out, the houses would be restored for family habitation again, and similar ones, but with indoor bathrooms, built on the rubble opposite. Except that the new ones wouldn't be quite the same; they would be built of nice red brick, not like the blackened dwellings built in the time of Queen Victoria, which remained.

But the women didn't want to move. They had heard all about council promises before. They wanted accommodation which they could move into straight away: houses or flats of their own – and no more high-rise blocks.

Every day Agnes wrote an article for the *Chronicle* in the form of a diary, and now journalists from other papers came to interview her, rather than the women for whom the squat was being organised. Not unnaturally, the squatters began to regard her not as one of them, but as a celebrity, an interloper.

Agnes was drying Clive's hand when his mother, Norah Drew, finished her cooking and came over, kneeling by the bucket.

'Thanks, Agnes. I'll give Alfred hell for playing with that hammer.'

'Well, there isn't much else for him to do.' Agnes looked out of the door. 'It's been raining all day. The thing that worries me about the squat, is that the children don't go to school.'

Agnes got on with Norah better than the others; Norah at least seemed to realise that Agnes was genuine.

'If we let them go to school, we'd never get them back. They'd take them into care.'

'No, they wouldn't. The children are restless and unhappy here; they're all crying upstairs.'

'I suppose it gets on your nerves, doesn't it, Mrs Holloway?' Doreen Livingstone always called Agnes "Mrs Holloway" as a way of setting Agnes apart from herself and the others. Agnes liked her least.

'Well, it gets on *yours*, doesn't it, Doreen?' Agnes got up from the floor.

'Yes, but I have to be here – you don't, Mrs Holloway.'

'I'm trying to help you by being here!'

'Yes, but how would you feel if you really *had* to be here, eh, Mrs Holloway? If you had no nice home to go to? If the squat was all you had in the world?'

'I'd hate it. That's why I want you to have a home, too.'

'A nice home like yours, Mrs Holloway?'

Doreen's husband was an alcoholic and regularly beat her up. Even now he was trying to get her back, and of all the women here she was probably the one with the most to fear. She had three small children, two of whom had had limbs broken by her husband.

'Oh give over, Doreen,' Madge Gordon said. She'd taken over from Norah at the stove, from which a pungent smell of fried sausages wafted from the large frying pan. 'You're always getting at Agnes. She can't help the way she is, any more than you can.'

Madge smiled at Agnes. She was a friendly young girl, with two children and no known husband. She was pretty and flirtatious and spent hours each morning plastering herself with make-up. 'Come on, let's all eat. Call them kids from upstairs.'

In the main room there was a ramshackle table and chairs, presented by a well-wisher. The women ate from the table, the children sat on the floor.

Agnes went out shopping every day for provisions and usually called in at the *Chronicle* to deliver her article and have a chat with Sam. She enjoyed these outings because, truthfully, as much as she sympathised with the women, the whole thing got her down. All the women seemed to want were the things which she felt trapped by: a safe marriage and a nice house.

'Going out this afternoon, Agnes?' Madge said, passing her plate.
'Yes.'

'Would you get me some shampoo? And a can of lager, if you can. They were so horrible to us at that pub last night I'm going to drink here.'

'Oh, *I*'m going again,' Jenny said. 'Just let them try and throw us out once more, the buggers.'

Agnes and Roman had babysat the previous night while some of the women went out to the pub. The landlord had doubted their ability to pay and had refused to serve them. A potentially ugly brawl had broken out between the women and the largely male clientèle, and in the end the landlord threatened to call the police and the women left.

'We don't want the police on us, Jen,' Norah protested. 'That's just the kind of excuse they need to get us out of here, and then we'd all end up in prison.'

'This isn't a police state!' Agnes exclaimed. 'You've got a legal right to squat on a deserted property and to drink freely in public houses.'

'*If* you can pay.' Doreen looked meaningfully at Agnes and sniggered.

'Doreen seems to think I'm very rich. I'm not.' Agnes retorted.

'I didn't mean that! I meant that Norah had no intention of paying. She went to pick up a feller, if you ask me.'

'What's wrong with that?' Norah bridled. 'I don't have to be pure and chaste just because I'm in a squat, you know.'

'As long as you don't bring him here.' Doreen giggled and nudged Agnes, who looked anxiously at the children. The four mothers had eleven children between them. Jenny had four, Norah two, Doreen three and Madge two. Five adults and eleven children, in a house that had hardly sufficed for a family of four. Another mother had been here, also an Agnes; but she had left the previous day to go back to her husband, who had given an undertaking never to batter her again. The thought of a man being brought into the house for the purposes of sex was amusing or gruesome, depending on your point of view.

Suddenly there was a loud knock at the front door and everyone looked up, frightened.

'Police!' Norah hissed. 'Let's go upstairs and barricade ourselves in.'

'They have to serve the repossession notice first, and they haven't done that yet.' Agnes quietly got up and went over to the door.

'Who is it?'

'It's Roman. I've got your husband with me.'

'Can you come round to the back? We don't open this door.' Agnes went slowly back to the table.

'Who is it, love?'

'It's Roman, with Barry.' Agnes got up as the two visitors came through the open kitchen door, Barry having to duck because the lintel was so low.

'Well, fancy you being back in Number Fifty-two, Agnes! I bet this is why you came!'

Barry, looking large and very handsome, put his hand up in his best Labour Candidate salute and waved at the women. 'Hello, ladies! Is my wife looking after you?'

The woman succumbed as one to his charm immediately and turned their chairs towards him, patted their hair or rearranged their clothes – much to Agnes's amusement.

'Tea, Mr Holloway?' Doreen looked ingratiatingly towards him and lifted the pot.

'If you could spare it, I'd love a cup.' His accent was now broad Yorkshire, the intonation just right, authoritative but brisk and friendly. In no time at all, the women gathered round him as he talked to them or listened to their stories, offering advice. Barry was in his element.

Agnes began to clear away while Roman helped.

'Your husband's going down very well,' Roman murmured. 'He *is* nice Agnes. He's terribly worried about you, how you're sleeping, what you're eating ...'

'Oh, you've talked to him, have you?'

'Yes. I showed him the other houses and I think he's very impressed. He really knows nothing about the housing shortage, you know, the jostling for places, the corruption in local government. Do you think he can do anything? He says he can.'

'He didn't seem very interested when I last spoke to him; but maybe he's been converted.'

Everything had been washed up and cleared away when Barry finally stood up, having drunk five cups of tea and smoked as many cigarettes. With people in crowds, Barry was undoubtedly very good indeed.

'Girls, I'll do what I can, I promise you. I'll go personally to the Chairman of the Housing Committee, whom I know – even though he's a Tory. Agnes's great friend Grace Calthorpe also knows the local MP very well.'

'Calthorpe!' Norah exclaimed in outrage. 'Them posh people!'

'Grace and Agnes were at school together,' Barry told her gleefully. 'They've been friends ever since.'

'Now, then!' Norah looked accusingly at Agnes. 'Tell *her* to come and see us at the squat.'

'I'm sure she'd be glad to.' Agnes glared at Barry. 'And she'd be very helpful. Barry, could you give me a lift into town? I want to go to the *Chronicle* and do some shopping.'

'I've masses of things to do at home,' Barry said. 'Lots of people are dropping by with boxes of things because of your articles. I've brought some. Given them to Roman.' Barry smiled a smile that he seemed to save specially for Roman.

'Well, could you drop me at the offices and go and fetch more? I can walk back.'

'I'd need help,' Barry said. 'Roman, do you consider yourself strong enough to help a mere man? Do you reckon you're *safe* with me?'

'Try me,' Roman said. 'I can match a man – any time.'

She met Barry's gaze with a bold, saucy smile.

CHAPTER TWENTY-EIGHT

'YOU USE YOUR CHARM SHAMELESSLY,' Roman commented, as they drove on after dropping Agnes off at the offices of the *Chronicle*. 'But I notice you're not so charming to your wife.'

Barry glanced at her as he changed gears. Suddenly he seemed to be driving as though he were at the wheel of a high-powered sports car, not his rather decrepit five-year old Ford. 'Well, first you tell me how you keep up with the charm through *nine* years of marriage.'

'But can't you at least be nice?'

'I am *very* nice. If you knew what I had to put up with, you – even you – would, I'm sure, consider me very nice indeed. Agnes isn't an easy woman, you know. She's stubborn and provocative. She's a terrible housekeeper and she spends her life opposing me.'

'I can see you don't get on – it's quite obvious. But the women loved you.'

'They're all looking for a man, that's why. Don't kid yourself, Roman. They're not interested in women's rights; just a man and a home.'

'That's what Agnes says. I think she's very disappointed in the squat. There's not a true women's liberationist among them.'

'That's why I get on with them,' Barry said with a smile. 'Here we are.'

They arrived at the house to find it a haven of peace, cleanliness and order. Kathleen Rivington loved housework, and in the few days she'd been there she had transformed it almost out of recognition. The hallway was now clear of toys and, for the first time ever, the hall table held a large vase full of spring flowers. Barry breathed a sigh of pleasure as he wandered through the house, pointing out the improvements to Roman.

'Well, Agnes isn't a housekeeper. She doesn't pretend to be. She wants to do other things than keep house. I don't blame her.' Roman looked quite indignant on Agnes's behalf.

'But her mother's a beautiful housekeeper *and* kept down a tedious full-time job in a woollen mill.'

'But her mother was a different generation, Barry. She was brought up like that.'

'So was Agnes.'

'Agnes is frustrated,' Roman said impatiently.

'Oh, she's not frustrated.' Barry puffed out his chest like a turkey and lit a cigarette.

'I don't mean sexually,' Roman said coolly. 'One is frustrated when one is deprived of anything that contributes towards fulfilment in life. Agnes wants to be a writer. She's in her element right now. Connie said Agnes was very bright and should have gone to university. Instead she had to marry you.'

'That's not true at all!' Barry said indignantly. 'She was working when she married me. She was twenty-three. *I* didn't stop her going to university. She was jolly glad to marry me, anyway.'

Roman gave a low laugh. 'You really are a male chauvinist pig, aren't you, Barry?'

Barry produced the sherry bottle from the cupboard.

'Drink?'

'Yes, all right. But I must be getting back soon. Where's your mother-in-law?'

'She'll be somewhere with the children.' He passed Roman her drink and raised his glass. 'Cheers!'

'Cheers!' Roman lifted her eyes and met Barry's. Her long gold plait lay across her shoulder and her large, sensual mouth was slightly parted. Barry felt a lump come into his throat, and swallowed.

'You're a bloody attractive girl, you know, Roman. Talk about turning on the charm – you can do it too. If I didn't know you were a Les, I'd think you rather fancied me.'

'That's a disgusting thing to say!'

'Why is it disgusting?'

'That term "Les". I find it offensive. I wouldn't say "if you weren't a hetero". For all I know, you might like men, too.'

'Well, I don't.' Barry grimaced with distaste and poured more sherry into both their glasses.

'And I don't like only women! I've had boyfriends, too, you know.'

'I bet you have. You don't seem like a Lesbian, frankly. Your eyes are too naughty ...' He bent and looked into them, and despite herself, Roman smiled. 'And you can't honestly tell me you get any satisfaction from going to bed with Connie Shilton? You're a most incongruous pair, if I may say so. I've never cared for Connie at all; she's a bitch. And she's never liked me.'

'I know.'

'Do you think she fancied Agnes?'

'Maybe.' Roman looked at him speculatively. 'You're really very unsure of yourself sexually, aren't you, Barry? Determined to prove yourself at all costs.'

He bent swiftly and kissed her. Roman didn't struggle; if anything, she twisted her body so as to make herself more comfortable. She was enjoying herself. And she was responding, too, one hand going round his neck and drawing him closer to her. Barry's hands moved down from her shoulders to her breasts, safely encased not only in a shirt but dungarees. They were quite large and bra-less underneath her clothes. The feel of them increased his desire, and he tried roughly to undo the fasteners of her dungarees.

Roman broke away, two cool hands firmly on his. 'Oh no, brother!'

'Come on!' His eyes had his pleading, little-boy look. 'I know you fancy me, Roman. I know you'd like to have it off with me. Let's go upstairs to bed.'

'To *Agnes's* bed?' Roman got up with a struggle and refastened the one button he had managed to undo. 'You really are a pig, Barry Holloway! I don't think you've got any morals, at all.'

'Oh, I've one or two. But don't think I've finished with you yet, Roman Payne. I haven't.'

They smiled at each other, as though each were anticipating a secret excitement to be shared in the not-too-distant future. Roman sighed, swallowed her sherry, and said: 'Where are all the boxes you wanted me to help you move, Tarzan?'

He liked the look in her eyes.

Kathleen Rivington had entered her old home with some reluctance, and stood for a long time looking about her.

'Well, I don't know,' she said. She kept on repeating it as Agnes took her round the house from room to room, bare of furniture now, but littered with belongings of various kinds. It was a fine day and the women had taken the children to play up at the slag, which had now been turned into a playground. Agnes and her mother were alone in their former home.

Kathleen gazed wistfully out of the window. 'I prefer this view to the one we've got now, however fine it's supposed to be. Every morning, in all weathers, I used to get up and look at the backs of those houses. When it was a nice day, the morning sun shone on the back and you could see just a bit of blue sky above. Sometimes they were shrouded in mist, and sometimes they were wet with the rain. I used to be able to tell what kind of day it would be by how the houses looked to me in the morning – *and* how your dad would be and how the children would behave. It was a barometer. Funny, isn't it?' She gave Agnes her rare, beautiful smile.

Agnes put an arm round her mother's shoulder. Kathleen, untypically, put her own arm round Agnes's waist, gripping it tightly.

'Your father thinks you should go with Barry, you know that, love. He's very upset about it. We think your place is with your husband.'

'*We*? Or just Dad?'

'Well, your father especially – but I agree with him. I really do.'

'I wonder if you *really* do, Mum.' Agnes turned and looked into her mother's eyes. 'You're so used to doing what Dad wants, thinking as he thinks. I don't believe you really know your own mind. Do you?'

'That's not fair, Agnes.'

Agnes went and leaned against the mantelpiece. 'You know, I spent a good deal of my life doing what my father wanted – and then a lot more doing what my husband wanted. When I thought about it afterwards, it seemed to me that their desires didn't always coincide with mine. Dad wanted me to leave school – and I didn't; Dad didn't want me to work at Calthorpes – I did. I didn't really want to get married, but Dad wanted me to. I didn't want to settle down and become a housewife, but Barry said it was all I could do. Now I certainly don't want to go to Aberdeen, and neither Dad nor Barry are going to make me. I'm going to assert my own independence, Mum. I'm going to do what I want.' Agnes's voice was quiet, forceful.

Her mother sat on one side of the low camp-beds and clasped her hands in front of her. Her whole attitude was one of resignation, almost of despair. Agnes was suddenly stricken with love for her.

'Agnes,' her mother said at last, looking up. 'I know you're modern and all that, but I don't think you're on the right lines. I feel, and your father does too, that you and Barry are thinking of getting divorced. We think that you're using this Aberdeen thing as an excuse to separate. Now, divorce may be very common these days, Agnes, but that doesn't mean people should approve of it. Your father and I certainly don't. It was bad enough having a daughter who *had* to get married, like you did; but to have you getting divorced is very hard for us to accept. We regard it as shameful, Agnes – and possibly harmful to your brother. We do beg you to think again.'

'You're not *still* thinking of Paul!' Despite herself, Agnes felt suddenly furious. She loved her brother – but why did her parents always put him first? *Why?*

'And why shouldn't we? Paul has never done a thing to hurt or annoy us. He's been a model of what a son should be. We're proud of him, and grateful. Oh, we're not entirely happy that he's marrying Grace, but if it's what he wants, we accept it. If Grace behaves herself and does as he wishes, she can be an asset to our Paul in his career. But if you and Barry get divorced, think how that'll reflect on Paul.'

'I don't think it'll reflect on Paul at all, Mum,' Agnes said shortly. 'We don't exactly move in his circles, you know. Anyway, Barry and I aren't anticipating divorce just yet.'

'I like Barry, Agnes. He's a nice, kind man, grateful for anything you do. He's not used to being looked after. You can tell that. And he's that good in the house! He'll help me wash up the dishes and ...'

'He'll *what*?' Agnes said, and burst out laughing, more from hysteria than amusement. 'Oh Mum, if you could see Barry normally ... Oh, I can't believe it. He helps you *wash up*, did you say? Oh my, oh my.'

'What's Agnes find so funny?' Just then, Barry came through the door, a pleased smile on his face. Behind him stood Roman with a pile of blankets.

Over the last few days, they had been back and forth between the house and various collecting points, where the good people of Beckersleigh had nobly responded to the crisis in their midst. The truth was that the squat had now become quite a fashionable cause. All the best people were to be seen visiting and leaving gifts, including the two Mrs Calthorpes – Mrs Rose and Mrs Grace. Mrs Malcolm Longley, the MP's wife, had even stayed to cook a meal – much photographed by the cameras as she did so, for the council elections were due in May, and it was considered of the greatest importance to the Tory Party that the squat should be amicably disbanded and magnanimously resolved. It was the unanimous opinion of all that it was a scandal for women and children to have to take such action in order to draw attention to their lot. Labour and Conservative were united on this point.

Money flooded in, and gifts of all kinds and even several homes were offered. Roman and Connie conducted tours round the houses, which had been specially cleaned for the occasion, while the squatters sat in carefully orchestrated poverty, hiding all the gifts that had been donated until the visitors had gone. Electricity and water were laid on free of charge until the problem was solved. The local butchers sent up the best cuts of meat several times a week; fresh dairy products and vegetables were delivered, telegrams, flowers and gifts of money continued to arrive. Not only the squatters began to think they were on to a good thing.

Gradually, those in the news were moved to the top of the housing queue and given flats and houses, and the protests of the many unknowns who had waited for a long time and who had now been pushed further down were quietly ignored.

By the time Kathleen visited her old home, there were only two houses left in the squat.

Some squatters were none too keen to leave. They found the houses comfortable, the food good, the companionship delightful and the siege atmosphere exhilarating. These women whom no one had ever taken the slightest notice of, who had spent their lives at the bottom of the heap and uncared for, now found themselves at the centre of attention, and understandably, they didn't want to give it all up. They knew that as soon as they were rehoused and off the front pages, things would be exactly the same as they always had been; no better, and perhaps even worse.

Roman and Barry stacked the blankets in a pile on the floor.

'Can we share the joke?' Barry said.

'It's about you washing up,' Agnes said, the mirth still showing on her face. 'Mum says you're ever so good in the house.'

'And you think that's funny, do you?' Barry was righteously indignant. 'You should see our house now. Sparkling like a new pin. It's a pleasure to help keep it like that.'

Roman smiled. 'You'll have high standards to keep up when you go back, Agnes.'

'*If* I go back,' Agnes said, turning to the window. 'If I don't decide to stay on the squat. Where are our kids?'

'Playing on the rubble with the others.' Roman began counting the blankets. 'They think it's marvellous fun. Better than any garden.'

Suddenly there was the noise of someone running up the stairs, and Connie burst into the room.

'Where the hell have *you* been?' she said, glaring at Roman.

Roman gave Connie one of her detached, superior smiles. 'Darling, we've been ferrying stuff back and forwards across Beckersleigh all day. Jenny and the children are being rehoused today, so I thought I'd give them these blankets.'

'There's still work for you to do here, you know!' Connie snapped. 'The Housing Inspector came, wanting to see you, and also the Chairman of the Town Planning with the architect who's going to convert the houses.'

'These houses are being converted?' Kathleen looked up in wonder.

'They're going to be made fit for people to live in again, Mum,' Agnes explained. 'Barry's had a lot to do with it.'

'So we needn't have moved at all,' Kathleen murmured, her face creased with pain. 'I doubt if your Dad would have taken so ill if it hadn't been for that high-rise. I wish we could come back again.'

'*Here*, Mother?' Barry said incredulously.

'I lived here all my married life, Barry,' Kathleen said wistfully. 'Me and Albert; we thought we'd die here, too.'

Connie stood between Barry and Roman, her large, bulky frame still quivering.

'Surely someone else could help Barry move the things, Roman? You *are* in charge here, you know.'

'Whatever you say, darling,' Roman said sweetly, stepping neatly over the pile of blankets and preparing to follow Connie. She glanced over her shoulder as she left the room and gave Barry her special smile. 'See you,' she said.

Albert Rivington died in his sleep a month after being admitted to hospital. He had no further words to say, no more advice to give to his family; he left no final message. And his calm, peaceful face in death seemed to suggest by its serenity that he was glad to be gone. He was buried in Beckersleigh Cemetery and Grace prepared a small family tea party back at the Calthorpe house.

'I'm insisting that Mrs Rivington stays with us,' she said, 'now that you're back at home, Agnes.'

'We've worked it all out,' Rose said calmly, passing a plate of cakes to Agnes.

'And we're bringing the wedding forward so that Mrs Rivington can come and live with us. It's to be the Ilkley house.' Grace smiled and looked at Paul.

'Ilkley?' Kathleen exclaimed, as though it was at the end of the universe. 'Oh, I could never live there!'

'But Mum, it's only fifteen miles away.' Paul took her hand.

'I don't care, dear. I was born in Beckersleigh and I want to die here; not in Ilkley!'

'But Mum, no one's talking of dying,' Paul said gently.

'We won't be in the house for at least three months,' Grace said. 'You can stay here until then, Mrs Rivington.' Grace's smile was tender and reassuring. But Kathleen looked round the living room as though the whole place terrified her.

'I don't know that I want to stay,' she said timidly. 'I'll have to think about it.' Her eyes appealed to Agnes for help. 'I think I'd really like to stop with our Agnes.'

'Mum can stay with us as long as she likes,' Agnes said quickly. 'There's plenty of room. Besides, Barry's used to having her now. She's transformed the house.'

'We shall miss you an awful lot, Mum, if you go,' Barry said, sounding sincere. 'Anyway, I'll be going soon.'

'You're really going to Aberdeen?' Henry took another cake, doing his best to ignore a warning look from Rose. He had been told to diet for his blood-pressure.

'Yes. I've decided not to stand for re-election. I don't want a second humiliation.'

'But you've done such a lot for the women,' Rose murmured, pouring tea. 'The papers have had some very fine things to say about you. Even the *Chronicle* has changed its tune.'

'Aye, it has.' Henry wiped his mouth carefully. 'More cake, Mrs R?'

Barry lit a cigarette and pushed his chair away from the table.

'Yes, I think I've done a lot for the squat.' Barry dusted his lapel where some ash had fallen. 'But I don't stand a chance of being re-elected here. The hard core Left are taking over – politics in Beckersleigh will never be the same.' He shrugged. 'I may seek a seat elsewhere.'

'You're leaving for good?' Paul looked sharply at Agnes.

'Well ... we'll see. First I want to see how the job turns out; then I want Agnes to come and see how she likes it. Houses are cheaper there, and we could afford to rent something much nicer than the one we've got now. Perhaps we could even buy a place.'

'They say Aberdeen's going to be quite a boom town, what with the North Sea oil,' Henry said. 'How will you like that?'

'I think it'll be good. It'll inject a bit of life into the place. And Agnes ...'

'I'm *not* going to Aberdeen,' Agnes said quietly. 'You know that, Barry, so why talk about it?'

There was a pregnant pause. Barry pushed his chair back even further and raised his eyes to the ceiling.

'You can see how unreasonable she is. She won't even see the place. Well, at least no one can blame me. I did all I could.'

'It was Albert's dying wish that Agnes and Barry should stay together,' Kathleen said tremulously. 'It was the one thing he really wanted. For all I know, the prospect of their separation finally killed him.'

'Mum, that's unfair! I don't know how you can say that.' But as she spoke, Agnes was aware that the mood of the gathering was against her. 'We don't know *what* Dad's dying wish was – and as for killing him, that's a monstrous thing to say.'

'I *do* know what he wanted,' Kathleen said in the same quiet voice. 'Each time I visited him, he said the same thing: "I do hope they don't split up, Kathleen. For the sake of those children ..."' Kathleen bowed her head and tears started to trickle from her eyes.

Barry, sitting next to her, put his hand on her arm. 'Now Mum, don't take on. You're upset. Don't upset yourself further. Agnes and I will work something out, you'll see.'

When they got up from the table, most of the party went into the garden to get some air, while Rose supervised the clearing of the table: Barry lingered in the dining room.

'I never even seem to get the chance of a quiet word with you, Rose,' he murmured. 'Let alone anything else.'

They hadn't made love for months.

'Barry, you know it hasn't been possible,' Rose said, anxious in case anyone else should come in. 'Besides, it made me so nervous that day with Grace. I couldn't contemplate it until she moves out again.'

'Grace saw me that day,' Barry said. He had never told her until now, because he had known exactly how she would react. But what he hadn't anticipated was that she would stop sleeping with him without even knowing the truth.

Rose had a plate in her hand, and Barry neatly fielded it as she tottered sideways, reeling with the shock.

'*Grace saw you leaving?*'

'She waited outside in the car. She wanted to know. She already suspected.'

'How?'

'She and Agnes got together. But Grace promised she wouldn't say anything.'

'Do you think she has?'

'I don't know; but then Agnes knew about you and me before, and Grace didn't.'

'Oh, my God! If Henry got to hear . . .' Rose looked apprehensively towards the door.

'I don't think she'd ever tell her father. Besides, why should she? She loves him, and she knows he's happy. It would be too cruel. I don't think Grace is that cruel, do you?'

'We can never start up again then, Barry!' Rose was dreadfully agitated.

'That's partly why I'm going away,' Barry said. 'You belong too much to Beckersleigh in my memory. I want a clean break.' It wasn't the truth; but he felt it was nice to make women feel important and wanted. There was nothing lost in being nice – his parliamentary career had taught him that.

Rose put a hand on his arm, close to tears. 'We had good days, Barry.'

'Very good. We'll always be part of each other.'

He looked at her tenderly. Then she hurried away into the kitchen with the rest of the plates, before she broke down. What with a funeral and now this it had been a terrible day for her.

Barry, on the other hand, thought it had all gone rather well. Old men, however regrettably, had to die, just as old mistresses had to be – gently – disposed of.

He wandered into the garden with his hands in his pockets to join the others, feeling quite pleased with himself.

CHAPTER TWENTY-NINE

AGNES HAD JUST BROUGHT THE children home from school when Connie rang, sounding frantic.

'The police are going to come and turf Norah and Doreen out!' she gasped. 'You've got to *do* something. Is Barry there?'

'Barry's away in Liverpool. But I thought they agreed to go?'

'They've changed their minds; you'll have to come. They've barricaded themselves in, and the police have got a warrant. They're going to move them forcibly.'

'Oh, my God! We can't have the squat ending like this. They'll lose sympathy. People have had enough.'

Agnes drove quickly to Enderby Street, where a small crowd had already formed. A fairly large force of policemen had surrounded the house and the usual clusters of photographers and pressmen were in attendance. The heads of Norah and Doreen poked defiantly out of the upstairs windows of Number Fifty-two. They were shaking their fists, hurling abuse, and clearly having the time of their lives. Everyone recognised Agnes and stood back to let her through. A policeman, with pips on his shoulder, touched his peaked cap.

'Afternoon, Mrs Holloway. I hope you can persuade them to be reasonable.'

'I'll try. Can I get in?'

The policeman shrugged. 'Miss Shilton here has already tried.' Connie gazed helplessly at Agnes and the police official. 'I'm afraid we'll have to break the door down,' the policeman concluded, rubbing his hands together.

'Oh, don't do that.' Agnes stood back and called up. 'Let me in!'

'Fuck off!' Doreen snarled. 'You've done enough harm already, Mrs High-and-Mighty Holloway.'

'Where's your husband, darling?' Norah sneered. 'We'd let *him* in!' Doreen screamed with laughter and gave Norah a playful shove; for a moment Norah disappeared from view.

'Let me come in!' Agnes begged. 'Think of the kids.'

'We're thinking of them. That's why we don't want to leave. I've got to go back to my old man, you know – and I've never believed *his* promises.'

'Let me in! The reporters are taking all this down.' Agnes felt hope rise when she saw them put their heads together and confer. Norah stabbed a finger at her and cupped her mouth in her hand.

'Just you, then. No one else. Promise?'

'I promise,' Agnes called back. She felt triumphant. Maybe they did trust her after all.

'Come in by the back door, then.' Norah's head disappeared again.

Agnes hurried round to the back where Norah was waiting for her at the door, a conspiratorial gleam in her eye.

'Come on in, love. Fancy a cuppa? The kettle's just boiling.'

'Norah, I don't think you're taking this seriously,' Agnes said censoriously. 'These men are going to arrest you.'

'Let them!' Norah poured water on the tea bags and stirred, her equanimity apparently quite unruffled by the commotion outside. She added milk and passed Agnes a mug. 'Come and talk to Doreen, but I warn you, she thinks like me.'

Upstairs, Doreen was still shouting obscenities out of the window, and the five children, ranging in age from three to eleven, sat on the floor, or took it in turns to run to the window and wave frantically to their friends down below. Obviously they were enjoying themselves enormously.

'Here's your tea, love.' Norah gave Doreen her mug. 'Milk's off.'

Doreen made a face and looked over the rim at Agnes.

'Now, what can we do for you, *Mrs* Holloway?'

Agnes's heart sank. If only it hadn't been Doreen. She had always been hostile to her.

'Doreen, I beg you to leave here quietly. The police won't arrest you or molest you. You did promise.'

'I've changed my mind. So's Norah.'

Doreen fluffed her yellow hair and looked defiantly at Agnes. She lit a cigarette and blew the smoke in her face. Both women smelt strongly of body odour and there was a dank, unkempt atmosphere throughout the house. It was three weeks since Agnes had stayed there. Now that the topicality of the squat was waning, she only devoted the occasional article to it. The battle appeared to have been won.

Agnes sipped her tea, her hands curled round the mug.

'Doreen, the council have done everything they promised. I know they were egged on to it by all the publicity, but that was the point of it. The squat, in human terms, has been one hundred per cent successful. These houses won't be torn down, they'll be made habitable again. Most of the women have got good accommodation. You've agreed to go back to your husband, who has given a pledge to the magistrate that he'll stop molesting you. He says he's anxious to start a new life in the new home the council have promised you both.'

'Tonight he'll beat me up, you know,' Doreen said, her eyes flashing. 'Sure as eggs is eggs.'

'But he won't! If he does, he'll be sent to prison.'

'But he will. I know him. Prison or no prison, he'll do it. Then where will I be?' She shivered, not dramatising now. 'Thinking about it made me change me mind.'

Agnes turned to Norah. 'Norah, please come with me.'

Norah looked doubtful. She had enjoyed the squat; now all that awaited her was accommodation in a hostel. She had stayed mainly to keep Doreen company, rather than through any conviction of her own. But it did look as though the game was up.

'Shall we, Doreen?' she said.

'No!' Doreen dragged at her cigarette and flicked the ash on the floor. 'Mrs Holloway is a fucking fascist just like the rest of them! Don't you know we've been *used*, Norah? Mrs Holloway here has had all the publicity she wanted. She'll probably write a book about us now – while my husband drinks himself to death and beats me and the kids black and blue every night. Mrs Holloway's a published writer. She wrote a novel. Do you think she really cares one fuck about us, or the likes of us? She's like all these bloody journalists and people crowding round: they don't give a damn about people like us.' She ground out her cigarette on the floor, folded her arms and glared at Agnes.

'We're staying,' Norah said firmly, and folded her arms too.

Agnes ran down the stairs and out of the back door, then leaned against the wall and wept. Behind her she could hear one of them, Norah or Doreen, turning the key firmly in the lock and once more dragging the table up against the door.

When Agnes went to the front of the house her tears were dry. She shook her head. 'No good, I'm afraid.'

'But why not?' Connie held her arm and looked at her.

'They think I'm a fascist. You should have gone in, Con. They always liked you better.'

'They threw a chamber pot at me this morning,' Connie said sadly. 'If only Roman were here.'

'Yes, where *is* Roman?' Agnes looked round.

'Don't ask me. She went off somewhere for the day. Very mysterious about it.'

'Oh.'

Behind them, the Police Superintendent had raised a megaphone to his lips:

'Ladies, if you do not come out of your own accord in five minutes – I will begin counting as soon as I have finished speaking – my men will forcibly break down the door and arrest you. Now please, ladies, come quietly.'

'Fuck off, you bastard!' Doreen and Norah shouted in unison, and shook their fists defiantly out of the window. One of the older children also appeared at the window and started waving a flag. The journalists licked their pencils and closed in as if for the kill; the TV cameras moved in towards the house. The Superintendent began counting.

As the police lined up, Agnes made for the front door. The big, burly police officer at the head would easily break it down, and his men would be in in no time. She wanted to try and get to the children before they were hurt ...

The tension was electric as the minutes went by, the Superintendent calling each one as it passed: 'One ... Two ... Three ... Four ... FIVE!' At a word of command the huge man splintered the door down with a massive shoulder and the rest of the column behind him hurled themselves in like a pack of rugby forwards. Agnes could hear shrieks and scuffling inside, then a child's scream. Without thinking, she dashed into the house.

Inside, it was bedlam. Doreen and Norah were standing at the head of the stairs, hurling down everything they could lay their hands on. But the first policeman, shielding his head with his hands, had already reached the landing. As he got to the top, Doreen and Norah backed into the front bedroom.

'Please, Doreen, Norah!' Agnes yelled, but no one heard her. There was a terrific commotion upstairs, more shrieks and screams, then a red-faced policeman appeared, grasping Doreen round the waist. She was kicking and pummelling him with her hands. Behind her were two very frightened children, their hands firmly held by two more policemen. The policeman struggled with Doreen down the stairs, muttering curses. By now Doreen was in hysterics and took no notice of Agnes, standing helplessly at the bottom.

The policeman got Doreen to the door and pushed her outside. She fell into the street to cheers from the crowd. A wailing siren added to the confusion.

Two more children fled screaming down the stairs and Agnes grasped one of them and picked him up, holding him in her arms. He was bawling, and she murmured to him, trying to soothe him. But the sight of his mother, Norah, struggling with the police at the top of the stairs was enough to set him off again. He wriggled in Agnes's arms, and Norah made a frantic bid to tear herself free and run to him.

'For God's sake, let her go!' Agnes cried. '*This is her child*!'

Norah finally managed to wriggle away from the policeman and ran to the bottom of the stairs. He, red-faced and swearing, went after her, catching her by the hair and trying to drag her towards the door. The child screamed and Agnes put him down, fetched a jug from the table and banged it over the policeman's head. She saw him stagger, but his helmet saved him. She was crying and screaming, too. Suddenly a strong arm came from behind, thrust itself round her waist, and dragged her to the door.

She found herself pushed roughly into the street, to be greeted by a furious Superintendent.

'Mrs Holloway!'

'Do you know what your men are? They're *pigs*! she screamed. And she spat right into the Superintendent's face.

'All you really wanted was a man,' Barry said, gently easing himself away from her inert, panting body. 'My God, how you wanted one!'

He thought he could see tears under Roman's closed eyes, but he couldn't be sure; and whether she nodded her head or shook it he couldn't be sure either. She was still a mystery to him, as much after sex as before. She was not the sort of woman who would reveal her true self lightly – if at all. He would find her endlessly fascinating.

Rose had revealed everything to him, her body, her soul, her mind; immediately he had felt a kind of familiarity with her which had left him with nothing more to discover. Agnes was like Roman;

he doubted whether he would ever know all there was to know about her; but now he was tired of trying to find out. Let Agnes reveal her mysteries to another man; Barry was past caring.

Roman still lay with her legs slightly apart, her breasts trembling, her breathing rapid. Barry sat on the bed and shook a cigarette from the packet on the rickety table. It was a terrible hotel, not far from the station in the centre of Liverpool. Barry had chosen Liverpool for this assignation, because he thought there was very little chance of meeting anyone he knew there.

Now he wished they had chosen the Adelphi – then they could have had lunch in style. After his conquest of Roman, he felt like opening a bottle of champagne.

She was a marvellous lay. They had made love for an hour, and already she was able to time her orgasm to match his. Such synchronisation at the beginning of a relationship was unique in his experience; it was as though they had a natural, mutual harmony from the start. She had been so hungry for sex that for one moment he had thought he would be lost, that the excitement would make him ejaculate too quickly and spoil the whole thing. But then she had settled down, and so had he, and the result had been tremendous.

'I'm very hungry,' Roman said. She put her arm under her head and opened her eyes. Their blue was startling. Barry was awed. Roman got more beautiful the better you knew her. Their frantic kissing seemed to have made her lips thicker, more sensual and strong. Both their bodies were covered in sweat from the heat of the room, and the odour of sex and perspiration was pungent and stimulating. Barry leaned over and kissed her, running his hand along her body, pausing on a large fruitful breast.

'I wish we'd gone to the Adelphi. We could have had lunch sent up.'

'I like this place,' Roman said, her eyes roving around approvingly. 'It's so terribly seedy and decrepit, it's sexy. Love in the morning in some rotten commercial hotel in Liverpool! I've often dreamed of something like this; it's straight out of Hemingway. It turns me on.'

'Something certainly turned you on, all right! You're the most extraordinary girl I've ever known.'

'You just say that because it's the first time.' Roman challenged him with her eyes.

'I don't. I've wanted you for some time, and I think you've

wanted me. You like a good prick inside you.' Barry leaned nearer, feeling like starting all over again.

'Well, put crudely in that way – yes. But my feeling for women is more emotional; I *like* them much better than men. You and I, for instance, would always fight if we lived together. Maybe as you and Agnes do.'

'Mmm, maybe. Agnes and I should have stayed apart, that's for sure.' Barry tried to put a hand between Roman's legs, but she pressed them together and sat up, leaning on one elbow.

'We can't start all that again until I've eaten. I didn't have breakfast.'

'Shall I go out and get something?'

'Yes.' Roman gazed at him, looking very serious. 'How long have you taken this crummy old room for?'

'The whole day.'

'Good. Then we have the whole afternoon left.'

'What would you like to eat?' he said, dressing quickly.

'Fish and chips,' Roman said, and turned to lie on her face, her hands stretched out on the pillow. She sighed deeply.

By three o'clock they had consumed fish, chips and a bottle of white Spanish wine, and made love again.

'I can't understand how you do it with Connie,' Barry said, lying facing her, watching that graceful, mobile face.

'Well, we don't do it much, for a start. Our relationship isn't primarily sexual. It isn't very important to either of us, except as an expression of our friendship and feminine solidarity. If you like, it's a symbol.'

'But you prefer this, don't you?'

Roman gave her fleeting, detached smile. 'That must, by now, be obvious. I was very bitter when my boyfriend left me, you know. I was pregnant, and he just took off for Sweden and left me on my own.'

'What a pig!'

'He was a pig. The abortion was horrible, too, and I felt I never wanted a man to touch me again. Well, that's over! And I'm glad. I'm glad to feel I'm normal.'

'Oh you're normal,' Barry said. 'You're normal all right.'

She had even provided herself with a cap; no spontaneity for Roman, no risking another abortion. Everything would be thought out, the pros and cons fully weighed. In this way she was very unlike

Agnes, who was impulsive. Agnes acted first and thought later.

'What are we going to do about this, Barry? I mean, we can't come to Liverpool every time.' Roman gazed at him frankly.

Aberdeen; oh God, Aberdeen. Barry leaned back and closed his eyes.

'I can't go to Aberdeen,' he said. 'Not now that I've got you.'

'But I thought you and Agnes were splitting anyway?' She took the cigarette out of his mouth and puffed at it, replacing it between his lips.

'For you I'd stay with Agnes! I could get a job in Leeds or Bradford if it's not too late.'

'But I don't particularly want you to stay with Agnes, Barry. I may be bisexual, but I'm also jealous, you know. I mean, I'm not laying down any laws, but if this isn't to be just a one-off, you've got to think, and plan. Do you want it to be a one-off?'

'Of course not! I want an affair with you, Roman, a long, lasting affair. Then we can see. Can't we?'

He looked at her and knew that she understood. She lay back, looking contented.

'There's a selection meeting soon; I'll stand for re-selection after all. What I did for the squat must have done my reputation some good.'

'I'm sure it has. And so have Agnes's articles, to be fair. You're both very well thought of.'

'I wasn't going to stand at first, because I thought Connie and Jeff and their henchmen were well organised enough to rout me. Now I feel strong enough to stand against them – and win. Despite its majority, the government's so unpopular there's bound to be an election soon; that's why they're having a selection meeting. If I get in, we can go and live in London.'

'*We*?'

'You and I.'

'Great! I don't really like the idea of you screwing Agnes too, you know.'

'Ditto with Connie.'

'Oh, don't worry. I shan't touch her!' She laughed. 'It won't be a deprivation, I can assure you. Promise to do likewise with Agnes?'

'I'll try,' Barry said, thinking how difficult it would be in that small bed. 'But it wouldn't mean much to me, anyway. Not after you.'

*   *   *

Before Barry had been back in Beckersleigh five minutes, he learned that his wife was in a police cell. Not only were there newspaper notices everywhere proclaiming 'AGNES HOLLOWAY ARRESTED', but the porter on the station told him, the ticket collector told him, and any number of people on the platform rushed forward to tell him. Thankful that he and Roman had agreed to travel back separately, he went immediately to the police station.

The Duty Sergeant inspected a document. 'Mrs Holloway has been charged with breach of the peace, disorderly behaviour and assaulting a police officer.'

'Oh, my God! But surely you're not going to keep her here?'

'No, she can go. But she'll be required to attend the Magistrates' Court tomorrow.'

Just as the sergeant finished speaking, Grace and Paul came through the swing doors of the police station, and Agnes appeared simultaneously with Norah and Doreen. All three looked very dishevelled, and Doreen and Norah had obviously been crying. Not Agnes; she looked very calm now, a hard, tense expression on her face.

'Hello, Barry.'

'What in Christ's name have you been up to?'

'Please don't let's talk about it now. Let's go home,' Agnes said wearily.

Barry looked at Doreen and Norah. 'Where are they going?'

'Connie's putting them up for the night. She's gone off to get her car.'

'You must come back to us.' Grace took Agnes's arm. 'You'll need looking after.'

'I'm OK, Grace. I just feel very angry and very tired.'

On the steps of the police station they met Connie. Roman was at the wheel of the car. Connie ran up the stairs and put her arms round Agnes.

'You were absolutely heroic! A champion of women.'

'I was bloody mad,' Agnes said wryly. 'Mad at the way they dragged Doreen and Norah from the house. I'm sorry I spat at the Police Superintendent, though.'

'You *what*?' Barry put his hands to his ears as though unable to believe what he'd heard.

'I was so angry' She looked at him apologetically. 'It just made me feel that way; but I'm sorry all the same.'

Roman got out of the car in a leisurely fashion and walked slowly up the steps, ignoring Barry.

'I hear you were a heroine, Agnes. Congratulations.' She kissed her lightly on the cheek.

Barry couldn't help thinking how odd it was to see his newly acquired mistress kissing his wife in such circumstances, and it gave him a curious kind of pleasure and pride to think how intimately he knew both these good-looking women; that now the aloof, haughty Roman Payne was his mistress. *Mistress*. It was a lovely, sensual word – an old-fashioned term that Roman would surely object to, but Barry relished.

Norah and Doreen came onto the steps with Connie and once more burst into tears. Their children had all been taken to a hostel for the night. They'd hardly stopped crying since they arrived at the police station. Agnes felt disgusted with them, because it was their stupidity that had brought the whole thing about in the first place.

Barry turned to Agnes. 'Let's go home and sort this bloody thing out. My God, I could have done without this after a busy day.'

He meant it, too; he was very tired. A whole day making love was enough to exhaust the most vigorous man.

The following day the three women appeared before the Magistrates. All three were pleading guilty, so the formalities were relatively simple. Grace got her father to get in touch with Parsoe, who sent a solicitor to represent Agnes in Court. An apology was hastily drafted, which the solicitor read out to the Court on her behalf. Doreen and Norah also apologised, saying that they didn't know what had got into them and promising never to do anything like that again. The Magistrates were mollified and after some consultation asked if any of the women wanted to say anything before they were sentenced. Agnes stood up and said she did – much to the alarm of her solicitor.

The Court rustled with anticipation as Agnes was led to the witness box. Looking very pale and solemn, she cleared her throat and began to speak.

'I do apologise to the bench, and I am sorry for what happened. I would like to say, however, that the police handling of the case was abominable. They treated those women like animals – pulling them by the hair and dragging them along. There were only two defenceless women and five young children in the house, and it was a terrifying experience for them. I only went into the house to save them; but I was appalled by what I saw. There were at least six burly policemen in there – perhaps if there had been fewer, the women might have come quietly ...'

'But Mrs Holloway, they were pelting the police with objects as soon as they came into the house,' the Chairman of the Bench said disapprovingly. 'If you are really going to carry on in this vein, I suggest the case be adjourned so that we can hear the police side.'

'No,' Agnes said quickly. 'I have no more to say. I'm sorry that I lost control of myself, and I accept whatever punishment the Court passes. There was no excuse for me to behave like an animal simply because the police did. I am truly sorry.'

Agnes stepped down and the Court Usher solemnly escorted her to the dock, at which point the Court grew so noisy that the Chairman had to bang his gavel three times before he could proceed to the judgment of the Bench. Mrs Livingstone and Miss Drew were each fined £25 and bound over for a year to keep the peace. Mrs Holloway, because of her assault on a police officer, was fined £100 and also bound over for a year. If she misbehaved again she would be sent to prison.

'Women's liberation is all very well,' the Chairman said in what seemed a measured after-thought. 'But it has its time and place. By behaving in this fashion you do your cause no good, no good at all. You bring opprobrium upon yourselves and lose the sympathy of the public. In the case of Mrs Agnes Holloway, a woman with some standing in this community, this breach of the peace is all the more regrettable. You may stand down.'

Outside, it was just like the heyday of the squat all over again – reporters, cameras and a television crew. The BBC wanted Agnes to go to Leeds to record an interview for *Look North* after the evening news, but Agnes refused.

'I might have something to say later,' she said, 'but not now.'

'What does your husband think of all this, Mrs Holloway?' a reporter asked eagerly.

'Naturally, he's not very pleased; but then he didn't see what I saw.'

'Are you *really* sorry, Mrs Holloway?'

'Yes, I'm sorry it happened,' she said. 'I think no one came out of it with dignity. I'm sorry the squat, which did have a very real point to make about housing conditions in this country, had to end that way.'

Agnes suddenly felt close to tears and indicated that she wanted to get away. Barry was standing on the steps between Roman and Connie. He'd hardly spoken to Agnes the night before and, as she looked at him now, she saw something in his eyes she had never seen before: dislike. She and Barry had reached the end of the road.

For the rest of the week they scarcely spoke at all. It was unlike Barry to hold back like this, and Agnes began to feel uneasy. They had been planning to go to Blackpool for two weeks with the children and Agnes's mother. Now Barry said he wasn't going. Agnes didn't ask why.

The night before their departure she told Barry she wanted to talk to him.

'Can't it wait?' Barry said.

'No.'

Barry lit a cigarette and poured himself a drink.

'This has been an awful time,' Agnes began.

'You can say that again.' Barry didn't offer her a drink.

'I wanted to say that, if you like, I could come home for the Selection Committee. If it would help.'

'I'm not standing, not now. You may think you were some kind of a heroine, but most of the town don't think like that.'

'I never thought I was a heroine, Barry. I was ashamed of what I did, but I was ashamed of the police too.'

'Well, spitting at a policeman *is* a bit much,' Barry said. 'People come up to me in the street now and say how sorry they are – for *me*. They think you made a fool of me, let me down. You've lost status in this town, Agnes, and because of you I've lost it too. The government's unpopular right now, but the Tory party here are sitting pretty. People think they did a splendid job over the squat, resettling all those blasted women; Malcolm Longley's well thought of too. They helped – those pictures of his wife cooking bacon and eggs and eating with the squatters. As for you and me, it's a very different story. I only thank God there *is* no picture of you spitting – that that priceless moment fortunately wasn't captured on film. But everyone knows what you did.

'If I stood and was selected, I'd always have you at my back to drag me down. So I'm making a break, Agnes. I'm going to Aberdeen in September and I doubt if I'll ever come to live in

Beckersleigh again. And if you think anyone's to blame for all this, I'll tell you one thing: it's not me.'

'So you're leaving?'

'Yes.' Barry looked her straight in the eyes. 'I'm leaving.'

'What about the children?' Agnes asked. Even in the muggy heat of July she felt cold and there were goose pimples on her arm.

'You wanted the children, you've got them; they're your responsibility.' Barry turned his back to her.

'And yours! You're a wonderful orator, Barry Holloway, but don't think you can lay all of what happened at my door. Or did you think that my reasonable suspicion over your relationship with Rose Calthorpe would help our marriage? Did you?'

'I think your irrational jealousy has certainly destroyed something,' Barry said bitterly, pouring himself another whisky. 'It's warped your mind.'

'Do you wonder? Hints here and there, visits to London, never satisfactorily explained. Perhaps I didn't want to know, Barry – perhaps I didn't want to force you to tell me the truth. Perhaps I hid my head in the sand deliberately and for too long. I didn't want to see.'

'There was nothing there to see,' he said. 'Anyway, you can forget about Rose. I haven't been to bed with her for months. It's quite finished. It's not because of Rose I'm leaving you.'

But neither did he tell her that it was because of someone else.

CHAPTER THIRTY

PAUL RIVINGTON STOOD BEHIND HIS WIFE, one of his hands on the clasp of her dress, the other proprietorially on her shoulder. He looked at her in the mirror and as she returned his glance his heart thudded. His fingers trembled on the clasp. He kissed her neck slowly, softly and, releasing the zip, stood back as she stepped out of the dress. She looked exquisite, with the dress and without it.

It had been a lovely wedding, a gloriously happy day. After the reception they had driven to this hotel on Lake Ullswater and enjoyed a long, leisurely dinner with champagne.

Grace stooped to pick up her dress and put it on a hanger. She did everything slowly and carefully, not a bit hurried or excited.

'I thought Barry might have managed to get down for the wedding,' she said. 'Or didn't he want to?'

'He sees the children every month. I think he saw them last week.' Paul undid his tie, doing his best to be casual, like Grace.

'I think they must be splitting up, don't you?'

'Well, whatever's happened, Agnes seems a lot happier. She's got her old vitality back again.' Paul didn't want to talk about Agnes – not now.

'She's going to be Chairman of the Women's Liberation Workshop,' Grace said.

'Chairwoman, darling.'

'Pardon?' She looked at Paul, uncomprehending.

'Not chair*man* – chair*woman*.'

Grace laughed. 'Oh yes, I see. I think it's all a bit ridiculous, don't you?'

Grace had her slip on and she was turning to study herself in the mirror. She had two strands of pearls round her neck and her beautiful thick hair was as it had always been, drawn back from her head without a parting and arranged in a coil at the nape of her neck.

Grace had maintained her poise all day, smiling, gracious,

slightly aloof. It was hard to tell whether she really enjoyed herself or whether she simply regarded it as something to be got through. She was an enigma to him – which was partly why he loved her so much. He sat on the bed to watch her as she revolved in front of the mirror. An arm came up and she pulled the slip neatly over her head. She turned again, spinning round, and tossed it on to the bed; it landed at Paul's feet. He felt the veins swell in his neck and head and began to undo his shirt.

Paul stopped undressing as Grace carefully undid her bra. Her breasts were thrust suddenly out, as though released from constraint, the nipples already erect, a deep red against the lovely white mounds. She cupped her hands under her breasts and gazed at herself in the mirror; then she looked past herself to him and smiled. Paul got up and removed his trousers. As he put them in the press his hands trembled slightly. When he turned round, Grace had taken off her tights and was bending down to remove her flimsy panties. Her breasts dropped towards the floor and Paul went over and put a hand on each of them, supporting them. Grace straightened and smiled, gently removing his hands.

'Not yet, darling.'

Paul sat on the bed in his underpants while Grace removed her knickers, leaving only the string of pearls around her neck. Paul was mesmerised by this performance – for it *was* a performance. There came to his mind the stories the boys used to tell of Grace stripping ... How he had wanted to see her then; but how much better to see her now. His wife. And today was her thirty-third birthday. What a woman – what a prize to wait for!

Her pubic hair was thick and slightly reddish, a darker blonde than her hair. It seemed to spring from her body, at once enticing and protective. He took off his pants and went over to her, his penis already erect and touching her before he could hold her in his arms.

To his surprise, Grace didn't yield, but stood there very stiffly, shivering suddenly as though she were frightened. He put his arms right round her and kissed her cheek.

'Come to bed, darling.'

Grace was shivering violently now, and he saw that her face was pinched and frightened. As well as disappointment, he was beginning to feel a slight alarm.

She lay stiffly on the bed, covering her pubic hair with her hand like a young girl. He lay beside her and looked at her for a long time, not touching her. The bed vibrated with her trembling.

'You're so lovely, Grace,' he said huskily, 'so indescribable ...'

Tentatively he touched her stomach with his hand and felt it quivering.

'Don't be frightened, my darling.' He eased a hand gently inside her thighs, but they tightened and he was forced to withdraw it. 'Grace, what is it?'

'It's been such a long time, Paul, since ...'

'I know, darling, but that's all in the past now. Long in the past.'

'I haven't slept with anyone since ... that time.'

It was the rape! The image of the rape was keeping her from him. She had never yet let him make love to her; her kisses had hardly ever been responsive. Why should he have expected her to abandon herself to him on her wedding night? Of course she was frightened. Some women took years to get over the effects of rape – and this one had been particularly horrible; her own husband, followed by his suicide. Well, he would be patient; he had waited so many years for this. And he loved her.

'There's no hurry, Grace. We can just lie together like this and then, if you feel like it ...'

'It still hurts, you know, inside, Paul.'

'Can I look?' Paul asked softly. 'Maybe there's something that still has to be done there. You know I *am* a doctor.' He touched her thighs timidly.

'You can only look,' Grace said, and opened her legs.

By the winter of 1972, Agnes had found a new direction in her life. Either people had short memories, or Barry had been wrong when he had said people thought less of her after the court case; for in the event, no one ever referred to it at all, nor did it seem to prevent her in any way from doing what she wished. If anything, she was more aware of people's problems now and more involved with the community.

While her mother looked after the house, Agnes was able to finish her second novel in six quick weeks and to her delight it was accepted. She also wrote a weekly column for the *Chronicle* and was now going out with Sam Armstrong. He was a mild, kind man, very different from Barry and a good deal older. It was the sort of understanding relationship she wanted. The sex wasn't much good – nothing to compare with her and Barry – but it was better than nothing. Whatever the other women's workshop members thought, Agnes found it almost impossible to do without sex. She didn't feel the need to torment herself with sexual thoughts so long as Sam Armstrong was ready to help her over them. They went to bed about once a week at his flat, and it was very nice.

One day, on her way home from the paper, Agnes called in to see Connie, who was secretary of the workshop, to discuss the agenda for the next meeting. Connie was going to stand for the council and she still lived in the small flat she had shared with Roman. Agnes found her sprawled on the rug.

'Hi!'

'Hi!' Agnes threw down a bunch of papers. 'I think we should bring all this up at the next Labour Party meeting. The adoption of a formal recognition of the place of the Women's Movement in the Party – equal pay and so on.'

'Equal pay was made mandatory by the Labour Government before its defeat in 1970. It's accepted in principle by both Parties.'

'I agree, but it's not enough. It's got to be put into practice. Shall I make coffee?'

'Please.' Connie started to read through the papers.

'I thought I'd devote one of my next articles to the real issues of the Women's Movement – equal pay, sex discrimination, the right to abortion on demand. Let's come out with it.'

'Let's.' Connie sat cross-legged and stirred her coffee. 'I hear you're going out with Sam Armstrong.'

'You *knew* I was going out with Sam Armstrong.' Agnes smiled. Nothing thrived in Beckersleigh like rumour and gossip.

'Don't you think that's weak?'

'Oh, don't be daft, Connie! I like sex as much as Sam. It's mutual.'

'I think it's a cop-out. A truly liberated woman doesn't need sex.'

Agnes grinned. 'The body, you know, has never heard of women's liberation. Barry once said that the sexes needed each other and, much as I resent having to admit it, I think Barry was right.'

'Do you miss him?'

Agnes shook her head. 'No. Oh, I sometimes miss having sex with him because we had a very good thing there. I mean, Barry was a really good fuck, as they say. But that's all I miss. Truly.'

'Are you going to get divorced?'

'If he wants to. I don't need him. I can rely on myself now. I know where I'm going, what I want out of life.'

'You look a lot better,' Connie admitted. 'Everyone says so.'

'Do you ever hear from Roman?' They hardly mentioned her these days.

'I only had that card from her at Christmas. Nothing since.' Connie's face looked sad and she brushed her hair out of her eyes. Roman's abrupt decision to leave the previous autumn, just after Grace's wedding in October, had been a terrible blow for Connie. Roman had said she was going back to the States, but she was still in this country, which made it worse for Connie. 'I could never understand the way Roman just up and left. But she was never the same after the squat, you know.'

'The squat changed a lot of things,' Agnes acknowledged. 'It really put the lid on things for me and Barry, and it finished you and Roman too.'

'I wonder if there was any connection?' Connie looked speculatively at Agnes.

'In what way, *connection*?' Agnes stopped sorting through the papers on the floor. 'I don't quite understand.'

'Between them. I always felt Barry fancied Roman.'

'He fancied anything in skirts!'

'Roman never wore skirts – but he seemed to like her especially. And I think she liked him.'

'You don't think they're together, do you?' Agnes was struck by the thought.

'Why don't you go up there and see?' Connie replied.

'I wouldn't lower myself!' Agnes finished sorting through the papers and stacked them together, fastening them with a rubber band. 'But it is a thought – I mean, him and Roman.'

It was the children who first told her officially about Barry and Roman; that Daddy lived with the lady who had once taken Agnes to see Terry in hospital. The children had spent Easter with him in Aberdeen, and since Barry had made no attempt to hide it from them it was obviously serious. Agnes didn't say anything to Connie.

'You remember that girl who lived with Connie – Roman Payne?' Agnes said to Sam as they got into bed at his flat before making love one day, soon after Easter.

'Of course; she was stunning looking.'

'Barry thought so, too, apparently; he's living with her.'

'I thought she was a Lesbian!'

'Well, she ain't. Unless Barry's turned into a Lesbian too, and I find that doubtful.'

Sam roared with laughter and drew Agnes towards him. He had a very thin body, and this Agnes found disconcerting. She liked bulk in a man, and Barry certainly had bulk. Sam began to make love to her in his delicate, fragile way, as though he hardly dared touch her; in this respect too, he compared unfavourably with Barry. But it wasn't any use thinking of Barry now. Was she jealous about Roman Payne? A bit; she had to admit it. A bit. She had it on her mind.

Sam slid into her and she pressed him very close to her, because she knew he needed reassurance. She felt guilty, thinking about Barry all the time. She didn't have an orgasm with Sam that day, but it was something he never asked about – again, unlike Barry, who would never come unless she had, and would make sure that she did.

She envied Roman Payne the sexual attention she was undoubtedly getting from Barry, but that was all she envied.

In May of that year, Labour again had success at the local elections, and in June the Chancellor, Anthony Barber, floated the pound to let it find its own level. Barry found Scottish politics very different from English, and soon came to the conclusion there was no chance for him in Aberdeen.

He and Roman had been happy enough, but he felt that their life was sterile. She hadn't enough to do, and she wasn't really interested in what he was doing. He wanted to be back in Parliament. He was only forty, and there was still time to make a career of it. One day he saw a job advertised for a vacancy at a Technical College in Bradford.

'It's Head of Department, too.'

Roman read it and passed it back across the breakfast table.

'I think you want to go back to your wife.'

'I don't, but I'd like to go back to England. I'd like to be in local politics again.'

'What about me?'

'Wouldn't you like that too?'

'I'd like a baby,' Roman said. 'I'm pushing thirty, you know.'

Barry opened the paper again and didn't say anything. He loved Roman, and in bed she was the most exciting woman he had ever known – infinitely diverse. But to marry her would be like being married to Agnes all over again. And a *baby* ... He shuddered, and Roman looked at the paper wondering why it shook.

Enderby Street, surprisingly, looked the same as it always had, except for the great stretch of rubble on the side where houses had once faced theirs. The rubble was being cleared before building work began on the new houses made of red brick and white wood. They would be better spaced than the old, each one with a back garden. No high-rise flats had been built since 1968. The fashion now was to restore old communities as they had been, and to try and restore the sense of community life that had once been so strong in Beckersleigh.

'I can hardly believe it,' Kathleen Rivington said, looking at the nice new bathroom that had been built in the yard onto the kitchen. 'They've made such a good job of it! It's hard to remember anyone ever squatted here. It's only a year, but it seems longer. Do you mean you *really* want to come back and live here, Agnes?'

'If you do, Mum, I do. I've never liked our house, to tell you the truth.'

'I don't like it either,' Kathleen said. 'It's got no character. Not like this.'

'We can begin again, Mum, here.'

'But Agnes, isn't it going back for you?'

'Back?'

'Why don't you marry Sam Armstrong and have a nice house somewhere, like Grace and our Paul?'

Paul had recently been promoted and was now a full Consultant.

'No, I'm not going to get married again. Anyway, I'm not divorced yet. I'm going to be a novelist and a journalist. I don't care what Mrs Thatcher says at the Ministry of Education, I think comprehensive schooling is going to push ahead, and I'm all for it. My kids can go to the old boys' and girls' grammar, which'll now be one big mixed school.'

'I'm not sure I approve of that, Agnes,' Kathleen said, her brow creased by a worried frown. Agnes hugged her.

'I'm *sure* you don't, Mum. And nor would Dad. But it's progress. Now – about rooms. I thought the boys could have your old room because it's bigger, and Miranda and I can have Paul's old room. The littlest one is my old room, and if you didn't mind ...'

376

'Of course I don't mind!'

Agnes felt very strongly the need to put down roots in old familiar places. Where better to begin again but in her old home, even if it was a bit small?

'I can't understand Agnes going back to that awful little house in Enderby Street, can you, Paul?'

'Mmm?' Paul had his head in the *Yorkshire Post* and Grace made a tetchy noise with her tongue.

'I *wish* you wouldn't read at breakfast, Paul. I see so little of you as it is. It's the one chance we have to talk.'

'Sorry, darling.' Paul put down the paper and smiled. 'But this is also my one chance to read.' He looked at his watch. 'I have to operate this afternoon, and there are my ward rounds to do first – it's time I was off. What did you say about Enderby Street?' He spread marmalade on his toast, but kept on glancing at the *Yorkshire Post* lying in front of him.

'Agnes and your mother are going to move into your old house. I simply can't understand it. Can you?'

'Yes.' Paul munched his toast. 'I can. It means a lot to both of them. I think it'll help Agnes to get over Barry, too.'

'I thought Agnes *had* got over Barry. She's sleeping with Sam Armstrong.'

'I know, but Agnes was very emotionally attached to Barry. He is also the father of her children. Barry was roots for her, and the Enderby Street house is the same sort of thing.'

'But they could come and live *here* – God knows, there's enough room,' Grace said, but without bitterness.

Paul got up and went over and kissed her. He still hoped that one day the house would have two or three children in it to fill its empty rooms; there was still time. But Grace had had enough of tests. Children, if they came, would simply be a bonus to their life together – and Grace was no longer desperate at her failure to conceive. The desperation was his, but he felt he couldn't insist. Besides, he had no complaints.

She had thrown herself first into making Paul a good wife, and then into her business. She entertained for him two or three evenings a week, and she was a great asset to his career. Not only did distinguished men from the medical profession come to dine, they stayed the night as well. The Paul Rivingtons lived in some style.

And everyone who met her thought that Paul was terribly lucky with Grace.

Grace's interior design business now had a branch in Ilkley, and she was consulted by some of the wealthiest people in West Yorkshire – and there were many of them. Her own home was ample evidence of her flair for decor, a model of elegance and opulence without vulgarity. Grace, it was generally agreed, had wonderful taste. A Grace Calthorpe house soon came to be recognised – and sought after.

She had kept her maiden name for business. There were still many advantages of being known as the daughter of Henry Calthorpe, because Calthorpe carpets had grown too. Much of Henry's push and dynamism in his later years was attributable to his wife, Rose. If anyone was ever the perfect wife and mother, it was Rose, and she also took a full and active part in civic affairs in the town. Rose was now forty-eight, and middle-age suited her. Her ten-year-old boys were well-behaved, well-spoken and rather dull. They went to a private prep school and had been put down for Giggleswick public school. Rose had no time at all for comprehensive schooling and deplored the abolition of the town's grammar schools.

After Paul had gone, Grace wandered into the garden, idling among the roses, clipping off a few dead heads with the scissors which she always kept on a small table by the French windows. Everything about the house, like Grace, was neat and in its proper place – things to hand, exactly where they were needed. It was a perfect June summer day, with the merest wisps of cloud in the sky and a gentle breeze teasing the leaves of the great elms on one side of the garden. The house was built on a slope, and before her lay the River Wharfe, and beyond that the town of Ilkley, shimmering now in the morning haze.

Grace shielded her eyes to look at the moor and realised how like Beckersleigh it was, with the moor dominating the town; yet how unlike it too. Ilkley was a prosperous middle-class town, whereas Beckersleigh had heavy industry and still spanned the extremes of wealth and poverty. Grace felt in an introspective mood. She didn't know if she could call herself happy; she was seldom visited by great heights of joy or depths of despair. Life, on the whole, had an even tenor, as a woman of her station and class might expect. She had a good and considerate husband, who was also a distinguished professional man of high standing in the medical world. She had a beautiful, even gracious, home and a flourishing business. She was well thought of. What had she possibly got to complain about? As far as everyone else was concerned she was a woman who had everything – well, *almost* everything – she could possibly want.

Barry sat in the sitting room and looked at Agnes. He had a longing for her that he didn't think he would ever feel again. His reaction had surprised him, made him tongue-tied.

'I'm astonished you're leaving the house. I thought we might buy it.'

'*We*?' Agnes turned and looked at him.

'I'm coming back to Yorkshire. They've offered me this job in Bradford.'

'I'm so glad, Barry. I'm sorry Aberdeen was such a disappointment.' But from her voice it was plain that she didn't care one way or the other.

'It's such a cut-off kind of place, and those North Sea oil people ... well, they've got too much money, for one thing.'

'Is Roman coming with you?'

Agnes said her name very carefully, lightly.

'It's up to you.'

'What's up to me?' Agnes sat down and stared at him in surprise.

'I thought we might try and make it together again.'

'Are you being serious?' She was amazed.

'Perfectly.' Barry got up and came over to her, standing by her side and looking down at her. 'I see things a lot clearer now. I think we could have another try. For the sake of the children.'

'Oh Barry, why *must* you bring in the children? That's sentimental.'

'Is it?'

'Yes, you know it is. The children see a lot of you, and they know a better me. You and I *can't* live together, you know that.'

'Well, I'd like to try again,' he said obstinately.

'But what makes you think it'll be different this time, Barry? Tell me.'

Barry sat down on the arm of her chair and put his hand on her shoulder. How he would love to see her naked again, feel her breasts in his hands ...

'You attract me terrifically, you know that, Agnes?'

Agnes got up quickly.

'Barry, I don't want to go back. I don't want to start all over again. I know that sex was always good with us, but sex isn't everything. It didn't make us happy before and it won't now – we'd still have the same problems. Besides, I've changed; I've grown. I *like* being a writer and a journalist. My time is absolutely full of things I *like* doing. I never do housework. Mum does all this; she's like a housekeeper and nanny and the kids love it. Everyone's satisfied. And anyway, I hate this house! I don't like it at all – fat, squat, ugly little box. Do you know, they've even got the old grate in Enderby Street? Mum's so looking forward to being able to black it again.'

'But you'll rent if for the rest of your life. You'll never own it.'

'I don't want to own it. Barry, I think I'm more of a socialist than you are!' She changed tack. 'Sam Armstrong's my lover, Barry. I'm not going to marry him, but I like him. We have a good relationship. It's calm and nice and productive. We talk a lot about books and we have a lot in common. We never have a row.'

'I hope he fucks you properly.' Barry's tone was scathing, his control slipping.

'There you are, Barry! That's typical. You think he probably doesn't fuck me as well as you; well, as a matter of fact, he doesn't. But he doesn't argue with me or treat me like an appendage either. He respects my work and me. You're too male, Barry, too chauvinistic to see a woman in that way. Obviously even Roman, with all her advanced liberationist views, hasn't changed you.'

'Roman hasn't changed me at all!' Barry said indignantly, 'For Christ's sake, that women's lib thing was a load of shit.'

'Your language hasn't improved either,' Agnes said acidly. 'Neither have your attitudes.'

As she looked at him, she felt the old tug, the old desire for togetherness, for tenderness; but she knew it wouldn't work. She had to steel her heart and, by doing so, keep herself free.

'It really is a *dear* little house,' Grace said carefully. 'A sweet little house. I like it. I really do.'

Grace trod around it delicately, as though she were walking on hot coals. 'It needs the Grace Calthorpe treatment, that's all.'

'Oh, Grace!' Agnes laughed. 'I don't think we could afford you!'

'I'd do it for nothing, seeing as it's you. Now we could have wallpaper here; and here ...'

Grace's hands began darting about as she sketched out ⸨
asking Agnes to imagine this thing and that, this object he
one there. But Agnes simply smiled, her heart full of affecti
frivolous Grace, her long-time friend, now her sister-in-
Grace, who had made Paul so very happy.

'It'll be very *small*,' Grace said at last, looking at her frankl⸥
'Have you thought about the children?'

'Yes. It's all arranged. It's all signed, with the Council, Grace,
and we've surrendered the lease of the old house. We're actually
moving in next week.'

Grace looked at her seriously. 'I do hope you've done the right
thing, Agnes.'

'I'm sure I have.' Agnes went to the window and gazed across the
rubble. In the distance she could see the tall tower blocks, which
both she and her mother knew had precipitated her father's death.

'And you really said "no" to Barry?' Grace shook her head,
teetering on her high-heeled shoes. '*That* I find hard to believe,
though I'm delighted. He actually wanted to get together again, and
you wouldn't have it? Good for you.'

'Well, a split now is going to be a lot less painful than later. I was
very sexually dependent on Barry, you know, and I think it was
wrong. It made me into someone I didn't really like. Now I'm
dependent on no one, sexually or otherwise. I'm my own woman.
At last.'

'But did you think about the children having no father?'

'They *do* have a father. Barry will see more of them than ever now
– he's going to work in Bradford. He spends more time with them
when he does see them, too. He seems to value them more. He's
going to marry Roman Payne, so the kids will have a new mother,
too. They seem to have taken to her already.'

'Oh, he's going to marry *her*, is he?'

'Barry wants a woman,' Agnes said, trying to sound casual. 'He
doesn't want to live alone; he's told me. He offered me the chance of
taking him back and I didn't take it. So he's going to marry her.
Having me would have been less trouble, but it comes to the same
thing; Barry needs a woman, even if she makes him unhappy. It
would never occur to him to live alone.'

'But does he *love* Roman?' Grace looked incredulous. 'It doesn't
sound like love to me. Either her or you, *very* rum.'

'Don't you think much of life is a compromise?' Agnes turned

[...]hat she had her back to the rubble. 'Roman's an attractive
[...] wants children of her own. Good luck to her.'
[...]ought there was something *funny* about her?' Grace screwed
[...]r nose, as though she couldn't bring herself to utter the word
[...]sbian'. 'She told me so herself.'

'Well, Barry's obviously put that right. The old sexual trick has
worked again. No, I think it's all turned our rather well. I have my
independence, Barry will have a nubile young wife, and probably
there'll be more babies on the way. For Barry it's the mixture as
before – but not for me. What amuses me is that we really split
because I was too independent – and now he's marrying an arch
women's liberationist! I think he'll find life is going to repeat itself
all over again.'

'Serves him right,' Grace said, and paused. 'I had to say what I just
said. I felt I had to say it, but he really was a swine, you know. I never
told you that I saw him come out of Roses's room at home, did I?
Well I did.'

'Oh, *did* you?' Agnes was silent for a moment, a feeling of shock
making her momentarily breathless, as though her heart had
skipped several beats. 'Then all the business about London and
everything was true?'

'I'm afraid so. Now you know.'

'He denied it. I asked him several times, because I wanted to
know.'

'I know he did. I had it out with him the day I saw him. I lay in wait
for him as he left the house. He said he didn't want to hurt you.'

'The hurt lies as much in suspicion as anything else. Didn't you
feel you should tell me at the time?' Agnes's heart had started to beat
normally again, but even so she found herself having to lean against
the wall for support.

'No.' Grace lowered her head and studied the bare, uncarpeted
floor. 'I couldn't interfere, or take the responsibility for you
knowing. If you and Barry had split up then, everyone would have
blamed me; they would have said what a bitch I was. I couldn't tell
Daddy, either, because I knew that he was so happy with Rose. I
thought that in your own ways you might each find out, and make
your own adjustments. You have, and now that Barry has left town,
I doubt if Daddy will ever know. I hope not, because I think it might
kill him.'

'All those years,' Agnes said, almost in a whisper. 'Who could have imagined it? All those years of lies, of evasion, of deception. Not very flattering to me, is it?'

'It's nothing to do with you! With people like Barry you can't apply normal standards of behaviour.' Grace went over and put her hand on her friend's arm, pressing it for comfort. 'I think, with them, it's a deep-rooted self-indulgence; their only concern is their own satisfaction and pleasure. I can't believe that Barry ever felt guilty about it, or imagined that he was doing anything very wrong.'

'I don't suppose he did. Years and years of lies,' Agnes said again, as if in wonderment. Then she brushed back her soft, curly hair, straightened up and smiled. 'What do I care now? The memory's hateful, but I'll put it away from me. I'm only sad that I knew so little about someone who seemed so close to me; but otherwise it scarcely touches me now. Obviously, one woman was never enough for Barry. Maybe he feels there's safety in numbers!'

Her tone was lighter and Grace responded to it, also smiling. She took her hand away from Agnes's arm. 'Much good may it do him and Roman. I think we should feel quite sorry for them both.'

The two friends, the two Graces, looked at each other and started to laugh – to laugh as they hadn't laughed since they were girls, the leaders of the school, the only two who really mattered. Agnes took Grace's arm and, still laughing, they stepped outside and paused for a moment while Agnes locked the door of Fifty-two Enderby Street, to which she would soon return. She felt enormously happy and grateful to life. As they walked towards Grace's car, she glanced up towards the slag, flattened now and no longer a threat hanging over Beckersleigh – if it ever had been. Aberfan seemed a long time ago, and so did her childhood. This year she would be thirty-four. It was a good age to make a fresh start – not too young and not too old, though people said you could make new beginnings at any age.

Soon the rubble would disappear under a sea of new dwellings, council houses like this one, which would once again recreate a community spirit in Enderby Ward. Families would grow up in the area, bringing children like hers, and once again the slag would come into its own. Surely there were a few rugged corners left? A few secret places where even this sophisticated, television-minded young generation of the '70s could still find adventure? Soon her kids, Terry, Miranda and Chris, would be tearing up the hill towards the slag, to play those wild exciting games all over again, just as she and Paul had done when they were children too.